~~~~~~~~~

ALMOST HUMAN

❧ THE FIRST TRILOGY ❧

VOLUME 2

LOST REFLECTIONS

BY

MELANIE NOWAK

~~~~~~~~~~~~~~~~~~~~~~~~~~~~

Praise for Melanie Nowak's Venomous Vampire series
ALMOST HUMAN

Top Pick Vampire Series - Night Owl Reviews
Top 20 Author of 2018 - Amy's Bookshelf Reviews
Best Vampire Series 1st place Winner by Public Reader Vote
in The Paranormal Romance Guild 2012 & 2015 Reviewer's Choice Awards

"An emotional rollercoaster that will have you sitting in suspense one moment, laughing out loud the next, and then crying your eyes out. ALMOST HUMAN is definitely a book series that should be read slowly and savored."
– www.NightOwlReviews.com

"Interesting and well written, giving a great depth to characters and the plot. I am captivated by the romance and desires of the vampires. I like that it is sexy and romantic, without being invasive or overly erotic. Great story."
- Amy's Bookshelf Reviews

"The reader is held breathless. Historical research is clearly evident in vivid descriptions and authenticity. The story twists and evolves with the relationships."
- www.ParanormalRomanceGuild.com

"ALMOST HUMAN is a series in which the characters are richly written in a way that helps the reader relate to all of them. Lost Reflections, *has wonderful historical backstory and natural romance unforced, making it a favorite of the three!"*
– www.BittenByBooks.com

"The story keeps getting better! All the relationships are changing, making for addictive reading!"
– www.ParanormalRomance.org

"I am one very addicted reader! I could not stop turning pages! I am totally invested in these characters and the twists and turns just keep on coming!"
- www.NerdGirlOfficial.com

"Stunningly good read. The story was finessed to a whole new level and is by far one of my favorites"
- Strawberry Reads: The Almost Human Diary (YouTube review channel)

*ALMOST HUMAN - The First Series was originally published as a trilogy of novels, now broken into novellas as an alternate format. The story is told in a serial succession - not stand-alone books. Each novella is meant to be read in order, as the story unfolds chronologically. Each series will be contained enough to be read on its own, with a certain amount of main storyline closure with the last novella, but there will also be some story-ties leading from one series into the next.

If you enjoy this book, please take a moment to leave a review online, on your favorite book review website! Questions and comments can be directed to: WoodWitchDame@aol.com

You can join author/reader discussions about the series, and get updates on upcoming book releases for this series on the author's web site at:

www.MelanieNowak.com

Copyright 2004, 2018
Melanie Nowak, WoodWitchDame Publications
Cover Artwork, Book formatting/Editing: Melanie Nowak
Cover Photo/Model: Natalie Paquette
http://natalie-paquette.wix.com/photos
http://fetishfaerie-photos.deviantart.com/gallery

LOST REFLECTIONS
ISBN: 978-9824102-4-7
ISBN-13: 978-0-9824102-4-0

~~~~~~~~~~~~~~~~~~~~~~~~~~~~~~~~~~

A Special Thanks to

~~~

My Mom & Step-Dad, Adele and David Weitzel
who have always given their love and support

~~~

My dearly departed brother, John,
who is loved, and missed each day

~~~

And to my wonderful and loving husband,
Scott,
and our sons, William & Eric,

who had patience when I was obsessed with writing,
gave me never-ending confidence and inspiration,
and for whom I am forever grateful
and blessed to have in my life.
I love you dearly.

~~~~~~~~~~~~~~~~~~~~~~~~~~~~~~~~~~

ALMOST HUMAN was originally published as a series of novels, now also broken into novellas as an alternate format. These are not stand-alone books - they are meant to be read in order, as the story unfolds chronologically.

ALMOST HUMAN ~ The First Series

FATAL INFATUATION
Part 1: Captivating Vampires
Part 2: Tempting Transgressions
Part 3: Venomous Revelations

LOST REFLECTIONS
Part 1: Persistent Persuasion
Part 2: Telling Tales
Part 3: Battles and Bliss

EVOLVING ECSTASY
Part 1: Ecstasy Unleashed
Part 2: Stakes and Sunshine
Part 3: Evolution of Love

ALMOST HUMAN ~ The Second Series

BORN TO BLOOD
Part 1: Vampiress Rising
Part 2: Exceeding Expectations
Part 3: Coping with Chaos
Part 4: Vampire Vertigo

DESCENDENT OF DARKNESS
Part 1: Determining Desires
Part 2: Undying Devotion
Part 3: Emotional Maelstrom
Part 4: Crossing the Line

DESTINED FOR DIVINITY
Part 1: Home of the Bloodthirsty
Part 2: Enemies and Allies
Part 3: Vicious Survival
Part 4: Divining Destiny

ALMOST HUMAN ~ The Third Series

VAMPIRESS REIGNING
Part 1: Uniting Vampires

ALMOST HUMAN ∽ THE FIRST TRILOGY

VOLUME 2 ∽ LOST REFLECTIONS

Contents

Part 1: Persistent Persuasion

Part 2: Telling Tales

Part 3: Battles and Bliss

Part 1

Persistent Persuasion

Chapter 1 - Morals

Felicity

Alyson's apartment
8:00, Sunday night

As the last blazing colors of sunset faded to deep violet in the sky, Felicity made her way up Alyson's front walk and knocked on the door. It took a long time for Ben to answer, but she trusted Cain's word that he was still there. He finally did appear, stifling a yawn. She must have woken him. She was glad he'd been able to get some rest and try to recover from his ordeal. She still had a hard time getting the mental image out of her mind, of his chest and stomach covered in bruises from his beating. She could barely even see evidence of Sindy's bite on his throat, but she knew that psychologically, Ben probably considered that trespass far worse than any more painful physical injury. "Hi," he said sleepily.

"Hi. Allie's not back yet?" she asked in concern. The sun had only just set, but she didn't find as much comfort in that as she used to. Cain had reminded her that this was real life, not a vampire movie, and she shouldn't be so confident that she knew all the rules of the game.

He shook his head. "No, but she called. She got stuck going in to work. She's going to try and get out early, but I doubt it."

She looked at him appraisingly. "You staying here? No more visions of Vermont?"

"For now. You wanna come in?" he asked.

"Do you want me to come in?" she asked back.

He gave her a look that said he felt bad that she should have to ask. "Of course I do," he answered, backing away some more to let her in. Ben eyed the denim jacket she wore, as she took it off and laid it on a chair. He didn't say anything, but he surely knew who it belonged to.

They went to sit in the living room, on the somewhat lumpy couch. Felicity fidgeted into the corner until she could get comfortable, as Ben sat down quietly next to her. He gave her a sidelong glance. "Sorry I flipped out before."

"It's understandable."

"Yeah, but I shouldn't have taken it out on you."

She shrugged. "It's okay." That sat in silence. She'd like to talk more about what was going on with Alyson and her vampire lover Mattie, but figured that she should let Ben be the one to start that conversation.

"You went to go see Cain, didn't you?" he asked.

"Yeah." He just sat there, waiting for more. "He asked after you."

"I'm touched," he said in sarcasm.

"He thought you might be planning some kind of revenge. He even offered to help." Why had she even said anything? She hadn't really planned to just blurt that out, but she was getting tired of Ben always thinking Cain was against him.

This got Ben's full attention. "What kind of revenge?"

She pondered for a moment whether she should even tell him. His expectant face wouldn't let her think of a way around it. "He knows where Sindy and her coven are sleeping. He followed them, even though it was almost morning and he could have gotten himself killed. As it is, I think he came much closer to being dust than he lets on. Anyway, he figured that if we knew where they were, we could plan to confront them in the daytime. They'd be at a serious disadvantage. Maybe we could even let the sunlight in on them somehow."

Ben was becoming more and more animated as she spoke. "Of course! It'd be easy! All of our problems neatly turned into dust!" he exclaimed.

"Hold on there, VanBuren, it's not..." Felicity began.

"Who?" Ben interrupted.

"The vampire hunter," she explained.

Ben groaned. "That's VanHelsing!" he clarified. "VanBuren was a president!"

"Oh. Well you know who I mean!" Ben rolled his eyes. She ignored him and pressed on. "It's not quite as simple as it sounds, this isn't the movies. If Cain can be awake during the day, they can too. What are you going to do, invite them to follow you outside for a stroll? Besides, they'd know you were coming from a mile away." He didn't seem to understand. She spoke as lightly as she could. "You're marked now, remember?"

He flinched and looked a bit sick. "So are you, right?"

She gave a little nod. "Anyway, I don't know about you, but I never really wanted to play vampire hunter. I just want them to leave us alone."

"Alyson could do it," Ben suggested.

"It's too dangerous," Felicity declared.

"Did she say that?" Ben asked.

"I didn't ask her," Felicity replied.

"Didn't Allie go with you?" Ben asked.

"To Cain's?" she asked in puzzlement. "No."

"I saw you leave together," Ben insisted.

"She dropped me off," Felicity clarified.

"You went to see him *alone*?" Ben seemed completely outraged, as though he thought that she had lost her mind.

"I trust him," she said simply.

He looked like he thought she was a fool. "I don't."

"Well, you're not me," Felicity told him quietly.

"He bit you, 'Liss!"

"Once, for a reason. Now that I'm marked, the others have to leave me alone," Felicity told him.

"Oh I see, it was a good deed. That couldn't possibly whet his appetite for more, even though now he's got his own private stock." She shook her head and turned away. "Are you *feeding* him?"

She turned back to him fiercely. "Want to check my neck?" she asked, sharply pulling her collar away from her throat on both sides.

"No," he mumbled.

She noticed that he still looked. She let go her collar and put her head down into her hands. They sat in silence. After a minute, she looked up to find him staring at her. She stared back at him for a second and then asked, "Think Alyson's got anything good to eat? I haven't had any dinner."

"The Chinese food place delivers."

She turned to him with a smile. She was so relieved to have something to divert their attention. "That sounds wonderful, I'm starved."

He got up and she followed him into the kitchen. "I think Allie's got a menu in here somewhere," he said as he began rifling through a drawer full

3

of papers, scotch tape, scissors and assorted odds and ends. He reached towards the back and winced as he stretched a sore muscle.

"Why don't you go lay down? I'll find it."

He looked at her in annoyance, although he was rubbing his side, under his arm, in pain. "I've been lying down all day. I'm sure I'm capable of getting a piece of paper out of a drawer."

"Sorry."

She stood watching him for a minute, until he looked up at her. "What?"

"Well, I wanted to ask how you were feeling, but I don't want to get counted at."

He tried not to smile. "I'm fine."

She wanted to ask more, but wasn't sure how to phrase it. "You haven't felt anything... weird, have you?"

He took a deep breath and let it out slowly before looking at her to answer. "No, I'm just very, very sore."

"I guess I should tell you..."

He didn't let her finish. "Could we have that talk after we eat?"

She nodded. "Yeah, sure. Hey, isn't that the menu?" She picked it up off the floor. It must have fallen out when they'd begun their search.

Half an hour later, they were sitting at the kitchen table with a bunch of open cartons. Felicity looked at Ben over her lo mein. She felt terrible about what had happened to him, but she knew he'd be okay. He seemed to have such a strong and confident personality. She wondered if he really was, or if that was just the face he showed the world. When he'd told her about his friend Mattie becoming a vampire, and even when he'd confronted Alyson about being Mattie's secret lover, he'd been angry, but she could see how hurt he'd been inside. He saw her looking at him. "What, is it time for that talk already?"

"What? No. I mean, unless you want to. Actually, I was just wondering something."

He looked as though he thought she was going to ask him something he wouldn't want to answer. He probably thought she was wondering about how he'd felt when he'd been bitten by Sindy last night. She wouldn't pry about that, it was not the kind of thing she thought he'd want to share. "So ask," he said with resignation.

She paused a moment. He just looked at her, patiently waiting. "Would you really have slept with Brenda last night? If she'd let you I mean."

He seemed bewildered, but relieved. "*That's* what you were wondering?" She just gave a little shrug and nod. He smiled and answered, "Yeah." He grinned at her obvious discomfort. "I'm a healthy, young, heterosexual guy and she's really hot. It's kind of a no brainer. I mean, I hope you don't think I'd be pushy about it or anything! But, if the opportunity presented itself? Yeah, I would."

"But you hardly know her."

He gave her a sly grin. "That's part of the allure." She gave him a look of disgust. "Well what did you want me to do, lie? Should I have told you that I would have turned her away, made her wait until we had a solid and lasting relationship? Because any guy who tells you he would have done that is either lying, or already sleeping with somebody else." She shook her head, dejectedly. "Hey, I never claimed to be anyone's knight in shining armor. I'm just a guy and I'm being honest. I told you men were from Mars."

She looked up at him almost pleadingly. "Doesn't it *mean* anything?"

He gazed at her steadily across the table and his eyes seemed to soften. "Of course it *can*. I'll bet it can be truly amazing, if it's with someone that you really care about." He chewed his lip for a second and then looked back down at his food to begin eating again. "But sometimes, it's just sex."

Felicity was still gazing back at him in puzzlement at his answer. "Have you *ever* been with someone that you cared about?"

"Don't make it sound like I don't care. It's not like I'm out collecting conquests or something; but have I ever been with someone that I might... love?" She gave a little nod. "No, not yet." He shrugged. "It'll happen. Until then, a guy's got to do something to pass the time, right?" She gave him a little smirk at that, just to let him know that she didn't fully agree. "So have you... ever been in love?" he asked. She was taken aback. "What, you get to ask me and I don't get to ask back?"

"No."

"No I don't get to ask, or no to the question?"

"The question. No."

He smiled. "I think that 'no' holds more than one connotation."

She felt herself blushing and looked down, before answering indignantly. "You don't get to ask me that."

He broke into a broad grin. "I don't need to." She played with the last of the food on her plate. "How old are you, eighteen?" he asked.

She looked up at him with an abashed little smile. She couldn't believe she was talking to a guy about this stuff. "Not yet, but I will be in another week and a half. My birthday is on the seventeenth."

He laughed. "Okay, soon to be eighteen then. A beautiful girl like you, remains untouched?"

Felicity's mouth fell open at his insolence. "This is rapidly leaving curious friend territory, and entering rude and obnoxious!" She got up from the table, amazed at his temerity.

"I'm not being obnoxious, I'm just making an observation," he protested with a laugh.

She hadn't planned to say more, but couldn't help herself. "It's not as if I've never had the opportunity." She brought her paper plate to the garbage and came back to begin closing up the cartons of food. Ben was grinning up at her as she moved around him.

He spoke to her as she tried to ignore him. "Now you're all embarrassed and disappointed in me, because you think I've got no morals, right? I may not be celibate, but I still think I'm a pretty decent guy. It's not like I'm out there cleverly tricking girls into being with me. It is a mutual kind of thing, you know? I should be a twenty year old virgin?" He caught her arm and made her stop to look at him. She'd been cleaning up around him, avoiding his gaze.

She looked down at him and smiled. "No. I don't think you have no morals, and I'm not completely naïve; or chaste..." She added naughtily. He raised an eyebrow and she laughed. She didn't want him thinking she was some kind of prude. "I think you're a good guy, who hasn't met the right person yet. Neither have I. And you're right, it'll happen."

She started to walk away, but he didn't let go of her arm. She looked down at him questioningly to find he'd turned rather serious. "'Liss, I know this is none of my business. You certainly don't have to listen to me, but since we're on the subject, I might as well give you my opinion, for what it's worth." He took his hand off of her arm, but she stayed, looking down at him solemnly. "If you've waited this long, don't give it up for a dead guy. 'Cause that's just not something that's going to last."

She wanted to be shocked and insulted. Certainly that flashed across her face, but after that first moment, she really wasn't. It was good to have someone to talk to and she saw an opportunity to maybe soften things for Allie as well. She tread gingerly. "How can you know, that it wouldn't last?"

He looked as though he couldn't believe she might defend such a relationship. "He's a vampire. What else is there to know?"

"I know you still don't want to accept it, but it's not like all vampires are these horrible mindless demons. We've seen *them*. Cain's not like that, and from what I've heard, neither is Mattie." He just stared at her coldly. She spoke gently, hoping he would listen, without being provoked to anger again. "I'm not saying it's a good thing, what's been done to them, but bad things do happen to good people. Don't you believe that the good people they once were could still be inside?" He looked away from her, silently. "I'm not saying that there's any kind of future there, as far as a relationship's concerned. To be honest, there's just too much that I still don't know. It's all so strange, but a friendship? Yes, definitely. Everyone needs a friend. Especially when they're going through a difficult time in their life.

What if Sindy had gone too far Ben? What if it had happened to *you?* What if you felt that you were still the same person inside, but now with this terrible curse upon you, this affliction that you never asked for; what would you do? Would you have me turn away from you? Would you take your own life? Or would you do the best you could, to live without hurting others and maybe try to make some kind of difference in the world? You don't have to like Cain, or even Mattie anymore, but I think that you have to accept them as people, instead trying to think of them as some kind of monsters. Especially knowing what they mean to us."

"Us? So now I've got Allie *and* you against me, huh?"

"We're not against you Ben. Look, I don't know what Alyson and Mattie's relationship is like, but I can tell that she really cares about him."

"Alyson can't even keep a relationship going for more than a month!"

"Maybe that's because she's in love with someone that she can't have!"

That seemed to frighten him. He was quiet for a moment. "She can't be." Those were the words that came out of his mouth, but even he didn't seem to believe them.

Felicity had meant Mattie and she knew that Ben also took it that way, but she suddenly wondered if Ben might not be included in that category as well. Alyson certainly loved Ben as a friend. She wondered if Allie was only not interested in Ben romantically, for fear of him rejecting her and ruining their friendship.

Allie had been romantically involved with Mattie though, at least she had insinuated that she was. "I don't know, she never actually told me that she was in love with Mattie, but my instincts tell me that, yeah she probably is. They were close before and she still cares now, three years later, after everything. She's so worried about him, Ben. Don't you think she'd know if he were *that* different; if he'd truly changed? Like I said, you don't have to like him. You probably don't even have to see him, but don't punish *her* for it. She needs *you* too, you know. Or at least to know that things are okay between you."

"She knows."

"You talked about it?"

"No, but she knows. What about Cain?"

"What about him?" He just looked at her. "I don't know. I'm not going to tell you that I'm not still attracted to him. I don't know where it'll go, or if I'll even let it go anywhere."

"It's not real."

"What do you mean?"

"The stuff you feel for him. It's not real. It's a drug, it's that... venom. Don't you know that?"

"It's not only that. It couldn't be. I know where the real stuff ends and *that* begins."

Ben laughed, but it was humorless and cold. "You think so? When did he first give you a taste of it? I know it's not all that long ago that he bit you, but what about before that? I wasn't unconscious during Sindy's little speech, as much as I wished I were. It's in their saliva, right? So when did he first kiss you? Isn't that when it really began? Let me tell you something, that's pretty potent stuff."

Somehow, she hadn't made that connection. The thought was both frightening and a relief at the same time. No wonder she had reacted so strongly to their one and only kiss! But at the same time, it showed her more about Cain's character than she had realized, because they had only

8

shared one kiss. She had kissed him and would have again, but he wouldn't let her. Now she knew why. He wanted her to know him, before she became under the influence of the venom. For the second time today, she felt both lucky and grateful at the same time that Cain was indeed a good man.

Of course, Ben didn't know what she and Cain had done together. Just because they hadn't slept together didn't mean she hadn't let him touch her. When Ben had said that Cain had kissed her, she hadn't denied it. She looked up with the thought of telling him of Cain's restraint, but the look on Ben's face made her lose the thought.

Her best guess would be that he was remembering being bitten. He certainly wasn't looking at, or thinking of her. After a moment, he swallowed hard and continued their conversation, although he wouldn't quite meet her eyes. He looked as if he were forcing himself to speak, through great difficulty. It came out as little more than a whisper, as though he didn't really want her to hear. "That stuff is strong poison. If it could make me *want* Sindy so badly... If my hands weren't tied, I can't even tell you what I would have done.

You don't know what's real, you can't. I know you liked him before he bit you. Maybe even before he kissed you, but now? How will you ever know how much is real? How can you ever trust that he's not just using you, bending you to his every whim? Because I haven't the slightest doubt that he could. In fact, the knowledge that he still hasn't, is making me think that maybe he's not such a bad guy after all. But you'll never really know, whether it's you, or just some subtle manipulation of you."

She lowered her eyes to the floor and tried to sort out her feelings. It was too difficult right now. She wanted to argue with him, but couldn't even try to think of how she could prove him wrong. She thought she knew how she felt. She wasn't being manipulated in any way right now, but was it just residual feeling, from the overpowering desire she felt for him whenever he was near? Was any of it really her? That was a very unsettling question. She would have to pay close attention to how she felt the next time that she saw Cain.

Until her mark wore off, she probably would have a hard time figuring out what *was* real. And even then, only if she refrained from kissing him. If she were to remain involved with him, how would she ever avoid the venom entirely? It seemed awfully complicated. She remembered how strongly she had desired him, just after that first kiss. That thought made her realize that she'd better try to prepare Ben for the evening ahead, just in case. She wasn't sure if Allie had really told him anything. "Sindy may come looking for you later."

"She can't come in," Ben said with assurance.

Felicity drew in a deep breath and sighed. "She may not have to. You'll feel her. It'll... call you."

Ben looked as though she had just taken his security blanket away. "Vermont's soundin' pretty good," he said in annoyance.

"I don't think it's the same for everybody, so I could be wrong, but *I* also didn't get as much venom as you did; and I feel it, pretty strong. I know it's not just me," she confided.

"Great. So what do we do? Tie me to the mast, like Jason and the Argonauts?" Ben questioned.

"Who?" Felicity asked in confusion.

"Jason and the Golden Fleece. When he wanted to hear the Siren's song? I've got to sit you down with some movies," he told her.

"Well, I don't think you'll require restraints," she said with a chuckle. "It's just kind of weird and uncomfortable, and I thought you'd want to know. I'd better stay until Allie gets home though, just in case."

"Thanks. Luckily, I kind of like having you around. You certainly make interesting conversation," he said with a mischievous leer. "Are you sure you want to subject yourself to being locked in an apartment with a crazed sex fiend? Could be dangerous," he teased.

She reached out and gave him a quick rap on the chest. It wasn't very hard, but it made him wince from his bruises. "I think I can take you." He gave her a look, which made her realize that her statement could easily be misconstrued. She made as if to hit him again and he backed away laughing. "Sindy may not even come. She probably doesn't even know where Allie lives, and she wouldn't know you'd be here anyway. What is she going to do, walk around the whole town, feeling for you?"

"She certainly could. It's not a very big town, and what else has she got to do?" Ben asked.

"Well, like you said, she can't come in. It may not be the best night's sleep you've ever had, but you'll survive," Felicity answered drolly.

Two hours later found them on the couch watching television. At least Ben was watching, Felicity was sleeping, until her head fell to the side and she jerked herself awake for the third time.

"'Liss, why don't you go to bed?"

"What? I'm awake," she said through a yawn.

"Go to bed 'Liss," Ben told her with a laugh.

"What time does Allie get home?" she asked.

"Last call's at 3:30, then she's still gotta clean up and stuff. She won't be back until after four," Ben said.

"What time is it now?" Felicity asked.

"Almost midnight. Trust me, you'll never make it. Don't even try. I'm going to turn in now myself," he told her.

"Okay, goodnight." She laid down and settled herself deeper into the couch, trying to get comfortable as he turned off the television.

"You're not going to sleep out here? This couch sucks. You won't get any sleep. Trust me, I've tried it," he said.

"I'm fine," she insisted.

"Do you want the bed and I'll take the couch?" he asked.

"No. I can't make you sleep out here with bruises like that. You need the bed," she admitted.

"Well, it's a big bed. And it's not like we haven't slept together before." He gave her an impish smile. "You have my word of honor that I will not seek to despoil your virtue," he said with overly dramatic flair. "I'm a little too wounded for such strenuous activity anyway."

"Shut up and go to bed." She didn't get up, or even look at him.

"At least get out of those clothes, you don't want to sleep in jeans."

Now she sat up. "And just what do you propose? It's not like I brought anything."

"Well it's a good thing. You know how much I like those sheep pajamas of yours." She made good use of a throw pillow. He caught it before it could do any damage. "Wear something of Allie's, she won't care," he said, tossing the pillow back to her.

"Ben, as sweet as it is that you think that I could, Alyson is at least two sizes smaller than me. I don't think so."

"Well, I keep some stuff here. It's mostly tee shirts and sweats, but they should do. Unless you're afraid that you can't squeeze into an extra large." This time the pillow hit him in the head.

He went into the bedroom and came back with the clothing. "I'm not going to lend you my underwear though. And I wouldn't recommend Allie's. I think hers are mostly made out of dental floss."

"How would you know?" she asked with an arched eyebrow.

"She does her laundry at my house," he replied with a chuckle.

"That's okay, I think I'll keep my own," she said, heading into the bathroom to change.

She came back to find that Ben had left a blanket and pillow on the couch. He must have gone to bed already, the lights in the bedroom were off. She arranged everything and shut the light.

"Goodnight." Ben called from the other room.

"Goodnight."

Felicity spent the next half an hour or so tossing and turning. Ben was right, the couch was awful. She thought maybe she felt Cain at one point, but it was fleeting. He must have just been passing close by. It was so strange to be aware of someone's location without seeing them.

She had classes tomorrow. It seemed weird that she should just resume normal everyday life. She couldn't imagine trying to concentrate on algebra. It was a good thing Cain didn't live very close to the school.

After a bit, she heard Ben get out of bed and come quietly to the doorway. "'Liss, are you awake?" he whispered.

"Yeah."

"I can't sleep. At the risk of sounding like a pervert or a total wimp, I've gotta tell you, I'd feel much better if you came into the bedroom."

She heard something in his voice that made her sit up to look at him. "Do you feel her?" she asked quietly.

She couldn't see his face very well in the dark, but he sounded uncomfortable to have to talk about it. "Yeah. I don't think she's real close by yet, but it's getting stronger, and I've gotta admit that it's freakin' me out a little. I know she can't come in and it's not like I'm scared of her or anything, but it's so weird and I can't sleep." He fidgeted a little in the doorway. "I know you can't be comfortable out here, and it'd just be nice to have someone else in the room, you know?"

She had to smile thinking of when she'd said that to him, the night he had asked him to stay in her room. "Yeah, sure." She got up and followed him into the bedroom. As he flipped on the light, she stood at the foot of the bed, trying to decide which side looked slept in.

He must have mistaken her hesitation. He looked amused. "If you want, I could build a little wall of pillows down the middle."

She laughed. "I don't think that'll be necessary, unless you're afraid I might elbow you or something. I know you're sore."

He smiled. "I'll risk it."

"I just didn't know which side," she explained.

"Oh. I don't care, whatever," he told her.

She climbed in on the left side and then he got in on the right. They both lay on their backs looking at the ceiling after Ben shut the light. She looked over at him in the dark. "What happens when Allie gets home? Where's she going to sleep?" Felicity asked.

"Let her sleep on her own crummy couch. Maybe then she'll finally be convinced she needs a new one. She won't listen to me. Then again, maybe she should just join us in the bed. Would you believe that for *all* my experience, a threesome is something I've yet to be a part of?" Ben asked teasingly.

She elbowed him, which probably did hurt a little, but he laughed. "Behave yourself, or I'm going back out into the living room," she threatened.

"Sorry, but I can't help it. You're fun to tease, and it makes for a good distraction," he said.

She suddenly remembered why he had asked her in here. "Is it strong?"

"I guess that depends, I don't know how strong it gets. I don't think she's right outside, but I feel her." He turned to face Felicity better. "Do you really feel this every time Cain's around?"

"I don't know if it's the same, but yeah. Only picture how powerful it would be if she were standing right next to you."

"No wonder you're always so distracted."

"Am I?" She could feel him shrug. "You know what's really weird? Whenever he touches me..."

"I don't want to hear about *that.*"

"Not like *that*. I just meant, like... regular touching. Never mind."

"I think it's going away," he told her.

"Good, go to sleep," she answered.

They did. For an hour or so, anyway. Felicity was awakened a little while later. Cain was nearby. Not very close, but she could feel him. It didn't bother her anymore really, now that she understood it. As she got used to the feeling, actually it was kind of nice... comforting. She wondered why it had woken her. It didn't seem to be getting any stronger or moving away, so wherever he was, he must be staying there for a while. She thought about where they were and what was close by. Tommy's maybe, that would probably be the only place close by that he would actually stay for any length of time.

She was drifting back to sleep when Ben mumbled something and rolled from his side to his back. He fidgeted restlessly and she realized that he was probably why she had woken up in the first place. He was still sleeping, but very fitfully. He was obviously distressed. Either he was dreaming, or it was Sindy. She was just wondering if she should wake him, when he woke on his own with a gasp. He lay still for a moment, breathing rapidly and trying to calm his nerves. After a minute, she asked, "Are you okay?"

He flinched a little at her voice. He must have thought that she was sleeping. "Yeah. I'm fine; I was just... having a bad dream. Man, Sindy must be right outside. I'm alright, go back to sleep."

He rolled over, to face away from her and try to go back to sleep. He fidgeted a few more times and Felicity felt bad for him. She remembered how odd and panicky she had felt the first few times she'd sensed Cain. Ben was probably having similar feelings, if not worse. Sindy had spent an awfully long time drinking from him. He'd probably gotten a lot of venom in his system. She wondered if it was much stronger than what she felt with Cain.

He fidgeted again and his breathing turned a bit ragged. Felicity moved closer to him, up against his back, as she had to comfort herself that night in her room. She put an arm around him, in kind of a hug. He put a hand up onto her arm and gave it a little squeeze. Then after a few minutes, he took her arm up off of him and slid away, out of her reach. "I appreciate the gesture," he said, lying on his back again. "But I think it's better if you stay over there."

"Oh. Okay."

After a few minutes, he hesitantly reached out and took her hand, interlacing their fingers. They lay on their backs, on opposite sides of the bed, each with one arm stretched out to the middle. He didn't let go of her hand, so she gave it a slight squeeze and lay there waiting for sleep to come. She could tell by his uneven breathing that he was still bothered and not sleeping. He squeezed her hand a few times, but he didn't speak to her again. If Ben suffered any other odd perceptions from Sindy, he kept them to himself. Eventually, they slept.

Chapter 2 - We have a problem

Cain

2:00, Monday morning
Tommy's Place

Cain pulled into the lot at Tommy's. He could feel Sindy moving away from him, towards Allie's apartment he assumed. He could feel Ben there, burning with Sindy's new signature upon him. Felicity was still there as well, shining with Cain's own comforting glow about her. They must be staying with Alyson this evening. They would be safe there. If Sindy wanted to sit outside and try to make Ben sweat a bit, then let her. Nothing would come of it, and at least it would give him a respite from her presence.

Cain walked through the front doors of the bar and looked around. There were no other vampires present, a fact for which he was grateful, as usual. It wasn't really crowded, but he was a little surprised to see that there were more than just a few patrons, considering it was late Sunday night. There really wasn't much else to do in a small town.

He didn't bother to visit the bar. He made his way towards the back to find a semi-private place to sit and think about his prior conversation with Sindy. He settled himself at a table and became lost in thought, until he was startled back to attention by someone addressing him from across the table. He looked up to find Alyson standing there with her little serving tray in hand. He was surprised; he hadn't expected to find her working tonight. She was looking at him expectantly with her usual mocking attitude.

"I'm sorry, what?" he asked sheepishly.

"Do you want a drink? From the bar," she added with a smile.

"Right. I'll take a rum and coke." She was turning to go when he called out, "Make it two."

"Two?"

"Save you a trip." She gave him an odd look and went to get his drinks. He stared after her, thinking of Mattie. He was still rather in shock over that. So Alyson was Mattie's chosen one? She had to be; it did seem to fall into place. Mattie had questioned Cain the year before, about how to properly change someone into a vampire. He was very excited, but worried about it. It seemed something that he wanted badly to do, but was frightened to try it. He'd never attempted it before. In fact, he'd never even killed a person that Cain knew of. In that, Cain envied him.

Cain had instilled supreme caution and care into the boy as far as turning someone was concerned. It was not something to be done lightly. Mattie had told Cain of the deep care and devotion he felt toward the one he had chosen. He had never given Cain their name, saying only that it was a childhood friend with whom he was still very close. Cain had never asked, because he'd felt that it was better if Mattie's past life remain somewhat separate. He was going to have to learn to let it go. If he turned his friend, there would be time enough for Cain to meet them then.

Mattie had made it clear to Cain that his affections ran deep for this friend and that he was terrified to fail them, so Cain did something that he had rarely ever done. He gave Mattie detailed and explicit instructions on how to properly turn his friend into a vampire. It was not so difficult to do, but to be careless was to create a horror. Far better to err on the side of caution. Usually he simply advised others against it, but Mattie was different. Cain knew that Mattie would never even think of attempting such a thing without the subjects express consent. Mattie was a gentle soul and he deserved the knowledge that he asked for. Cain believed that he had the good judgment to use it wisely. Mattie was very attentive and somber. He asked numerous questions and had many worries. It was a good sign that he would heed Cain's teachings. Cain was confident that when the time came, it would be done well.

Cain had always assumed from Mattie's attitude, that it was a girl, until that night in the woods with Ben. That had made him wonder. He'd had no idea that this was Mattie's home. He was shocked to find that the young man who had served him coffee nightly for three months, had been one of Mattie's very good friends. He'd begun to worry for Mattie, because if it was indeed Ben whom he wished to change, Mattie would be sorely disappointed. Ben would never want such a life. He gradually came to realize that it could not possibly be Benjamin though. Mattie could never be so blind, as to think that Ben would come around to embrace such an existence. It just was not in him. Besides, Cain had been sure that Mattie was still seeing his friend on a regular basis, whereas Ben said he had only seen Mattie but once since his change. No, it had to be Alyson. Cain approved. Alyson had just the personality to make her tough and strong without being cruel or heartless. He was glad. Mattie needed someone like her.

Cain was extremely proud of Mattie, although Cain had merely shown him the way of things. Mattie's character and way of life were his own accomplishments. Cain felt that only divine intervention could have placed him in the boy's path at so perfect a time in his development. Mattie had been newly turned and horrified at the prospect of living as a creature of the night. He was starved and alone, having run from the ones who had sired him. He had been changed against his will by brood of vampires who were trying to gain advantage over another coven, by increasing their own numbers. Such territorial wars were rare and never lasted long. Most vampires were happy to be left alone with their chosen few companions, and would rather flee than fight, if given a choice. Vampires with warlike tendencies usually managed to kill each other off rather quickly.

Mattie was very lucky to have been so well made. Most vampires were not so careful or thorough, but from what information Cain could glean from the boy, his change had been somewhat of a 'group effort' on the part of several vampires together. It had been a sort of 'gang bang' affair, that they had indulged in for fun as well as to turn him. The result was that Mattie had been drunk from and then fed by his captors many times. His rebirth as a vampire had been traumatic but thorough. He had run from his siring brood as soon as he'd been able. They had surely given chase, but apparently met up with their enemies along the way. There were few survivors after it was done and none were interested in Mattie any longer.

Cain had found him on the steps to the church, of all places, shortly before dawn. His heart had immediately gone out to the boy, who had obviously been contemplating suicide. He had taken Mattie into his home, seen that he was fed, and had then begun to teach him a new way of life. Mattie had stayed with him on and off for almost a year, traveling every couple of weeks to visit a friend that he'd had in his past life. Cain had never taken such time with any other apprentice, other than those few that he had made himself. In fact, most other vampires simply accepted his suggestions or asked his advice and then encouraged him to move on. Mattie was eager for knowledge and friendship, something that filled a need in Cain also, but once he was confident that Mattie could be independent, Cain also felt the need to travel, to continue to help others. He had of course invited Mattie to join him, but had known that Mattie wouldn't care to venture too far from his home. He still had ties there that he was unwilling to give up just yet.

They had kept in touch, meeting in various places over the next two years, never leaving each other without setting up a place for future contact. Cain had drilled Mattie relentlessly in the art of cloaking his presence from others. Mattie was such a kind and peaceful young man, he could gain nothing from associating with most other vampires, Cain had assured him.

When last they'd spoken, Mattie had told Cain that he would be found in a town nearby this one, come early December. But it was just another town, one of dozens they had inhabited. Cain knew that they were in the general area where Mattie had once lived, but had not thought that he would be in the very spot, with people from Mattie's past. Cain had been traveling in this general direction anyway, following rumors of rogue vampires needing to learn discretion. Those vampires had of course turned out to be Sindy and Ernest. Shortly before he arrived, Sindy had also added Luke and Chris to her little family. Cain had thought to make contact with Sindy and the others, teach them to lead a less destructive existence and then go on to meet his friend.

So here he was in the local pub, being served drinks by the very girl that he had calmly sat and discussed with Mattie, how to turn into a vampire. He wondered if Mattie had approached her about it yet. Had she turned him down? Or perhaps he had become afraid that it would not go as planned.

Of course, it was possible that Mattie had been thinking of someone else entirely, but Cain didn't think so. Mattie was quiet and shy, and Cain couldn't imagine him being close with more than a few select people. Cain watched Alyson move through the crowd to return to him with his drinks, and wondered just how much Mattie had shared with her.

She put down two napkins on the table in front of him, and then placed a drink on each. "It's thirteen."

He handed her a twenty-dollar bill and she began to dig into her apron pocket for change. "Keep it," he told her.

She looked down at him with curious appreciation. "Thanks."

He smiled as he took a sip of his drink and then gestured towards the other glass on the table. "You want one?"

Now she really seemed bewildered by his attitude. "I can't, I'm working." She just stood there and watched him for a second. "You're in a friendly mood."

"I've just found out that we've a mutual friend."

Her eyes widened and she quickly looked about to see if she was being watched by her boss. Apparently, she decided it was safe to sit. She took the chair opposite his and leaned over the table towards him, anxiously. "Do you know where he is?"

"No, I'm sorry." He noted her look of concern. "But you needn't worry. Mattie knows how to keep out of trouble."

"I'm surprised you even know him. He usually hides himself from other vampires."

Cain smiled. "Who do you think taught him how to do that?"

Allie stared at him with a look of uncertainty that quickly turned to suspicion. "Are you... Did you *do it* to him?"

"No! No, I'm not Mattie's sire. Just a friend." So, Mattie hadn't told her of his beginnings. Perhaps he hadn't wanted to frighten her, although Alyson was hardly a girl of delicate sensibilities. More likely, Mattie had been afraid that given information about the vampires who had abducted him, Alyson would probably try to hunt them down and kill them. That would only lead to her bringing more danger down upon herself than even she could handle. Cain could see that for all of her oddities and outspokenness, she was a most loyal friend. He wondered how long Mattie'd been away from her. "How long has it been?"

She actually took on a quiet and shy demeanor, very unlike herself. Yes, she and Mattie were intimately close. She didn't even have to think to answer his question. "May. I used to see him at least one weekend a month. Sometimes he'd even stay longer. The last time I saw him, he told me that he wanted to travel around a little, and that he might not be back until Halloween, but it's a long time, you know?"

Mattie must have meant to spend the month here with Alyson before going to meet Cain in December. Cain wondered if Mattie had expected to turn her during that time, and then bring her to meet Cain. It certainly seemed plausible. Cain knew that Mattie had drunk from her, although he had never yet tasted human blood at the time Cain had found him. Mattie existed on animal blood, as Cain did. Cain had certainly hoped that it would remain Mattie's prime source of sustenance, but had spoken to him about having control when drinking from a person, just in case. He was not so naive as to think that Mattie might never be tempted. Better to give him preventative cautions on how to be sure not to hurt the one that he drank from.

Not long after that talk, Mattie had come back to speak to him about it again, almost as a sort of confession. Mattie had told him of the few times that he had dared to sample a human's blood. He had told Cain in hesitant whispers of how he'd drunk from his very best friend, a willing offering. Even if Mattie hadn't told him, he might have guessed it from Allie's attitude. Most likely, it had become a regular thing. She definitely cared for him, but there was also a great need in her voice. If the victim were willing, it could be an amazing experience. Cain gave Alyson a sympathetic nod. "It must be difficult. He kept you safe too, didn't he?"

She returned his small nod with one of her own. "I can take care of myself, but things have been getting pretty rough around here." She rubbed the back of her head, where Sindy's thugs had clubbed her, Cain assumed. "It's a little overcrowded in this town, don't ya' think?"

"Definitely."

"I never had to worry much about it before, but lately I feel like I'm seein' 'em every other night." She lowered her voice and seemed as though she were very happy to have someone sympathetic to confide in. "It's gettin' to be nervous business just gettin' home from work, now that my mark's gone."

Cain stared at her long and hard. "Are you... You're not... asking for my protection, are you?"

It took her a second to realize the implication. "No! I mean, no. Um, thanks? I think I'll just wait for Mattie."

He smiled. He found the whole exchange rather amusing actually. He'd thought she might be asking him to bite her and she was basically thanking him for it, while trying to decline without offending him. He wouldn't have anyway, even if he were so inclined. She was Mattie's, marked or not. "Good. No offense. I mean, not that I wouldn't if... but, no. I think it's best if that does not occur. I will keep watch for Mattie though. I'm sure he'll be around soon."

Just then, the bouncer walked by and gave Allie a playful little shove as he passed. "Hey Allie, flirt on your own time."

She looked a little embarrassed as she rose from the table, but still flashed Cain a big smile. "Thanks."

She left, but was sure to keep a full drink in front of him all evening. Cain found himself half listening to the conversation at the next table. Two young men happened to be discussing a movie they must have just seen. It turned out to be a film that Cain had just recently sat through, twice. He soon introduced himself and was drawn into their conversation.

A short while later, he noticed that Sindy was on the move again. He had felt her presence, just barely, all along, but had ignored her. Now she seemed to be striding purposefully straight towards him. Even if she was unsure that he was here, she would find him soon enough. There was nowhere else to go at this hour.

Sure enough, she strode through the door minutes later. She was made to pause for words with the bouncer, who apparently did not like her behavior the last few times she was here. Cain saw that Alyson had noticed her arrival. She looked to Cain, but he gave her a shake of the head to indicate that she should leave Sindy to him. Alyson looked as though she'd rather go throw Sindy out and stake her in the parking lot, but the bouncer seemed to have come to some agreement with her and was letting her enter. Alyson went into the kitchen to avoid trouble.

Cain turned to his newfound friends. "If you'll excuse me gentlemen, I believe we're about to be interrupted."

They looked up to see Sindy bearing down on them. "She can interrupt me anytime," one of them remarked.

"You don't want *her* attentions, believe me," Cain replied as she approached. She looked beautifully murderous.

She stopped directly in front of him and paused to glance at his companions. She turned back to Cain and put her hands on her hips. "We have a problem."

"What else is new? Would you like to have a seat?"

She looked as if the very idea was ridiculous. "No I don't want a seat. I'll take that drink though." Without waiting for him to give her leave, she snatched his full glass from the table and proceeded to chug it down without a breath.

"Help yourself," he remarked, dryly. "Weren't you meant to be out tormenting Ben this evening, so that I might have some peace?"

She finished the drink and slammed the glass down on the table. "Well, I gladly would have, if your slut of a girlfriend hadn't beaten me to him!"

This drew an 'Oooo', from the guys he'd been talking to. He fixed Sindy with an icy glare. "Do you think we might take this outside?" he asked through gritted teeth.

She gave the guys a sharp glance, and stalked towards the back door. "Whatever."

Cain faced the young men who were giving him amused but sympathetic smiles. "Excuse us."

He followed Sindy out the back door and before he was barely outside she spun around to glare at him accusingly. He shut the door behind them and addressed her. "Now, what are you going on about?"

"I am talking about Benjamin. Your little Miss Priss is sleeping with my Ben! I guess she's not as innocent as I thought."

Cain looked at the ground as he stretched out his awareness to them once again. Yes, Ben and Felicity were still together, and of course Alyson was here, but that didn't have to mean anything, did it? Although they were close, their traces were distinctly separate, they did not overlap or even really touch, that he could tell.

Sindy gave a little stomp on the ground and groaned like a child deprived of a treat. He looked up to see her gazing back at him, sullen and forlorn. "Oh Cain, I did him *so* good too. That boy's got me coursin' all through him. I think he must be my best handiwork yet! I'm tellin' ya', I had him squirmin'! Hell, if he'd been alone, I'll bet he would have met me right out on the God damned driveway!"

At this, Cain had to laugh, although she didn't seem pleased by his reaction. "I think you overestimate our abilities, my dear."

She moved closer to wave her finger in his face. "Oh no. Don't you try to tell me." He shooed her hand away with a wave. "This is one area where you have no experience, but since you taught me to leave 'em breathin', this has become my favorite pastime. I know what I'm capable of. If I dose 'em up right, I can call them right out of their sweet safe little houses and into my waiting arms! It's a beautiful thing. I've had guys sleepwalkin' all over this town! But Benjamin is special; Ben is mine! That boy's got the temperament and body of a wild stallion and I'm ready to ride!"

He rolled his eyes at her ridiculous metaphor. "Oh please." He then gave her a hard stare. "So you only agreed not to go after him, because all along you believed that you'd put him in thrall and he'd just come right to you? Well, you'll have to excuse my lack of sympathy that it didn't quite work out for you."

She stared at him resentfully. "It would have worked out just fine. I was feelin' him real strong and I *know* he was feelin' me, but the closer I got, the more I had the sense that something wasn't quite right. I reach the house and lo and behold, what do I see? But your little shinin' star right there with him; in his very bed! I spent over an hour feedin' that boy the best vibes of his life and your little whore is in there reapin' the rewards!"

"Watch your tongue."

"You don't believe me do you? Come and see for yourself! I'm tellin' you we're both gettin' screwed and not in the fun way." She tugged at his arm to follow her closer to Alyson's house, but he shook her off.

"I don't need to go anywhere. I can see them from here."

"That's impossible!"

He raised his eyebrows and gave her a look to remind her that he was over three centuries her senior and she should not presume to know what he might be capable of. "They *are* together. They are still; they're sleeping."

"*Now.* What do you *think* they were doing in bed together?"

Cain took a deep breath and expelled it slowly. She didn't know anything. So they were together, that didn't have to mean they'd had sex. Sindy didn't even know for sure that they were in a bed. So they had been close to each other for a long time, they could be sitting on a couch watching television for all she knew.

Even if they *had* been romantic, as much as Cain wished for that not to be true, he had no right to judge their actions. Whatever his own feelings, he certainly wasn't going to show them to Sindy. He kept his voice neutral and steady. "Felicity has made no pledge of devotion towards me; she may do as she pleases. And certainly neither of them owes anything to you! It's none of our affair."

"Are you kidding? Don't try and act like this doesn't bother you! You've put in a lot of time on that girl and she's obviously steppin' out on you Cain. Doesn't that make you just wanna drain her dry?"

He fought to keep level headed and calm. "Statements like that, will hurt no one but you. The fact that they are together means nothing." She just stared at him mockingly.

Felicity wouldn't have chosen to give herself to Ben, would she? The two did seem awfully close. She'd shown such concern for him last night. Perhaps it was strong feelings for Ben, which gave her such resolve to keep from acting on any desires she might have for Cain. It did seem odd that although she had shown such interest in Cain before, she was now able to hold herself so aloof from him. Considering what he himself felt for her from the marking, the urges she felt for him from the venom alone, must be at least equally as strong. And she had felt for him even before that, hadn't she? It was she who had kissed him. Had he spent so much time being cautious and worried for her, that she had decided not to wait? Had she become attached to Ben while he had worked so hard to keep himself away, so that he wouldn't hurt her? "Are you telling me that you actually observed romantic activity between them?" Cain asked.

She looked petulant and sour. "Cain, I know Ben. I also know that my feedin' from him was a guilty pleasure that he'll never forget. He *wanted* me Cain, bad. I've got that boy so worked up I could probably get him off with a touch," she said with a lewd little chuckle. "Now I may find Felicity sickeningly sweet on most occasions, but I've got to admit, as far as the physical stuff goes, you've got good taste. Don't think that's lost on my Ben, he's not blind. I've got him all wantin' and you think they're just laying there? Wise up."

He stared at her coldly. "And what exactly would you have me do?"

2

She stopped pouting to give him a hopeful suggestion. "You could *call* her. Make her leave him. It's real easy, you could do it. I could show you how."

"I've no doubt I could accomplish anything *you've* so easily mastered, but I've certainly no need to call a woman from another man's bed. They choose of their own will and that's the end of it."

"You're just going to leave her there?!"

"Sindy, go home and play with your boys. They are yours, as Ben never will be."

She glared at him as though her discontentment was all his fault. "So I get no Ben *and* no hunt, and I suppose *you* still don't want to play?" she asked crossly.

He didn't bother to answer that. "You really haven't fed this evening?"

"From a plastic bag. How do you find *that* at all satisfying?"

"Put it in a glass in the microwave."

She looked disgusted. "I'm talking about the experience! Don't you miss it? You never have any fun! At least I can feed off my boys when they get home."

"That's cheating," he reprimanded her mildly.

She eyed him appraisingly. "You want some?" She moved her long black hair away from the side of her throat and turned her head to expose it to him. "I'd let you."

He never entertained the notion that he actually would, but it was tempting. "Go home Sindy."

She gave him a long time to change his mind, eyeing him wantonly and absently playing with a thin gold chain she wore around her throat, winding it about her finger. He found himself staring at the light glinting off of the chain as though mesmerized. He gave no outward sign, but was a little surprised at himself by how much he actually wanted to drink from her. Marking Felicity had been a dangerous reminder of what he was missing. Drinking from Sindy would be all reward with no regret.

He ignored her as best he could, and turned his attention back to Felicity and Ben. They hadn't even moved; they must be asleep. Sindy eventually gave up on him. He was very glad when she finally left.

The back door opened, rousing him from his thoughts. It was Alyson holding his jacket. She glanced around to see if he was alone. Sindy was gone. "We're closin' up and I'm goin' home. You left this at the table. Nice leather, be a shame to lose it."

He walked over and took it from her. "Thanks."

"Everything alright?"

He sighed. "Besides my usual nightly torment? Fine." Alyson looked at him warily and took an unconscious step back. He looked up and gave her a weary smile. "Relax, you're not my type. Not anymore anyway."

She thought about that for a minute. "Do you... live like Mattie?"

He grinned. "I suppose it'd be more accurate to say that Mattie lives like me, but yes, I buy my blood." He fixed her with a steady gaze. "I have for centuries, but it's not always easy," he added in a whisper.

She studied him for a minute. He wondered what she was thinking. He wanted to tell her more, of what it was like, what to expect. It was not the sort of life that everyone could handle, but he thought that she could, if she chose. However, it was not his place to offer such information unsolicited. Any questions she had, remained unasked. "You'll be alright getting home?" he finally asked. "Sindy was by there earlier, but I don't think she'll return. It's getting late."

"She knows Ben's there."

"Felicity's with him."

"Good, I was hopin' he wouldn't have to ride it out alone. I was thinkin' I'd get out of here earlier, but..." She shrugged. "At least they're okay. I'm sure Ben didn't take it well." Either she didn't think anything would happen between Ben and Felicity, or she just didn't care. The fact that they'd been alone together all night obviously didn't interest her, except in protecting Ben's well being. Alyson stifled a yawn. "Well, I'm gonna split. See ya."

"Goodnight." She went back into the bar and he heard her bolt the door from the inside. He walked around the building to his waiting motorcycle in the nearly empty parking lot. He mounted the bike and sped off towards home.

Chapter 3 - Give her what she wants

Felicity

Alyson's apartment
4:20, Monday morning

Felicity awoke with a start as she heard Alyson come in the front door. She had a terrible wave of guilt as she realized that she probably should have waited for her; met her at the door, knowing that Sindy was nearby, but she'd fallen back asleep. Ben was also sleeping and Allie seemed to have made it in okay. Maybe Sindy had left. Alyson came to the bedroom doorway and peeked in. Felicity let go of Ben's hand and sat up a little, though she was still half-asleep. "You want your bed back?"

"Na, that's okay." She entered the room and grabbed a nightshirt from her drawer. "Is he alright?"

"Yes, he's finally sleeping."

"Cool, I'll see you in the morning."

Alyson went back out into the living room. Felicity lay back down, but planned to get up and go out to Alyson. She felt as though she should take the opportunity to talk to Allie alone. She was so exhausted that she fell back asleep before she hardly finished the thought.

The next thing she knew, she was hearing what was surely designed to be absolutely the most annoying noise in the world. It was Alyson's alarm clock. It was on Ben's side, he must have set it. She lay there cringing and wondering how Ben could possibly bear to hear that for another minute without shutting it off.

Then a horrible fear came across her, that something was wrong. A fear that Sindy had come back; that somehow she had gotten inside and done something to him. No one could sleep through that horrible noise. She sat up and looked at him in dread. He was still, his features calm and peaceful in sleep. She put a hand on his chest; he was breathing. She felt relief wash over her, and she left her hand there for a moment, feeling his heartbeat. He looked so sweet and vulnerable; she felt bad about his problems with Sindy and couldn't help but feel a bit protective over him. Of course, it was much easier to feel that way when he was sleeping and not arguing with her.

Allie yelled from the living room, startling her. "Somebody shut that damn thing off!" She looked down at Ben again, nothing. It was 7:17 a.m.

Felicity practically had to lie on top of him to reach the alarm clock. It took her a minute to find the right button. She wanted to make sure she didn't just hit snooze, or it would go off again. She finally got it to be quiet and then looked down to find Ben looking back up at her. She hastily withdrew.

"Time to get up I guess," she said a little awkwardly. He just closed his eyes again. She got up and went into kitchen. After some searching, she managed to locate some cereal and a bowl. Alyson got up off the couch and dragged herself into the bedroom. A few minutes later Ben stumbled into the kitchen, barely glancing at her and looking very weary. He fumbled around at the counter behind her.

"Kicked you out did she?" Felicity asked.

"Coffee?" Ben asked sleepily.

"No thanks," she replied.

He finished setting up the coffeemaker and slumped into the chair opposite her. "How can you be awake with no coffee? You can't have gotten more than a few hours sleep. I know I didn't."

"Why don't you go back to bed?"

He sighed. She got the feeling he would rather not have to talk until after he got some caffeine. "I've got class."

"You're going to classes today?" Felicity asked incredulously.

"They beat up my body, not my brain." He got up to watch the coffee perk. "Besides, if we're not going to scrap the whole semester and go to Vermont..." He shot her a hopeful glance. She shook her head no. "Then mid-terms are coming up and I can't miss." He got impatient waiting for the coffee and finally just poured what little was in the pot so far, into a mug. He mixed his coffee and stood drinking it at the counter. He turned to face her. "Don't you have Algebra with Ashley this morning?"

"Yeah, at 8:45," she told him.

"Make sure you tell her I had a wonderful time at the dance," he said sarcastically. "Well, I've got until 9:00. I figure that's just enough time to run home for a quick shower and change. I'll give you a ride," he said.

"Your car's still at school," she reminded him.

He grabbed a piece of paper and a pen out of the drawer. "Well, that wasn't *my* idea." He wrote Alyson a note and put it on the table in front of Felicity. It read:

> A-
>
> I'm taking your car. Will pick you up for lunch.
>
> -Ben
>
> (P.S.) If anything happened to my Mustang, it's coming out of your paycheck!

He looked down at her cereal. "You done?"

"Yeah." She got up and put her bowl in the sink.

She began to walk past him, back out to get her stuff. "'Liss," She stopped to look at him. "Thanks. For staying."

She smiled. "Don't mention it."

~~~~~~~~~~~~~~~~~~~~~~~~~~~~~~~~

Lunchtime found Felicity sitting at a table by herself, eating a sandwich and a yogurt. She saw Karen across the cafeteria, rushing on her way somewhere else and gave a quick wave, but no Ben and Allie yet. She wondered if Alyson had even been awake when Ben went to pick her up.

Finally, she saw them enter and stood up with a wave for them to find her. They made their way to the table. Ben dumped his books with a timid 'hey', that made her wonder if he was embarrassed that he'd asked her to stay with him last night. He hardly made eye contact with her, but quickly turned to Allie. "Let's go get something to eat."

Alyson handed him some money from her back pocket and then slumped into a chair, evincing no further plans of moving. "My treat, get me something."

Ben looked surprised that she wasn't coming. "What do you want?"

"Whatever. Juice, some snack cakes or somethin'. You know, stuff."

"Why don't you just come pick out what you want?"

She looked over at Felicity for a moment and then fixed him with a steady stare. "I don't want to." Ben looked from one girl to the other. Obviously, they planned to talk about him when he left. Alyson waved a hand towards the lunch counter. "Shoo."

Ben looked at her in annoyance. "Just for that, you're getting salad." He turned to leave.

Alyson called after him. "You bring back a salad and you'll be wearing it!" She watched him go and then turned her attention to Felicity.

"Everything okay with you guys? About Mattie I mean." Felicity asked.

Allie shrugged. "I'm never supposed to mention him again."

"That's it, just avoid the problem?" Felicity asked.

"That's just the way Ben does things, but he also knows that I don't listen to him anyway. When the topic comes up, he'll deal. He just wants to be sure that I know he doesn't approve. Anyway, enough of that. I've got limited time and lots of questions. All I'm getting from Ben is avoidance and denial, so I need you to fill me in. What happened last night?"

Felicity became flustered. "Nothing! We were sleeping!"

Allie rolled her eyes. "Not with *you*. Ben would've told me if you were *doin' it*. I'm talkin' about Sindy. She came by, right?"

Felicity wasn't sure whether to be happy that Allie believed her, or disgruntled by the fact that Allie was so sure that Ben would've shared it with her. "Oh. Yeah. I felt really bad; we should have warned you that she was there."

"Like I couldn't figure out that Sindy wouldn't pass up the chance to get Ben all hot and bothered? Anyway, she was long gone by the time I got home. So, how'd he take it?"

"He didn't say much. Just that she was there."

"Well of course not. Mr. Prideful. What do you think I'm askin' *you* for?"

Felicity tried not to get annoyed by her attitude. "Well, it must have bothered him, because I started out on the couch, but then he came out and asked me to join him in the bedroom."

Alyson burst out laughing. "Strange behavior! Because there could be no other possible reason, for Ben to have been asking you to join him in the bedroom?"

Felicity gave Allie a withering look and glanced around uncomfortably for Ben. He was still on line. "No. I mean, not that the thought hadn't crossed my mind, but no. Judging by the way he acted once I got there, I'd say he was freaked."

"How'd he act? Come on, I don't have time for subtle! I need details!"

Felicity sighed. "Well, I don't think it was so bad at first, but it must have gotten worse later. It woke him up. He seemed really agitated and kind of spooked. So I moved closer and put my arm around him." Allie began to smirk and raised an eyebrow. "Like to comfort him! But then he pushed me away, like he didn't even want me to touch him."

"Now that's not normal Ben behavior." Felicity looked at her questioningly. "Not that the man can't control himself, but let's face it, I can't exactly see him *fending you off.*"

Felicity became insulted. "Well it's not like I was trying to..." she broke off in a huff as she looked up to find Ben approaching with his lunch tray. He was met with silence as he put it down on the table. It was piled with the usual junk food and stuff that Allie would have bought.

"It's always so comforting, when all conversation stops as soon as I arrive."

Felicity looked up at him, ashamed. "We weren't really talking about anything important."

Ben sat down and gave her a condescending smile. "I know exactly what you were talking about, I'm not stupid. We're all adults here and we've all three of us been bitten at one time or another. It's not exactly a big secret." He looked from one to the other of them. Alyson looked almost smug, Felicity felt terrible. Ben continued, "She's going to do that to me every night, isn't she?"

Allie answered. "Yep, I'm sure she will."

Ben looked disgusted. "Great, so I can basically look forward to nightly torture for the next three to four weeks."

Alyson grinned. "Torture? Oh, come on Benji. It wasn't that bad, was it?"

He stared at her coldly. "Don't call me Benji, you know I hate that."

Alyson kept after him, undaunted. "So, is it just like a weird and repulsive blood thing for you, or is it really sexual?"

He glared at her fiercely. "If I didn't answer you in the car, what makes you think I want to talk about it now?" He looked over to Felicity. "We may have all been bitten, but I'm betting that they were three very different experiences."

Alyson still wore a smug smile on her face, but Felicity sympathized with Ben. At least she and Allie had liked the guys who had bitten them. She couldn't imagine what it would be like to feel the effects from a bite from someone you loathed.

That reminded her, she would have to let Allie know that Cain did indeed know Mattie, but this was probably not the time. The next time that she could get Allie alone, she would mention it.

Felicity suddenly realized that Alyson had also been bitten by Sindy once herself. She wanted to remark on that and ask what the effect had been, but didn't quite have the courage. Allie softened her tone and answered Felicity's unasked question on her own. "Come on Ben, I've been bitten by Sindy too you know. She didn't get me as good as she got you, but I felt it. You wanna talk about unwanted urges? She did you good. I know it must be strong." She gave Felicity a mischievous grin. "I guess Felicity and I will just have to keep you distracted and otherwise occupied nightly for the next three to four weeks."

Felicity looked at her as though she were insane. Ben just smiled. "As delightful as that sounds, I think I'd rather take Cain up on *his* offer."

Allie looked bewildered and amused. "You'd rather sleep with Cain? I didn't think he was your type."

Felicity spoke up about Cain's 'offer' as Ben glared at Allie in annoyance. "You can't do that, it'll never work."

Allie looked over at her. "Do what, sleep with Cain?"

Ben ignored Allie. "It could work, if we're careful."

"What could work?" Allie asked.

"You know she'd feel you coming." Felicity retorted.

"Alyson could do it," Ben suggested.

"**Do what?**" Alyson yelled.

Felicity answered Allie while shaking her head at Ben. "Cain knows where they're sleeping. Ben thinks that we can go over there in the daytime and just open the blinds on them or something."

Alyson looked at Ben with much the same sarcastic attitude as Felicity. "Yeah right, because I'm sure that Sindy has conveniently pushed her coffin up against the window for us, so that we could just open the lid and watch her burn."

"They don't sleep in coffins," Felicity said quietly.

"Some do," Allie corrected her.

"Cain doesn't," Felicity informed her.

"Well neither does Mattie, but that doesn't say anything about Sindy. Some vampires prefer it," Allie replied.

Ben banged a hand down on the table for attention. "Ladies, instead of spending the rest of lunch telling you how disgusted and appalled I am by your thorough knowledge of vampire sleeping habits, I think I'm just going to scrap that whole plan and try something much more simple. Sindy wants me, right?" Alyson looked as though she'd like to make a rude comment, but Ben stared her down. "So tonight when she comes, I'll just give her what she wants."

Allie laughed, Felicity was confused. "What are you going to do?"

"I'm going to go outside," Ben told her.

Allie smiled. "And let off some steam?"

"With a stake," Ben clarified forcefully.

Felicity touched his arm in concern. "You can't do that, they'll kill you. She wouldn't be stupid enough to come alone."

Allie looked thoughtful. "She might. She was goin' on about wantin' to *take* you in private."

Ben didn't look thrilled with her phrasing. "I wonder if she came alone last night? We should have looked out the window."

Felicity shuddered at the thought. "Too creepy. She wasn't alone when she took you from the dance. She knew you'd fight her. What is she going to think, that you had a sudden change of heart? I don't care how much venom is in your system, she knows you hate her."

Ben looked at her thoughtfully. "Yeah, but she doesn't think like you. No matter how much she knows I hate her, she'd still believe I wanna fuck her."

"Ben!" Felicity said in shock.

Allie interjected. "He's right. She would." She gave Ben a disapproving look. "Some guys are like that."

"Well I wouldn't *do it,* but she'd let me get close; close enough."

"Still, she'd probably try to lure you someplace else first, and that's not good. What do you think she's gonna do, let you take her right there out on the lawn, like a dog?" Allie asked.

"She might. She thinks I've got this fantasy about us out on the grass, remember?"

Felicity spoke up. "Ben it's too dangerous. She'll probably bring that huge guy with her. Look what she had him do to you last time! What if you can't get her?"

"Then I guess she'll get me. I'll survive. I did before."

"And if she decides to go a little further this time? We should get Cain. Just for back up, in case things get out of hand and she tries to go too far, or if she sics that guy on you. She wouldn't even have to know that Cain was there unless you needed him." Felicity placed her hand on Ben's arm again, to emphasize her alarm over the issue.

He looked into her eyes and she could tell he appreciated her concern, but he spoke quietly and firmly against the idea. "I don't want Cain's help. Besides, I've got Allie," he added with a smile.

Alyson was caught off guard. "What am I supposed to do?"

"You're the one who spent all of her money on those jui jitsu lessons. Take him out for me," he said with a challenging smile.

"What am I, Buffy the Vampire Slayer?"

Ben laughed. "Relax, it won't come to that. I'm telling you, she'll be alone. Even if she's not, I don't need you to kill anyone, just distract them. If I do it right, I can stake her before she even knows I don't want to play. Then we just have to get into the house, where they can't follow."

Alyson looked as though she might actually be considering it. Felicity tightened her grip on Ben's arm. "Ben, you're going to get yourself killed! Just stay in the house until she goes away. The mark will fade, what's the big deal? Wait it out, please."

"You just don't get it 'Liss, I can't. You were right. It's like she was *calling* me. And God help me, but I wanted to go to her, *badly*. If you weren't there, I probably would have. I'm not going to let her do that to me every night. I can't. And you can't be anywhere near us. She'll never buy it if you're around. You're marked. She can feel you, so she has to know that you were there last night. She probably figures that's why she couldn't get to me. If you're there again, but I come out, she'll know something's up. You're working tonight anyway. After work, you have to go back to your room and stay there. One way or another, one of us will come and let you know what happened in the morning," he said with a glance to Allie.

"No way!" Felicity said indignantly. "I'm not going to just sit in my room by myself, waiting to find out if you guys got yourselves killed!"

"Then why don't you go sit with Cain?" Ben asked with a sardonic edge. She gave him a wounded look and he softened. "If you come, you *will* get me killed. She has to believe that I'm alone, or she wouldn't think that I'd give in to her. She'd know it was a trap. Stay home, okay?"

"Are you really going to do this?" Felicity asked incredulously.

He nodded. "I feel like I have to."

She looked over to Alyson. "And you're going to let him?"

Allie shrugged. "I may tease him about it and piss him off, but I know it'll kill him if he doesn't do something. He's like my brother, I've gotta back him up."

"You guys are being so stupid!" Felicity sat sulking and looking from Ben to Allie. Obviously, they weren't backing down. She glanced up at the clock. It was almost 1:30 and she should be leaving for chemistry class. Instead, she began calculating how long it would take her to walk to Cain's. She had to be to work at four, but that should give her enough time. It was a long walk, so she wouldn't have enough time for a long visit, but it would be enough. She had to do something. She hoped Karen wouldn't mind lending her the chemistry notes.

Chapter 4 - Persuasion

Cain

2:30, Monday afternoon
Cain's house

Cain was awakened from a deep sleep by a strong surge of hunger, the thirst for blood. He lost fleeting visions of Felicity in a dream he'd been having. It was probably better not remembered. The need for blood washed over him again like a great wave.

Felicity. She was very close, probably at his door. He sat up and rubbed the sleep from his eyes. Her nearness was awakening the vampire within him. It had tasted her before and it wanted her again, fiercely. He hadn't fed since early the evening before. His body wanted blood and she was right here. The rich, remembered taste of her was tantalizing, beckoning him.

He arose from bed as he heard her knock at the door. He wasn't sure if it was the first time she'd knocked. He fought to suppress his vampire nature, and tried to awaken his humanity instead. He wore only a pair of black sleep-pants. He groped at the end of the bed for his tee shirt, his eyes still half closed in sleep and pulled it over his head as he started for the stairs. She was just knocking again as he opened the door.

Another bright and sunny day. The light made him cringe, as it assaulted his sensitive eyes. He backed away a step and blinked for his eyes to adjust, so that he wouldn't have to squint at her. She was lovely, as always. She wore a simple white gauzy top, a little eyelet pattern worked all around the neckline, with a pair of jeans and white tennis sneakers. Her long hair was falling in beautiful waves over her shoulders. He was so used to seeing her in the darkness of night; he was taken aback by her radiant beauty in the day. The sunlight shone on her, making the usually dark reddish brown of her hair, seem alight like crimson fire. He was so thrilled that she had come to him again, that he hoped he wasn't grinning like an idiot. He was still half-asleep, and hardly thinking clearly.

She looked at him expectantly, seeming unsure of her acceptance here. "Hi." He hadn't even said anything; he'd just been standing there, awed by her beauty.

"Hi. I wasn't expecting you," he said by way of apology for his hesitancy.

"I know. And I woke you up again, sorry," she said timidly.

He smiled. "Don't apologize, come in." She moved inside and he closed the door. He turned back to her with a smile, but quickly realized that she was in a solemn mood. "Is everything alright?"

"I don't know. I hope it will be. I wanted to talk to you... about Ben."

He froze, trying to keep his expression blank. She'd been with Ben the night before. The fog of sleep fled from his mind as he remembered. That was why she had come? She wanted to tell him that her heart lay elsewhere now? His stomach became a cold hard knot. It almost felt as though the beast inside of him began to pace and want to claw its way out. She was his! She was marked! How dare another touch her and take her away from him! He fought for peace and silence within himself.

She hadn't even been looking at him; she was staring at the floor, lost in her own thoughts. She looked up at him now, distractedly. "Are we going downstairs?"

"Oh. I didn't know if you'd want to." The vampire within him seemed so strong, as it fought for control; he almost wanted to yell at her. Are you so naïve as to shut yourself up down there with me? Don't you know what I am? You plan to put yourself in such a compromising position and then tell me that you're not to be touched! Don't be a fool! But he couldn't actually bring himself to say anything that might cause her to leave. He clenched his fists and made himself very still, consciously pushing back the beast within him to the far corners of his mind where he was normally able to keep it locked away.

She did actually stop and think about it for a moment. "It's alright, we can go down." She had such trust in him. He wished he knew if he could trust himself. Why did she cause such an intense reaction in him, that he seemed in such a precarious position? He'd been in similar situations before in his life and he'd always had confidence in his control. His feelings for her were far stronger than he could remember feeling for anyone in quite some time. Truth be told, it frightened him a little. He resolved to start keeping himself better fed, it would help.

She led the way down the stairs and he followed. He tried in vain not to notice her scent as she descended the stairway in front of him. She smelled sweet, of citrus and fresh fruit... some sort of body spray. She spoke to him over her shoulder as she walked. "I don't really have much time. I have to be at work by four and I walked, so I haven't even got an hour before I should leave, but I really needed to speak to you."

She stopped and turned to face him as they reached the bottom of the stairs. It was practically pitch black, with all of the windows boarded. He could see her clearly though. She looked as though she had just stepped out of his dream. He crossed the room and lit the small lamp next to his bed. She came and put down her purse and book bag. Rather than sit, she glanced towards the closed doors at the other end of the room. "Mind if I use your bathroom?" Felicity asked.

"Of course not, go right ahead," Cain answered.

She entered the bathroom, beyond the door that he indicated, and he went to the bar, flipping on its lights. He opened his small refrigerator, as he heard her close the door. The fridge was bare save for a bottle of soda, another of rum and three plastic deli type containers filled with blood. He took out the container of blood that was half-full and put it on the counter.

His thirst for Felicity was so strong, he felt almost tormented by her presence. He could control it, he assured himself, but it was uncomfortable and distracting to say the least. He thought perhaps if he could drink, he could quiet the thirst. If she were here to tell him that she would not return his affections, he did not want his need for blood to fuel his reaction.

He poured the blood into a coffee mug and put it into the microwave for a minute. He put the container away and was just retrieving his cup as she exited the bathroom. He took several large gulps before coming out from behind the bar to her. It seemed so pale and distasteful compared to his memories of drinking from Felicity. There was absolutely no comparison. She observed him for a moment before speaking. "You really need that morning coffee too, huh?" she asked with a smile.

He leaned back against the bar and gazed at her levelly over the cup. "It's not coffee." As comprehension washed over her face, she seemed very confused. As though she'd never imagined he could drink from a cup. How did she *think* he lived? She looked at it as though it were something obscene. He hadn't the patience for discussions of his daily habits at the moment. Other thoughts were far more pressing.

He forced himself to be blunt and to the point. He wouldn't try to stretch out her time here. Let her say what she had come to say, and then leave without further tempting him. "What did you want to say, about Ben?"

She broke her gaze from his cup. "Oh, Sindy was hanging around him last night, outside. He had kind of a difficult time with it. I think she was sending him like a... summons; like she was calling him. It must have been hard to resist."

'Lucky you were there', he thought fiercely. He could hardly blame Ben, but he'd thought *her* better than to succumb to such urges. She certainly evinced self-control with him. Did she really care for Ben so much?

Suddenly a new and much darker thought occurred to him. What if she hadn't succumbed... willingly? What if Sindy had driven Ben to such desirous distraction that he had taken it out on Felicity, *by force?* Cain would kill him. He hadn't a moment's hesitation at the thought. His reaction scared him a little, but if that were the case, Sindy and Ben would both suffer for it.

He studied her for a moment as she searched for the right words. She did seem distressed, but she appeared more worried than degraded or abused. Perhaps he had been right in his first presumptions after all, that she was only worried for his reaction to the news that she belonged to Ben now. She shook her head with a sigh and then looked into his eyes, as if to stop beating around the bush. "He's going to try and kill her."

Cain was momentarily perplexed. This was not the conversation he'd been expecting. "What? Now?"

"No, not *right* now. I convinced him that wouldn't work; he can't try to surprise her in the day. She'd feel him and it's too dangerous, but tonight, if she comes to him... He's going out to meet her, as if... like a trap. I tried to tell him not to, that she wouldn't come alone, but he won't listen. He'll have Allie out in the bushes to help him, *her* mark's gone, but what if Sindy brings that huge guy with her? Ben and Allie'll both get killed."

"Marcus. The huge guy, his name's Marcus. What does Ben think Alyson's going to do?"

"I don't know. Distract him? I know she can handle herself pretty well, but it's still a really bad idea."

"I agree. Ben has no right to ask Alyson to put herself in such danger for him."

"I tried to convince him to ask you for help, but he won't. Cain, you have to go, please. They wouldn't even have to know that you were there, but if things get out of hand, you could… step in. To make sure it works out alright."

He put his mug down on the bar behind him. He did not like where this was going. "You want me to help him kill her?"

Felicity looked contemplative. She seemed to realize that he did not entirely embrace the idea. "I don't really want to kill anybody; I just don't want Ben to get hurt again. The way she bit him was bad enough, but you should see what else they did to him Cain, the bruises. It was horrible."

He tried to feel bad for Ben, but he couldn't get past the idea of Felicity looking at his body; tending his hurts and showering him with sympathy.

She moved closer to him, seeming desperate for his understanding. She put her hands on his chest and looked up at him pleadingly. "Please, you can't let them hurt him again."

Even through the fabric of his shirt, he could feel the slightly electric tingle of his mark in her touch. He looked into her eyes and breathed in her alluring scent, as he wondered what he should do. He felt as though he would do or say anything to make her happy, and gain her favor. He was such a fool. She was better off without him anyway.

But was he really ready to disregard them all; to leave Felicity, and to let Ben and Sindy kill each other? He certainly couldn't let Alyson be harmed again if he could help it; it would break Mattie's heart. He felt gratefully lucky she hadn't been permanently harmed the last time. No, this could not take place. He would have to do something. He wouldn't promise her Sindy's death, but the safety of her friends he would ensure. He wasn't sure how he'd accomplish that, but he must.

He looked down into her large and hopeful green eyes. They sparkled with unshed tears. She was terribly worried that he would neglect her wishes. She held herself so close to him, innocently, without hesitation. Did she really belong to Ben now? He was no longer so sure. Her words showed great care for Ben, but then she brought herself so close to him, without thought that it might be unseemly. He was certain that she was not the type to share her affections with more than one man.

Again, he was incredibly conscious of her body and blood. Memories of marking her flooded his mind. His body was desperate to claim her once again, in any and every way that he could. He fought back the urge to take her into his arms. She implored him once again. "You won't let them hurt him, will you?"

He felt as though he were drowning in need for her. "You have my word." He kept his voice steady and even, although it was little more than a whisper.

Her face brightened and she beamed at him as she breathed a sigh of relief. "Thank you!" She lifted herself swiftly on tiptoe and gave him a quick kiss on the cheek.

He knew that it was just a sweet and simple gesture to her. A spur of the moment thing, but as her lips touched his skin and triggered the thrill of the mark they shared, it made him shiver with wanting her. She had to feel it. As soon as she did it, she stopped to look at him with new awareness of the innocent act. She looked at him for a long time. She wanted him too; he could see it in her eyes. He waited for her to come to his lips, but she only stared at them, longingly and unconsciously moistened her own.

Sindy's words rang in his ears, that he was not a saint, nor was he meant to be. As much as he did not wish to vindicate Sindy in any way, he knew that she was right. He wanted Felicity far too badly.

He could stand it no longer. There were worse things that he could do. How long was he meant to wait? Denying the thirst was bad enough; must he deny his human needs as well?

He pulled her to him and kissed her. He forced himself to be gentle and unthreatening, lest the intensity of his desire frighten her. He needn't have worried. She quickly gave herself over to it and returned his passion with even more fervor than he'd expected. She was not timid or shy as he usually found her to be. She pressed herself against him and kissed him with an urgency that betrayed her own need for him, which she had hidden so well. The vibrant thrill of the mark they shared ran like a current through their kiss, making the experience more charged with desire than he ever could have expected. It seemed to go on forever.

So badly he wanted to scoop her up and bring her to the bed, but he forced himself to accept only what she offered. She crushed herself to him as though she could not get close enough. Surely, she felt how urgently his body longed for her, but she showed no signs of stopping... or of taking things further. He was caught in a pleasant and yet torturous state of purgatory.

It was quite a struggle to keep his lips from moving to her throat. He could hear her pulse pounding as her blood rushed through the veins there, enticing him. Finally, he knew that it needed to end. If it would go no further, then he needed to end it now, both his need and his thirst were too great and if she did not leave, one of them *would* be satisfied.

Even as he ended the kiss, she would not leave him. Her lips hovered over his and she covered them with sweet little whispering kisses that finally moved down his chin to his throat as she came down off tiptoe. Even though she was human, this provoked almost a stronger reaction than the kiss. It may only be psychological, but as a vampire, the throat seemed the most vulnerable and sensitive area that one could place their lips. He kept waiting for and wanting the piercing pain of a bite that would never come.

She seemed unaware of his torment and was taken with trying to bring herself back under control. He knew that to taste the venom in his mouth produced a dreamy sort of euphoria. Not nearly the effect of introducing it into the bloodstream, but she certainly felt it. Coupled with the heightened sensitivity of touch brought by her mark and physical desire that seemed as intense as his own, she was surely fighting strongly to keep herself from him. She rested her forehead against his breastbone, as her breaths came in quick little gasps for air. He could feel her heart racing. She turned her head to the side and laid her cheek against the top of his chest. He wondered if she were listening for his heartbeat. She would be disappointed, as he had none to hear.

He tilted his head to look down at her. After a moment, she met his eyes. He knew that his own eyes must be begging her for more, but he said nothing. She looked as though she was having a very hard time, keeping herself from kissing him again. "I have to go." She tried to say the words with a forceful certainty that she obviously did not feel.

He made himself remove his hands from her. "You *really* do." A tremor in his voice seemed to betray his thirst to her. She appeared a little frightened by his bold honesty. She looked as if she would say something, but instead she turned and grabbed her things. He commanded his body to remain standing at the bar, although he could easily see himself rushing to meet her at the bed. She gave him a brief glance and then fled up the stairs.

Instinct wanted him to give chase. He closed his eyes and clenched his fists. 'You are a man, not a predator!' he scolded himself. He waited to hear her out the front door, before he opened his eyes. She was safe, outside, bathed in sunlight. He turned and retrieved his mug off of the bar behind him. He forced himself to drink its full contents, although his stomach threatened to reject it entirely. 'Be satisfied and leave me alone!' he silently begged his thirst.

He could feel Felicity receding. He wished she would walk faster.

~~~~~~~~~~~~~~~~~~~~~~~~~~~~~~~~

Would the sun never set? He hadn't been able to go back to sleep. Once Felicity had left he'd tried, but it was hopeless. Every time he closed his eyes, his senses would torment him with vivid reproductions of her.

Her scent would fill his nostrils and he could feel her mercilessly pressed up against his body. The whisper of her lips against the soft, tender skin of his throat was maddening, but when he thought of her kiss, the taste that seemed to flood his mouth was that of her blood. Her kiss had been heavenly torment, but it was nothing compared to drinking her blood. No matter how he tried to separate the two acts, it was impossible. He desired her as a man, but the vampire within him desired her more.

He paced the floor. He tried to read, but could not concentrate. He showered, shaved and dressed. He thought to drink more blood from his refrigerator, to ease his cravings, but could not seem to force it down. It tasted such a poor substitute, when his memories of the sweet nectar flowing through Felicity, were so sublime.

Why was this so difficult? Three hundred and thirteen years he'd been doing this! He'd drunk from humans before and he knew that it was far better than any animal blood that he might buy, but it had always seemed well worth his piece of mind, an educated and civilized choice. He'd never considered drinking from a person *for the blood;* not since his early years anyway. His heady years of shameless excess and selfish slaughter as a novice vampire were quite far behind him now. Now he rarely drank from living vein, and never without great care and significance.

He had drunk in passion and for marking, and they were always exquisite experiences, but he had taken them for what they were and then went back to his daily sustenance. Why did she tempt him far more than he was prepared to face? Was it because she was passion and thirst together, undifferentiated? He had dealt with situations like that before, but they'd never been as severe as this.

She would have to choose, and soon. If she wanted to explore a real relationship with him, he could indulge with her, in body anyway. He could be satisfied with that, for a while. Then he would have more time to approach the question of other experiences with her. If she were open to it, they could have a relationship that would be unadulterated bliss, for a little while anyway. However sinful it seemed, he must admit to himself, that that was where he really wanted to be. He craved that stage in the relationship where she would allow him to drink from her and he could give her pleasures like she would never know again. It would be amazing. Of course, after a time it would become dangerous and they would have other choices to make. That's when things always went wrong.

He began to realize that his young friend Mattie was perhaps far wiser than he in this respect. For surely, he and Alyson had explored the pleasures that he longed for with Felicity, blood and sex went hand in hand for a creature of the night. As far as Cain knew, Mattie and Alyson had been seeing each other for three years now, but Mattie was smart. He never let it go on for more than a few days at a time. Mattie gave Alyson time to live in reality, instead of constantly basking in the venom induced dream state that such relations would surely put her in. Perhaps she'd begun to want it too much, like an addict seeking a fix. Was that why he had left her to travel; to give her time to decide what she wanted with a clear head, planning then to come back with an offer for eternity? Yes, Mattie was far wiser than Cain had ever been, with a woman.

Still, he was not at that point yet. There was much to be considered before such choices were put before them. Felicity had only freely given him a kiss, not her body or her blood; not yet.

She wanted to be with him, but she wanted the troubles around them cleared first. Apparently, she did not want the decision to be reached under such duress. Of course, that's what had happened with the kiss anyway. He had grown weary of fighting his feelings for her. He'd given in, just slightly to his desires and she had not turned him away. The smallest sign of resistance would have stopped him, he'd like to think; but she had not resisted, quite the opposite. She had been very responsive. However, the tension of the moment, the distress over her friends' safety, and her heightened desire for him through the venom were all factors that hardly made for fair gauges of her true feelings.

Still, as much as he wanted her to desire him for himself and not his vampire nature, his need for her was strong. At this point, he was beginning to think that he would take what he could get. He would never be able to truly remove all of the outside factors that could influence her feelings for him. It would be impossible. He wanted her, if she returned his affections, he would not question her motives and influences. She'd certainly had ample warning to remove herself from the situation.

So he would do his best to resolve the problems around them, but in the meantime, he would hold himself back no longer. He was not going to sit here and watch her gravitate towards Ben, just because he was afraid to rush her. He would rather she reject him, than simply choose someone else first. If she came here, it was by her own choice and he would not continue to keep himself from her.

He had always been level headed and calm, slow to anger and never hasty to judge a situation, but lately it had been grating on him. He was becoming impatient. Why could he not take charge of things and put them to rights in his own fashion; chase off Sindy and her boys once and for all; find a way to convince Arif to leave as well?

Once those outside fears were removed, surely Felicity would find herself drawn back into his arms, unafraid. She wanted to be with him. The passion of her kiss betrayed the desires she had so cautiously kept in check thus far. It was fears placed in her head by Sindy and the others that gave her such caution. Without that fear, Felicity would have given herself over to him by now. She had been attracted to him from the start, but now… his venom within her was too strong a lure for her to fight for long. Why couldn't he just settle everything in the quickest manner possible and bring Felicity to him, unhindered?

He forced himself to halt his thoughts. He knew why, because it was wrong. Sindy and her boys needed his help. He was still unsure whether her boys might be beyond his assistance. They may not have been made well enough to exist independently, but Sindy was desperate for guidance, whether she would ever admit it or not. If he let her be, she would surely drive herself to destruction, taking many more lives along the way. He'd known others like her. He had done this before and it wasn't easy to change a rebellious vampire's ways, but to stand back and let them self-destruct was unthinkable. He could not fail so miserably in the task he had set for himself. If he did not help those in need, who would?

And Felicity, he would not deny himself her company, but it was wrong to let her be so driven to him by his mark. She hardly knew him. Who was he to assume that she should want to completely give herself over to him? Who was he to make that decision for her, the way he had made the decision to mark her? He wouldn't shun her, but she needed to be given the freedom to determine her feelings uninfluenced by venom if at all possible, or it would be unfair. It was not for him to ordain her future. It was not for him to determine her path. He made himself look down at the tattoo on his arm. Genesis 4:7. '… Sin is crouching at your door; It desires to have you, but you must master it.'

'Stop walking down the path of least resistance', he admonished himself, 'for surely it will lead to places that it were best you not go.'

It was nearing sunset. He would go to find Sindy. He would try to persuade her to leave Ben alone, for her own well-being. It would be better if he kept one simple and clear goal at a time. Right now, his purpose was to save Ben's life, *again*. That boy caused him more grief for less thanks than anyone he'd ever known, but at least Felicity would appreciate it, even if Ben did not. How he was going to accomplish it, he was still unsure.

He was not going to hide outside Alyson's apartment waiting for Sindy to come and for things to get violently out of hand. That was just not a smart plan. Ben and Sindy would both be feeling the effects of their bond, and both would be emotionally charged and unwilling to back down.

He would go and find Sindy before she ever visited Ben. Somehow, he would convince her to leave him alone. He was undecided what he would be willing to offer her for such a favor, but he would have to work something out, when the situation arose. He was pretty sure that he knew her well enough to be able to turn things to his advantage.

Sunset, finally. He put on his leather jacket and sunglasses, as proof against the sun's dying rays. He set out into the blazing orange sky, started his motorcycle and rode off towards Sindy's last known resting place. As he neared the place the others called home, he could feel them. They were sleeping still. Young ones were always afraid to venture out before full dark. He rarely bothered to inform them that it was possible. Why not keep the advantage for himself? They could wait the hour more.

Now to find Ben. He was a little surprised to discover that Ben was not at Alyson's apartment, but then he realized that Ben was practicing smart tactics. Sindy couldn't feel Alyson anymore, she knew that. If he stayed at Alyson's apartment, Sindy would expect her to be there. Last night was exploratory, but if she were to try again tonight, she would not give up so easily. If Ben wanted her to think that he would succumb to her call, he was best off pretending to be alone.

A little reaching out with his senses helped him to find Ben easily enough; he wasn't far from Allie's. At least now he knew where Ben lived. He assumed that Alyson was there with him, hiding so as to attack from ambush if needed. Cain found a field not far from Ben's house and parked at the edge of it, on the wood line of the forest. The spot where the others lay was still just within his range. He didn't want them to know that he was aware of their exact location, or they would probably move. He just wanted to be sure that he could intercept them before they went to Ben. He could feel Ben as he lay in wait. Cain waited as well.

As the last glow from sunset disappeared and true darkness fell, he felt them awaken and begin to move around. It was interesting to observe, from his limited awareness of their traces in his mind. He could sense Sindy moving about; seemingly visiting each one to give them individual attention. Most likely, she drank a little from each, to more firmly cement their loyalty to her. They did seem to each glow a bit brighter with her signature, mingled with their own as she left them.

It was Chris and Luke she spent the most time with. He knew them well enough to recognize the shape and hue of their marks in his mind. The others were just menials, pawns and bodyguards, to be used for protection. Chris and Luke were the only ones that she had made well enough to be worth his notice. It was questionable whether their intelligence was dimmed by lack of blood, or if this was simply their normal state. Sometimes they did evince some traces of independence. Chris more than Luke, he'd noticed. He knew she'd found them out in the woods doing drugs around a little campfire they had made behind the school. She'd offered them her body and then stolen their blood. She had kept them as pets, before eventually turning them. They were loyal and bound to her ever since. He was unsure whether they had sufficient free will to leave her. Perhaps they stayed by choice, but more likely she made sure that they were terrified to try and live without her.

She seemed to take forever with them. He could imagine what they'd be doing; he tried not to. Finally, they began to move out into the night. None were left behind; there were seven of them in all. Sindy, Luke, Chris, Marcus, and three football players that remained, of those that she had recently abducted.

At the time, he had thought that her taking such a large and prominent group of young men was supremely foolish, an act that would certainly not go unnoticed as foul play, but apparently, he had underestimated the ability of people to concoct explanations for things that they did not wish to face.

Sindy must have had Luke and Chris do something with some of the boys' cars, for they were missing, along with the contents of their football lockers. It would look as though they had taken some things and went on a trip; although where they would go with only gym attire, Cain couldn't guess people should believe. He assumed that a greater investigation was taking place, out of the public eye, but there had been no headlines yet, and for now, people seemed to believe that the young men had gone off on some fool adventure together.

Unfortunately, it was an adventure they would never return from. A fresh reminder of why Sindy should be brought down. Why didn't he just kill her? She had killed so many others. If he had killed her at the outset, he could have prevented those deaths, but he just couldn't do it. When he tried to see her as evil, instead, to his mind she simply seemed lost and in need of help. He'd better do something soon though. He could not allow her to kill again. Things had already gone much further than he should try to justify.

Their marks grew stronger in his mind. He had guessed correctly, they moved in his direction. He waited until they were fairly close and then gradually let his presence be known. They moved in on him as moths to a flame. Eventually they appeared, materializing out of the woods like wraiths in the night. They were eerily silent for such a large group. Sindy went before them, Luke and Chris after her and then the rest ranged out behind.

She looked sinisterly seductive in the waning moonlight. She wore a dress of all black this evening, to match her hair and the dark shadow around her eyes. It made her skin seem all the more pale, as though she were carved from alabaster. The bodice of the dress was cut in a deep V, to show off far more cleavage than was strictly proper. Its belled sleeves were so long that they seemed to be dripping down from her, hiding her hands, but the skirt was very short, to show off her fine legs. Her skin there seemed made up of little white diamond shapes, as it was glimpsed from between the strings of her fishnet stockings. On the whole she looked ethereal, but in a wicked and sinful manner. Like a succubus, risen strictly to tempt men to surrender to her. The thick-soled black combat boots she wore ruined the effect a bit, but he'd seen other teenagers dressed in similar styles and knew it was the fashion in some circles. Besides, it would be rather impractical to try and hike through the woods in high heels.

She stopped a short distance from him and raised her hand for the others to pause as well. She put her hands on her hips and studied him with a smile. "Well, hello there."

"Good evening." He eyed the others around her warily. If she chose to have them all attack him at once, he would have no choice but to flee. He would never survive such a battle. That's what they were for.

"Can I do something for you?" she asked.

He gave her a seductive smile. "I was hoping," he answered, suggestively. If he was going to get her to dismiss these others, he needed to get her attention; to make her want to be alone with him.

She was pleasantly surprised by his attitude, but knew he was probably teasing her. "What exactly did you have in mind?"

"Well, some privacy for a start."

She laughed. "Can't say I'm not curious, but I'm kind of busy."

He fixed her with a steady smoldering gaze. He tried to make his eyes lie to her, to tell her of how incredibly sexy he found her and how badly he wanted to get her alone. Come to think of it, they weren't really lies. She seemed to be posing for him, inhaling a bit and tilting her head just so. She didn't know what to make of his request. She was too suspicious to believe that he would suddenly give in to her so easily. He gave her a desirous smile. "I'll try to make it worth your while."

That convinced her, that whatever he wanted, he should not be dismissed. She didn't really believe he wanted *her*, but she did know that he was not in the habit of making empty promises. His request was worth investigating. She called out to her boys, although she still gazed at Cain. "Chris? Lukey?"

As they moved towards her, she finally broke eye contact with Cain and turned to them. They stood side by side, and she rested a hand on each of them. "Be good boys and see that these guys get fed, would you?" She nodded her head towards those behind them. Chris was obviously displeased, "You can come and help me play with Ben later," Sindy said soothingly. Cain groaned inwardly. Just as he'd suspected, she had no intention of forgetting Ben.

Luke grinned with excitement. "We get to be in charge again? I like to be in charge." Sindy smiled at him and ran her hand through his thick, unruly curls.

She spoke to Luke with a patronizing tone, treating him like the simpleton that he surely was. "I know you do," she said, as she wrinkled her nose at him and then made as if to snap at him with her teeth.

She looked up to address the others who stood behind, only dimly aware of their surroundings. "Now you behave for Luke and Chris. You know I won't stand for disobedience." Watching her with them made Cain feel ill.

She looked back to Chris and noted the disappointed resentment on his face. He was staring sullenly at Cain until she blocked his view. She moved in front of him and put a hand on his cheek. "Oh, Chris. Don't be sad. I'll see you later." She leaned closer to speak into his ear, although Cain could still hear her clearly. "Feed well. I'm going to be hungry when I get back," she said in a sultry whisper. Chris was apparently thrilled by the prospect of her drinking from him. Most men probably would be. That's what made her so dangerous.

She pressed herself up against Chris and began to kiss him passionately. The others shifted restlessly behind them, but were ignored. Luke was on the other side of her and after a moment, ripped her away from Chris so that he might pull her to him. He didn't kiss her though; he gave her a playful nip on the neck with his human teeth. She seemed pleased. She gave them each a quick parting kiss and moved a step away. "Go on now."

Cain wondered vaguely how she managed to keep them all from killing each other. And wasn't she kept busy enough trying to make them happy? How could she possibly still have desire left to want Cain or Ben?

But Cain knew that it wasn't really sex that she wanted. It was power; the power to make a man want her. That's why she found Cain and Ben so irresistible. They didn't really want her. Easy men she had, she craved a challenge. She wanted to try and rule someone who could stand up to her and prove their dominance over her. It gave him an idea how he might handle things tonight.

Chris looked back at the others in annoyance. His eyes fell upon Marcus. "We don't have to take *him* do we?"

"No, he should stay." She noticed Cain's disapproval. "Cain, you know I can't let him go feed without me. He's not really a team player." The others began to leave and she went over to Marcus and made him understand that he was to stay. He seemed content to just stand there. Cain wondered if he'd any mind left at all. Sindy came back to him and glanced again at Marcus. "Just ignore him. He's useful sure, but you were right, he really is too stupid to know what's going on half the time. It's a good thing he likes me, or we'd have some problem on our hands huh?" she asked in amusement.

Cain stared at Marcus in distaste. "We?"

Sindy began to walk a little away from where she had left Marcus standing. Cain followed. She stopped and turned to him in expectation. "So, what's so important that you're willing to lower yourself to try and seduce me away from my boys?"

He smiled. "Sindy, if the night comes when I finally do decide to seduce you, I won't have to *try*. And you certainly won't have the presence of mind to question it. I just wanted your full attention."

She seemed amused. "Well, you have me all to yourself now." She glanced back at Marcus. "More or less. So, what do you want?"

"Only what I've asked before. I want you to leave Ben alone."

She rolled her eyes and seemed very disappointed in him. "That's what this is about, Ben? Aren't you over this yet? So I've got yet another college boy pantin' after me like a puppy, big deal."

"You know that Ben is different. He knows very well what you are. He is smart, he is resourceful and he won't stand to be made a fool of."

"What's he gonna do? Kill me? I'd like to see him try!"

"Be careful what you wish for."

Sindy widened her eyes with a chuckle. "Well, that's what I've got my boys for, isn't it? Once he comes to me, I wouldn't want him getting cold feet."

"I thought you weren't hunting anymore, anyway. Your resolve isn't weakening already, is it?"

She smiled. "I'm not huntin'. What do you think I want to make sure my boys get so well fed for?" She gave him a sly wink.

"Then why are you visiting Ben?"

"He doesn't count! Besides, it's not really a hunt when they come right to you." He stiffened and gave her a look of warning. "Relax! I don't have to take his blood, I'd accept other offerings."

He lowered his voice and gazed at her steadily. "I promised Felicity that you wouldn't touch him."

She laughed at him. "Well that's your problem, isn't it? You don't really think I'm gonna give up playing with my favorite new toy, do you? I wanna see that boy beg! Or did you put your girlfriend back in his bed, to keep him busy?"

That drew from him a silent pause and a cold stare of contempt, before he spoke again. "Felicity will be sleeping in her own bed this evening, thank you. I don't need *her* to keep you away from him. I'll do that myself"

She actually laughed at him. "Oh please, why am I wasting my time with this crap?" She began to walk past him as though totally unconcerned by anything he might do.

"Don't do it Sindy." He reached out and took hold of her arm. He would not be so easily dismissed.

She looked at him in amusement and then shook her head condescendingly. "Cain, let's face it. I love it when you try to stand up to me! You're so hot when you're all stern and demanding, but we both know by now, that you are all threat and no follow through. There's just no bite behind your bark. I used to think you just hid those tendencies well, but, I've come to the conclusion that it's just not in you. You really are the decent vampire that you claim to be. It's kind of boring. So step aside and let me have my fun."

"You're not leaving."

"What, are you gonna try and kill me too?" she asked sarcastically.

He looked into her eyes to catch her full attention. "If I wanted to kill you, I would let you go." It seemed lost on her.

She tried to pull her arm from his grasp, but he wouldn't release her. She turned and glared at him, trying to make him back down. His eyes played over her face, the mocking amusement in her eyes, the fullness of her lips, and then they settled on her throat. She still wore the thin gold chain. He fixed his stare on those delicate links, trying at first, not to look at what lie beneath them.

The hunger rose within him, he still hadn't fed since the cup he'd drunk after Felicity had left. That was hours ago and had barely been enough to curb his thirst for a short while. He glanced up to her face again. She was smirking at him and shaking her head. He had tried to do things his way and she did not take him seriously. Maybe it was time to do things in a way that she would understand and respect. He made the conscious decision to let his thirst come forth.

He willed himself to shift into his vampiric visage and tightened his grip on Sindy's arm as he felt his mouth widen to accommodate his newly unsheathed fangs. He watched Sindy's form begin to take on strange hues as his new vision sought to find heat and blood within her. Other vampires always stood out strangely with his vampire sight. Her body took on cold tones of bluish green, but the vampire blood within her fairly glowed in crimson red, thriving within her, giving her life where none should be.

Her eyes went wide with shock, that he had actually allowed himself to change before her, but he could see that she was not entirely displeased. He was also aware that Marcus had noted his transformation and was bearing down on them both. He quickly pulled Sindy in front of him, so that he held her in much the same way he had held Felicity that night in the cemetery. Sindy was up against him, facing outward to Marcus, as Cain held her arm in one hand, out to the side. He put his other arm around her waist.

"Tell him to leave us, Sindy," he whispered in her ear. She was unsure what to do. Threatening as he must seem, she'd waited a long time for him to take any sort of interest in her, but she was not certain what he had in mind. She knew it would be stupid to let herself be left alone with him like this.

He used the arm around her waist to crush her close against him. Shameful as it seemed, his body was reacting strongly, not only to her blood, but to her own fine body as well, and he wanted to be sure that she could feel it. He was certain that it would please her, to know that she had such an effect on him.

He was right. She felt his body's readiness pressed against her, and it made the decision for her. "Marcus no! It's okay. You can leave us. Cain only wants to play. Go on, go home. Now, go!" He seemed very confused and Cain worried that he wouldn't listen, but Sindy stared him down and finally he turned around dejectedly and left.

He held her fast as he tracked Marcus in his mind, making sure he did not return. She squirmed against him. "So, are you just gonna stand here like this? Keeping me distracted for as long as possible, so Ben can get some sleep?" Cain saw that she felt she knew him well enough, that he wouldn't really hurt her.

He released her waist, but not her arm and spun her to face him. She stared with undisguised wonder at his vampire face and smiled. He rarely ever let her see him this way; he knew it turned her on.

She tried to pull away from him again. He knew it was feint, only designed to draw a reaction from him, but he reacted to it all the same. She just wanted to see what he would do, but he couldn't help it, his instincts took over. He pulled her closer by the arm and wound his other hand into her hair. He jerked her head roughly to the side to expose her throat. He stopped himself to look at her face. Now he knew that he had surprised her, by the expression that she wore. Perhaps she had thought that he'd wanted her body more than her blood. She became very still, her eyes wide, her lips slightly parted, not quite believing that he would do, as he seemed to be threatening.

He would. He wouldn't turn back now, he would do this. He would stop her and force her to heed him. She would know that he was serious and he would taste... ecstasy.

He sank his fangs into her throat with a savage snarl. He was not gentle, but he knew she wouldn't want him to be. She let out a sweet moan as his teeth entered her flesh and he began to pull and draw the blood from her body. It was like liquid fire. Human blood was sweet, thick and rich, but this was different. This was the blood of a vampire. It tasted of spice, strength, and the dry smooth fire that vodka and rum could sometimes try vainly to remind him of.

It had been a very long time since he'd drunk from another of his kind. He planned to drink long and well, unlike the little play drinks that she was probably used to. She would make him strong as he drained her.

Her free hand grasped and struggled to open his pants but he bit down on her harder with a warning growl. He fought to control himself enough to pull away from her and speak. "Only blood. This is not for your pleasure, but mine."

"But what about yours?" she asked weakly as she groped to feel him hard and ready, restrained by his clothing.

"Sex, I can get elsewhere, your blood I cannot." She tried to answer him but he went back to feeding from her and the words were lost.

She began to swoon beneath him, although he wondered if she were simply choreographing it that way. She wanted to lie down. He indulged her in this; he planned to leave her too weak to stand anyway. She strained to keep herself pressed close against him, as he lowered her to the ground without leaving his feast. She began to writhe and moan beneath him, pressing her hips to him with a force that surprised him. He had denied her the full pleasure of his body, but it seemed his presence at her throat would bring her to orgasm all the same.

He felt her tense beneath him as she climaxed and he fought to hide the fact that it pleased him as well. His body shuddered and his mind was lost to thought. Her blood, it was all consuming. The more he drank the more he wanted. This was exquisite, sinful ecstasy that he had scarcely ever allowed himself. He let it engross him.

She was thoroughly spent and seemed unable to do more than whimper lightly in his ear. This was surely far more than she had expected of him. It would do her good to be under another's control for a change.

Her slight sounds made him wonder if his venom was affecting her strongly. Even her unnatural body would hardly be proof against such poison. He was far older than she was, and was sure that his venom was much stronger than anything she was used to receiving from her younglings. He let her have no respite. She thought that she was experienced in domination? Let her know how truly *he* could master *her*.

He drank still, it seemed unending. He had no need to hold himself back, no fear of hurting *her*. He felt her come to life again beneath him. She tensed and squirmed, but not in pleasure this time. Her struggle renewed and he understood she was trying to gather the strength to shift into her vampire state. He didn't know how he could tell she had shifted, but sure enough, he felt her fangs graze his own throat as she sought purchase there.

He ripped away from the wound at her neck to fiercely admonish her. "No! You don't get to drink *my* blood." She looked up at him, changed. Even like this, she seemed beautiful to him. The humanity left within him, cringed at the thought. Her eyelids were heavy over her bright red orbs as she gazed at him pleadingly. Yes, not only was she suffering lack of blood, she was fighting the venom, and losing.

"Cain, please. I need it. I haven't fed," she begged him in trembling whispers. He was unmoved.

"Good. Perhaps you'll learn some respect. You *will* mind me."

He went back to the wound and she tried to struggle again beneath him. It was hopeless; she was no match for him like this. If it were any other, he would be horrified at himself, guilt ridden, but somewhere beneath her haze, he was certain that she was pleased. She seemed to faint beneath him. She had given up, he would leave her only when *he* would, and not before.

Finally, he could take no more. He left her throat, and let his face return to its human visage, as he licked the wound clean. He looked down at her; she also had lapsed back to her human state, when he would not allow her his blood.

She lay still like death, but she was strong, and he knew that she would recover well before dawn. He was unsure what possessed him to do it, but he placed one soft and tender kiss on her lifeless lips before rising from her.

She startled him by opening her eyes. They were soft and brown, without the feisty spark that usually inhabited her. She looked up at him dreamily. "Cain, please…" she beseeched him. "You can't leave me like this." She hardly had the strength to speak.

"Call someone else to come and give you a drink. I hear you're quite good at it." She simply closed her eyes.

He stood and left her. He walked to his waiting bike, and as he climbed upon the seat, he scanned the area for others. Her boys were not far away, and yet they did not come. She hadn't called them. He had no doubt that she could have. She must still drink from them often. The bond they shared and her hold upon them was strong.

Cain had never explored that effect of the venom himself, but if she could call humans as easily as she boasted, she could surely call her younglings as well, as long as her venom was fresh within them. He looked back at her. She had not moved. He wondered if she would want them to see her like this. She might not even tell them of what had occurred, if she could at all hide it from them.

He wondered how it would change the way that she saw him. He began to wonder also how it changed the way that he saw himself. Here he was, engorged with her blood, seeking her submission and obedience. How could he tell himself that he was any different from her? Or from Arif, for that matter? Weren't they really all just the same?

He saw her stir in the grass. She probably didn't even know that he was still there. She hadn't the strength to sit up yet apparently, but she would definitely be recovered before dawn. There were at least six hours left before she would need to seek shelter and he could keep track of her in his mind, to know if she had moved by then.

He had spoken truly to her. If he had wanted her dead, he would have let her go to Ben, but why did he value her life? Was it for the pure and chaste motives that he had so often professed? He would never be happy with one such as her. She needed his guidance, but *he* could gain nothing from her but grief, he was sure.

He started the engine of his Harley Davidson, making her flinch noticeably. She still did not try to rise though. As he left her, he found himself glad that dawn was still half the night away.

He went home. He wanted to shower. He felt dirtied by his actions, inside and out. As he toweled off and went to put on fresh clothing, he knew that he could not stay inside. He had thought to stay home until going to sleep, but he realized now, that he never could. Now that he had left the site of the act, he felt as though he had also left his sinful culpability behind as well. He had done what he needed to; he would no longer dwell on it.

Meanwhile, his body was surging with the power and vitality that he had gained from her. Sindy's blood was coursing within him. It made him feel strong, elated and high almost. It had been a very long time since he had given his body so much blood, and of such quality no less. He felt as if he were an old car, used to running on never more than the most minimal amount of economy gasoline and had now filled his tank with racing fuel. He needed to be outside experiencing the night.

Felicity. At first, he thought it would be distasteful to go to her. Technically what he had done to Sindy would not be considered 'being with another woman', but no matter how he tried not to think on it, in his heart, he felt as though he might as well have raped her.

His conscience was eased by the fact that he knew deep down, Sindy was probably thrilled by the act. In fact, she had even offered it freely the night before. Of course, he was sure she'd never expected him to take things to such extremes, but as he had said to her this very evening, 'be careful what you wish for'.

It's not as if he had given her *his* body or blood, for whatever that was worth. He and Felicity did not even have a relationship or agreement that he could be considered to have been unfaithful to.

Sindy and Felicity lived in two separate worlds. Felicity was human, and he wanted her and treated her as a human woman, worthy of his love and respect. Sindy was a vampire, and he treated her and disciplined her as such.

He loathed the idea that he had behaved like an animal, but it was not by his design that such instincts and patterns were imprinted upon him to bring her under control. He had tried to do it in human fashion first, but he was ignored. He certainly would not be laughed at! Anyway, it did not matter now. It was done and she would take him more seriously from now on. He may even have some slight control over her, strictly through his venom that now invaded her bloodstream. Her body would heal her of it before long, but psychologically, it might be very effective far beyond its physical consequences.

He turned his mind to Felicity again. He realized that while the thought of seeing her did excite him, it did not awaken his thirst. His hunger for blood was thoroughly sated. Visions of her in his mind produced no more than a normal desirous reaction, uncolored by blood lust. Yes, he would definitely go and see her, if only to feel that he could truly relate to her as a man and not have to fight the monster inside him with every fond glance or touch she might bestow.

He should have thought to go to her anyway, just to let her know that things were all right. She surely worried for her friends. It was well after eleven, a little late to her, but the night was long. He was too taken with the idea of seeing her, to resist following through with it now.

He finished dressing and brushed his hair. It was still wet from his shower, but would dry with the wind from the motorcycle ride to her dorm, before long, he was rushing towards her building, feeling her presence. She still moved about, she was not asleep.

He cut the engine just before entering the lot, so as not to disturb anyone. He walked the bike in and parked it, looking up at her window. A dim lamp was lit, as though she were reading in bed. He would not go to the door; it was too late for open entry. He thought at first to attempt to call her, as Sindy had suggested last night. Surely, he could, but then he realized that it would probably be regarded as uncouth, after what she had seen Ben go through the night before. It would frighten her and push her away from him. What approach would she look upon fondly?

He looked up again at her window. It would not be easy, but it would be fun. His body seemed eager to use the extra energy it had been given and it's not as though he could really hurt himself.

He set about finding a way to climb up. Eventually he found a tree around the side of the building that would give him access to the roof. He then found his way to the spot over her window and managed to drop down, perching himself on the slight ledge at her windowsill.

Meanwhile, he could feel her within. She had risen from bed, she definitely felt him as well. Her mark was a week old and he hadn't given her much, but although it was beginning to dim, it was still effective.

He endeavored to strike a suave pose, and gave a few slight taps on the window. She was there almost instantly. She looked shocked and amazed as she pulled the string to lift the blinds away, and raised the glass of the windowpane. "Hi," he said, with as much casual charm as he could muster. She was suitably enchanted.

"Hi," she replied hesitantly as she looked around to try and see how he might have gotten there. She was mystified.

"I thought I'd come and let you know that you needn't worry about Ben. Sindy will not be visiting him this evening. I don't think she'll be bothering him any time soon, either."

Felicity was visibly relieved. "Thank you, I was worried. How did you manage that?"

He smiled. "I can be quite persuasive, when I've a mind to be."

She eyed him thoughtfully. He wondered if she was trying to fathom what he might have done, or if she was simply thinking of the times that he had purposely *not* tried to persuade *her*. A little of both, he decided. "I'll bet you can be," she agreed. She looked around again to see if she might gain some clue as to how he had reached her window and gave a little laugh. "This is so weird. I feel like 'Juliet'."

He leaned back a touch, being careful not to fall out of the window, to look her over, as if to assess her. "Oh no, definitely not." Her brow furrowed at his words and he smiled. "Even her description pales next to your beauty. You're far lovelier than anything Shakespeare could have dreamt of." She rolled her eyes and looked away shyly to hide the heat rising in her cheeks. He had to smile. He knew he was being terribly ostentatious, but he couldn't help it. He was so joyful to see her and eager to gain her favor. It felt wonderfully good to be close to her without even really noticing her pulse for a change. He laughed a bit at her bashful pose. "Come now, hasn't anyone ever told you that you're beautiful?"

"Not like that." She laughed a little and shook her head. "Did you want to come in?"

"Unless you'd like to come out."

She peered over the edge to the ground far below. "Not *that* way," she answered with another laugh. "Come in, please, before you fall."

She backed away from the window as he began to climb through. He pretended not to notice as she quickly and discreetly fixed her hair and adjusted her clothing before the mirror. She was dressed only in her nightgown. It was a large tee shirt of sorts, with a deep v-neckline and was awfully short. She had very nicely shaped legs, he observed. She had tugged down her hem, self consciously as he was entering the room, but he noticed as he stood that now she seemed transfixed. He realized that she was still peering into the mirror, and that he was not reflected there. She looked to him and then back to her lone reflection again in wonder. She hadn't noticed the oddity the last time that he was here. It was a long-standing habit of his, never to stand near a mirror when he could help it.

As she looked back at him again, he smiled and shrugged. "How do I look?"

She giggled a bit as he tried to comb his hair with his fingers, pretending to preen in front of his invisible image in the mirror. "You look..." she paused, evaluating his appearance, "*really* good."

He gave her a grin and raised his eyebrows as if to question her seriousness. "Well, I guess I'll have to take your word for it." He glanced over to her bed; the covers were a rumpled mess. "I hope I didn't wake you."

"No, I couldn't sleep anyway." The mirror kept distracting her. She finally moved to turn her back to it and looked only at him. "Thanks again, for handling things with Sindy. I know you and Ben don't always get along, but I do appreciate your help."

"I've no problem with Ben... that I'm aware of." He looked at her questioningly. She seemed perplexed. "Are you and he, involved?"

Her face brightened as she realized what he was asking. "No," she answered immediately, with a shake of her head.

He smiled at her suggestively. "Then I've no problem with Ben at all." She was blushing again. She was so easy to fluster, he found it adorable. "I want you to know, that when I kissed you earlier..." she became even more flushed at the memory; he went on, "I hope you don't think that you... owed it to me, for my help. They are separate acts." He stumbled a bit for words. "You're not indebted to me, or obligated in any way, for anything. You know that, don't you?"

She smiled in demure appreciation. "Yes, but thanks for saying it."

He gazed at her in silence for a moment. She simply looked back at him, trying not to obviously run her eyes too far down his body. He raked his hand through his hair. "Do you want to go out? We can use the door if you'd like," he said with a mischievous grin.

She seemed a little shocked at the idea. "It's after midnight and I'm not even dressed." She became self-conscious again, trying to smooth down her nightgown with her hands.

He endeavored to keep his eyes from her perfect legs, to avoid making her uncomfortable. "I'd wait. Or else... tomorrow evening?"

She was very happy with the idea. "Yes, I'd like that. I'm working until nine."

"Shall I pick you up at the bookstore?" She gave him a little smile and nod. "Alright then. I should leave; let you get some sleep, now that your mind's been put to ease." He went back to the window and sat on the ledge, making ready to leave.

"You can use the door."

"That's alright, this way has a much more dramatic effect, don't you think? And it's kind of fun." He laughed and she shook her head and smiled. "See you tomorrow."

He spun around to put his legs out the window and perched on the ledge again. He was deciding whether to disappear over the roof or simply try to jump to the ground when she rushed to the window.

"Cain!" He looked back. She gazed at him, unsure what to say. "Goodnight." He realized that she wanted to kiss him. He ducked down to lean his head and shoulders back through the window. She took his face into her hands and met his lips with her own. It was sweet and soft; uncolored by thirst and blessedly normal. Still passionate to be sure, but the intense urgency that had driven him before, was replaced by sincere contentment. Not that he didn't desire more from her, but he could wait. He thoroughly enjoyed it. The kiss ended, and a moment after, he pulled himself up to the roof and was gone.

Chapter 5

Thanks for bringin' down my day

Felicity

Felicity's dorm room
8:30, Tuesday morning

Felicity found herself singing as she got dressed for class. She couldn't help herself. She was still riding a high off of last night's visit from Cain. Brief as it had been, she couldn't wipe the smile from her face. He was so romantic! And overly dramatic and a little silly, but she found him delightfully charming and was very excited to see him tonight.

She put on a lovely skirt and blouse, of hazel green, just the same shade as her eyes. She was just fixing her hair, and was almost ready to leave for some breakfast, when there was a knock at her door. She went and opened it, while trying to clip up her hair with one hand. It was Ben. "Hi," he said with a smile.

She just gave him a casual, "Good morning," and went back to the mirror to finish her hair. From the corner of her eye, she saw him enter the room looking a bit disappointed. Apparently, he had expected a more enthusiastic reception.

"I just figured I should come by and let you know that everything was alright. I mean, in case you were worried... since we weren't at Allie's."

She finished her hair and turned to face him with a smile that hardly matched her scolding tone. "I know. Stayed at your place huh?"

"Yes. And see, that is exactly the reason why. I knew you were going to go over there and I didn't want you getting yourself into trouble."

"I didn't go there. You told me not to, remember?" she reminded him.

"Like you were going to listen to me?" he asked with a smirk.

She smiled. "Well, I actually did listen to you, and I sat here and worried, after I called like twenty times! Thanks for letting me know where you were!"

"Why didn't you try my house?" he asked.

"Because by the time I realized you weren't answering at Allie's, it was after ten o'clock. I didn't think your dad would be very happy to hear from me."

"It's my own private line," he clarified.

"Well, I didn't know that. Besides, he still would have heard it ring."

"Remind me to give you my cell number," Ben told her.

She refused to let him change the subject. "Why didn't you guys just call me and let me know you'd changed tactics?"

"Did you want me to call and wake up the whole dorm? Anyway, she didn't show."

"I know, Cain told me." Unsurprisingly, he was not thrilled to hear her mention Cain. "And good news, he doesn't think she'll be bothering you again anytime soon either."

"I told you I didn't want his help."

"Well, he wasn't helping *you*. He was doing a favor for me."

"Gee I wonder why?" he asked sarcastically.

She gave him a look of annoyance. "Look, you wanted Sindy to leave you alone, mission accomplished. So why do you care?"

"Is she still alive?" he asked.

"I would assume!" she exclaimed.

"Well, maybe I wanted to stake her myself!" Ben told her.

"Yes, I'm sure that would have been very satisfying to your bruised ego. It also would have made you very dead! The girl has created her own private army. Do you really think she's going to let herself get killed by someone like *you*?"

"Someone *like me*? What, you don't think I'm capable? I notice you didn't have any problem sending Cain after her!"

"I didn't *send* Cain after her! And all I meant was that you're human! I just didn't want you to get hurt again."

"Thanks, but I don't need you to get Cain to protect me!"

"Ben! It's not so much that I was afraid that you *couldn't* kill her; I was terrified that you would! You're right. She would let you come to her. She would have let you get real close. And you would have staked her, and she would be dust right now," she said.

"Sounds good to me," Ben replied.

"But Ben, no matter how brave, or strong, or clever you are; six to one is just really bad odds. Even if she came alone, Chris and Luke would know it was you. Let me tell you something, the mark that you have from her will fade, but I'm thinkin' their desire for revenge would last a long time. We've seen enough of her guys to know that they're pretty single minded. If you kill their mistress they will hunt you down until the day you die!"

He stared at her for what seemed like a really long time. Finally, he lost the angry scowl he wore and began to look a bit chastened. "Well, I guess that's a pretty good point. Why didn't you just say that yesterday?"

"Like you would listen to me," she answered with a smirk.

"Still, just because she didn't show up last night, doesn't mean she's going to give up so easily," he pointed out.

"Well, Cain seemed pretty confident that we shouldn't worry," she told him. Ben obviously didn't put much stock in that. "If she does try for you again, and you can't manage to keep yourself from going outside, then you can stake her. But for now, let's just wait it out, okay?" Ben still did not seem satisfied. "Was it really so hard to resist?" He just looked sullen and shrugged. She smiled. "Alyson seemed more than willing to help distract you. I bet she'd even tie you to the bed if you asked."

That made him give her a grudging smile. "She probably has her own hand cuffs, but no thanks."

"It'll fade. I think my mark's going away already. I still feel it, but it's not quite as intense as it was in the beginning."

He gave her a level stare. "When did he do it?"

She realized that they were moving into an area that it was probably best not to discuss, but he held her gaze and she felt forced to answer. "It was the night we met Arif," she said, thinking back. "The night after the cemetery, so... Monday? Wow, was it only a week ago yesterday? It seems like longer."

"So... what? Were you like, making out and he just lost control?"

She looked at him with disgusted irritation. "No. It wasn't like that at all. He was afraid that Arif would hurt me. Hell, I'm afraid of Arif too! He is so creepy. He told Cain that I didn't *belong* to him, as if I were up for grabs or something. You should have seen the way that he looked at me," she said with a shudder. "If I'd understood about this whole marking business, I might have *asked* Cain to do it, right then and there."

Ben was very thoughtful, and did seem to sympathize a little. Then he asked, "But you *didn't* know, did you? He just, *did it*. Am I right?" She didn't say anything, but the answer was obvious. "Weren't you scared?"

Why was he bringing this up? Couldn't he just leave it alone? It was over. "I didn't press you for details about Sindy."

"You didn't have to! You had a front row seat." He looked as disgusted as she felt.

"I didn't watch."

He seemed a little surprised, but she thought he appreciated hearing it. "So what happens when it's gone? The mark," he clarified.

"What do you mean?"

"Your mark. Think he'll want to give you a new one?"

That was a disconcerting thought. "Well, things are different now. I think he and Arif have come to some kind of agreement, so I shouldn't really have to worry about him anymore. And Cain did say that Sindy would stay out of our way. So, he shouldn't need to."

"Yeah, let's see what Cain has to say about that in another week or two."

She thought about that for a few minutes in agitation, and then looked up at Ben with a frown. "Thanks for bringin' down my day."

He gave her a sympathetic, half-smile. "Sorry, I try to live in reality. It's a lot less fun, I know." He paused for a moment, as if something had just occurred to him. "Have you ever actually *read* the bible?" She only answered him with a strange look. "Cain was *not* a good guy. Just so you know."

"Look, I'm going to be late for class, as it is I'll have to skip breakfast. I'll see you later, okay?" He held her gaze for a moment longer. He didn't really want her to be able to dismiss the thought so easily, but finally he relented and went out into the hall. She gathered her things and went out to walk to class. She found that he was waiting for her, and they walked together.

~~~~~~~~~~~~~~~~~~~~~~~~~~~~~~

Evening. Felicity was working with Ashley in the bookstore, but when Ashley went home, she would be closing with Harold. She was very glad that Cain would be meeting her. Not that she was frightened of Harold, but she certainly didn't relish the thought of spending time alone with him.

She and Ashley were up at the registers around 7:45 p.m., when Alyson entered the store. She wore what Felicity believed was probably one of Ben's tee shirts, which was way too big on her, with a pair of ripped and faded jeans, and big pink basketball sneakers. She leaned on the counter in front of Felicity and pointedly ignored Ashley. "Hey." She glanced over at the cafe and spotted Harold. "Ew, what's the grease ball doin' here?"

"He's working," Felicity said.

"Where's Ben?" Alyson asked.

"Ben's not on tonight," Felicity informed her.

She looked at Felicity in confusion. "But he didn't answer his phone."

Felicity gave her an amused smile. "Maybe he's busy."

"Well, how dare he go and have a life without me!" Alyson's tone was joking, but Felicity suspected that she truly felt that way. "Besides, I even texted his cell! He didn't answer me."

Ashley spoke up. "Alyson, when are you going to give up and realize that Benjamin will never be interested in you?"

Alyson moved to speak to her directly over the counter. "Ben and I are friends Ashley. I realize that's a foreign concept to you, but try to understand. It's when two people hang out and have fun together, *without* having sex. You should try it sometime."

Ashley looked down her nose at Allie. "Well of course Ben wouldn't want to sleep with you; you have the body of a twelve year old boy!"

Felicity stepped in. "And you've got the maturity of one." She knew by the look on Allie's face, that if the counter hadn't been between them, Ashley would have been laid out on the floor. "Cut it out, Mr. Penten is here and you're going to get us in trouble."

"I'm goin' for a cup of coffee." Allie began to head for the cafe. "Slut," she muttered as she passed Ashley.

"Freak," Ashley responded mildly. As soon as Allie left, she turned to Felicity. "I will never understand why Benjamin spends all of his time with that refugee from the fashion police."

"They're good friends, Ashley. Not everyone judges people by their appearance."

"Obviously, but that's the worst part; she would actually be pretty if she didn't put ten pounds of multicolored goo in her hair. And did you get a load of those shoes? Ew!"

Just then, a customer approached the counter and Felicity backed away a bit to let Ashley take him. Partly because he was a young cute guy, and Ashley had made it quite plain that customers like that were hers, a point Felicity did not have the patience to argue, but mostly because she had begun to feel Cain approaching.

Sure enough, a few moments later he walked through the door. Her mark must be fading; she hadn't felt him until he was practically here. He looked very handsome this evening. The fairly long layers of his sandy blonde hair had been windswept back from his face with the motorcycle ride. He was dressed much the same as he had been the night of the dance, wearing his black jeans and boots, but his shirt was a deep shade of purple, that made his eyes seem all the more bright, Caribbean blue. He looked to Felicity as though he could have walked right off of the cover of one of the romance novels they sold.

Ashley was still taking her time with her customer, and hadn't noticed Cain. Felicity saw that Allie had gotten her coffee 'to go'. She had definitely seen Cain, and was on her way over. He approached the counter.

"You're early," Felicity said with a smile.

"I couldn't wait to see you," he replied.

Felicity glanced around to see Mr. Penten doing some sort of inventory towards the back of the store. He looked up to eye her and Ashley at the counter now and again. "I can't really talk, Mr. Penten's here."

Cain shrugged with a smile. "Then I'll just have to find myself a book to gaze at you over."

Felicity rolled her eyes at him. Ashley's customer left, and both she and Allie gave Felicity and Cain their full attention. "That won't be at all distracting," Felicity said with a sarcastic grin.

"Well, you couldn't expect me to try and read. Your beauty is distracting."

Felicity glanced up at the ceiling as Ashley looked annoyed and Allie snickered. Felicity turned back to Cain. "Aren't you laying it on a little thick?"

Cain smiled at all three girls. "I'm only being honest. So, could you recommend any books for me to *not* read?"

Felicity smiled. "Sorry, all of our books have words in them."

"Well, I guess I'll just go browse the shelves then," he said.

"You do that," she said with a patronizing tone.

As he began to leave, Allie followed and put a hand on his arm for his attention. "Dude, just a tip. I think you're in, stop trying so hard. Your 'aloof' image is gettin' blown to hell." She gave him a pat on the back and then waved to Felicity as she left the store. Cain just laughed and started towards the bookshelves.

"He seems to like you," Ashley muttered.

Felicity smiled as she watched him wander among the aisles. "I guess."

Ashley turned on her, almost viciously. "What did you do?"

"What?" Felicity asked.

"I have been flirting with that guy for *months*, and *nothing!* That does not happen to me! I was starting to think he was gay! Now you've got him coming in here spouting crap about your distracting beauty; what the hell is that?"

"Maybe he just doesn't like blondes?" Felicity asked with a smile.

"As if. You must have done something. When did you first talk to him? How'd you meet him?" Ashley inquired sternly.

Felicity looked at her thoughtfully for a moment. "I was attacked, actually. He rescued me," she answered with a fond smile at Cain, far down an aisle, off to the right. She almost thought she saw him acknowledge the memory with a little smile of his own.

Ashley looked at once relieved and disgusted. "The 'damsel in distress'? How obvious is that? *I* could have done *that!*"

Felicity shrugged. "I certainly didn't plan it that way. That's just what happened."

Ashley sighed in resignation. "You are so lucky. Cain is such a catch!"

Felicity laughed, aware of the fact that Cain could most likely hear their entire conversation, even though to Ashley he probably seemed well out of range. "He is, but everyone has their faults," she said quietly.

"No way! Look at him! Cain is a totally delicious stud! He's so much more mature than any college guy," Ashley observed.

"That's true," Felicity answered.

"And he is so totally cool and confident! Don't you find that just amazingly sexy?" Ashley asked.

Felicity smiled and answered as quietly as she could. "Yeah." She tried not to laugh as she pictured Cain straining to hear her response. He had moved behind a shelf where the girls could not see him, for the moment.

"Not to mention the fact that the man obviously has money!"

That one caught Felicity off guard. "What?" she asked skeptically. "Why would you think that? It's not like he dresses flashy or wears jewelry or anything."

"Real wealthy guys don't have to flaunt it. He always totally over-tips in the cafe, and I know it can't be for Ben's crummy service."

Felicity laughed. "He doesn't even have a car Ashley."

"So, have you seen that sweet motorcycle? Harley Davidson's that fine do not come cheap. And he buys these overpriced books every night and he doesn't even keep half of them. Anyway, I don't need to see material stuff. I'm telling you, the man smells like money!"

Felicity laughed at her again, trying to imagine what Ashley would make of Cain's bare house. "I don't think he's rich Ashley. That never mattered to me anyway." Another customer came to the counter as they talked. It was an older woman, Ashley gestured for Felicity to ring her. "I thought you liked Ben?"

Ashley smiled and seemed to think about him for a minute. "I do, but you can't expect me to go out with him again, after what he pulled."

"What'd he do?" Felicity asked.

"You know, you were there," Ashley insisted.

Felicity looked at her in confusion as she finished ringing up the books. "$42.25," she told her customer. She looked back to Ashley as the woman paid and Felicity gave her the change. "Are you talking about him not asking you to the dance?"

"Well duh," Ashley said condescendingly.

"Didn't you say someone else had already asked you anyway? Your date certainly didn't look like a 'second choice' kind of guy."

"Well of course I had other offers." She looked at Felicity as though she should know better, and began explaining her 'system'. "All the boys I date for like three weeks before an event invite me to go with them. Then I choose who I want to go with, but I was waiting for Ben. I dated that boy three times before the dance. He owed me an invite!"

Felicity tried not to laugh. "Maybe he didn't like the fact that you were dating all those other guys! Besides, what do you want with Ben? He hasn't got any money!"

Ashley gave her a reprimanding tone. "Oh, come on! Have you seen his car? Besides, Ben is pre-law. That's like being pre-money! He is so suave; couldn't you just see him in a court room?"

Felicity laughed. *"Ben, suave?"* She always saw him as pushy and argumentative.

Ashley looked dreamy eyed. "Oh yeah! Put that boy in a suit, and he cleans up *real* nice! Didn't you see him at the dance?"

"I guess. I mean, yeah. He's definitely a good looking guy."

"Understatement of the year! Trust me, I've done my share of sampling the stock at this school and that boy is totally top shelf."

Felicity laughed with a little shake of her head. "Isn't 'playing the field' supposed to be a way to find out who you like? Once you like someone, why would you keep dating all those other guys?"

Ashley gave her another condescending look. "Well you can't stop dating other guys right away! Otherwise, the guy you like will know how much you like him! Once he thinks that he means more to you than you mean to him, he's got all the power in the relationship. You have to leave them wanting more."

Funny, Ben had seemed to insinuate that Ashley hadn't left him wanting for much. Felicity knitted her brows. "So, when do you drop the other guys?"

Ashley looked as though she felt bad for poor Felicity, who obviously lacked basic dating skills. "When the guy you like starts buying you jewelry!"

Felicity tried to cover her mouth with her hand and couldn't help but laugh. She knew that she was blushing fiercely, knowing that Cain was listening. Ashley got very serious and made Felicity look at her. "Oh my God! Has Cain bought you jewelry?" she demanded.

Felicity's laughter softened into giggles. "Yes."

"Oh my God! When?" Ashley demanded.

"It was like, almost a month ago," Felicity said, shaking her head dismissively.

Ashley's mouth fell open. "He hardly knew you then! I told you he had money! And you're not even sleeping with him yet, are you?! "

Felicity felt as though her face was on fire and her cheeks hurt from smiling. "I kissed him when he gave it to me."

"Well I should hope so!" Ashley exclaimed.

Mr. Penten began making his way back up to the front of the store; Cain was still browsing, with his back to them. Ashley glanced up at the clock on the wall. "It's eight, I've gotta go."

"Hot date?" Felicity asked with a smile.

"Pretty hot," Ashley answered as she took off her nametag and came out from behind her register. "He's not quite Ben or Cain caliber though. Ah well, better than staying home." She gave a little wave and left to clock out and get her stuff.

Cain came back up to the counter with a book, as Mr. Penten went into the office. Cain was grinning like the cat that ate the canary. Felicity tried to compose herself and not smile too broadly as he addressed her. "Found a book. Look, no words!"

He opened it for her on the counter. It was an art book, filled with prints of famous paintings. He seemed very pleased with himself. Felicity laughed. "You going to buy it? It's $68.95."

"Might as well, being that I'm *rich* and all," he said with a broad grin.

Felicity shook her head. "You know, it's very impolite to eavesdrop on other people's conversations."

"I know, it really is, but it's rather hard not to when you can hear *everything*," he said apologetically.

"Are you actually buying that?" He put a hundred dollar bill on the counter as he pushed the book towards her. She looked at him questioningly as she rang it up. "You're not really rich, are you?"

He smiled. "I thought it didn't matter to you?"

She gave him back the change. "It doesn't."

"Then you don't need to know." He gave her a little smile as he took the book and went over to the cafe. He spent the rest of the night flipping through his book and making a great show of staring at her whenever she happened to look up. His stares began as smoldering gazes, but as the night wore on, they dissolved into silly faces that became more and more distracting. By closing time, she was barely able to look at him without breaking down into giggles. Luckily, Mr. Penten remained in the office.

At nine, she changed the sign on the door to 'closed' and went back to close out her register. Cain came over to meet her, but Harold followed closely behind. He haughtily announced that only employees were allowed to remain in the store as the registers were counted. Felicity began to protest, but Cain held up a hand to silence her and shook his head. He didn't want to cause her any trouble. He would wait outside.

Felicity was very annoyed, but let him leave. Mr. Penten was still in the office, so it wasn't as if Harold could really bother her. He just wanted to be a prick. Fine, she would be done quickly anyway. She finished in record time and went to get her things to leave. On her way to the lounge, she noticed Cain had left his book on the table. She picked it up and brought it into the back. She'd keep it in her locker for him. When she emerged from the lounge, she saw that Harold looked far from finished. She came out from behind the counter and hardly even paused as she put on Cain's denim jacket to leave. "I hope you don't think you're goin' anywhere," Harold said as she passed.

"I'm done," she told him.

"So? You have to wait until I'm done. That's the rule."

She didn't even bother to argue with him. She gave him an angry glare and then stalked over to Mr. Penten's office and tapped on the door. "Mr. Penten? I'm finished with my register. I know I'm supposed to wait until the cafe is closed out, but since you're still here with Harold, would it be alright if I left?"

"Sure, that'd be fine. Goodnight."

Felicity gave Harold a little smile and a big wave, and was out the door. Cain was leaning against his motorcycle in front of the store. Felicity came out shaking her head. "He acts like such a jerk."

Cain smiled, "Of course he does. Why wouldn't he rather have you in there with him, instead of out here with me?" He patted the seat of the bike and got on.

She looked down at her skirt and then back at the bike. "I didn't plan this very well, did I?"

He looked to see what she meant and smiled. "You could ride 'side-saddle'."

"Yeah right. You have way too much faith in my coordination. I'm a klutz. I'd fall off before we left the parking lot."

He smiled. "I doubt that." He looked at her skirt appraisingly. "But if you aren't comfortable side-saddle, you could always just hike it up. It's cut full enough." He smiled at her chagrin over the idea. "Unless you'd rather walk. Come on, I won't look." He said it teasingly, but did turn to face forward, waiting for her to get on.

She grabbed a handful of material in her hand and got on. She draped and arranged her skirt so that her legs did not really show. "Okay, I'm ready."

He turned to look at her, and laughed. "I don't think so."

"Why not?" she asked.

"Well you look lovely, but this is a motorcycle, not a horse. If you left your skirt like that, it would get caught up in something and be ripped *off* you before we left the parking lot," he informed her.

"Okay, that would not be good." He gave her a smile, which made her think that he might disagree, but he didn't say anything. "So what do I do?"

"You have to tuck it in around you." She fidgeted and attempted to fold it under her. He shook his head and looked at her. "May I?" She was sure her face was red. No one else had ever made her blush so much in her life.

She avoided his eyes while raising her hands into the air as if to surrender, and answered with a smile. "Go ahead." He arranged her skirt for her, tucking it in well under her thighs. He did it very discreetly, but she still thrilled to his touch. He seemed to think it was nothing. It was, but she couldn't help it, she was still blushing.

"Well, it'll be terribly wrinkled when we get there, but at least you'll still be clothed."

"Thank you. Where are we going?" she asked.

"Well, according to Ashley, I should head to another jewelry store," he said with a mischievous grin.

"Very funny, but jewelry will get you nowhere," she said.

"Good. That's why I don't pay much attention to girls like Ashley. We can go anywhere, but I thought maybe you'd like to visit Venus?" He noticed her slight look of apprehension. "Don't worry, it'll be fine. I think you'll like it."

When they entered the club, Felicity was suitably impressed. In fact, awestruck was more like it. The place was wild! So far, she'd only been to the little places they had around her town. They were just bars, like Tommy's. This was something entirely different. There was fog, and bubbles and flashing lights, brightly painted murals on the walls, great music and an actual dance floor. It was huge! "Wow! This place is so cool!"

Cain smiled as they paused just inside the doorway. "It's not bad. Never been to New York City have you?"

"Twice in my life and not to go to a club, believe me. I've been pretty sheltered, it's pathetic I know."

Cain laughed sympathetically. "The city's not that great. It is convenient for someone like me, who's better off as a face in the crowd, but there is definitely something to be said for quiet country life as well." She had the feeling he was just trying to make her feel better, but it was sweet. "So, are you still shy of dancing?" he inquired.

"I thought *you* didn't like to dance?" He shrugged. "Are there any other... I mean, there's no one else here we should worry about, is there?"

"No. I don't think so," he answered.

"Well, maybe we could dance a little." They made their way to the dance floor and had fun dancing to three or four fast songs. Cain wasn't nearly as 'bloody awful' a dancer as he had originally claimed, but he wasn't nearly so polished a dancer as to make her feel awkward either. It was almost comforting to see him not be perfect at something; it made her feel that they were more on level footing. Sometimes he seemed so impeccably flawless... well, except for the whole blood sucking thing.

After a while, she motioned to Cain that she needed a break. They made their way off the dance floor and Felicity leaned closer to speak to him. "Maybe we could find someplace to sit for a little." He smiled and took her by the hand. He wove his way through the crowd, to a staircase in the back corner and she followed him up. She hadn't realized that there was a whole upper level. This place was awesome!

There was a balcony that overlooked the dance floor and another bar up here too, but the best part was that further back from the balcony, where the volume was actually conducive to conversation, there were large couches and armchairs scattered all about with little tables for drinks. She was delighted! There were very few people up here. It felt private and cozy. She headed for a little sofa up against the back wall. Cain followed but didn't sit. "Can I get you something?"

"I'll just have a coke. Straight up," she added with a smile, remembering the last time he'd brought her back a drink. He left for the bar and she snuggled back into the overstuffed sofa. All of the furniture up here was done in terribly loud colors and patterns that seemed to have been made to clash. Neon orange and green zebra stripes, yellow and purple polka dots, and other odd hues that glowed in the black lights. There were even colorful lava lamps on many of the tables. If someone had described it to her, she would have thought it sounded hideous, but being here, she loved it!

Of course, she had good company. She was so enjoying being with Cain, she had almost forgotten that he was not just a regular guy. In the past, he had seemed sort of mysterious and gallant, very mature and reserved. But lately he seemed different, freer and less sedate. It was as though he'd stopped trying to present an image, and was just having fun and simply being himself.

He also seemed to be trying to impress her a bit, coming up to her window and saying such flattering things, but she didn't mind, because it was done with a humor that told her that he knew he was being a little over the top. He was having fun and being honest about it. He wasn't trying to trick or persuade her. The things he said, no matter how flowery, did seem sincere. He had such a chivalrous manner; it usually put her off guard as to how to react. The boys she was used to associating with just did not act that way. As he came back with the drinks, he looked the perfect gentleman. "Your drink my lady," he said with a smile. Quite inappropriately, she started laughing. Undoubtedly, it surprised him. "Are you laughing at me?"

She looked up at him abashed, but couldn't quite stop giggling. "Yes. Yes I am."

"Do I want to know why?" he asked hesitantly.

She gave him a smile and put her hand on his arm, to assure him that he shouldn't worry. "I'm sorry, it's just... sometimes you are so... charming."

"That's funny is it?" he asked in amusement.

"No, but I was just thinking about how, here you are... all sophisticated and dignified, but a few hours ago you were sitting in the cafe making funny faces at me from across the room and acting so silly. Then other times you seem kind of stoic and withdrawn. I never really know what to expect from you. It's kind of disconcerting. Not in a bad way, but I don't know... it just struck me as funny."

He put the drinks on the table as he sat down next to her. "I can't say I mind putting a smile on your face, but I hope you won't be disappointed when you discover that I'm really rather predictable. I just don't get all that much opportunity to actually enjoy myself these days. Have you any idea how long it's been since I've acted truly silly? I hadn't realized how much I miss just having fun. It's not very pleasant having to act the brooding task master all the time."

Task master? "So you basically travel around, looking for vampires who need to be taught a lesson?"

He laughed. "Well, I guess it doesn't sound very nice when you say it like that! I'm trying to stop the killing. Arif calls it my own personal 'crusade'. I try to teach them a way to live their lives without so much violence and torment."

"But I'm thinkin' most of them would probably like you to mind your own business, right? So you end up having to spend most of your time being threatening and scary?"

He seemed to become very serious. "Well, I try *not* to be actually. I don't much like myself that way." She was afraid maybe he didn't really want to talk about it. Maybe she should have let him forget that he was a vampire for a while, if he could. "Though it is true that as a whole, vampires are not exactly a friendly lot," he said with a laugh. "I do my best. Some listen, some don't. I've been attacked, and I've killed when I've had to, but there are those who *are* grateful for my help; those who sorely need it."

He seemed so melancholy, that she felt bad for bringing it up. Time to change the subject. "Would it be alright if I asked you one of my rude and straightforward questions?"

He chuckled. "Wait, let me prepare myself." He took a deep breath, expelled it slowly and smiled. "Proceed."

She giggled at his formal attitude. "Now, it really doesn't matter, but I have to ask. How is it you always have money? Are you working the night shift at Wal-Mart or something?"

He laughed. "Not at the moment, although I have been known to take the odd job from time to time." He took a sip of his drink and turned to face her more fully. "My father owned quite a large estate back in England. Herald Manor. It's really quite beautiful. You'd like it. Well I don't live there, obviously, but I do still hold the deed. It's been made into sort of a tourist attraction, declared a historical monument and all of that. They hold functions there as well, weddings and whatnot. The gardens alone are absolutely breathtaking.

Anyway, the proceeds are more than enough to take care of the Manor and those who run it for me; the rest goes into my account. I hold other properties as well, here in the states. Houses that I've bought or inherited along the way. I rent them out when I'm not using them. It's enough."

"Then, you *are* rich?" she asked.

"On paper I guess. I've got holdings, properties and such. In a life as long as mine, you do tend to collect things and accrue interest, but as far as liquid assets..." He shrugged. "I try not to take more than I need. I'm not wanting for anything to be sure, but I don't much like money, as strange as that might sound. It's played a part in my life that I'd rather forget. To be honest, I give most of it away."

"To who?" she questioned.

"Other vampires. Young ones who don't know what to do, how to survive. Ones like Mattie, who never even dreamt of such an existence. There aren't that many who need it, unfortunately, but those I do give to, I give all that I can," he explained.

"*Un*fortunately?" Felicity asked in confusion.

"We're talking about beings who steal blood from their victims nightly. Do you think they are above stealing a little money as well? I'm so much more fortunate than most. I've never had to, and even if I had nothing, I'd like to think that I wouldn't do that, but how hard must it be for them?" He seemed to become lost in thought, his expression was kind of sad.

"I'm sorry. Here we've been having a fun evening, the perfect date. And now I'm bringing it down with this dark and depressing conversation."

He looked up at her with a sweet smile. "Darling, I've seen dark and depressing, believe me, this hardly qualifies." He became thoughtful for a moment. "Do you realize that it's been... *decades* since I had an actual date? I hope I'm not too rusty."

"*Decades?* Now that is depressing! Not to mention a little pressure on me," she told him.

"I'm having a wonderful time," he assured her.

"Good. Sounds like you could use a little fun." She found herself gazing into his eyes in one of those moments that seemed to stretch on forever. He was so sweet and so incredibly attractive. How could he actually be interested in *her*, and why did he have to be a vampire?! "Want to go dance some more? I think you've got me hooked." He smiled broadly and stood up, reaching for her hand.

They danced the rest of the night away, until at one o'clock she reminded him that she was in fact not nocturnal, and had classes in the morning. He seemed to feel bad, but she assured him that she had thoroughly enjoyed herself. Unfortunately, it was just time to wind it down. They rode back to her dorm. He cut the engine as they turned in and coasted into the parking lot, as had become his habit, so as not to attract undo attention from those inside.

As they got off the bike and began to walk towards the steps, she noticed that he immediately went straight past the pillars to sit on the third step. It seemed a conscious act, to break any unwanted reminders of the night he had bitten her. That was impossible of course. Here they were in the very spot, under the moonlight. She eyed the pillar for a moment and then went to sit beside him. He had turned and was sitting with his elbows on the step above where he sat, his long legs stretched out in front of him. It seemed a very purposeful pose, as though he was trying to appear as non-threatening as possible. He was watching her as she passed the pillar, and then looked up at the sky full of stars as she came to join him.

She sat next to him in silence for a moment. He looked very casual and at ease, but she imagined he was terrified to do something that she might interpret as menacing. After a few minutes, she very purposefully took his hand. There was still a slight magical sort of tingle there, like a very low voltage current; just the barest humming feeling across her skin. She turned to look at him and he met her gaze with a small smile. "It's almost gone isn't it?" she asked. "My mark."

He looked thoughtful for a moment. Maybe even... ashamed? "The physical aspect fades more quickly. The psychic mark's still got a good week left I'd say."

She kept her eyes on the ground, her voice quiet and neutral. "Is that going to bother you? When it's gone, are you going to... feel the need to give me a new one?"

He dropped her hand and in her peripheral vision, she could see him turn to face her. She finally looked up at him. His face seemed to crumple as he looked into her eyes. "You're scared to death aren't you?" he asked in quiet shame.

"No. Should I be?" she asked.

He shook his head and then put his face down into his hands for a moment. "With all of the explaining, running, fighting and dancing, did I ever even tell you that I was sorry?" he asked, looking back up at her. "Did I ever actually ask for your forgiveness?" She just gave a little shrug. "Why do you even grace me with your presence?" He took her hands into his own and made her look into his eyes. "I'm sorry. I am so sorry. It was wrong, unforgivable really. I should have spoken to you, tried to explain my fears, said something! I shouldn't have just..." She almost thought there might even be a sheen of tears over his eyes. "Please, you *must* forgive me. I give you my word, *never* again will I ever touch you, in any way, without your express consent; my solemn promise."

He seemed desperate for her to accept his word. She gave his hands a little squeeze and then let them go, taking her own back into her lap, without breaking eye contact. She wanted him to know her true fears, as much as she could express them. "I believe you. I trust you, but you're not really alone in there are you?" He looked away from her to the ground. "Will you even have a choice, or will it just be some... overwhelming instinct; the need to let the others know that you think I *belong* to you?"

"I am not an animal. I do have control." He was offended she was sure, but she didn't plan to let it go so easily.

"But is it *total* control, really? Because I would much rather have you tell me now, than find out for myself later. If you were to tell me that it was difficult... If you told me that there were times that it was really hard and maybe it would be better for me to leave, like yesterday; I would respect that and I'd be much more apt to come back, than if you scared me by losing control. But if you pretend that you're infallible and hope for the best... You might pull it off, or the next time, I might not be able to forgive you, if I even survive. That might be a risk you're willing to take. I guess *you* really don't have much to lose, but I hope you'd tell me."

He lost his defensive expression and just stared at her. When he spoke, he had a little smile playing around his lips. "You are a very smart and perceptive girl. And much more accepting than anyone I have ever met, or even deserve to know."

"Why do you always sound like you're carrying out a penance or something? You didn't ask for this did you? Why shouldn't you deserve to have friends or be happy?" He was silent, and she wondered if perhaps his past was even darker than she had imagined. "I don't know what you think you're trying to redeem yourself for and it doesn't matter. From what I know of you, you're a good man now. Aren't you the one who said to me, that we can only try our best to do the right thing each new day? Stop spending all of your time trying to punish yourself for your past. These past few days you finally seem to be happy for a change. Do you always have to be on a 'crusade', or hiding away in seclusion? Can't you just take a break and have a life for a while?"

He gave her a little shrug and a smile. "I suppose I'd like that, though I don't know how attainable it is." He took a deep breath. "One day at a time, right? I will tell you, if I need to; and I can honestly say that I haven't thirsted for you even once this evening. Although I can't say you haven't awakened *other* desires," he said with a mischievous smile. He shook his head and laughed. "Such a weighty discussion, when I was simply hoping for a nice kiss goodnight."

She gave him a coy smile of her own. "Well, *now* you can have one." He had leaned back onto his elbows again and she rested herself on one elbow next to him, as she leaned towards him for the promised kiss. As she came down to kiss him, he didn't come up to meet her, but let her more fully lean into him; so that she felt almost as though she should be lying on top of him. She was amazed at how much she wanted to. She was usually very reserved and almost stingy with her affections, if she were to be honest with herself; intimidated and afraid to act out the daydreams of a romantic teenage girl. But now as she met his lips and lost herself in kissing him, she felt as though things were moving far too slowly for her liking. The caution she had been practicing seemed to fall away, and she could scarce restrain herself from wanting more.

Lying on the steps as they were could not have been very comfortable for him, but the kiss went on and on. He certainly wasn't complaining. In fact, he eventually put his arms around her to pull her over onto him, as she had so wanted to do, but had been afraid to act out. She lay atop him and tried, self consciously not to push him too strongly into the cement stairs beneath him, but she could hardly stop herself from pressing firmly against him as unsated passions awakened within her.

Finally, she broke from him and rolled aside to let him up. She was surprised at herself. She was not usually one for such ardent displays. Obviously, she just hadn't ever been with a guy who warranted such affection from her before. He turned back towards her before she could get up from sitting, and took her face lightly into his hands. He gave her a few more sweet and tender kisses, his tongue only just teasing her lips. She was again amazed at how much she just wanted to pull him to her and love him, unrestrained. She was also aware of the lightheaded haze that his venom was inducing in her, but she was confident that although enjoyable, it wasn't really effecting her thinking at all. This was her, not just the outside catalyst in his saliva causing her desire. Grudgingly he let her go, looking into her eyes. "I hope you had a nice time," he said, sitting up more on the steps.

She laughed a little. As if there was any doubt? "You know I did. I'll be sleeping through English Lit. tomorrow, but it'll have been worth it."

"I don't suppose you'd like to stay out a while longer, sleep through a few more classes tomorrow? Or perhaps, blow off the day entirely?"

She laughed at him as her cheeks heated again. "My grades are suffering as it is." She answered, although they both knew that worry over her grades was the furthest thing from her mind right now. She'd almost like to just say, 'What the hell?' and give in to being with him, but no, it was far too soon.

"I guess I am a bad influence in that respect. I should leave you to your studies during the week and let you catch up. What are you doing for the weekend?"

Felicity groaned in annoyance. "I have to go home this weekend. Family stuff, birthday party."

"Who's?" Cain asked.

"Mine," she said with a shy and embarrassed little smile. She hated to remind him of how young she was.

"It's your birthday? Why didn't you tell me?" he asked with a chuckle.

She shrugged. "It's not until Monday, actually."

"And how old will you be?" he asked with a quiet smile.

"Isn't it impolite to ask a lady her age?" she asked.

"Not when the person asking is well over three hundred years older than the lady! No, I don't think that applies. 'Fess up, how old?"

She sighed. "Eighteen," she said quietly.

He leaned in and put his hand to his ear. "What was that?"

She laughed and swatted at him playfully. "You heard me perfectly well. I must seem like a little kid to you."

He ran his eyes down her body, seductively. "Hardly. You must be aware that you are far more mature than other young ladies of your age. I love that you are both mature and yet still unjaded and hopeful enough to see the good in people. Funny you should find my 'maturity and cool confidence' sexy." She was so embarrassed that she couldn't keep eye contact. "It's your quiet and honest insecurity that I'm so drawn to."

He put a finger to her chin, making her tilt her head to look at him, and leaned in to give her a tender little kiss. She looked down again smiling. "I have really got to find you some ear plugs," she remarked on his quote from her conversation with Ashley.

He grinned. "Goodnight. I shall do my best to carry on without you. Study hard and I'll see you soon."

"When?" she asked eagerly.

"When I can't manage to keep myself away any longer," he said with a chuckle. He stood and took her hand, helping her up. "Goodnight."

She started up the steps and turned back to wave, half expecting him to be gone. He still stood just where she'd left him. On impulse, she ran back into his arms to kiss him again. He caught her eagerly and held her tightly as they kissed. After a time that seemed far too short, she pulled back and he let her go. She smiled at him, a little surprised at herself. "Goodnight." She turned and fled up the stairs, this time forcing herself not to look back.

~~~~~~~~~~~~~~~~~~~~~~~~~~~~~~~~~~~~~

Felicity reached the cafeteria a little earlier than usual. Her class had let out a bit early. She was looking forward to some quite time alone before Ben and Allie would arrive. Once she bought her lunch however, and was walking with her tray trying to find a place to sit, she noticed Alyson was already here, sitting alone. Felicity sighed and went to join her.

Alyson sat picking apart, but not really eating a muffin, and seemed very grateful to see Felicity heading her way. "Have you seen Ben?"

"No, I've had classes all morning," Felicity told her.

"You haven't talked to him since yesterday?" Allie asked.

Felicity shrugged. "Not since lunch. Why?"

Allie looked very annoyed. "No reason. And what did you do last night?"

Felicity couldn't help but wear a smug smile. "I had a date."

"Oh yeah. Count Cain, right?" Allie joked.

"He's not a Count... I don't think." Alyson rolled her eyes. "Oh, I forgot to tell you, I talked to Cain about Mattie. It turns out that they're pretty good friends," Felicity told her.

"Well thanks for the news flash. I found that out like three days ago," Allie said dryly.

"Oh, sorry. I just didn't think I should bring it up in front of Ben, and you're always with Ben," Felicity explained.

"Speaking of Ben, aren't you just a little worried that we haven't heard from him?" Allie asked.

"We just saw him yesterday Allie, relax. I'm sure he's fine. You don't expect him to keep you apprised of his every move, do you? Cain said we shouldn't worry so much about Sindy anymore anyway. Ben probably had a date of his own."

"Do you know a girl named Regina?" Allie asked her.

"There's a Regina in my dorm, but I don't think she knows Ben," Felicity said in confusion.

"I know *that*, but *you* might wanna avoid her for awhile."

"Why?" Felicity asked.

"Well, I called over there looking for you last night."

"So?" Felicity asked.

"So, the last time I called it was like one in the morning and she sounded pretty pissed," Allie informed her.

"Great. Why were you calling me at one in the morning?"

"I was looking for Ben," Allie said simply.

"And you thought he'd be in *my* room?" Felicity asked incredulously.

"Wouldn't be the first time," Allie said with a grin.

Felicity let out an exasperated sigh. "He really does tell you everything, doesn't he?"

Alyson smiled. "Don't bother trying to beat him at Monopoly, he always wins."

"Finally accepted that, have you?" Ben said from behind them. After enjoying their surprise at his arrival, he went around to sit at the other side of the table. "Why are we discussing Monopoly?"

Alyson turned on him with almost furious relief to demand an explanation for his whereabouts. "Where were you all night?!"

Ben was taken aback. "I went over Pete's. He just got a new pool table."

"I thought you were lying dead and drained somewhere, and you were playing pool all night?!"

"What are you, my wife? Allie, what is your problem?"

"I didn't know where you were, and you ignored my texts!"

"So? I forgot to check my phone. Allie, I go out without you all the time. Hell, when you've got a boyfriend, you disappear for whole weekends without telling me, what's the big deal?" he asked.

"The big deal is that I have very few people in my life that I consider important to me. And I would like to know where at least **one** of them is at all times!"

Ben stared at her for a minute. "Ever since you broke up with Greg, you've been hovering over me and making me nuts. You need to find yourself a new boyfriend."

Allie sat back in her chair, folded her arms and took on the expression of a pouting child. "I don't want a *new* boyfriend."

Felicity suddenly realized what the problem was; Mattie. He still wasn't back and Allie was terribly worried. She'd probably broken up with Greg because she was anticipating Mattie's arrival, but he still wasn't here. He must have been gone for a long time, to have her so distressed over it. Felicity felt bad for her, that she couldn't even talk about it with her best friend. Allie shared everything with Ben, but not this. She was all distraught, but couldn't say a thing. It must be hard for her. Felicity thought to try and make her feel better. "Don't listen to him. You don't need anyone else. I'm sure everything will be just fine."

Alyson didn't take kindly to her attempt at comfort. "Easy for you to say. You've got a boyfriend."

Ben gave her a discriminating stare. "Who?"

Allie answered before Felicity could find a way around it. "Who do you think? She's dating Cain."

Ben gave her an angry glare. "You're actually *dating* him?"

"We had one date," Felicity clarified.

Allie smirked at her. "It must have been a doozy!" she laughed, turning to Ben. "She was out well past one, because I called and called."

Felicity looked at her in annoyance. "Thanks for your thorough reporting. See if I'm ever on your side again!"

Allie just shrugged. "Just tellin' it like it is."

Ben spoke quietly and coldly. "You spent the night with him? Couldn't even make it to your eighteenth birthday huh?"

She stared at him in a mute rage. Finally, she just stood and began to gather her things. Allie and Ben exchanged looks, but said nothing. When she was ready to leave she turned back to them. "You are unbelievable! You know, not everyone sleeps together on the first date! I really don't see how my social life is any of your business, anyway! I'm tired of taking this crap from you guys. Date whoever you want, stake whoever you want. Work out your own stupid problems." She stalked outside to a picnic table, although by this time it was a not so comfortable 60 degrees outside, with the wind making it a little too chilly. At least she was alone.

Chapter 6 - Satisfaction

Cain

DownTime cafe and bookstore
8:30, Wednesday night

Cain sat in the cafe, drinking his coffee and flipping through the art book he had bought the night before. Felicity had thoughtfully saved it for him and brought it out when he had arrived. She'd seemed surprised to see him. "I thought you said I wouldn't see you for awhile? Not that I'm disappointed, but you were going to stay away so I could concentrate on my school work during the week, remember?"

"Actually, my exact words were 'Until I couldn't keep myself away any longer'," he had answered with a smile.

"You couldn't even last 24 hours? And you're always going on about your self-control." She paused to give him a dark smile. "I'm doomed aren't I?"

That had made him laugh. "You aren't doing homework at the moment are you? Anyway, I thought you'd appreciate a chaperone to get you home safely."

"Oh, I see. You were being self-less."

"Alright, you caught me. I did have an ulterior motive. I really needed a cup of coffee."

She'd given him a big smile and brought out his book, saying that for $70 he ought to at least get two nights out of it.

So he sat and thumbed through it as he drank his coffee and tried not to be too distracting to her, although he did find himself gazing at her more than the artwork in front of him. She was beautiful, in body and in personality. Could things possibly progress to a level that could be acceptable to both of them for any lasting amount of time? She made him hope.

She made him want to forget that other vampires even existed, or that he ever felt the need to perform a service or carry out a duty to others. She made him want to live for himself again. That could be dangerous.

He probably shouldn't have come to see her again so soon, but it was true that he was doing no harm in being here. He spent practically every other evening sitting here reading for an hour or two before heading out into the night. He really didn't plan to keep her out this evening. He would walk her home; that was all. He had other plans for the late hours of the night.

Truthfully, his being here was a bit of a test. He was astounded by the degree to which Sindy's blood had sated him. He had spoken the utter truth when he had told Felicity that he had not thirsted for her last night. He hadn't thirsted for blood *at all*. He had made himself drink a cup before leaving the house to see her last night, as a precautionary measure, but he hadn't really needed it.

He had always drunk only what he badly craved and needed to survive; just enough to keep himself functioning at his normal capacities. A vampire could not really perish from lack of blood, but to deny oneself, was to be weak and incapable. He had never denied himself to that extent, after his initial experiments with his tolerances in the beginning. He knew how much he generally needed, but he had certainly never satisfied his cravings to the extent that he had with Sindy's blood. The benefit from it was still amazing him.

Not only did he feel absolutely wonderful physically, but also his cravings for blood had been non-existent since. A vampire would normally drink at least once every night. It was not uncommon to need to drink two or three times, if the first victim was not drained to death. Cain had drunk from Sindy early on Monday evening. He'd had a cup of blood out of habit more than anything else last night, but had felt no cravings. This would be the third night since he'd drunk a full measure. He had again drunk a cup of blood at home, as a prevention, but that should not be enough to satisfy him.

He'd wanted to come and be near Felicity, to see if she awakened the thirst in him yet. He did feel vague stirrings of it within him, upon seeing her, but they were faint, and he almost wondered if they were the psychological expectation and remembrance of drinking from her, more than the actual craving itself. He almost wanted to spend the whole night with her, just because he could, without fighting for normalcy; as though this were an opportunity wasted if he did not, but no. He did have other things in mind.

Sindy. There had been no evidence of her last night, although he knew she had survived her ordeal. He had kept track of her in his mind for the rest of the evening after he'd left her. She had lain there for some time, in fact he had begun to worry when she still had not moved by four a.m., but just as he had started wondering if he should go to her himself, he had felt Chris move in upon her. He had approached alone, her other boys were heading back to their sanctuary for the day. Chris had gone to her and after a time, they had moved together, to get home before the coming dawn.

She must have drunk from him, just as she had promised him she would. Cain would bet however, that Chris had not been prepared for the thirst his mistress would have had *that* night. Cain hoped that the boy had drunk well before going to her, for Chris' sake.

Tonight he had some experimenting in mind. He had never had the stomach, or even the desire to really test the powers that his venom provided over a victim. Being that Sindy was a vampire, he knew that its effects would not last long. Her body would probably rid her of it in less than a week.

Right now, it was still strong within her though, it had to be. His venom had grown potent over the years. However many times she might let herself become infected by her boys, she could not possibly be immune to poison as powerful as his. He was not even certain that she ever did let them drink from her anymore. For her it was a power thing. After making them, her blood would probably only be given as a special reward, even though she probably drank from them often. So while the vampire's she had made were certainly infused with Sindy's venom, it was unlikely that she was very used to receiving venom herself.

Cain had certainly given her enough. What little blood he had left within her was surely saturated with it. A new infusion of blood from Chris would try to dilute it, but he knew that his venom had had enough time to entirely infiltrate her body. Long before Chris had gone to her, it'd had a chance to adhere to and infect her nerves and cells where it would not be dislodged, but if he were going to explore its effects, it would have to be tonight. It would begin to fade in the next day or two and after the extent to which he'd drained her, he doubted she would give him the opportunity to try it again anytime soon.

This was not entirely new territory for him. He had, in the past, had vampire lovers; however ill fated their relationships may have been. To drink from another was a very erotic and intimate phenomenon that he had explored on occasion.

He knew from experience for example, that he could not effectively hide himself from her now. Something that he had not really considered before the act, but it probably didn't matter anyway. The ability would return as her mark faded, but for now, although he could still cloak himself from others, *she* would feel him, as Felicity did.

He did have to admit to himself, he was a bit anxious to try out his influence over her though. Could he summon her, as she did others? Could he bend her to his will at all; cause her to be unable to go against his wishes? Most vampires elicited very few psychic powers, either because they were not strong enough, or more commonly, simply because they didn't know it was possible, no one had ever shown them how. He had heard of this power, to hold a victim in thrall, a power bordering on mind control, but truthfully, he had always dismissed such tales as legends and folklore.

There were so many myths and claims of power that he had found to be untrue, but Sindy's boasts of being able to bring men to her, almost unbeknownst to them, against their will? This was something he thought deserved investigation. He had heard such stories before, but never had the opportunity to truly observe the power in action. He hadn't ever been curious enough to try it on a human victim himself. Curiosity seemed a poor excuse to go against the careful limits he had set for himself. Of course, Sindy was a poor subject, being a vampire, but he could not even consider that he might experiment with this on a human. Besides, it was time for a visit with Sindy anyway. He wanted to see what her reaction to him would be.

But first, Felicity. Let Sindy do what she would, start her evening off with her boys. He would find her when he chose, the night was young.

Felicity eyed him every so often, from across the store. He would smile and return her fond glances with his own. Harold was closing again tonight. He glanced over at Felicity almost as often as Cain himself did. Cain watched him warily and eventually took the opportunity to give the man a warning glare. Cain decided that Harold had better start keeping his attentions to himself, or a more explicit warning might be required. Cain did need to remind himself now and again, that there were other predators in this world besides vampires.

As closing time approached, Cain took his book and went to see Felicity at the registers. "I'll be waiting outside," he informed her gently. He gave a glance back to Harold in the cafe. "Don't let him treat you with anything other than the respect that you deserve." She gave him a little smile and told him that she would try not to be long. He went outside and sat on the stoop under the lights, paying closer attention to the paintings in the book than he had given them in the store.

Eventually she emerged and he walked her home as promised. She seemed a little surprised that he hadn't brought the bike. "We're walking? I've kind of gotten used to the motorcycle," she admitted.

"Used to or spoiled by?" he asked with a chuckle. "I do plan to leave you to your homework this evening, but if I brought the Harley, our time together would be over all too soon wouldn't it? At least this way, I can claim innocent necessity in the time we spend."

"You really expect me to go back to my room and stay there... alone... doing homework? You are a severe taskmaster aren't you?" she asked with a smile.

He gave her a disapproving look that soon melted into a smile. They reached the dorm steps all too soon. This time, he put his book atop the pillar, where he had bitten her that night, and then leaned himself against it. She stood in front of him and awkwardly stared at the ground as two girls passed by on their way into the dorm.

She looked up at him, almost shyly after the girls had left. "I don't have all that much homework," she said with a timid grin.

He laughed and shook his head at her. "Then you'll get a good night's sleep for a change."

She pouted at him. "Wasn't it just last night that you were trying to persuade me to blow off all my classes and stay the day with you?"

He smiled. "It is a very tempting idea, but if I had really been *trying* to persuade you, you probably would have done it, and we wouldn't even be having this conversation."

She pretended to be shocked and disbelieving that he thought that he could indeed persuade her. Then she laughed. "Probably."

"As good as that might sound, I know it's wrong of me to expect you to shirk your responsibilities for me. I've been reflecting on things and I deserve a severe reprimand for endangering your school success. You shouldn't neglect your daytime life in favor of our time spent at night."

"Stop acting so mature and responsible, it's very annoying," she teased.

He fixed her with a steady and appraising gaze. "I am most definitely a bad influence on you. I *am* leaving you to your studies, so if you'd like a kiss goodnight, you'd better take it, before I go."

She raised an eyebrow at him. "So sure I want one, are you?"

Now he pretended to be the one timid and shy. He tipped his head down and then peeked up at her bashfully. "I was hoping."

She may have thought to tease him, but it didn't last. She moved in to kiss him almost immediately. With the passion of their kiss, he did feel his thirst acknowledge her presence, like a sleepy lion, vaguely aware of the antelope around it, the day after a feast. When the time came, it would seek to pounce, but for now, it was still satisfied.

Another girl approached. She dutifully ignored them as she climbed the steps. Cain had of course been aware of her all along, but Felicity was startled when she came by, and broke off their kiss in embarrassment. Finally, she looked back up at him. "Will I see you again tomorrow night?"

"Are you working?" Cain asked.

"No. In fact, I can probably even finish all of my school work before nightfall," she told him gleefully.

He laughed at her eagerness to see him. He felt that way himself, but hadn't really expected it from her. "Tomorrow then. Shall I come to your room?"

"Okay, on one condition," she warned.

"What's that?" he asked.

"Use the door!" she ordered.

He laughed and kissed her again, and again. Finally, he found himself putting his arms around her waist and holding her tightly to him as they kissed. Maybe he should just forget his experiments with the venom and stay here with Felicity. She did seem anxious for him to remain.

She seemed to read his uncertainty. "Suddenly you don't seem all that eager to leave," she teased him.

"You do make it hard." After a moment, she began blushing fiercely and looked away from him, smiling. He realized the unintended pun and smiled himself. "I thought you were an innocent maiden? You should be naive to such double entendres."

She laughed and nerved herself to face him again. "Who told you I was innocent?"

He blinked at her in surprise. In his day, women defended their virtue, not a lack of it. "I just assumed."

"Because I'm so much younger than you?"

"No. I admit, I may be a little *old-fashioned,* but I'm not *so* out of touch as to believe that youth promotes innocence. But you, my sweet, have the bearing of a pure and virtuous lady. Whether it is true or not, you needn't reveal. Simply know that *I* see you that way." She smiled and kissed him again. "And not only am I a bad influence on your school work, now I seem to have become a corruptive influence as well."

She consciously pressed herself closer to him. "Trust me, I'm not complaining." She gave him a few playful, darting kisses about the lips and then kissed fully him once more.

She certainly was making it difficult for him to leave, but then he began to feel Sindy, just coming into his range, on the verge of his senses. It was the first time since he'd drunk from her, and he was startled by how bright and clear she seemed to be in his mind as she moved closer. He didn't think she was aware of him yet, but it reminded him of his plans.

As delightful as his distraction with Felicity was, he should leave. He knew it was only play and she wasn't really ready to stay the night with him... yet. If he were to test his command over Sindy, it should be now.

He disengaged himself from Felicity's attentions, as gently as possible. "Best we not start what won't be finished," he told her sincerely. She seemed almost offended that he assumed she *would* leave it unfinished, but after a moment seemed to concede that it was true. She put her arms around him, held herself close for a simple hug for a minute, then let him go, and backed away. She looked as though she thought that perhaps he was disappointed in her.

He smiled at her lovingly. "It's alright. I don't mind the wait. Time spent with you has its own worth. No need to look to the future before we're there. *If* and when the time comes, it'll have been worth waiting for." The look in her eyes alone, told him she was swaying towards thinking the time was now. He smiled, it was only the moment. She wasn't ready, and he knew in his heart that if she had reservations about being with him, they were best dealt with before things grew any more serious.

He reached behind him to retrieve his book off of the pillar. "Why don't you keep this for me? I've looked at it all I want, and I'll only have to carry it."

She took it from him with a smile. "Thanks."

"I'll see you tomorrow. As soon as the sun permits."

She nodded and slowly backed up the first few steps. Finally, she gave him a little wave, turned and disappeared inside.

He closed his eyes for a moment, and tried not to think where his spending so much time with Felicity may be going. It was sure to be fraught with difficult decisions, and he wished that he could just be blissfully unaware of the future and live for each night. But that approach was what had caused him to become the man that he was before he died; a man that he never wished to be again.

Sindy was moving again. He was lucky to have found her. He had thought that he might need to go back for his Harley. He'd thought that she would have hidden herself far from town, to avoid him. He knew that she did have access to a car, and had Chris drive them places now and then. Hunting for so many was an endeavor that did require a bit of travel, but he was fairly sure that they never left in hunting parties of larger than three or four.

He had worried that she might bring the entire brood to a different town to inhabit now, just to keep away from him, but fortunately, they were still around. Six guys would probably be difficult for her to move permanently, especially when they were mostly creatures of habit and instinct. Apparently, she wasn't willing to leave them to their own devices.

He began to walk towards her, and thought about what he should do. He didn't really want to *control* her. Even if it was possible, that just did not sit well with him. He just wanted her to stop killing people and to take him seriously.

He thought to try and call her, but then decided that he should get further from the dorms first. He was inexperienced in this sort of thing, and he worried that in being attuned to him, Felicity might somehow pick up some unintended influences. He walked a little further down the street and headed for the woods in Sindy's direction.

He stepped into the dark and silent forest. In moving forward, he was quickly enveloped in its cover and the town was left far behind. Autumn had definitely arrived, as evidenced by the blanket of leaves covering the forest floor. It was almost impossible to walk silently, so he crunched and crackled his way through the trees, stopping every so often to study the silence for evidence of others. Once he felt that he had sufficient distance, he decided to try and call her, as he continued moving towards her.

He wasn't sure how to begin. He cleared his mind and thought of Sindy. He pictured her face and form, her long dark hair, her high and prominent cheekbones and her full and pouting lips. He pictured her large brown eyes and the glint of pride and self-assuredness that was usually reflected there. Having died at little more than the age of sixteen, her body was that of a budding young woman, lithe and thin. Her figure was not quite as fully endowed as it might have been in another year, but it *was* that of a woman, and not a child.

He knew that chronologically she was a little older than Felicity. And she acted as though she were superior to any other she might meet. She was proud and strong; a girl of outspoken temerity and unafraid of a challenge. She was tenacious, beautiful and as much as she would hate it, for now she was *his*.

She wanted to be his, but only on her own terms. Like this, unwillingly, she would hate it. Good, teach her a lesson, he thought with a sinister little grin. He wouldn't be cruel. He just wanted to know the effect and it certainly wouldn't hurt her to have a taste of her own medicine.

He imagined a line drawn between her mark in his mind and himself; a gossamer thin, yet infinitely strong thread, stretching across the space between them. He imagined the line pulling her to him, reeling her in. He called her mentally, as strongly as he could. He continued to walk through the woods towards her and broadcast his summons. Eventually he reached a large outcropping of rock and decided to sit and wait.

The forest around him was silent at first, but once he stopped moving, the night call of insects picked up and sang to him as he waited. He heard slight noises coming towards him, but could not imagine that Sindy could possibly move so quietly. Certainly, she was still some distance away. Sure enough, it was only a raccoon. It came waddling out of the brush, already fat, fur full and ready for the coming winter. It paused to look at him for a moment and then hurried on its way. He stretched out his senses to Sindy once more, tracking her progress and urging her closer.

She was definitely coming to him, although her boys seemed to trail along as well. Disappointed that she was not alone, but still gratified by her response, he even strengthened his efforts. He imagined himself mentally cajoling and persuading her to come. 'I need you to come. I desire your presence, you belong here with me.' He continually sent these messages, although he was unsure exactly what she would be receiving.

Finally, he heard her physical approach. She still was not alone. A fact that she loudly complained of with a wicked temper. Her broods' obstinate refusal to obey her, coupled with Cain's beckoning call, had obviously put her into a foul mood. Cain decided to fade back a bit, to see if she might actually rid herself of the others, so that he could approach her alone.

"I don't care where you go, as long as you take them with you! Jeez, can't I ever just be alone? I just want to be left by myself for a while." The others kept a respectful distance, afraid to disobey her, but not sure where to go. Luke seemed to be trying to keep them together and away from Sindy, lest she get even angrier.

It was Chris who kept after her persistently. "Even Marcus? Don't make me take him. He doesn't listen to me."

"There are five of you and one of him. Somehow, you'll manage."

"He doesn't know when to stop drinking, and he gets all pissed off if you take someone away from him. We'll be all night just trying to calm him down again."

"I don't care! Just get the hell out of my sight, **I want to be alone**! I'm sick of all of you!" she screamed. They all seemed to freeze and her voice rang in the silence.

"Even me? You sick of me too?" Chris asked, after a moment. Even Cain felt a little bad for him. He sounded heartbroken. It seemed that, of all of Sindy's toys, he was the only one smart enough to actually understand and take offense at her outbursts.

She actually did stop and turn to look at him. She too had heard the vulnerability there. Cain suspected that he functioned at a much higher level than she usually gave him credit for. She went to him. "Oh Chris," she cooed quietly in his ear. "I could never be sick of you. You know you're my favorite."

He seemed more perplexed than comforted. "What else did Cain do to you? Why did you let him?"

Sindy stiffened and drew away from him. "You know *why* you're my favorite? 'Cause even though you're smart enough to take care of stuff for me, you're also usually smart enough **not to ask why**." He cringed like a dog expecting to be hit. She abruptly changed her voice to a tone that was light and sweet, but she still spoke with measured precision that showed she was not to be questioned again. "Take them, and go. I will see you in the morning."

She was trying to stare at them stonily, but seemed very distracted. Chris turned and walked away. "Come on," he said to Luke quietly as he passed. Luke seemed relieved just to be given a direction. They all moved off into the woods and Sindy was finally left alone.

Now that they had left, she dropped her arrogant facade and was obviously uncomfortable and distressed. It must be very difficult to fight, Cain thought. He renewed his efforts once more, just to see if she would come.

She actually did take a few steps towards him, although he was sure that she didn't know he was so close. She could feel him, but she hadn't seen him yet. Finally, she sat down on the same rock where he had sat before, unwilling to move if it killed her. He waited a moment and then came closer, into her view. She noticed him almost immediately. She shot him a look that was perfectly ferocious. He smiled and continued towards her until he was only a few feet away. He did not relent in his summons, but simply folded his arms across his chest and waited for her to respond to him in some way.

"You think you're pretty clever don't you, using my own trick against me?" she asked.

He grinned. "Working well, is it?"

She answered him with another angry glare, until she shuddered and looked away. "I'm right in front of you. You can shut it off now."

"I thought you were to come right into my waiting arms?" he asked, quoting her boast from the other night.

She sneered at him. "Don't hold your breath."

"What's the matter? Didn't you enjoy being there the last time?" he asked.

She gave him a thoughtful little smile. "Not as much as you did. Did it *please* that sinful nature, you try so hard to hide?"

He smiled and looked at the ground for a moment before answering. "You have said in the past, that you've only wanted to satisfy me in some way. Congratulations, but as delicious and satisfying as you certainly were; what I did was not only for my pleasure, but also to prove a point. Do not go against my wishes. You will not win. You'll not find safety in numbers either, next time I'll find my way around them without your cooperation. And don't think running to Arif will protect you; he's no match for me if I truly wished to oppose him. He may be old, but I am older still and I'll not let him think to command me. If you, *or* your drones at your behest, should seek to anger me in the future, you'll not find my next reprimand to be so gentle."

"That was gentle?" she asked with an arched brow.

He moved closer, to speak to her more intimately. Holding her gaze with his own. "That was only a warning. I know you. I know what you like. I also know what you wouldn't. While it's true that I don't usually care to be cruel or indecent, don't be fooled into thinking that I don't know how. I know you've thought it might be fun to try and awaken the darker side in me, but trust me, it's something that you don't want to see. Play your games of being the puppet master, have your fun, but stay away from my friends. That includes Benjamin, and if *anyone* else dies, your ashes will join them." Once he had begun speaking to her, she never took her eyes from him. he wondered if perhaps he *was* holding her in thrall. She didn't move. "Do you understand?" he asked.

She began to nod her head slightly, and then blinked and seemed to come back to herself. "Yes," she said quietly.

"Good."

She closed her eyes and shivered slightly. After a moment, she looked back up at him in disgust. "Would you stop already?"

The summons. He hadn't even been aware that he was still projecting it. It must be far easier and stronger than he'd thought. He made a conscious effort to end it. "Not so much fun to be on the receiving end, is it? Just thought you should know what it was like."

"I know what it's like. Trust me." She stood from the rock and began to pace a little as she spoke. "Amos tortured me for weeks before he brought me over. Let me tell 'ya, ain't nothin' *you* could do to me that could be any scarier than what he dished out."

Cain gazed at her thoughtfully. "You never told me."

"Pfft! What for? I already got my revenge. Last thing he saw before Arif turned him to dust was my smilin' face. And if you think I'd be lookin' for your pity, you *don't* know me."

He stood watching her for a minute. Then he became very still, giving no outward sign, but very strongly and clearly in his mind, tried to push her away from him. He had no idea what would come of it, if she even felt it at all. He just wanted to see what would happen. It was nothing dramatic, or even definitive, but she did take a few steps back from him. She didn't even seem aware of it. He wondered if it were coincidence. He now thought to make her sit back down. He gave her very clear and precise mental commands to sit down. She did nothing. She didn't look as though she were resisting him either. Nothing. Ah well, just checking.

Finally, she looked up at him again and sighed. "So, can I go now, or are you gonna be callin' me all damn night?"

He laughed. "I've said my piece. I've certainly no need to force my company on you. One question though, have you fed this evening? Still trying it my way?"

She gave him a sly smile. "I'm not drinkin' anymore of that bagged crap! But no, no humans. Good thing I've got a lot of boys in my brood. Who says it's better to give than to receive? Although I must admit, both have their rewards." She licked her lips and moved the hair from her neck, smiling. She knew how much he'd enjoyed drinking from her, and she loved it. She'd probably remind him of it whenever possible. She stared at his throat and he knew that she wished she could have drunk from him as well. 'Sorry, not going to happen', he thought sternly. She smiled at him.

He could tell that she also thought that she had impressed him with her abstinence. "That's still cheating," he said disapprovingly.

"A girl's gotta have *some* fun," she said with a shrug, then turned and walked away. He let her go.

Part 2

Telling Tales

Chapter 7 - Courting trouble

Cain

Sunset, Thursday night
Cain's house

Cain paced the entryway of his house, impatiently waiting for sunset with eager anticipation, so that he could go and see Felicity again. The sun dipped below the horizon and he forced himself to wait a few minutes more, for the blazing hues of the sky to dim. Finally, he couldn't stand it any longer and went out to his Harley, though the fading sunlight still irritated his sensitive eyes and made his skin twitch with the anxious anticipation of pain. He knew he was courting trouble, in more ways than one, as he ducked his head and mounted the bike, but he still couldn't wait to see her. *I'm going to end up with sunburn again,* he thought to himself as he pulled out of the drive and onto the road.

He decided to take a different route to the dorms, so that he might stop for a few things on the way. By the time he reached Felicity it was fully dark. He felt a pang of regret upon his approach, as he saw that her mark was fading. It was still evident though, and she still felt it as well. She opened the door before he even knocked. "Hi, come on in."

He entered the room as she turned to put away the schoolbooks she had left scattered on the bed. He watched her straightening up, amazed at how comforted he felt just to be near her; as though looking upon her loveliness and being in the presence of her pleasant spirits lifted the pall of darkness he could never otherwise seem to shake.

She noticed him watching her, and he sought something normal and practical to say, rather than speaking the phrases of poetry that drifted through his mind like a love-struck fool. "I see you've been working."

"I didn't want you to have an excuse to bring me home early. I'm done."

"If you were truly done they wouldn't still be out," he responded with a laugh. As he came further into the room and closed the door, the distasteful smell of some fried food assailed his nostrils. He tried to ignore it, but she noticed the unsavory expression on his face. "I'm sorry," he began, "but I have to ask, *what* is that smell?" She seemed startled and sniffed a bit to see what he was even talking about. It must not seem as strong to her.

She giggled in embarrassment. "My dinner, I guess. I'm sorry, does it bother you?"

He got the distinct impression that she thought it might be distasteful to him *because* he didn't need to eat. "Food in general doesn't, but *that* smells only like burnt onions in a great deal of grease."

"It was a Philly cheese steak. Not a stunning example of its kind, I'll grant you, but I can't believe you can even smell it anymore. I finished it over an hour ago."

"I've got a rather keen sense of smell. Lucky me. Remind me to take you out for a real dinner sometime."

She laughed, and then looked horrified. "Oh my God! You'll probably think I smell like that too! I'll be right back." She grabbed a toiletry case and headed out the door, to the bathroom he assumed. He smiled and shook his head. He wandered around the room, which was a bit messy but not terribly so. He loved to look at her things. Scarves and jewelry were strewn about her dresser. Schoolbooks and papers with little doodles around the edges were piled there as well.

Pictures were stuck into her mirror frame. One was of her, with her parents at her high school graduation, another of Felicity and another girl in swimsuits at the beach. Cain's glance lingered on Felicity in a modest but still alluring bronze bikini. She practically glowed with the sunlight upon her, her long hair, blowing in the wind. The other girl was lovely too, with short dark hair and a mischievous little smirk on her face, but to him, Felicity shown with a radiant beauty unlike any other. To him she was just beyond compare.

He forced his eyes from that photo and moved on to the next. Two others were of her with Ben and Alyson at the dance. In one, they had all posed sedately, wearing their mandatory 'photo smiles', in the other, Ben had an arm around each girl's waist and must have been tickling them. They were all laughing and both girls seemed to be trying to squirm out of his grasp.

In both pictures, Felicity looked absolutely gorgeous. Cain envied Ben terribly for the fun they seemed to have had. He looked into the mirror, and of course saw only the contents of the bedroom reflected back at him. There would be no pictures of him in her frame. Film wouldn't accept him any better than the mirror itself.

He also noticed that the boy he had seen escort Felicity to the dance, was not in either picture. When Cain had seen the boy there, he hadn't even been with Felicity. Obviously, it had been nothing serious.

He observed a stack of books on the dresser. The top one had caught his eye. It was entitled *17th Century Life, Tales of a Quaker Community*. Curiously, he flipped through a few pages. There were many pictures of a recreated village, with players costumed to the period. It was a very basic description of everyday life in a farming community of the time. It was strange to look at; the village could have been his own.

He closed the book and perused the other titles in the pile, more of the same, with a few witch trial accounts thrown in. He smiled to himself. Homework? He doubted it. She was studying him. He wandered over to the other side of the room and was looking at one of her anthropology texts when she came back through the door.

She returned, smelling of mouthwash and the citrus body spray that she had worn the other day. She came close to him and smiled. "Sorry about that. How do I smell?" She leaned in for him to sample. Of course, stepping in close to a vampire and tilting your head to bare your throat, so that they may *smell* you is normally not a wise thing to do. He knew she was teasing him, seeing how he would take it, he assumed.

He dutifully leaned forward to breathe her in and then whispered into her ear. "Delicious." He chewed his bottom lip a bit, as she looked up at him and smiled. Yes, he was definitely bringing out some new, daring tendencies in this girl. She, who had first struck him as so timid, was now beginning to like a little taste of danger. He glanced about the room again, his gaze lingering a bit on her bed. Indecent thoughts flitted through his head, but no, he would keep to his previous agenda. "Let's get out of here, hmmm?" he suggested.

"We don't have to *go* anywhere. I'd just like to sit and talk."

"You read my mind." He walked in front of the spare bed and took hold of the end of its comforter. "May I?"

She looked confused, but agreeable. "Go ahead."

He pulled it off of the bed and draped it over one arm. He held out the other arm for her to take. "Shall we?"

She laughed and grabbed his denim jacket off the chair before they walked out the door. "What are we doing with that?"

"You'll see."

Chapter 8 - What's in a name?

Felicity

The Dorm Parking Lot
8:00, Thursday night

Felicity took Cain's arm as they made their way out to the parking lot and his waiting motorcycle. He held the comforter draped over one arm, and she wondered where they were going and what exactly he might have in mind. It was a challenge to fold and store the blanket on the bike, while leaving room for the two of them, but they managed. She noticed he had a picnic basket strapped to the back as well; obviously, he had their evening all planned.

He took her to the park, deserted in the darkness. There was an area of grass in front of the little spillway that let the stream fall into a pond for the ducks. To Felicity it all seemed terribly romantic, to be picnicking out here next to the little waterfall alone in the dark, just the two of them. It was like something she would read about in a novel, not actually be out here doing with someone, but then, Cain himself often seemed a little surreal compared to other people in her life. The grass was damp from the mist off the pond, but he had anticipated that. He pulled a plastic tablecloth from the picnic basket to spread on the ground and motioned for her to sit.

"It's a bit colder than I'd hoped, but that's what this is for." He shook out the comforter and draped it over her shoulders. She laughed and then looked at him thoughtfully as he began to unstrap the basket from the back of the bike.

"Do you feel it too, the cold? I mean, does it bother you?"

He stopped and looked at her in surprise. "I feel everything, same as you. I might not notice it quite as much. My body doesn't take the cold as the warning sign that yours does, but I feel it. I'm not going to die of exposure, but I'd rather not sit out here and shiver." She gave him an embarrassed little smile.

Cain put the picnic basket onto their ground cover and began to go through it. He took out a bottle of wine with two glasses, cheese and crackers, a bunch of grapes, some paper goods, a large pillar type candle and a book of matches. He wedged the candle into the dirt next to them and lit it. Then he put out the grapes, cheese and crackers before her, on a paper plate with a little plastic knife. She stared at it all for a moment. "Okay, another rude question. Can you actually eat that?"

"Sure I can. Vampires are a sophisticated predator, meant to mimic their prey. Not a very good disguise if they can't do all that the prey can do, besides, my body really hasn't changed all that much.

I don't know why some things continue while others do not. For example, my hair and nails still grow as always, but my heart no longer beats. Perhaps it's an outward appearance thing. The force that keeps me animate doesn't waste energy on that which doesn't show, but if I eat something, it'll pass through my body normally. I just don't really get anything out of it. Blood supplies all that my body needs now. I don't *need* food and I don't usually bother to eat, but I can."

He sat across from her on the cloth and she held up an end of the comforter, an offer for him to come and snuggle next to her. He gave her a sly smile. "That's alright; I'm not quite shivering yet, but don't think I won't take you up on the offer later. If I come over there now, I will be sorely tempted to forget my original plans for the evening, and you won't get a chance to ask me all the other questions that I can often see hiding behind your shy smiles. You wanted to talk and *I* had planned that we should talk as well. I'm giving you free reign, ask me anything."

She gave an abashed little giggle. Was her curiosity about him so obvious? She thought for a moment and then leaned forward to swipe his hair back out of his eyes. "Who cuts your hair?"

He looked at her strangely and laughed. "Of all things to ask, that's your question?"

"Well, I can't imagine what would happen if you walked into a salon full of mirrors! They'd faint! Your hair's a little long, but it's nicely cut. It'd be pretty difficult to get such nice even layers when you can't see yourself. I can't even cut my own bangs!"

He chuckled. "There's a woman in Connecticut, she cuts it at her house. She thinks it's against my religion to see my reflection."

"You're teasing me!" she accused him with a smile.

"No it's true! She's not the brightest, but she's sweet. She does the job and she doesn't question it. I pay her rather well not to. When I'm passing through, I stop by her house. Usually about twice a year. Unfortunately, I'll have to find someone else soon though."

"How come?" she asked.

"I've been going to her for over twenty years now," he said.

She was still confused. "So?"

"So, people do tend to notice when two decades go by and you haven't aged at all," he explained.

"Oh, right." He poured her a glass of wine. He almost looked as though he thought she might refuse it. He'd never known her to drink alcohol, but she accepted it without comment. "Wow, you'll never look any different, huh?"

"Nope, unless I change my hair of course, but you'd be surprised how little such things seem to matter when you can't see yourself." He poured a glass for himself and put down the bottle.

"How old were you?" she asked.

"27." He didn't even hesitate, he seemed to know just what she meant.

"No you weren't! You don't look it," she insisted.

He shrugged. "So, you've got a birthday coming up, big party at home?"

"Not really, just a birthday dinner. I'd invite you, but besides the obvious obstacles, I wouldn't want to subject you to a weekend with my family anyway."

He laughed. "I'm sure they're delightful."

She rolled her eyes at him and shook her head. "They're okay I guess. So when's *your* birthday?"

"I don't really celebrate it anymore," he told her.

"Why not? Everybody deserves to have a special day. When is it?"

"To be honest, there's enough celebration going on that day without me. It's Christmas."

"Really? It isn't on the actual day is it?"

"Sure it is. That's where I get my...name." He trailed off and looked seriously shaken. It seemed almost as if he'd forgotten. As though he were human and just having a regular conversation. She was looking at him in confusion. He shook his head a little and sighed as he looked back up at her, as if to apologize. She held his gaze. "Christian. That was my name, before. I was born on the very same day as our Lord Jesus Christ. Guess you can see why I had to change it. Not exactly a fitting name for someone who can't even touch a cross."

"Christian." She whispered the name quietly to herself while studying his face, 'trying it on him', as it were. "I like it," she said quietly.

"Me too. Pity it doesn't fit any longer, not that it ever really did."

"Why 'Cain'?" she asked.

He looked as though he'd swallowed something bitter. "Thought that'd be obvious."

She had searched out her mother's bible, the last time she'd been home, and read those few passages in Genesis, regarding 'Cain'. "Because Cain slew Abel, just as vampires kill humans?"

"I suppose that would loosely fit. Unfortunately it's much more literal," he said.

She swallowed and forced herself to say it. "You killed your own brother?"

"Charles. Yes, I did. I killed my own brother, after having a very long and sordid affair with his wife," he confessed.

She was staring at him. Not judgingly or with horror. Just an empty sort of stare. Waiting to try and understand why. For a moment, he looked as though he wanted to try to give her some plausible explanation, a justification that would hold the blame from himself, but then he just shook his head in resignation. He took a slow, deep breath. "I don't really want to start the story there, but I thought it best I get it out, before I lost the nerve. Now I'll *have* to tell you, the story complete."

She had prepared herself for this. It was something she had often thought about, lying alone in bed at night and thinking of him. She had assumed there were dark things in his past, he'd even hinted at them before. He was a creature that drank blood to survive and was over three hundred years old. It would be very naive to think that he hadn't a single death on his hands.

She had imagined the time when he might feel close enough to her, to actually trust her with the confessions of his past, but she had never thought it would be this soon. Wasn't he afraid that he would frighten her away from him? He certainly wasn't trying to sugarcoat it. She realized that was the reason he had blurted it out the way that he did, so that he would not have an excuse. So it wouldn't sound like something that could be rationalized into an act that she could sympathize with; it would sound the cold and hideous act that it must have been.

He stared at his wine glass and began to tell her, very slowly and deliberately, about his life. A sentence he had passed upon himself, that she should know the man that he was. "I suppose I should really begin ten years *before* I died. Just after my seventeenth birthday. January 1682, that was when my father disowned me."

"For what?"

"Well, I'm sure he could give you many answers to that question, all of which would be perfectly justified, but to sum it up, I'll just say, for being a rebellious teenager. Of course, that saying would hold a little more weight back in those days. Children were not considered children for long. We were expected to grow up all too soon and rebellion was not accepted. At the age of seventeen, I saw myself as very much a man, even if the reality was that I was a very spoiled and disrespectful child.

We were still in England then and you have to understand, my father was a man of some prestige. He held a title, and connections to the King. He had wealth and power, things that as his son, I enjoyed very well. But with those things came responsibilities, obligations and a certain image to be maintained, all of which I couldn't care less for.

I had always been a troublesome child. Luckily my older brother Charles could always be counted upon to 'cover my trail', as it were. He would keep father from knowing the full extent of my transgressions when he could. Charles could usually get his hands on enough money when needed, to help smooth over whatever trouble I'd gotten into or replace things broken.

'Round about my sixteenth birthday however, I had discovered that money could buy much more than just material things. It could easily buy the favors of women as well. By the time I reached seventeen, I was living quite the life of sinful excess. My father was too busy with his own business and affairs to tend much to me. My mother had passed away some years before, and although my brother cared for me greatly and tried to advise me, I never listened to him, and he couldn't dictate my actions. He had his own life to keep in order.

Charles was five years my senior, and in fact he was newly married that year, to Maribeth. She was a delectable young beauty, but from a humble family and had no notable connections. She did have grand designs however, and an unshakable determination. She endeavored to put herself into my brother's path and once he laid eyes on her, he was lost. Charles thought that the sun rose and set in that girl.

I don't know if she ever loved him. Charles was handsome and charming to be sure, but it was clear to me from the start that Herald Manor was her goal. Charles was the eldest son of a Lord, set to inherit title, estate, wealth and status. She was enamored of the idea, more than my brother, I do believe.

But Charles loved her, of that there was never any doubt. So as you can imagine, he was kept rather busy that year, what with the wedding, moving Maribeth in and establishing her as the new Lady of the Manor; introducing her into the social circle of the court and doing all that he could to make her happy. Far too busy to worry much about me.

Let me try to describe an average day of my life back then for you. On a typical day, I slept and lay about until tea, 4:00 p.m., dressed and attended dinner with the family, then went out for the evening. As a young man of some social status, there was never a shortage of invitations. I spent my early evenings at various social engagements, balls and benefits; my design, to impress the young debutantes there. Often Charles and Maribeth would attend, but at some point I always endeavored to escape them. Then I would wander out to spend the rest of the night with liquor and loose women, until staggering home with the dawn."

"At seventeen?" Felicity asked incredulously.

He shrugged. "Such was my life. One particular evening, there was some party or other that was significant to my father. He was always being invited to attend important events. I don't remember what it was for; in fact, I don't remember much of it at all, but apparently, I arrived drunk out of my skull, with a woman of extremely questionable morals on my arm. I'd probably staggered in straight from the local brothel I imagine."

"They let you into a brothel at seventeen?" she asked in disbelief. She was still having a very difficult time picturing this, especially from Cain.

He let out a breath of a laugh and shook his head. "Things were different then. I think I was sixteen when I became a regular. The 'ladies' there were quite enamored of me. You can imagine what it did for my ego. They had me convinced that they liked the look of me, and my 'manly charms', but looking back I know it was my father's money that they really liked."

Cain paused to refill his glass, which caused Felicity to realize she'd hardly taken a sip of hers. She had been sitting as though spellbound. Now she did take a sip of her own, in fact she drank it half-empty.

"Anyway, I'm sure I said outrageous things and embarrassed father terribly. It wasn't the first time either, but he was determined that it be the last. So he cut me off, kicked me out and told me that I was no longer worthy of the 'Herald' name.

I'm sure he expected only to impress the significance of my actions upon me. Everyone, including father expected me to come crawling back with apologies I'm sure. What else could I have done? I'd no skills or any idea of life in the real world. I'd been schooled by a private tutor of course, so I could read and write, albeit not well. I'd only performed to the absolute minimum that was required of me. Learning was not a love of mine then.

I did gather what little money I could lay my hands upon and take a room at the local inn, thinking to stay there until fallen pride or some unimagined cleverness allowed me to regain my place. While I was there, taking a meager meal downstairs in the tavern, I overheard a conversation that was to change my life. There was a man there, telling another of a journey he was to take. Come the summer, he was to sail to the colonies, to start a new life.

I eagerly introduced myself and asked that I might learn more of his plans. It turned out that he was going to join a community already established, but in need of supplies and eager for growth. It was a modest farming village, but they were prospering, and asked for nothing from new members, but a willingness to assume a productive role in their community. You needn't be a member of a specific branch of the church or have any special skills. They simply wanted the freedom to live a Godly life, apart from the rule of the King. They believed that God would call those who would come, and that they would be joined into the group only if it was his will. They had faith, trust and open hearts to any who would be eager to unite with them.

They would expect me to work and earn my place somehow, if I went, but, at the time it certainly sounded more appealing than begging back to my father. I was very prideful and arrogant, and unwilling to accede that I might have gotten just what I had deserved.

And so, the very next day, I snuck back to the estate and pilfered whatever I might get my hands on. After visiting a few pawnshops, I booked myself passage upon 'The Lamb'. It was a ship of Penn's fleet, destined to leave Liverpool the end of June, bound for Pennsylvania. It was a small ship, mostly carrying cargo for the colony; nails, glass, gunpowder and the like, but they did have some forty passengers or so, and I was to be one of them."

Cain paused for some more wine and Felicity all but finished her own, and then popped a few grapes into her mouth. The evening had taken a far different turn than she had expected, but now she realized that he had probably planned it this way. He would not be telling her his story at this time, if he hadn't truly been ready for her to know. Now she understood that he had conspired to tell her of his past now, purposely, at just this point in their relationship.

The last few times she had seen him, she had begun to think that regardless of the doubt that lay in their future, she still wanted to get closer to him. She couldn't help it; she was so terribly drawn to him. It wasn't anything as unnatural as the venom in his bite or his kiss, it was simply him. However unwise, she was falling in love with him and seemed powerless and even unwilling to try and prevent it. Her resistance against him was fading even faster than her mark and she knew that soon she would want to take things further than she ever had with another. He must know it too. So he had planned to tell her his past before things went any further. He was such a good and decent man. Could he really have done something as awful as killing his own brother?

She could easily picture him among nobles and debutantes in 17th century England, but patronizing brothels and arriving places so drunk that he could hardly even remember it? That just was not the Cain she knew.

She was very glad of that though, because she never had any doubt that he spoke only truth. The fact that these acts seemed so unlike him, showed her how much he must have changed.

But *do* people ever really change *that* much? She remembered her friend Deidre telling her once, that people are incapable of drastic personality change. They may find a way to cover up and hide their tendencies to do things that got them into trouble in the past; but that those tendencies never really left them. They always wanted to do the things that were bad, they just controlled the urge or made sure that others never knew. Of course, Deidre had come to this conclusion after her boyfriend had cheated on her… again, but what if it were true?

If that were the case, then just how stupid was she, to think that she would want to get close to a self-professed murderer? Someone who had betrayed the trust of people that were close to him and then ended his brother's life?

No, she could not be so rigid as to think that people couldn't change at all. She would have to let him tell her the rest of his story, before she could decide. He'd lived ten more years from where he'd started the narration, before being turned into a vampire. Obviously his life had changed a lot, perhaps his character had too. And if not… well, dying had to change a person for sure. Also, any opinions people might have, about the ability to change were based on humans, in their lifetime. How much more could a person learn, to change their outlook, if they lived centuries longer?

Cain seemed lost in thought himself, and to be drinking quite a bit more wine. She caught his attention and nodded towards the bottle. "Not planning on getting 'drunk out of your skull' tonight I hope?"

He seemed a little embarrassed, but smiled. "It might make for an easier telling and a more interesting story, but I couldn't even if I wanted to. Doesn't work very well on vampires. I feel it a little, but my body cures it in me, like any other disease or poison, before I could ever get more than a slight buzz anyway."

"Oh. So go on. You were planning a voyage on 'The Lamb'," she laughed. "On 'The Lamb'. Isn't that slang for like, 'on the run'? And you were running from your father, that's kind of funny."

"I hadn't thought of that. Of course, that expression didn't even come into being until at least two centuries later. No, I believe the ship was named as 'The Lamb Of God', a sort of humbled sacrifice. There was a saying prevalent back then, that 'God tempers the wind to the shorn lamb'. Meaning that God is merciful to those humble and unassuming, like a lamb. That's why 'The Lamb' is also another title for 'The Christ'." He looked perplexed. "Which also sort of fits, being my name was Christian then," he laughed. "Whatever. I hadn't made any of those connections then; that was just the name of the ship.

Anyway, to tell you the truth, I began having serious second thoughts about even going. As much as I wanted to show my father that I didn't need him, I didn't really want to have to *work* for a living. I began to think that I would try to use the boarding pass as a sort of threat, to get my father to change his mind. I still had over four months before we'd set sail. As tired as my father was of my shenanigans, I was sure he wouldn't want me to partake of such a dangerous journey and perhaps be really lost to him. I was also vaguely aware that the colonies had always been a bit of a sore point with him, although I never paid much attention to his rambling arguments with Charles over dinner. Politics were not an interest of mine either.

I requested a formal dinner invitation, at my own house. Then, I sat at the table with my father, Charles and Maribeth, and announced my plans to voyage to the new world. As I had expected, my father was outraged. He ranted and raved about how he was a staunch supporter of the King, and he thought the colonists were fools who didn't know a good thing when they had it here in the mother country. If they wanted to help expand our borders and bring wealth and resources to England, fine, but he wouldn't have his own son as one of them! I should be reasonable. I should be willing to take on certain responsibilities, conducting myself in a manner befitting a man of my position. Then he would accept my return.

What I did *not* expect was my brother's enthusiastic response. He thought the whole thing to be an absolutely brilliant idea! He was thrilled at the prospect of beginning anew. Owning and working your own land, edging out to new horizons. He defended me vehemently and as you can imagine, I was not particularly grateful for his help.

Maribeth seemed to abhor his excitement as much as I. Especially when Charles announced that he thought perhaps a move to the new world would be in order for she and himself as well. Father began protesting anew, about a total lack of responsibility in his sons. Maribeth looked at Charles in shock, as though he'd gone insane.

What I did not know at the time, was that Charles and Maribeth had been having their own troubles at home. You have to realize that Charles had been considered quite the catch in our circles. He never cared much for impressing others, but he was one of the most coveted of the eligible bachelors of our time. The debutantes and ladies of class that we knew were none too happy to find that Charles had given his hand to a very young girl of no account. So you can guess how unwelcome she might have been made to feel.

Not only was she the target of much whispered slander and backstabbing among their peers, but as it turned out, the household staff could not stand her either. Apparently, she took her role as 'Lady of the house', much too literally. She was turning the manor upside down to suit her own wishes and the servants were none too happy about it. My father hadn't really paid it mind as of yet, he was always wrapped up in business. Charles had followed along behind her though, trying to smooth ruffled feathers and keep peace. So a change of scenery probably sounded rather good to him right then.

Maribeth had a simple solution to her own problem however, if no one else's. She cut him off about the idea of a move right quick, by taking the opportunity to announce that she could not possibly make such a journey. She was with child.

As she had doubtless expected, this caused quite a stir and flurry of excitement. Charles was beside himself, eager to become a father. My own father also was glad to hear the news. It didn't make much difference to me, but at least it took the focus off my trip for a while. I had accomplished what I'd wanted; I'd laid the foundation of the idea. I knew that I would discuss it again with my father another time, and then let him convince me to stay. I had thought that would be the end of it, but things worked out a bit differently than planned.

Over the next three months, Maribeth's belly began to swell, and she and Charles began to make arrangements for a nursery. Meanwhile, I was still living out of the inn, but was convinced I was making progress with each visit home. Of course, I hadn't changed my ways out of repentance, but without much money at my disposal, I couldn't carry out my old habits anyway. I found my brother had paid the innkeeper, that I might have my room until leaving for the colonies. Charles discreetly gave me a small allowance for food, which I must admit was mostly spent on ale, but he saw I was taken care of. For that at least, I was grateful.

Then, in May, disaster struck poor Charles and Maribeth. She'd begun to bleed. They'd had the best physicians money could call, but there was nothing that they could do. The baby was lost.

Charles was crushed. Maribeth was treated with great sympathy from my family of course, but in society, under the proclamations of sorrow for their loss, there was much whispered contempt and speculation. There were rumors that Maribeth's outspoken manner and lack of self-discipline caused the death of their unborn child. It was whispered that she was so busy trying to be sure that she was in charge of everything at home and arranging various social events to further her own image, that she had put the baby into jeopardy. They speculated that poor Charles would have done better to choose a woman of stronger breeding and proper etiquette, who would have known to rest and take better care of herself. People can be so cruel.

We were still reeling and trying to recover from this terrible loss, when disaster struck our family yet again. My father. He died suddenly, of heart failure. We were left in disbelieving shock. My father had always seemed a strong and unmovable figure, impervious to such things. And yet, now he was gone.

Everything was left to my brother Charles. I was yet to be reinstated; in his anger, my father had been quick to strike me from his will. I wouldn't have inherited as much as my brother anyway, he was the eldest and had first choice of our holdings, including the manor, but I should have received a nice sum for myself. Yet now, I was left penniless.

Of course, I knew my brother would not let me starve. He had always endeavored to take good care of me and guide me in the past. Unfortunately, he was certain that he knew what was best for all of us, whether or not we agreed. When I requested that I return to my rooms at the manor, he declined. 'You may come to pack your things,' he told me. 'But we leave in three weeks to sail for the new world.'

I was confused to say the least. I had truly discarded any adventurous notions I might have had. Living away from home without the comforts to which I was accustomed, for even this short time, had shown me that I would not be eager to try and support myself. Certainly I could, I was a healthy and able young man, even if unskilled, but I had never really worked hard at anything in my life other than impressing women and avoiding real labor. I had fully expected Charles to give me my share of our father's leavings. I would then set myself up in a modest home somewhere and try to find a way to make the rest of that money work *for* me, so that I would not have to.

Charles had evidently anticipated this and announced that I would not be given any money, for I would only waste it on women and wine, and never actually make anything of myself. He declared that purchasing passage on 'The Lamb', was the wisest thing that he had ever known me to do. It was an incredible opportunity to build myself into the fine man that he knew I'd the potential to become.

He was right of course, but I hated the very idea, even if it had originally been my own. Who was he to tell me how to plan my life? He should give me my damn money and sod off! But he wouldn't debate the issue.

In fact, he announced that I should not approach the opportunity with trepidation, for I would not have to start this new adventure alone. He and Maribeth would be joining me. In the wake of all that had happened, he could sense that Mari was unhappy among the Ladies of the court at Canterbury. The baby's nursery at the manor was only a cruel reminder as well. Charles also confessed that he himself was never entirely at ease playing the entrepreneur.

He found the prospect of owning and running a farm, very uplifting, if you can believe it. It was something filled with promise and encouragement, at a time when the prospect of trying to take my father's place in society filled him with anxiety and dread.

He would still hold the deed to the manor, and he'd put some money aside for me, into a trust fund. The money would not be accessible to me independently until I reached the age of twenty-one, or until he himself withdrew it and gave it to me.

The manor he would leave in the care of cousins, with the understanding that he would reclaim it if he were to return. In the meanwhile, we would sail to the New World. Charles would use his money to set us each up with a house and to purchase farmland that we would work together. We would give it a go; see how it felt to be independent for a change. Of course, we had a lot to learn, and we would need knowledgeable farm hands and such, until we understood the workings of it all, but it would be good for us, he said; a growth experience.

I was shocked and outraged that my brother would make this decision for me! Then another thought occurred. 'How was Maribeth standing for this?' I wondered. For as difficult a transition as this might be for me, she would surely flounder as a fish deprived of water. Maribeth was young and inexperienced in the ways of the ladies of high society, but a 'farmer's wife', she most certainly was not. She was far too fond of her silk fans and satin slippers. And to be made to give up the manor that she had finally truly obtained? I could not even imagine her response. Harder still was it for me to imagine Charles directly doing something that would so displease her.

I asked Charles as much and was not surprised to hear that he had not yet advised Maribeth of his decision, but he assured me that although initially Mari would resist, he must convince her that it was for the best. He could stomach society life no longer, and would not bear to watch her suffer the slings and arrows of the ladies of the court. Their slander would kill her spirit far more surely and swiftly than honest work could ever do. He was her husband, and where he would go, she would follow.

This was going to be a difficult and interesting venture. We would fail miserably, I was sure, but Charles said we were to give it four years. That was time enough to get crops established and truly figure out what we were doing. If by that time, I was dissatisfied, I could take my money and make myself a life elsewhere. Of course, I was welcome to do whatever I pleased. The money would be mine in four years, on my twenty-first birthday regardless, but what else was there for me to do? He would not allow me to remain at Herald Manor without him. If I went with them, at least he would purchase me a house and supplies. Charles and Maribeth were going, no question. He showed me their boarding passes for my very ship. He was extremely eager for me to join them. I agreed, and our new life began."

Chapter 9 - Remembering

Cain

The park
Thursday, 9:30 p.m.

Cain put down his glass and stretched, breaking the narration. Once again, Felicity looked as though she were awakened from a dream; she was so entranced by his tale. "It sounds like your brother really cared about you."

Cain tried to smile, although it felt an almost painful gesture. "He really did, as much as it provoked me at the time. I'd like to say he was right, that the move was best for us all. It did seem so, at first. Of course, knowing what I do now, I often wonder what might have happened had we simply stayed put. Though we probably wouldn't have fared any better. Charles and Maribeth were the people they were, no matter where they would go. Their problems certainly did not start or end with me.

I myself would never have become the man that I am today. I suppose you could argue that to be better or worse, depending upon your point of view, but most likely, had Charles given me any amount of money, I would have lived the life of a 'playboy' until I drank myself to death. They do say that 'there's no great loss without some gain'. I just find it unacceptable to think that my gain might be worth the multitude of loss that purchased it."

Felicity shook her head. "You can't try to analyze things that way. I'm sure things happen for a reason, but we can't think that we know or understand those reasons. I don't know whether the things that happened to you in the past, were a purposeful path to lead you to where you are now. And your life now shouldn't be dictated by actions and deeds from back then. We learn from the past and we shouldn't make the same mistakes over again, but you can't think that you know why things work out the way that they do. You can call it fate, destiny or God or whatever you'd like, but you can't say that you know for sure why."

"I know you're right. I've said it to you myself, 'I'm not the one making the plan'. It's just hard to accept sometimes. If things had been different, the people's lives that I would *not* have touched... Wouldn't they have been better off never knowing me? A fruitless line of thought I know, but nagging and torturous all the same."

"And what about the people's lives you've touched more recently? How many people would have become just another victim? How many vampires would know of no other way to survive, other than killing people?"

"What do you think I tell myself every night? Those are the thoughts that keep me going. Otherwise guilt and remorse over the past would have weighed me down beyond the capability of carrying on," Cain explained.

Felicity watched him as he filled his glass with the last of the wine, and put the empty bottle back into the basket. "Did we finish that already?"

"You mean did *I,* you've only had one glass. Not to worry though, I came prepared." He pulled a second bottle from the basket with a smile.

Felicity took the last sip that was in her own glass and held it out for him to refill. "It's so hard to comprehend, that the things you've lived through, all that's happened to you, are things that happened long before my great grandmother was born. It's so very long ago and yet they actually happened, to *you*. Does it get hard to remember? I mean, there's only so much room in our heads, right? Do you forget a lot of stuff?" she asked.

He'd been struggling a bit with the stubborn top to the wine bottle. Now he finally got it to open and poured her another glass. "Sure I do. You don't remember every day of your life, I could certainly never remember every day of mine, but I do remember the general succession of my life. Some of my memories are bit foggier than I'd like, but there are days, moments, that are so burned into my memory, that they could have happened yesterday. I can close my eyes and feel them, even now, as though they were happening at this very moment."

"Like what?" Felicity asked.

He sighed; the stronger images were not ones that he was yet ready to share. Their time would come. For now, he would keep to the timeline of his story for her. "Like the day I caught my first glimpse from our ship of these once foreign shores, for one."

Felicity settled her glass onto the ground and then lay back, wrapped in her comforter, to look up at the stars. "Tell me."

Cain closed his eyes and felt himself transported back in time as he tried to relay for her, the feel and excitement of that day. He described for her, his impressions, from the image in his mind.

"It was just after dawn when I emerged from below deck and approached the rail with a stomach full of butterflies. Today would be my first day in the New World. The wind was brisk, the air smelled of salt and I could see land. 'Twas far off in the distance, but looming ever closer, through the early morning fog. We should reach it before nightfall. Already it seemed foreign and exotic. I leaned forward on the rail to try and make something of the dark forests, across the water. Still too far.

I looked down to the dark waters rushing past, and couldn't help but feel so terribly far removed from everything I had known. But where this had often filled me with fear and dread these past months, I began instead to find myself expectant and excited. Before these four months at sea, I had never been on a ship, much less made a voyage such as this. I wondered if I ever would again. How would our venture fare? Would I be headed home on a ship much like this one, four years into the future; being glad to have this time behind me and eager to return to a life of luxury back in Canterbury? Or would I stay, this foreign land becoming my new home? Would I take to this life well, and meet my destiny here, living simply, as a common man?

Perhaps the woman I was destined to marry awaited me here. That was a sobering thought. Marriage and responsible family living were not notions I had ever seriously entertained, only worries for a far distant future. That was much of my problem. I'd always lived for the enjoyment of the moment, a habit I would do well to try and leave behind.

I'd spent much time with Charles and Maribeth these last few months. It did make me view them each differently then I had in the past. My brother, whom I had always seen as responsible and level headed, now looked a bit different to me. For although Charles reasoned that this move was something that Maribeth and I sorely needed to revive our deficient lives, I did suspect that for Charles this was nothing loftier than an escape from responsibility. Of course, the endeavor would take much courage, work and planning on Charles' part, but it was running to unknown troubles rather than face the ones that he knew.

Charles did not care overly much for life at court or the effort and canoodling that went into keeping father's investments and contacts working for us. To run the household and carry out father's obligations was something that Charles had looked upon with dread. He would much prefer the simple and straightforward challenge of managing fields and livestock, to managing the people and properties of the more 'civilized' world. Leave the rest to hired secretaries, accountants and our ambitious cousins. I don't know if I really thought less of him for it, but he no longer seemed my wise and infallible big brother.

Maribeth on the other hand, had gained some slight favor with me as time went on. When first she was introduced to me and for the year after, I had seen Maribeth as a very beautiful, spoiled and manipulative child. Very like myself, if I would dare to admit it. We were the same age, she being only a few months my senior. She did exactly as she wished and worked her wiles on my brother to gain anything that she might want, in the very same way that I would do as I pleased and gain things from my father most of the time. That is, until my father had had enough. I wondered if Charles had had enough as well. Was that part of his thinking, when he planned this endeavor? Did he plan to take her out of the world that she knew, so that she might be forced to grow into a woman, instead of remaining a spoiled child?

I had to admit that I'd been rather impressed by the way she had held her head high and refused to be beaten down by the attitude of the other ladies of society towards her. Once she'd lost the baby, I had thought she would be much humbled and broken. It was a terrible thing, to be sure. Maribeth had taken it much harder even than Charles had. She had seemed so depressed, that I'd wondered if she would ever again be herself. Yet, as the time for our journey neared, she seemed to have picked herself up and carried on with life. It was out of necessity more than anything else, but at least she was more herself again. In that, I thought perhaps Charles was right in saying that she needed this new life to focus her energies on.

Yes, Maribeth seemed her old feisty self once again, carrying on with the grace and dignity of royalty, and expecting to be treated as such.

However, being that we both were forced upon this journey almost unwillingly, she treated *me* differently now. In the past, she had always viewed me as a person of no importance. If anything, she had seemed to regard me as a nuisance who took Charles' attention away from her, but now, we were prisoners of fate, comrades in our complaints and resentfulness. She had begun treating me more like a secret confidant. Nothing untoward, but someone with whom she could share glances of discontentment and roll her eyes to when Charles went on overly long about his hopes for our future.

But there would be no discontentment today, I decided. One glimpse of that distant shore and I was filled with an excitement that I could not deny. If we were going to do this, I should try to do it right. Maybe Charles would be vindicated. Perhaps we would be successful, build ourselves a new life in which to thrive, instead of living out our stagnant and shallow existences back home. It would be hard work, something I was unaccustomed to, but I resolved to try my best. I figured Charles deserved at least that much from me. I hoped that Maribeth would not give him too difficult a time.

I knew that my brother and his wife had positively warred over the prospect of coming. It was quite grudgingly that Maribeth had finally let herself suffer to be brought along. Over the time spent on board, she had finally stopped her complaints and become more accustomed to the idea, but she was still in for a rude awakening to be sure. She was stunningly beautiful, but that would not get her very far when it came to running a household on a farm. This girl, who was used to getting things done by giving the right man a hopeful smile and batting her eyes, was in for an education.

The lady of my thoughts appeared on deck, quickly followed by my brother, who immediately rushed to the rail, some distance away. Maribeth spotted me and ventured to my side, while her husband heaved the contents of his stomach into the sea. The waters were a bit rough and walking was treacherous at times, but she managed without event. I remember her, approaching through the damp and mist, and then the sun cut through the morning fog, to make her red hair shine like a halo of fire. There's something about a woman with red hair that's always piqued my interest. They seem more exciting and passionate somehow."

He was drawn from his thoughts to realize that the lovely girl in front of him at the moment, was becoming a bit red in the face. Felicity's hair was not nearly the hue of flame that Mari's was, but would definitely be considered a dark red. She was giving him an amused but embarrassed grin. He laughed and gave a little shrug. He leaned forward to run his fingers through her long hair. He rubbed the ends together between his fingers, holding them to make the candle light shine on them and bring out her hair's auburn glow. "Guess my taste's haven't changed all that much." He dropped his hand and let himself become lost in her eyes for a moment. "But regardless of hair color, who could blame me for being attracted to such an exceedingly lovely woman?"

She was giving him an increasingly disapproving stare. Finally, she leaned back a little. "She was your brother's wife," she reminded him coldly.

He lost his smile and answered her very seriously. "A fact which I was very much aware of at the time. I would have to have been blind not to notice her as a man, but I never treated her with a familiarity unbecoming of our relationship until years hence." He gave her a little grin. "So stop jumping ahead. When I spoke of my attraction to a lovely woman just now, I was talking about *you*."

She was properly abashed and looked down with a smile. "Oh." She took a rather large sip of her wine. After a moment, she looked back up to his eyes, still smiling. "Don't think flattery is going to soften my judgment on you."

She said it teasingly, but it struck a painful cord in him. He took a large swallow of his own wine and prepared to continue. "As well it shouldn't." She seemed regretful of admonishing him and put a hand on his arm. He gently shook it off with a forced smile. It's not as though guilt were new to him.

He began again with strong and measured words. "As I did notice, she was a magnificently beautiful woman, but the only thoughts that came to my mind at the time were that I could only hope that I should find a wife of my own, half as lovely someday. I hailed her with a smile as she approached. 'Good morning. Up for a bit of air?' I asked.

She returned my smile and then turned to look after her husband, still doubled over the side. 'You would think he'd nothing left by now. How much more of this are we meant to endure?' she demanded of me.

'You can see land there, if you look carefully through the mists. I heard Master Tench say that it's only a short while now before we land. You should be stepping onto solid ground by this evening before the sun has even set.'

'Well thank the good Lord in heaven! This has been a bit more than I had thought to be subjected to.'

I gave her a raised eyebrow and a smile. 'Well, I hope you've a bit more left in you madam. This is only the beginning you know. We are debarking into a new world and it may be quite trying at times.'

'Oh really Christian! You know as well as I, that this company is simply joining a colony already formed. It's not true wilderness into which we go. I've been speaking to the goodwives of this ship and they all agree that there aren't even any natives living where we'll be. It's really all quite civilized.'

'I can only hope that it will live up to your expectations my lady.' I said this last with a humorous grin and a little mocking bow. To which she gave me a disapproving little smile and laugh.

My brother staggered over to join us, still looking rather pale. 'How you two are so completely unaffected, I can't begin to understand. I shall never be so pleased as when I might set my feet to solid ground once again.'

I smiled and put an arm around Charles to steady him. 'And what ground it shall be! Look you there brother, it shows even now through the fog. Our new home!' Charles looked a bit surprised at my new found enthusiasm, but as soon as he spotted land, he forgot all else. He was mesmerized. He hung over the rail so that I thought almost we would need to hold him back from falling overboard.

Charles pulled Maribeth to him and squeezed her tightly. 'Have you seen it Mari? Our new home! Doesn't that just sound the most wonderful phrase?' He spun her around and then quickly steadied himself at the rail as he began to look a bit green once again. Maribeth was laughing and I'd felt a bond between the three of us stronger than ever. Hope and excitement tied us together more than sharing a house or family ties had ever done. It seemed such a momentous occasion, a beginning of great times and dreams realized." Cain paused for a moment in thought. "If we had only known what really lay in store."

"Wasn't as good as you'd hoped, huh?" Felicity asked.

"Actually it was, for a little while. We had a few good years anyway. Charles set us up well. He purchased us a good amount of land and had two houses built, within walking distance of each other. We did need help getting started, but had no problem finding others to hire until we felt sufficient expertise to handle things on our own, with only minimal farm hands. As for the work itself, would you believe that I loved it? It sounds bizarre I'm sure, as I'd spent most of my life until then trying to avoid work, but understand that I had never felt the thrill and pride of real accomplishment before. In fact, I don't think I'd ever even broken a sweat, if not through the efforts of pleasing a woman in bed." He stopped to smile at Felicity's reaction to that comment. He hadn't meant to be crude, but was being truthful. She was so easily shocked, it was rather amusing.

He went on to tamer descriptions. "To take bare soil and seeds, and through nothing more than my own efforts, turn them into a viable crop, seemed almost magical! Food for our tables and enough to be sold for profit as well, come right from the ground. It was just amazing to me.

Once I learned the way of things, I threw myself into the work with a passion I'd never felt for anything else. It was a good thing too, besides supporting us, it kept me out of trouble's way for at least a little while.

I hadn't ever really thought about it, but until then I had taken very poor care of myself. I had never eaten more than one meal a day and barely picked at that. Not for lack of food of course, but simply because I spent all my time with alcohol and unseemly activities. For the first time in years, I'd begun eating three square meals, of hearty fare. I wasn't drinking anymore, but for ale or wine with dinner. I finally began to fill out my large frame a bit. Running that farm saw me grow from a lank and gangly youth into a well muscled, hard working young man. My face seemed to lose all of its hard and arrogant angles, to become that of someone healthy and happy."

Felicity leaned forward to hold her hand to the side of his face, lovingly. He closed his eyes for a moment, just enjoying her touch. Then he turned a bit, to give the palm of her hand a little kiss, before she took it back. He opened his eyes to see her sweet smile.

"I hope you don't think that I speak of myself this way out of vanity or pride. I'm just trying to help you see the changes that took place in me. Thinking back to those days in England, when I thought I was a man, I realize now that I was really like a large and awkward puppy. I had the height and frame of a man, but not the poise and stature of one who is truly in command of one's facilities.

You know what I look like now, even better than I do, but you should have seen me *then*." He smiled and looked down at himself, shaking his head. "I do remember the reflection in the mirror well enough. I feel a pale shadow of myself now."

She tipped her head to catch his gaze and looked at him in disbelief. "Are you kidding? You look pretty good to me." She actually did run her eyes over his body with a smile, as he laughed. Finally, she took her eyes away to finish her wine and have him refill her glass. He noticed her gaze did still return to travel the length of his body now and again as he spoke.

"Blood does not build muscle. It only maintains the minimum necessary to keep up the 'appearance' of health and provide me with the strength needed to hunt. If you notice, after a time, most vampires do begin to turn quite thin. Never shockingly so, but they would need to constantly exercise their muscles if they want to convince the demon within that they are in fact necessary.

With you, was the first time I'd set foot into a gym... ever. I usually get enough exercise keeping myself from getting killed by young ones who don't like my views, or feel they have something to prove, but maintaining myself is not exactly high on my list of priorities these days." He laughed again to see her open admiration of his appearance. Perhaps it was the wine. She usually sought to sneak glances at him when she thought he didn't know.

"The point is... I had changed. The girls of the village began to notice as well. You can imagine how frustrating that was. Remember, I'd had quite the education with the fairer sex up until our move. Now, I found myself in a Quaker village surrounded by girls of high moral standards and guarded virtue. It was frustrating to say the least. Their demure glances and shy giggles as I passed were hardly enough to satisfy.

I hadn't found anyone in particular that I thought could hold my interest for more than passing fancy, and I wasn't prepared to offer anything of a more committed nature as of yet. In fact, that may be one of the reasons I threw myself into my work as hard as I did. It proved a welcome distraction. Unfortunately, those girls were not the only ones to notice me. I began to see Maribeth's gaze linger a bit too long upon my form now and again. I ignored her, of course.

Charles worked hard as well, though he didn't seem to have quite the knack with the crops that I did. He took up the care of our small bit of livestock instead and put himself in charge of bringing our excess to town for sale and to barter for things we might need.

Maribeth did have some trouble adjusting at first, as we had feared she would. Cooking and keeping house were not her strong suites, to be sure, but after a few months of floundering difficulty, she did find her place. It seemed that sewing was an art for which she did have great skill. Her mother had been a seamstress in London, and she knew well the ways of cutting and stitching cloth. It came back to her well enough and she soon found her services in some demand as other ladies of the village viewed her fine work. Charles was thrilled that she had found a way for herself to be useful. So he hired a girl, Alice, to come and help with the baking and cleaning, so that Mari could sit and sew to her heart's content. The money earned from her labors paid for the girl and some. It was all working out even better than we might have dared to hope, theoretically anyway.

But Charles and Maribeth had other problems than those of running a household and farm. We lived and ran our farm that way for the next four years. Maribeth conceived children three more times in those four years and birthed none. Each new conception would bring new hopes, only to be dashed as she would find their baby's life running out from between her legs with her blood.

It sorely embittered her towards her husband, who seemed to feel she had failed him. I watched Charles and Maribeth, as their marriage turned cold and they became like strangers living in the same house. Of course, I tried to comfort them in every instance, but there was nothing that I could do. For Charles the best I could help, was to lessen his burden of work, so that he might attend to and comfort his wife. That was something he did less with each loss, I did notice.

Maribeth, at first too proud to let anyone see her discomposed or distraught, eventually at the end, did cry and sob upon my shoulder of her inadequacies as a wife. She wept of how she was not a true woman, a fact that I thoroughly disputed.

I remember her leaning back to look at me, wiping the tears from her face with the back of her hand. She was so disheveled and broken, but she was lovely still. She was very much a woman of not only beauty, but great strength of character as well. I told her so, though I never meant it in an improper way. She looked at me a bit oddly, and then whispered in a hushed and enticing manner, that I'd no idea how much a woman she could be. That Charles did not appreciate her wiles as he should, for he saw only her shortcomings now, but that pleasing a man was an art she knew well, and if ever I should care to find out just how well... Perhaps she could make me feel more of a man even as I could help to remind her of her worth as a woman.

I gently removed her from my lap as I stood and handed her my handkerchief; one that she had embroidered for me herself in fact, for my last birthday. I told her that I had indeed always admired her for her beauty and spirit, and that there was no doubt in my mind that she could transport a man to heaven and back in her bed if she'd the desire. However, she *was* a married woman. My brother was a fool if he did not appreciate the good fortune that he had, in being wed to such a glorious woman, but that she was still his, all the same. I would forgive her, her transgression and I understood her need for appreciation, but she did need look to her husband, not to me.

Never again did I seek to comfort her, not for years anyway, though my heart did break for her with every unkind glance or harsh word from my brother. I tried to speak to Charles, to convince him to heal his marriage, before he lost her love altogether, but my brother had become bitter and did not take kindly towards the idea that his 'little' brother, five years younger, should think to know more of life than he did.

I think that Charles resented how well I did adapt to this life. Charles was happy for me, but although he did try hard, it just didn't come as easily for him as it did for me. I think that was grating to him at times. I often wondered if he thought we should return to England. I had decided that I would stay, but when I brought up the prospect of he and Mari returning, he told me to mind my own affairs. He maintained that he would rather live here among true and honest people who shared his ideals. His wife should appreciate that and want him to be happy. She would be happy as well if she weren't more concerned with what others thought, than the happiness of her own husband. There was no talking to him on Mari's behalf and I had to let it alone.

Meanwhile, also during that time, a sweet young girl of the village had caught my attention. She was Elizabeth, daughter of our own Parish Priest. She was a pretty and petite little thing, with long blonde hair and a very quiet and modest demeanor, but every Sunday at services, I would see her, apart from the gaggle of giggling young girls who seemed more eager for my notice. She was different. Her shy smiles seemed far more worth my interest, than the girls who preened and posed for me.

Maribeth did not speak of indiscretions to me again for some time, and I endeavored never to let her find me alone to give her the chance. But after a short time, she did begin to look upon me with improper desire once again, and this time, I couldn't pretend not to understand the intent behind her wanting eyes. As the illicit glances from Maribeth increased in frequency and desire, I became much more aware of the fact that I was sorely in need of a woman of my own. So I did ask Elizabeth's father for her hand, and in due course, we were married."

"Married?" Felicity seemed surprised and almost alarmed by the news.

"Yes," he confirmed.

"She became your wife?" Felicity asked.

"That is how it works." He smiled at her concern. "You needn't worry for your own propriety; she's three hundred years gone, remember?"

Felicity shook her head as though to dislodge her foolishness. "I know. It's just this ingrained thing about staying away from married men, I guess." She took a sip of her wine, and then suddenly seemed to realize what it would mean to him, that she was gone. "I'm sorry. Do you miss her terribly? I mean, is it hard to talk about?"

"Not as hard as it should be, I suppose. Elizabeth was a good woman. She kept a fine house and attended to me, as a wife should. But I had married her because I'd felt that I needed a wife and I liked her better than any others, not because we had fallen in love. I suppose I did grow to love her, but if I'm going to be entirely honest, she never set my heart to racing in the way that Maribeth could.

Just a subtle, but undeniable look of wanting from Mari could make me forget to breathe. And those glances did not stop simply because I became another woman's husband. I always managed to ignore her and to seek solace with my own wife, but it was no easy feat I can assure you. As I said, Elizabeth was a fine woman, with a pleasing face and figure, but although she never denied me, her own appetite for my attentions and for such bed sport seemed sorely lacking. Shortly after we were married however, Elizabeth did find herself with child. We were very happy for the news, of course. And I did rightly assume that having a child would be one of the most changing and wonderful experiences of my life."

Felicity's face immediately seemed to melt into an expression of happy wonder. "You had a child?"

He fought very hard to keep the tears from his eyes, even as an unstoppable smile spread across his face. "A little girl. Amelia." He felt as though he could scarce contain the incredible surge of love and loss that enveloped his heart. Tears were going to flow, but it didn't matter. No one could ever take from him, the amazing love that he would always have for his little girl. He recognized that the proud excitement that was reserved only for Amy was beginning to infuse his voice. "In three hundred and forty years, I have never experienced happiness like she gave me. She was the most perfect and beautiful child. Her hair was like the softest corn silk. Not truly white mind you, but the palest blonde that you ever did see. Her eyes were blue as the sky on a clear summer day, and her smile seemed something that could heal all the ails of the world."

He took a deep breath and sighed. "But I get ahead. I should first tell you of things before she was born. Things between Liza and myself, that's what I sometimes called her, Elizabeth, the depth of our relationship was often less than I desired, yet I endeavored to be a good husband and our lives carried on. Things between Charles and Maribeth grew even more strained. Charles deliberately lost himself in the work of the farm, hardly attending to his wife at all. There were times when I did feel for her, for he treated the serving girl with more warmth.

To her credit, I must say that Maribeth did try to befriend Elizabeth and kindle a strong relationship there. Elizabeth was never unfriendly to her, but she shied away from Mari with an almost instinctive dislike of her. It was almost as if she sensed Maribeth was an influence best kept out of our house. I don't believe she ever witnessed anything to give credence to her suspicions, but our households were kept very separate, even though we still jointly worked the farm.

It was sitting at Charles's table to discuss the sale of crops and purchases of supplies that I most often saw Maribeth. She would hover around us, seeking to serve us tea or something to eat. It was most unlike her and I knew she was just positioning herself to be closer to me. Maribeth had begun to cast those indecent glances my way all too often, after Liza had taken to bed under the burden of pregnancy. I was sure that *I* would never seek to disgrace my brother or my own wife, but Mari was obviously unsatisfied and Charles seemed oblivious.

My own wife refused to let me touch her, once she found that our baby was growing within her womb. I knew that she was terrified to undertake any activity too great, lest she risk losing the child, as Charles and Maribeth had lost all of their own. For her own reasons and distastes, she would never touch me either. As time went on, Maribeth's beckoning glances became almost intolerable.

Finally, I succumbed. Maribeth found me in the barn late one afternoon, storing tools of the field after a day's work. Charles was in town on business and the farm hands had all gone for day's end. Elizabeth was coming near her time and hardly left her bed these days. We had a young hired girl named Nan in the house to help with her needs. There seemed little risk of being found, and as Mari advanced on me wantonly, her deep blue eyes promised pleasures I'd not known in far too long a time. I found my character weak, and could deny her no longer.

I thought I'd known all there was of the ways of a man with a woman. Indeed, I thought I'd quite the romantic education, but really, what I'd known was anything *but* romance. Even what occurred between Mari and I was not *romantic.* There is very little true *romance* in the world... you know? But still, Mari did give me an experience that I had not known I'd lacked. As I mentioned, Elizabeth was not really one to initiate such play, and the women I had known back home were mostly paid lovers. They surely did earn their money, and I daresay that I made sure they enjoyed their tasks, but Maribeth was different.

I had never been beset upon by a woman with such sheer desire in her eyes. Mari positively *hungered* for me as a man. She was desperate for my touch as no other woman had ever been. The effect was absolutely beyond compare.

Am I embarrassing you?"

Felicity was a bit startled from her trance. She shook her head and remembered to breathe again. Then she smiled. "A little." She took a sip of her wine and stared at the glass. "You're always so, reserved and composed. It's just hard to picture this story being about *you*. Little did I know that the reason you're so passive is because you've already had enough excitement to last three lifetimes."

He laughed. "*Most* of my life has been very boring, I can assure you."

"Really? Because so far most of it has revolved around sex."

He shook his head. "It hasn't really. I guess it just sounds that way."

"You have probably slept with thousands of women!" she exclaimed.

"Not *thousands!*" he replied in defense.

She gave him a disapproving look, daring him to do the math. "Even if you slept with less than ten a year."

He thought about that. "Maybe *a* thousand," he teased, with a grudging smile. "Why does it matter? Just so you know, I may have gotten off to quite the head start in my youth, but in recent *decades*, my life has been rather celibate, if that knowledge makes you feel any better."

He stared at her, trying to convince her of his seriousness, until she began to smile again. "How did we end up on this tangent anyway?" she asked.

"Your dirty mind," he supplied teasingly.

"It's *your* story. So you slept with Maribeth, I get the gist. Move on," she told him sternly.

He laughed. "I only wanted you to understand the difference between *that*, and what I had known."

"I get it," she said shortly.

"Do you? Let me phrase it so you'll see what I mean." She rolled her eyes at him and shook her head to show that further explanation was unnecessary, but he carried on, unheeding.

"I've no doubt that your own virtue is more closely guarded than mine was." She gave him a warning look for teasing her. "But surely you have had many suitors, at least; those vying for your *valuable* attentions." She smiled. "And from at least some of those, you must have allowed a kiss."

He stared at her with a smile until she acceded this with a nod and a chuckle. "Among those, I'm sure, was an unlucky fellow, whose kiss was simply a touch of the lips and nothing more. And perhaps, there were a few... very few," he added at her raised eyebrows, "whose kisses were sweet; something warm and enjoyable, as a kiss should be. But then maybe... just maybe, you have experienced a kiss filled with such passion... such electric and undeniable fervor, that it begs to go on and on. A kiss after which you can barely restrain yourself from wanting *more*. Might you know what I mean?"

She said nothing, but gazed at him with a hint of longing from over her glass as she sipped her wine as he went on. "Would it be fair to call each of these separate experiences, by the same name, as a kiss?" She looked as though beneath her amused acceptance of his description, she might like to refresh her memory of such kisses again, but she made no move, except to drink more of her wine. He continued with his story.

"And so, I *did* commit adultery with Maribeth. We had sex, but it was *not* like sex that I had ever known before. I found myself unable to resist her charms thereafter. For the last few weeks of Elizabeth's pregnancy, whenever there was a time of opportunity, Maribeth and I would secretly steal away."

"As your wife lay bedridden, pregnant with your child."

He hung his head. "I know. I wasn't trying to justify it, only to help you understand how I could have been so weak. It was unforgivable. I knew it was wrong, reprehensible and lecherous. And yet, she won me over, again and again.

That said, let me describe for you another momentous day in my life. It was September the 23rd, and I was out working in the fields, as always. I had put in a hard day, bundling hay for the livestock over the winter. I'd paused to wipe the sweat from my eyes, yet again. When I looked up, I saw Maribeth, coming out to the fields towards me from the house.

Although she was still far off, I knew her by that flaming copper hair of hers. Even with the condemnation and guilt that her visage brought down upon me, I could not deny that she was still the most beautiful woman that I had ever seen. And as she came to me now, I assumed that her insatiable appetite for my intimacies were what had driven her to the fields.

I felt terribly shamed that I had been so weak in character as to accept her affections these past weeks, but I have to admit that I was still excited by the sight of her nonetheless. It was with mixed feelings that I noted her approach. My guilt had weighed heavily on me of late and I found that although she pleased my eye, she plagued my heart. I thought to tell her that our infidelities should come to an end. I had thought this in the past however and her wiles were always such that I could not bring myself to end it.

As she crossed the fields, the wind tugged and played with her skirts and threatened to unbind her long braid of copper hair. I felt myself tense with the expectation of her advances. Surely she wanted more of my illicit attentions. Why else would she have come? However, as she drew closer, the stern set of her face convinced me otherwise. I dropped my scythe and went to meet her.

'Mari, what is it, has something happened?' I asked.

"Tis only your wife, 'Lizabeth. Her time has come at last and she calls for you.' Maribeth was obviously less than pleased to have been the one to bring this news. We did have that young girl Nan, to help care for Elizabeth in these end weeks, but she would certainly be at Liza's side during this time. The other hands of the house and farm were quite busy preparing for the harvest, and so it was Maribeth who was sent to bring the news.

I knew that Mari was sorely covetous of my own wife. As Liza's' stomach grew, it became obvious that she would succeed where Maribeth herself had too many times failed, but until now, I had not seen such undisguised malice on her face. I'd no time for thought on this now however, the baby was arriving!

As I ran back to the house with Maribeth trailing behind, I began to feel my guilt press upon me again. I had wronged my wife terribly, though I hoped she never knew it. I decided things would change. Our baby would come and our marriage would strengthen. My attentions would be for Liza only from now on. Mari and Charles had their own marriage to heal. I would be a new man, a faithful husband and devoted father.

I stopped before we reached the house and turned to tell Mari as much. I didn't want to waste time with many words or explanations, but I wouldn't be too abruptly harsh with her either. I simply told her that things would be different now and that the sins of our past should not be repeated. That she knew I did appreciate what a fine woman she was, but it was wrong for us to be so untrue to our spouses. It was a new time in my life, and perhaps she and Charles could rekindle their own love, even as Elizabeth and I rekindled ours.

She didn't say anything. Not a word. She just gave me a very steady stare. It was vaguely haughty in nature, almost as though she was amused that I should think that Elizabeth could make me happy now. After a moment of silence, I dismissed her from my thoughts and raced home to await the birth of our child.

Some hours later, I sat at Elizabeth's side as she held our new baby girl. She was the most amazing creature that I ever did see. To think that her life came from me, that Elizabeth and I, however imperfect our love might be, had created this truly perfect being! We would name her Amelia Catherine Herald, and she held for me hope that our life would begin anew once again. We would be a true family, and whatever difficulties life held, we would face them together.

The years passed and our family prospered, even as poor Charles and Maribeth conceived and lost yet another babe. In those first few years, I did hold true to the promise I'd made to myself on the day of my daughter's birth. I was a devoted husband and father. Elizabeth and I had no other children as of yet, but we did have hopes of rearing a son one day as well. Although she did not seem any more interested in such pleasures, Elizabeth was the only woman to receive my attentions.

Secretly I did wish she could be more like Maribeth. In fact, shameful as it was, as time went by I came to find that only remembered visions of Maribeth could please me. So although I stayed true to my wife, I felt an adulterer still. Though I tried to never let it show, Elizabeth surely noted that I was unsatisfied. She didn't seem anxious to fulfill my needs however, and eventually turned all of her attention towards caring for our child and house. I tried to make her feel special. I tried to show her that I felt she was a good wife and mother, but perhaps it was guilt that drove my devotion more than pure love.

I'd no idea how I could turn her to be more like the woman I craved. Most likely, I never could. I guess it was wrong of me to think so, but our marriage was unwell and obviously something needed to be done. I wanted to tell her. I wanted to confess my sins, so that we could purge our relationship of it and move on. I don't think she knew. She never even hinted she might, but she was always a bit colder after Amy was born and I did wonder. Then again, perhaps it was the pain of childbirth that had turned her from wanting to conceive again.

I was afraid to throw myself at her mercy. I was terrified that she would not forgive me, that she might take Amelia and go home to her parents' house, a ruined woman. *That* I could not bear. I'd like to say that I was worried for Liza's emotions and reputation, but really it was my own selfish comfort I thought of. How would I live alone? And what would I do without my precious Amy? Amelia was the light of my life. I could never risk letting her take Amy away. Even if she stayed, I was frightened that she might turn Amelia against me somehow, keep her love from me. So I said nothing.

All of my happiness came from my sweet Amy. I indulged her in everything, though it never spoiled her. No matter how exhausted I was after a long day of work, I always had time for her. We would play for hours. I attended all of her tea parties. I never complained as she dressed me in fancy hats or put flowers in my hair. Her giggles were worth more to me than anything else in life. I used money from my account back home, which I now had the control of, to buy her dolls and dresses. I bought things for Liza too, but she was not one to put much store in material pleasures. She had a good head on her shoulders, my wife. She ran our house as a well-oiled machine; frugal and smart with our expenses so we wanted for nothing. I should have appreciated her more, at the time.

And so, my gifts to her she did accept, but they did not really gain me her favor. I thought I'd done all I could to be a good husband, but I began to feel our marriage turn cold just as surely as Charles and Mari's had. Perhaps if we'd had more heartfelt talks... discussions of our hopes and fears, instead of simply exchanging pleasantries and 'playing house', as it were, things would have been different.

I have to admit that I did begin to treat her more as someone who cooked and kept the house for me, than a woman that I should love. Something that I had rebuked Charles for so many times in my mind years past, but I saw myself as totally unlike him. Charles was lucky enough to have Maribeth, a woman of great passion and beauty. How could he be so foolish as to be blind to her charms? It was his own short sightedness that killed the love in his marriage.

I felt that my own wife however, did bring upon herself any coldness she may have felt from me. For I gave her only that which I received. If she had ever been more loving, and treated me as the prized husband and virile man that I should want her to see me as... Well, perhaps I would have seen *her* differently and treated her differently as well. Or so I told myself. I don't really know what might have been, if either of us had been a bit more giving, but once again I began to notice Maribeth's hopeful glances. As she saw them have effect on me, she tried all the more to lead me astray. After four and a half years, I did finally give in again and our illicit affair was rekindled.

It was late January, not long after my twenty-seventh birthday. Charles was away from home for the day in town, when it suddenly began to snow heavily, out of nowhere. I went over to Charles and Maribeth's barn, to make sure the animals were in, and then I stopped at the house to see if all was well. I knew Charles was not back yet, their carriage was still out, and perhaps *I* should have stayed away as well.

I can't really say what my intent was. I told myself that I was only checking in, as a good brother should be expected to. I did think their girl Alice would be there, so it would be innocent. She'd been sent home however, and Maribeth was alone. I suppose to Mari's eyes, I was there with impure intent. She seemed to expect that I'd come for *her* and she was very glad of it. I did protest, but she wasted no time in stripping me of my defenses, winning me over with kisses and such. I must admit that I did not fight it as hard as I should have.

That tryst was our last transgression. I hated myself when the act was through and I promised myself t'would be the last. As I dressed and readied myself to leave, I became more and more disgusted with our wickedness. I told her that she was to leave me alone thereafter, to look to her own life and stop ruining mine, as though she was the only one at fault in the affair. I was harsh, and it hurt her terribly I'm sure, though she'd never show me.

She wouldn't cry. She held her pride above tears when she could. I guess that's what made it easier for me to keep flinging cruel words at her as I did. In fact, I think I'm the only person who's ever truly seen her cry, other than tears designed for effect of course, but not at that time. I was the one hurting her and so she would shed no tears before me. I called her an evil temptress and threatened that she best stay far away from me from now on. She never even said a word in her own defense. I suppose because she knew that I spoke truly, but still, I was at fault as well and yet I gave her all of the blame. I don't even remember all of the awful things that I said, and I don't really care to. She just took it, until my anger was spent and I stormed away.

Again, I felt as though I should tell Liza, but at the same time, I knew it would only hurt her. If I weren't to commit the sin again, should she still know, or should I try to let it fade into the past? I was undecided.

What happened then, seemed the very next day, although I don't know if it really was, but I know that I was still agonizing over whether to talk to Elizabeth and confess what a poor excuse for a husband I'd been... when it started." Cain felt as though he were growing positively nauseous, but forced his expression blank and his voice steady. "Amy got sick."

Cain could see the fear and foreshadowing of what would be said next, come over Felicity's face. He forced himself to tell the story, instead of just breaking down over his own remembrance of it.

"The winter after Amelia's fourth birthday was a particularly cold one. There had been a wet and ailing summer that had turned the fields to mud and the crops reflected it. We were coming upon hard times, to be sure. The harvest of fish from the sea helped to ease the burden of hunger in the villages, but without the provisions of a strong crop, the winter looked to be long and difficult.

Of course we were far luckier than most. We still had money banked in England that could be used to send for supplies from overseas and that did get us through. We couldn't get much; ships were hesitant to run in the harsh winter. We could have the things we needed bought for us, but getting them sent was a trial. We did get some though. We had dried goods shipped over for our household and were generous as we could be to our neighbors as well, but food was not our community's only problem.

With the cold, the illness came, and no amount of money could keep it from visiting our families just as it plagued the others. It began with a dry harsh cough that racked my daughters' chest and woke us in the night. Soon it developed into a heavy fatigue and ague that affected not only Amy, but Elizabeth and many of the other villagers as well. Fevers raced through the townsfolk and many of them were sent home to the Lord by the time the winter was through." Cain took a deep breath but when next he opened his mouth to speak, no words would come. He could see by her face that Felicity already knew, but this was a story he seldom told, and he felt that he needed to say it aloud, however difficult.

"She was only four. Four short years is all we had together, my sweet Amy and me. She was the light of my life and the sickness put her out. It took her away, just like that. She died, February 12th, 1692." He stopped talking because it seemed there was nothing left to say. A wave of grief he had spent many a night holding at bay, washed over him with such force that he could scarce hold himself silent. Rather than weep he grabbed for his wine.

He drank down the contents of his glass, even as he felt sick from the grief. After it was finished, he threw the glass aside in anger. "Stupid wine doesn't do a damn thing." The weight of loss overcame him then. He did something he had not allowed himself in too long a while. He openly and overwhelmingly mourned the loss of his daughter. He hadn't told anyone of her in so long. Of course, she was always in his heart and he did think of her, but he couldn't speak of her to others usually. Even people he was close with over the years, he usually did not share her with. She was his, his private joy and also his deepest despair.

He'd been so overcome that he had almost forgotten Felicity's presence for a moment. He did not know what it was about this girl that made him want to share his life with her. He had known many others in the past, in longer much more serious relationships, that he had not told, but he wanted to share everything with Felicity. For some reason he felt it very important, that she truly know him right from the start. Maybe that was where he had gone wrong in the past. Holding things too dear to share. He had known that he would speak it all to her even before this evening, but now he found the task even more daunting and difficult than he'd expected. He tried to gain control of his sorrow to go on. "She died... and..."

"Oh Cain, come here." He glanced up to see tears streaming down Felicity's cheeks as well. She reached her arms out to him from across the blanket.

He felt so weak and angry with himself for being unable to just tell her, without all of this. He wiped his face, although new tears simply replaced the old ones. "No, I'm fine. I just need a minute. I'm sorry."

"Cain, please." Again, she reached out for him. She tried to wipe his tears and bring him close, but he pulled himself away.

It seemed that she wanted to hug and kiss him. He did not want her kisses right now. "No, I don't need..." She had taken hold of him and did pull him to her, but not to kiss, as he'd assumed. She made him lie down, putting his head into her lap, facing away from her body. He tried to get up, "You needn't..." but she pushed him down again, gently but firmly.

"Just stay." She began to run her fingers through his hair, brushing it back away from his face. She did it over and over in a methodical and strangely soothing gesture. He stopped fighting her and lay there, silent. "Don't say anything else right now. It's late, and you can tell me the rest tomorrow if you want. It's enough for now. Let's just stay quiet for a little."

She kept playing with his hair, and had begun to hum a bit. It felt so odd, that someone should be trying to take care of him. He spent so much of his life worrying about taking care of others. It seemed that others always saw him as strong and removed from emotion. He set it up that way, he knew, for other vampires anyway. To appear weak was to have his advice dismissed. Humans, on the other hand always saw him as some all-powerful creature, good or bad, never as someone in need of comfort.

He lay there for awhile, in bewilderment, as the sorrow for his daughter's death took its place back in the corner of his heart where its ache was something that he had grown accustomed to and could go on with. His thoughts turned back to Felicity. He turned just a little to look up at her face. He expected to see her studying him, wondering what he was thinking, but she wasn't even looking down at him. Her eyes were closed and her face was tipped towards the sky, as she gently rocked a little and hummed a snippet of some song he'd heard somewhere before. In the candlelight, her cheeks sparkled with the wetness of her tears still, and it gave her a slightly ethereal appearance when seen from below.

She was such a beautiful soul. It wasn't even her physical form he thought of now, although he found that lovely as well, it was her gentle, generous manner. He loved the way she sought to see the good in him and tried to empathize with him. She obviously disapproved of his past, as well she should, but she did seek to understand, honestly, without trying to fit him into some preconceived notion she might have. She made him feel that even where she would disagree with his actions and as the story furthered, surely be horrified by them, she may still forgive him of them. It would change the way that she saw him, but she was a smart girl. She had to have had some idea of things he'd done, by his nature as a vampire at least. She seemed prepared to accept his story and then carry on, as his friend if not more. Many others would have rejected him by now, he knew.

He spent a long time just lying there, gazing up at the stars as she rocked and hummed. Her mark was a pale glow. It was almost gone, but it still seemed to surround and connect them both, and he felt the tingle of it in her fingers when they brushed his skin. She'd ceased stroking his hair and was now just winding her fingers within it, every once in a while taking her hand from it to stroke the side of his face. He couldn't remember a time when he'd felt so at peace. It was probably the greatest gift that she could bestow upon him right now; acceptance and a quiet sharing of his grief. He did hope that she could forgive him, when his tale was through, for he knew now if not before, that he truly loved her.

Chapter 10 - A few quarts shy

Felicity

In the park
early Friday morning

Felicity was unsure just how long they sat that way, Felicity sitting on the tablecloth spread over the ground, with her legs curled under her and Cain lying stretched out, with his head in her lap. She stroked his hair and closed her eyes, thinking over all he had said so far. The terrible grief that he'd had for his daughter had broken her heart. She'd felt almost panicked during his telling of it, as though she were desperate to do something to change it. Of course that was foolish, but that was how she'd felt, all the same.

So, she had done all that she could think to do. She had made him lie still and try to be at peace. She had comforted him the only way that she could think how. With someone else, she might have felt inadequate or silly, but somehow, for Cain, it seemed right. He had resisted at first, as though he didn't need or maybe didn't deserve consoling, but she had insisted, and now he seemed content. Every once in awhile she dared to brush her fingers across the side of his face and feel the fading electricity between them from her mark. Of course, there was also still a very real natural spark between them, she thought so anyway. As exciting as the effects of his bite made contact between them, she was glad that it was almost gone. It made things a little confusing, because a kiss from him was wonderful in its own right, just as he had so vividly and accurately described.

She had been almost afraid to let things go further while her mark was in effect. It would be amazing she knew, but a little overwhelming too. The thought of losing her virginity and being with someone as experienced as

Cain was scary enough. She was unsure whether she would decide to sleep with him, but would much rather wait for her mark to be gone before she let things go too far. She could too quickly and fully lose herself and all judgment in feelings like that. It would be better to feel somewhat in control.

They had been like this for a while, just quiet and content. She wondered if he was truly happy to remain, or was just waiting for her to allow him up. He'd been so quiet and still, he seemed content to stay with her indefinitely and she certainly wasn't in a rush to end it. She was glad that he seemed calm now. She'd felt so helpless to see him before. Finally, she looked down at him and was very surprised to see him gazing back up at her. "I thought maybe you'd fallen asleep, you've been so still," she said quietly.

He smiled. "No. Just enjoying your quiet company."

She didn't mean to remind him of it, but she suddenly felt tears welling up again over the death of Amelia. "I am so sorry... for the loss of your daughter."

He gave her a watery smile. "Me too. Enough said." He lay there smiling at her for another moment, then sat up and looked at her appraisingly. "It's late, you must be exhausted. Do you have early classes tomorrow?"

"Yes. Why are you suddenly so worried about my education?"

"Because you aren't. Someone should be," he told her.

"So I miss a class. It's not that big a deal," she insisted.

"I beg to differ. Your future *is* a big deal. Don't you plan to live in it?" he asked discerningly.

She laughed. "I guess."

"So, it's time I took you back. When do you leave for home?"

"Oh, not 'til Saturday," she assured him.

He seemed relieved. He must have thought she would leave tomorrow. "Alright then, we'll pick it up tomorrow evening."

She smiled at first, but then groaned and tilted her head towards the sky. "I have to work tomorrow night. I'm closing... with *Ben*." She was not looking forward to seeing him again anytime soon. She'd had enough of his judgments and snide remarks.

Cain chuckled. "I thought you liked working with Ben?"

She rolled her eyes and shook her head. "Lately, not so much."

After a thoughtful moment, he smiled. "Good."

Now it was her turn to chuckle. Jealous was he? He shouldn't worry. "You don't like Ben, do you?"

"I like Ben. Ben does not like me." He pondered that for a second. "That's the problem isn't it? Is he giving you a hard time about me?"

She sighed and gave a little shrug. "He's just being… Ben. You know, arrogant, aggravating, annoying, obnoxious…"

Cain laughed. "Would you like me to speak with him, remind him of his manners?"

"That's okay, I can handle it," she assured him with a smile.

"Alright then, I suppose I'll pick you up at work?" She nodded with a smile. He smiled back and nodded towards the remains of their 'picnic'. "Let's pack this up." He began putting things back into the basket.

"This was nice," she said, gesturing over the tablecloth, and everything, "the way you set this up."

He grinned. "Yes, a very romantic evening, which I wasted no time in turning to tales of deception and depression."

She smiled at him in the waning candlelight. "I'm glad." He looked very confused at that remark; it hadn't really come out right. "I mean, I respect that; that you want me to know, more than you want… well... that you want me to know." She smiled and blushed at the awkward statement. She hadn't meant for it to come out quite like that, and had a hard time re-wording the sentence halfway through.

He gave her one of his little lop-sided sort of smiles. "I guess it was a bit different from the evening that you'd expected." She just shrugged. "I don't suppose you might grant me a kiss anyway? Come the end of tomorrow night's tale, I certainly don't expect one. In fact, you may decide that I'm not worth your time at all. If I still hold some slight favor with you now, perhaps, just one kiss? Shame to let the wine and candlelight go to waste."

"That depends... How difficult is it going to be, to keep it from turning into something that would make me miss my first class in the morning? Seeing as you're so concerned about my education."

He grinned at that. "I think I can control myself, if I *must*."

She leaned forward a little. "Maybe just a touch of the lips..." she teased. She gave him only a peck on the lips, and then came away to see his reaction. He was obviously disappointed, but made no move. She laughed at him and then leaned in for a more rewarding experience. She teased him with a few more darting little kisses, made into magical little thrills by the remainder of the mark they shared; then she gave him a real kiss. At first, she sought to make it deliberately short and sweet, but the moment it truly began, she realized that would never do.

She knew that she should probably see him differently, in light of the things he had done in the past, but she couldn't help it. It seemed like a story about someone else. He'd changed so much since then, hadn't he? This was not some seventeenth century farmer who was sleeping with his brothers' wife. This was Cain, her strong and confident rescuer, who kept her safe and made her feel so special. Quiet, handsome, mysteriously charming and gentle; this was the man she was falling in love with, not some awful adulterous murderer.

She just couldn't make herself see him that way, not right now. In the candlelight, with her head slightly buzzing from the wine, his kiss was so sweet and disarming. She'd planned to lean over for a short, simple kiss, but she should have known better, before long she found herself melting into his arms. After a moment, she actually found she was lowering herself to their ground cover, and pulling him down to her. It was as if something had come over her and she could not help herself. It might have been the wine, but more likely, it was just him. He lay lightly on top of her, not truly pressing her down with his weight, but she did feel a little indecent thrill as she recognized the hard length of his member stiffen against her. She had never been so sexually aware of someone in her life.

She allowed herself another minute or two of tasting his lips and pressing herself against him, and then she pulled back. As the kiss ended, she felt him take a very deep breath and tip his face up to the sky for a moment. She gave him several parting kisses down the length of his throat, before tucking her head into the crook of his shoulder and just holding him to her for a moment. He rolled over off of her and lay down to look up at the stars with his hands behind his head.

She sat up, thinking to stand, but as she looked at him, she couldn't help but bring herself down for another kiss. He eagerly greeted her lips with his own, wrapping his arms around her, but she forced herself to keep it short. She rose from him and looked down. He was in the most seductive possible pose to her. He lay there unmoving, splayed out and vulnerable, looking up at her with heavy lidded eyes. Those eyes did seem to beg for her attentions, but he left *her* in the position of control. To her that seemed far sexier than boys of the past who tried so hard and always sought to initiate things and be in control themselves. He was so handsome and sweet, no matter what his past. She fought back her urge to lie with him again, stood and lent him her hand to rise. He took it with a smile. He seemed more resigned than disappointed, although he obviously would have been content to stay.

"And so, the evening ends," he said. He rose beside her and then turned and took her face into his hands. He gave her one more very deliberate and seductive kiss, fully tasting and teasing her with his tongue. It wasn't long, but even as he sought to end it, pulling slowly away from her, he sucked just a little on her lower lip. It sent a thrill through her that made her feel as though she should simply like to lie down and pull him onto her again.

That was most likely what he wanted her to feel, but she knew she needed to leave. This was not the night, not yet. She felt a little tipsy from the wine and now the venom of his saliva was beginning to affect her as well. She was very much starting to wonder what she was waiting for. Why not just give in? Was it such a big deal, such an important decision? Maybe not, but if she did it now, she knew that in the morning she would wonder about her real reasons for being with him. Was it only the moment? This was not the time for such a commitment. Let him finish his story, let her have time to think and for her mark to truly fade away.

As he released her, she stepped back from him a bit, almost tripping over the wrinkled edge of the tablecloth that she stood on. He laughed and held out a hand to steady her. "Well, I think that's enough for you, young lady," he teased. "Three glasses of wine and you can barely stand."

"It wasn't the wine; it was *you* that put me over the edge. That venom of yours is dangerous stuff."

She smiled at him, but he seemed a little chastened, as though he was embarrassed by the mention of the unnatural agent in his saliva. She came back to him and gave him another quick kiss on the lips, to try and erase his

151

concerns and show that she was unworried by it. "Not that I'm complaining, but I think that it is time for me to go." He smiled and gave her a little nod.

He walked over to retrieve the larger broken shards from his glass that he had thrown earlier, wrapping them in a napkin and dumping them into the basket. She then helped him to fold up the tablecloth and then blew out the candle. She held it out to him and he finished closing up the basket. He could see much better in the dark than she could, she knew, so she let him fasten everything to the bike and then come back for her hand. She could see a little, but he led her carefully to the motorcycle.

On the ride back, she held tightly to him and thought about what he had said. Mostly she pondered his comment about how he thought she would not want to be kissing him tomorrow after hearing the rest of his story. Did he really think that it would affect her so strongly; that she would be so disgusted by his actions? She already knew that he must have killed his brother, what more was there? How much worse could it have been?

She searched her feelings about him now. She knew that he had slept with his brother's wife and then killed his brother. Yet, as absolutely horrible as that was, she still felt she could forgive him and she was certainly still attracted to him. Did that make her a bad person, that she could so easily forgive such horrid acts? Time passed, did not mean that he was any less guilty of the things he'd done. His poor wife. His poor brother! What had they ever done to deserve such treatment? If he'd treated his wife and brother that way, why should she think that he would be any better a person in *her* life?

It was becoming confusingly muddled in her head. The wine, mingled with the loud engine of the motorcycle was giving her a headache. She'd have to think on these things more tomorrow. She may attend her classes in the morning, but she'd a feeling that she would have a difficult time actually paying attention.

He coasted into the dorm lot and she hopped off the back of the bike. He remained in the seat, but turned to watch her as she strapped the helmet back onto the bar on the back. She looked up at him when she was finished, and then moved closer to him, resting her hands on his leg. As she looked into his eyes, he seemed a little sad. She wondered what he'd been thinking about on the ride home.

"Goodnight, I'll see you tomorrow. We close at ten on Fridays," she said.

He grinned. "I know. It'll make for a late start and there's so much left untold. I hope you won't mind being up all night."

"That's alright, I'll take a nap," she said with a giggle.

"Mind if I come early?" She smiled and shook her head. "Alright, then I'll see you tomorrow."

"Can we spend the evening just the same? I mean, go back to the park, and bring some more wine?" He laughed.

"As identical as you like." She leaned in to kiss him, but he turned to make it only a kiss on the cheek. "Sleep well." She was a little bemused by his refusal to kiss her again. She smiled at him and then looked at the comforter on the back of the bike.

"I guess I'll leave that with you, then. Oh, do you want your jacket?" she asked, grasping the collar of his denim that she'd worn again.

He gave her a little shake of his head. "Keep it," he said quietly.

She smiled, gratefully. She hadn't really wanted to give it up. She loved wearing it. She loved that it was his. "Thanks. Goodnight," she called as he walked his Harley to the road. He gave her a wave and then started the bike and rode away.

~~~~~~~~~~~~~~~~~~~~~~~~~~~~~~~~

The next morning's algebra class found Felicity in a very tired and grumbling mood. She'd woken up with a bit of a headache. She hadn't gotten nearly enough sleep and she couldn't help but feel that she had far more important things to think about right now. The last thing she was in the mood to do, was fill her head and strain her mind with linear transformations, matrices and determinants.

However, she was unwilling to miss the class because she knew Cain would ask her if she went. She wouldn't lie to him and then he would be disappointed in her for not going. Besides, if she were going to skip class anyway, then she might as well have stayed with him later last night. At least she felt that attending class would help her justify her decision to leave him. She was still a little annoyed with herself for being so indecisive.

Part of her really was bothered by the things that he had done in his past. Cautions and warnings that she would rather not heed, flitted about in the back of her mind. She could not believe that he would ever really hurt her, emotionally or physically, but Charles and Elizabeth had probably thought that too, and look at what he'd done to them. It was disturbing to say the least, but she felt that she knew him now and he was not that same person at all anymore. He was a man who would never do such things again, wasn't he? She hoped she was not just being naive. Although she was unwilling to really admit it to herself, she knew she would be better off to forget about him. There were plenty of other guys in the world, with much less dangerous concerns.

At the very same time, she was so incredibly attracted to him that she could not imagine ever wanting anyone else. If not for his past, she loved everything about him. Alright, maybe not everything. She hadn't really forced herself to come to terms with the vampire issue. Was that really something that could be ignored or worked around? She was being really stupid wasn't she?

But if not for the fangs, he was the most wonderful guy she had ever met. He was so handsome and charming and sweet and... he needed her, didn't he? He was so alone if not for her. He deserved someone that would accept him for what he was. He needed someone he could share things with and not be afraid to be honest with. Of course, the fact that he was so incredibly sexy was something that could not be ignored either.

She was becoming impatient even with herself. Physically, their relationship was the most exciting she'd ever had, and they hadn't even really *done* anything yet. What was she waiting for anyway? She had never wanted a man so badly in her life. If he wanted her as well, then why shouldn't they enjoy being together to the fullest extent possible? Was there really anything wrong with that? It's not like she was really waiting for marriage was she? She just wanted to know that it meant something to both of them; that it was not a one night stand or just some passing fling. Cain obviously cared enough for her, to wait until she was ready. She already knew, that however unwise, she was falling steadily and deeply in love with him. What more could she ask for?

She was almost afraid to hear what he had to tell her tonight, because she knew that she would want to be with him, no matter what he said. To find out worse things about him now would only hurt. If she was going to be truthful with herself, she should realize that it was too late to believe that she could just simply walk away from him. She already cared too much. If she really felt that she *had* to leave him, for her own well being, of course she would, but it would not be easy. In fact, she would probably feel devastated. She hoped he had made things out to be worse than they were.

All of these thoughts, combined with a lack of sleep and no lack of wine the evening before, had put her into a fairly grumpy mood. Amazingly, she still made it to algebra on time. Then it turned out that the professor was late anyway. As she slumped into the seat next to Ashley, she hoped she might go back to sleep until class started. Of course, Ashley made that impossible. "Hi!"

She looked over to Ashley, groggily. "Why are you always so chipper?"

"Because *I* recognize and respect the value of a good night's beauty sleep. Look at you. Did you even *go* to bed last night?"

"Yeah, I think I finally got to sleep around three."

Ashley broke into a broad grin. "Out with Cain huh?"

"Yeah, he's... kind of a night owl."

"Where'd you go?"

"We had sort of a... picnic in the park, wine and cheese anyway. You know, by the waterfall."

"Wow, romantic! Finally showing the man some appreciation I hope?"

Felicity tried to look annoyed, but it was ruined by a yawn. "We spent all night talking."

"*Just* talking?"

"Pretty much."

"What a waste! What is wrong with you girl? I've got to be honest, if he ever gets tired of waiting around for you, don't expect me to give you a grace period. That man is so yummy. I am all over that, first opportunity."

"It's not like I ignore him, believe me. It's just, kind of complicated."

"No, it really isn't. He is a totally gorgeous and worthy guy, who I still think has money, no matter what you say, and he totally wants you. All else is secondary and works itself out, believe me."

Felicity just shook her head. She was too tired to try and dispute. It'd just be easier to get Ashley talking about her favorite subject, herself. "So, I suppose your date book is full for the weekend?"

Ashley gave a sly smile. "Of course it is... full of Ben."

That news was unexpected and woke her up a bit. "Really?"

"*Oh yeah,*" Ashley confirmed.

"Finally decided to let him know that you still like him, huh?"

"I didn't even have to, he called me. I knew he would eventually. He is so hot for me," Ashley informed her.

Felicity tried not to roll her eyes. "Where are you going?"

"Tonight we're going to Venus, one of the few hot spots around here. Then tomorrow he wants to take me to the Debate Luncheon."

"What's that?" Felicity asked.

"They do it every year. It's a big fancy lunch at the country club, over in Oxford. Ben was chosen as captain of the debate team this year, you know."

"I didn't know that. Although I guess I shouldn't be surprised, he certainly loves to argue. Wait, isn't Ben closing tonight?"

"Yeah, that's okay. It'll give me some time to find an outfit that'll really rev his engine. Ben appreciates that sort of thing, you know? And Venus is the only club around here worth dressing for. You ever been?"

"Yeah, Cain took me once," Felicity told her.

"You guys should come," Ashley offered.

Felicity smiled at the thought of she and Cain on a double date with Ben and Ashley. The professor arrived and Felicity gave Ashley a hushed answer as class started. "Thanks, but we have a more private evening planned."

~~~~~~~~~~~~~~~~~~~~~~~~~~~~~~

Felicity arrived for work on time at four o'clock. Thank goodness her school schedule was light on Fridays, and she'd had time for a quick snooze before heading over to the DownTime for her shift. Closing with Ben would probably be aggravating enough, without being tired as well. She also assumed she'd be out late with Cain again and she certainly didn't want to fall asleep during his story.

Friday nights were always pretty busy, so she had Lucy helping her in the bookstore until eight. She noticed that Harold was working with Ben in the café. Oh joy. She made her way to the counter while both guys were busy with customers, so she could slip into the back without having to address them.

Unfortunately, when she came back out, Ben was standing right there. She wasn't sure if he'd planned it that way. Rather than give her an angry look or a rude comment, he just said 'Hi', as though she weren't mad at him. She stopped for a second, caught off guard, and then returned it with her own 'Hi'. Just then, Harold approached, giving her a look that was an obvious assessment of her body. "Hiii," he cooed in what he seemed to think was a seductive manner. Felicity rolled her eyes and shared a disgusted look with Ben, who then handed Harold an empty dirty bowl he'd been holding.

"Go wash the dishes," he said, nodding towards the full sink. Harold gave him an annoyed glance, but went to the sink as directed.

She didn't say anything else to Ben, but went right over to the registers. At six thirty she had a break for dinner. She'd brought her own sandwich to try and save some money. You weren't supposed to bring outside food into the cafe though. There were two chairs and a tiny table in the 'employee lounge' behind the cafe, where the lockers were. So she resigned herself to having dinner back there, with a magazine. She was about halfway through, when Ben entered the room, with a plate full of pasta salad from the cafe and a drink.

He put his dinner on the table next to hers, although there was barely room for it. Felicity looked at the plate, then up at him. "What are you doing?"

He sat down across from her. "Eating my dinner."

"You bought that here, why don't you just go eat it out in the cafe?"

"Do you have a problem with my eating back here?" he asked.

"No," she replied defensively.

He just shook his head at her and started eating. After a few minutes of ignoring him and reading her magazine, he started trying to get her to talk, as she'd known he would. Benjamin was just not the type of guy that would let you ignore him. He either made you comfortable or pissed you off, but he just couldn't ever leave things alone. "So, I didn't see you at lunch yesterday. Are you avoiding me now?"

She barely looked up from her magazine. "I felt like McDonald's."

"Kind of a long walk, don't you think?" She just shrugged. "Well, if it makes you feel any better, Alyson's mad at me too," Ben informed her.

Lucy came into the break room just then, to get something from her locker. Felicity had been about to speak and wasn't going to let Lucy's interruption stop her. "Gee, I wonder why? Maybe because you're incredibly intolerant and judgmental?"

Ben looked insulted. Lucy seemed to have planned to grab something and leave, ignoring them, but instead stopped to put her hand on Ben's shoulder. "She's right honey. I love ya' but... you are." Without waiting for a reaction, Lucy went back out into the store.

Ben looked at the table with his mouth open in an expression of disgust. "Thanks." Of course, Lucy was already gone. Felicity just chuckled and finished her sandwich. She gathered her garbage and threw it away as Ben spoke. "You know, it's not like I just... don't *like* the guy you're dating. *That* would be judgmental. Sometimes Cain can be an okay guy, I guess. And hell, Mattie used to be my best friend! **But they are not human anymore!** There is something fundamentally wrong with them. Do you even get that? Something that could easily get you killed!"

"Cain's not going to kill me," Felicity said dismissively.

"How do you know?" Ben asked.

"Don't you think I would have been dead by now?"

"Maybe he likes to play with his food," Ben suggested.

She stood there for a moment, just glaring at him. "Benjamin, just... stop talking," Felicity replied in disgust.

She walked out the door, but he followed. "You just don't want to admit that I could be right."

She spun around, startling him, because he'd been following closely behind her. "You could be right. You could also be, oh I don't know... jealous?"

"What?" he asked in disbelief.

"Never mind." She turned and began walking away, but he kept following. He put a hand on her shoulder to try and spin her back around, but she planted herself so that he couldn't unless he really forced her. After a minute he took his hand away, then she turned to face him. She crossed her arms and waited for him to speak.

"Jealous of who, Cain? Over *you*? Please! If that were the case, why would I have a problem with Mattie and Alyson? You've got some ego," Ben accused.

"Careful, you're livin' in a glass house," she warned.

"Very cute. Excuse me for not wanting to see my friends in the newspaper as just two more missing girls, found a week later in a ditch, a few quarts shy," he said forcefully.

She sighed. "Not going to happen, so just butt out, okay?" She didn't let him answer, she just turned and went back to work.

Felicity spent the rest of her shift avoiding Ben's annoyed glances from across the store and waiting for Cain to arrive. He said he'd come early, but it was already almost closing time. She kept thinking she felt him, but it was faint and she couldn't really tell if it was just wishful thinking. Where was he?

Ten o'clock arrived, and she went to flip the sign on the door to 'closed'. She paused at the door. Cain was definitely out there. She couldn't see him, but she could feel him. It was slight. Her mark was almost gone, but she was sure he was there. Why wasn't he coming in? She didn't really think that he would stay away because of Ben. Well, all she could do was close out her register and wait.

After she finished she went to look out the door again, nothing but dark. She walked dejectedly over to the cafe to sit at the counter and wait for Ben so she could leave. He was still counting his register. He glanced up as she sat. "Would you go put up the chairs for me?"

She gave him a sour look. "That's not my job." As he looked up at her, she noticed that he looked very pale. She wondered if he felt sick.

"Whatever," he said in annoyance. He slammed the drawer and began to walk around to get the chairs.

She stood and felt bad for being so bitchy to him. He really did look ill. "I got it." She went and lifted all of the chairs to the tabletops as he finished cleaning up behind the counter.

"So, you getting picked up by Count Cain this evening?"

She gave him a condescending look. "Did you get that one from Alyson? You should at least try to be original."

"Thought I was. Good one Allie," Ben said with a chuckle.

"Not really." He stopped what he was doing for a minute to lean on the counter with his head in his hands. "Are you okay?"

He looked up at her and then went back to work. "I'm fine. Cain *is* picking you up though right?" he asked.

She studied him for a minute. Why did he care? "He's already outside."

Now Ben stared back for a moment before answering. "Well, I wish you would have asked him to come alone."

Felicity's eyes widened a bit. No wonder Ben looked so nauseous. "You feel Sindy out there?"

"Nice and strong. Thanks again for not letting me go to Vermont. This is so much more fun," he pointed out sarcastically.

She disregarded him and went to the door. Still nothing. She could still feel Cain though, so they must be close. Just around the side, out of view of the door probably. "Why doesn't he come in? What are they doing out there?"

Ben laughed. "Yeah, I wonder what Sindy could be doing out there, all this time with *your* boyfriend?" She gave him an annoyed glance and then went to the lounge for her stuff, ignoring him. He followed her and went to get his own jacket. "Let's see, either they're killing each other, which *I* would certainly appreciate." He came closer to her with a smile. "Or, they're making nice, which I might also enjoy the results of."

He stood in the doorway. She put a hand to his chest, to lightly push him away. "Very funny, get out of my way."

He backed out the door with a smile and shut the lights for the cafe. "Well, I hope Sindy won't be too insulted if I don't stick around, because I've got plans." He waited for her to come to the front of the store before turning off the rest of the lights. "I still can't believe that you're dating a dead guy."

"At least *he's* got a brain in his head," Felicity said pointedly.

"Are you calling me stupid?" he asked.

"Not *you*. You are obviously a pretty intelligent guy, even if you are an obstinate pain in the ass. I'm sure there must be plenty of room for a brain in that swelled head of yours. I was talking about your date."

Ben looked like he was trying to decide whether to be insulted that she thought he was a pain in the ass, or pleased that she thought he was smart. Eventually he decided to dismiss the whole subject of her feelings about him for now. "Why are you always so down on Ashley? She's a very nice girl."

Felicity started laughing. "You barely even like her! But I'm sure you're looking forward to having a *very* nice time tonight all the same. Here's a tip, buy her jewelry."

Ben just gave her a shrewd smile. "Sounds like someone's got some jealousy issues of her own."

She gave him a sharp laugh. "As if. So are we leaving... or are you too afraid to go out into the parking lot?"

"Ladies first," he said with an outstretched arm.

"No problem. Oh, did you want to go get your cross first? I'll wait," she offered snidely.

Ben just gave her a condescending sneer and pushed open the door for her. She made sure to give him a sweet and unconcerned smile as she stepped outside into the dark parking lot.

Chapter 11 - Indiscretions

Cain

8:30, Friday night

Cain started up his Harley Davidson and rode out into the night. He'd awoken almost two hours ago, but he had spent a good deal of time just lying in bed, trying to decide how he would word the rest of his story to Felicity. He truly did want to tell her everything about himself. She should know what she was getting into, in being with him.

At the very same time, he *so* wanted her to stay, that he was afraid to have things come out in too harsh a light. He would be honest of course, but just how detailed did he really need to be, in order to feel that he'd given her a factual and legitimate account of his life? She didn't need to know every detail of his past, did she? It would make for a rather long story and there were aspects of his life that should really have no bearing on her feelings towards him.

For example, his past relationships. Felicity had to know that she was not the first girl he had cared for in over three hundred years, besides his wife and Maribeth, but did she need names, dates and full accounts? Probably not. Some things should be kept private, he decided. What of the relationships that had ended badly... fatally? Wasn't it his duty to tell of those that had come before her? There had not been many, and most of his relationships had not really failed through fault of his own. As far as those who had trouble adapting to a life like his... he better understood now, what was needed in a person. He knew what kind of personality was necessary to make them strong, to help them bear the burdens of this existence. He would never turn her if she were not suitable, if he were not convinced that she would indeed thrive. He would not repeat past mistakes, of that he was sure. He sincerely hoped he would also avoid making any new ones.

Truth. This relationship needed to be grounded in truth. He was never a liar in his life, not in words, but he had often refrained from telling girls of the past, things they may not look upon fondly. He needed to tell Felicity the truth... all of it. How detailed it should be, he was undecided. He was not thrilled at the prospect of describing certain things to her. He didn't want to frighten her more than necessary, although she had a right to know.

He would tell of his worst transgressions, so he would not feel he had anything to hide. The rest of his life he would then tell in broad generalizations. Did it even matter? He had been quite serious in saying that she may decide after tonight that he was no longer worth her time. What he had to tell her would be bad enough without petty concerns of ex-loves and such.

The very real truth of it was that he might not even see her again after tonight. The thought made him feel a bit ill. It caused a desperation that made him want to edit his narration to his own advantage, but that was why he'd told her the bottom line of it the night before. She knew he was a murderer. There was more to tell of course, but she had the idea of it. At least he felt that if she came back tonight to hear the rest, then he still had a chance. She *had* kissed him after. Then again, that may just have been a combination of her mark and the wine. Now she'd had time to think...

As he approached the DownTime, he was a bit surprised to feel Sindy drawing near. She had thoroughly disappeared after he'd spoken to her on Wednesday night. Last night he hadn't felt her at all. She was purposely staying away from him, he assumed. Yet now, here she was, and alone too! Very strange. She must want something. She seemed to be waiting for him. As he drew near, he saw her sitting on the guardrail at the bend in the road, just before the DownTime. He slowed as he approached her and then cut the engine and rolled up beside her. She stood as he neared. Yes, she'd been expecting him. After a moment's startled realization, he remembered that she could feel him as well as he could feel her, cloaked or not. She was marked... as his.

"Evening," he said with a casual nod.

"Hi there."

"Aren't you missing like, half a dozen people?"

She laughed. "I sent them to follow after Chris for a while. I thought I might want some privacy." She said this last with a coy glance at him that spoke volumes of what she might want that privacy for.

Cain smiled and thought to himself, 'sorry luv, not tonight'. "Good luck with that." He got off the bike and began walking it the last of the way to the bookstore.

She followed after him, obviously irked by his lack of interest. "Well, what are *you* doin' tonight?"

He kept walking as she fell into step next to him, on the other side of the motorcycle. "I've got plans."

"With that pet of yours, right?" she pouted.

He stopped walking to give her a level gaze. "Don't call her that."

Sindy smirked at him. "You can *call* her whatever you want, but we both know that *a pet* is exactly what she is."

Cain stared at her, unmoving. "Considering that you've no protection this evening, in fact even if you had, I rather think that you should be speaking to me with a bit more respect. Wouldn't you agree?"

She stared back at him for a moment. She wasn't really frightened of him, but at least she wasn't smiling. "Sorry," she said quietly.

"I should hope so. Why is it that you've decided to forgo the protection?" he asked, with a slight smile playing about his lips. "Don't you think it's a bit risky for you to be out here waiting for me, all alone? Your boys aren't even within hailing distance, I don't believe."

She shrugged. He started walking again, slowly and she fell back into step beside him as she spoke. "The way I see it, around me you're usually *firm,"* she gave him a promiscuously sly smile, just to be sure he caught the double meaning, "but fair. As long as I behave myself, I should be safe, right?"

He smiled. "Indeed. In that case, why don't you just dismiss them altogether? Still planning on misbehaving?"

She laughed. "I haven't decided yet, but you know, I don't think that I could get rid of them if I tried. They really like me, and most of them couldn't even survive on their own."

"Maybe you should have thought of that before you made them all."

She smiled. "They do need me, but I need them too. Where else do you expect me to get my evening meals? I've been off humans ever since… Ben." At the mention of feeding from Ben, she seemed to give a little shiver. They were nearing the DownTime and Cain could feel Ben quite clearly inside, bearing Sindy's mark. Surely she felt him very strongly.

He shook his head disapprovingly. "Why do you assume that you're gaining any sort of favor with me this way? How is it that you think feeding off of those boys of yours is any better than feeding off of humans directly? You're just sending six others out to attack people, rather than do it yourself. I'm not impressed. I much prefer to associate with those who do not harm others, in any way."

Sindy furrowed her brow as she thought about that and they crossed the road to the lot of the DownTime. Finally, she gave him a very fond appraising look and declared, "I *could* live like that. It's just boring. Now if you promised to keep me entertained…"

He looked at her oddly for a moment and then lightly laughed. "It was simply meant to be a statement, not an invitation." He kept walking, not waiting for her response.

Cain glanced through the front doors across the lot. He saw Felicity, busy inside. She hadn't noticed him yet. He could just barely feel her. Ben's mark was much brighter. He found that a little depressing. The store was still open for almost an hour yet. He could go right in, but he knew Sindy would be unwelcome there. He wouldn't so blatantly dismiss her yet. Rather than approach the doors, he walked his motorcycle up along the side of the building and parked it there.

Sindy watched him and then sat on the grass next to the building. She seemed to take for granted that he would join her. "Okay teach, I've got a question for you." He went to sit beside her. "What if I were… *involved* with another vampire, exclusively," she eyed him seductively, "and we were in the habit of drinking from one another? You know like, nightly give and take relations." She smiled and eyed his throat, seeming very aroused by the idea. "If neither of us ever drank from anyone else, could we go on that way? I mean, couldn't we just feed off of each other, indefinitely?

"As neatly solved as that sounds, you know it would never work. If you never drank blood from an outside source, eventually you would both become depleted. I don't suppose it would kill you, but you would both become far too weak to function after a time."

She didn't want to accept it and pouted at him. "How do you know?"

He gave her another level stare, as a smile hovered about his lips. "I've tried it." She seemed very surprised and amused. "Don't look so shocked. A life as long as mine leaves a lot of room for experimentation. I wasn't always as *boring* as you seem to think I am now."

"You know, I always suspected that. You go through a lot of trouble to prove me wrong though."

He laughed. "How else can I ever get you to take me seriously?"

"Because my *salvation* is so important to you, right?"

He didn't answer her, after a moment he just lay down to look at the stars. He spent so many nights staring at the sky. He could recognize practically every constellation at a glance. Sindy lay down as well and they silently studied the star patterns across the heavens for a while.

This girl was a bit of an enigma to him. They had such an odd relationship. He *was* a sort of teacher to her, and he was so much older and more experienced than she was. Yet in many ways, he felt as though they were almost equals. She was so confident and self-assured. She often did things purposely to anger him, and yet she also seemed to desperately seek his approval.

When they'd first met, he'd had it in the back of his mind that she might make an interesting partner for him, someone that he could spend his time with, without fear of bringing her corruption and harm. After being in her company for awhile, he had decided against the idea. He found her personality rather abrasive and irritating at times. He thought that he wanted to assure himself that she would live in a passive manner and then have nothing more to do with her.

He told himself that it was for the sake of her well-being and the safety of others, that he invested so much in trying to teach her to live peacefully. It was for The Lord that he tried to prepare her now. That was what he told himself. It would take patience and be difficult, but eventually she would see the truth in his ways and adopt his more civil practices. He'd no earthly personal stake in her future, though. He didn't really think that she would ever submit to him in any way, not really. He'd believed she could never truly please him as a partner.

He knew now that he had simply not given her enough time to come around. She was proud and stubborn, but she was still all of the things that he had seen in her from the first as well; beautiful, smart, playful, strong and he must remember, she was still young. As he had once told her, he did believe that she would truly grow be a splendid creature as she matured.

But he'd met Felicity. He'd been lonely, vulnerable, and unwilling to wait and distance himself as he should. Now he'd lost his heart to her. Sindy, perhaps someday he could love, but Felicity he loved already. It might sound cruel but in his mind, compared to Felicity, Sindy seemed almost a poor parody of a woman.

But Felicity was human and in that, the problem lie. To keep her, he would probably ruin her life. For all of his beliefs and his desire to be a 'good' man, he must admit that he had worn mental blinders where she was concerned. He was so lonely that he had let his personal desires override his moral responsibilities. It was a pattern that he actually did recognize in himself, after all these years. He tried to change it and did go decades without succumbing to the urge for such relationships, but after awhile he grew weak and managed to deceive himself, that it would be different... *this time.*

At first, he had sought to try and ignore the fact that she had a true life beyond time spent with him. School and family were things easily dismissed, things to try and distance her from, so as to more easily bring her into his own world. But now, he loved her, he truly did. This was not the sweet infatuation that he had initially felt with her. He really did care for her, with all of his unbeating heart. He was so angry with himself for being so intentionally blind! How could he ever risk hurting her? As he did fall deeper in love, he was forced to realize that she had a very real future in the world from which he would be taking her away.

That was why he'd almost begun to try and show her that, to hold her at arm's length. His actions and desires seemed almost to yo-yo between bringing her close and pushing her away. He savored her kisses and dearly wanted her body along with her heart, but he would not let her dismiss her schoolwork. He would not try to persuade her to stay with him rather than visit her family. She should remain grounded by the world. It was unfair to expect her to give that up for him.

When he told her the rest of his tale, she might decide that the world was where she belonged and not with him. He was unsure whether he could coexist in her life with everything else. Her world was just not a place where he really belonged. How could he ever think that she could live a normal human life, with him? How impractical and unrealistic was it to think that he could fulfill a need in her life as she did in his?

And, if he did not continue his self-appointed task, of educating other vampires to live a peaceful and non-violent existence, what would he do, 'play house' with Felicity until she grew old and died? What of all the deaths he could prevent in that time, if he were not tied to her? How could he ever justify that to himself? Besides, he could never sit by and idly watch her die of age or disease. He knew that it was not in him. He would feel forced to act, to prevent her from fading away, and doom her to undead eternity instead.

That was an existence that could certainly be rewarding in itself in some ways, and then they could be together, but would she want it? Was it right? It was with an almost masochistic determination that he had resolved to tell her all of his wrongs. As badly as he wanted her, he also almost wished for her to turn him away, so that he couldn't hurt her. No matter how pure his intentions, surely, eventually he would.

As he lay here, looking up at the stars, he found himself doing something that he had not truly done in far too long a time. He prayed. He honestly and unconditionally asked God for guidance. He asked forgiveness as always, and repented past sins, but then he sincerely tried to open his heart and mind. He cleared his thoughts and prayed, for direction, for help.

How would he know The Lord's will from his own selfish wishes? He was unsure and hoped that even if he did, he would have the strength to obey. He took a deep breath to clear himself of these thoughts now and simply prayed for strength and the desire for obedience. He would move slowly and carefully these next days and see what unfolded.

He would see Felicity, and enjoy this night with her, as much as he could, but he would remain true to his intentions and tell her all. Then, if it seemed the only course true to the Spirit, he would steel himself to accept that he must leave her.

He had made some thoughtful insights to Sindy's personality traits the other evening, but her own insights regarding he and Felicity had been unfortunately accurate as well. As much as he had not wanted to admit it, Sindy was right. He hated that fact. It messed up their careful relationship; the order of things as he saw them. *He* was supposed to be the elder, the one with the knowledge. *She* was childish, indecent, immoral and she was not supposed to be right!

Sindy brought herself up on one elbow to look at him, as he lay on his back next to her. He noticed that even beneath the garish artificial blush that she wore, she did look a bit flushed. "I don't think I can stay here for much longer. Ben is too close, too tempting. How do you stand it? You see her like, every night don't you? You hold her and you kiss her, and her blood just... calls to you. How do you do it?"

Normally he didn't let himself enter into such conversations with Sindy. It always turned out that she was simply baiting him, verbally trying to turn things to her own ends, but she wasn't speaking in a mocking tone. She seemed to really be asking. She sounded almost in awe of his control. He didn't answer right away and she went on.

"Blood always calls you, no matter who it's in. Isn't it weird? It could be the skeeziest guy. Ugly, dirty and old, it doesn't matter. The blood is always good, no matter what the package, but when it's someone you like, someone you really want, well that's just *special.*

I've known Ben my whole life you know. I've always wanted him. That's why drinking from him, was sooo good, special. You *know* Felicity. You want her. Drinking from her must have been so intimate, delicious. But, you hardly even took any, did you? Even when her mark was new, it wasn't really all that strong. How did you stop? How could you control yourself? You must have such command, be sooo strong." She leaned over a bit, slipping her hand under the edge of his open jacket and rubbing it across his chest.

He'd been lying on his back, with his hands under his head, but now he reached out to quickly and firmly grasp her wrist. He gently moved it off of him and let go. "Don't touch me."

She was unfazed. "You didn't seem to mind touching me, when you drank. Was it... *special?*"

He propped himself up, as she was, on one elbow to face her. "Blood always is, no matter the package." As he saw her face crumple, he felt unnecessarily cruel. "But with our kind it's always *extra special*. You know that."

That seemed to mollify her. "It was good wasn't it? Bet I kept you for a while too."

"What do you mean?" he asked.

"Satisfied. Didn't you say you found me very, satisfying?" He just smiled. It was amazing to him and almost a little sad, how badly she wanted please him, in any way. "How could you go back to something packaged in a little plastic container, after that?" she asked incredulously.

"That's just what I do. It makes me feel good, to know that I'm doing right." He'd made such statements so many times in his life, as explanations to young ones such as her. Why did it suddenly feel so false? As though he were using 'good deeds' to hide larger sins.

She shook her head in disbelief and then sighed up at the sky. "When you drank from me, that was good, at first anyway. Found I don't really care for being... emptied, but thanks for the new experience." He chuckled. "But that was nights ago. Now you're going to see *her*." She nodded towards the store to indicate Felicity. "Hold her and be with her. Won't you wanna drink her?" He lay back down to look at the sky again. "It's gotta be like torture!"

"It can be trying at times," he agreed.

Her voice took on a hushed and hesitant quality. "You know, if you wanted, I could help you out with that. Give you a little, to hold you over. I mean, as long as you promised not to get carried away."

He looked up at her in disbelief, and then laid his head back again and smiled. "No thanks."

"It's not like it would make any difference to anyone. And wouldn't it make things so much easier for you, with Felicity? Besides, I'm already marked by you, so it's not like I can give it to anyone else at the moment."

That was something that hadn't occurred to him. Of course she would be unable to give blood to Chris or Luke, or any of her others. She was his, marked for them to see. She couldn't hide it. "What do they make of that? Your boys. I hope I haven't caused you to lose credibility with them."

"Like you care," she said with a huff.

"You're right, maybe I don't, really. Just curious," he added.

She shrugged her shoulders. "They're too stupid to notice."

"That's not true. Not of Chris anyway. Does he feel you've betrayed him? That was not my intent."

"What *he* feels really shouldn't concern you, or me even. He's just a follower, like all the others."

"He's not like the others; don't try to pretend that you can't see it. You made him better, whether or not it was by design. He does understand. Do you care for him at all?"

She shrugged again. He thought that she did, but she wouldn't admit it to him. "Not like you care for *her.* Why don't you let me make being with her, easier for you? It's not like *she's* givin' you any." Sindy must have noticed the steady fading of his mark upon Felicity. He wished his personal relations were not so clearly evident to her. She went on baiting him. "You *like* torture? Isn't there a word for people like that?"

"Masochistic. And yes, I suppose at times that does apply to me," he replied with a little laugh. They sat in silence for a moment, as he left her repeated offer unanswered. He certainly had no intention of accepting it, tempting as it was. "I thought you wouldn't remain for long, with Benjamin being so near?"

She lay back down beside him again, very close, but not touching at all. "Guess I'm a little... masochistic myself." He laughed.

They lay there in silence again for a few minutes. The bookstore would be closing soon. He should probably go inside. Felicity would be wondering where he was. She might even have felt him out here by now. He could feel her, although her mark was now very faint. He became aware of a change in Sindy. She was shifting, he could feel it. He looked over at her, in slight alarm, although he didn't sit up. "What are you doing?"

She did sit up a bit, but not in a threatening manner. She brought her own wrist up to her mouth and very deliberately, bit it. She tore the skin a little more than usual, to make sure it would bleed easily. Once she had an open wound there, she brought it away from her mouth, holding the inside of her wrist pointed up to the sky so as not to lose the precious blood from inside. He lay there, watching her in disbelief as she licked the blood from her lips.

"Helping out a friend," she said quietly, stretching out her wrist towards his face.

Now he did raise himself up on his elbows, craning his head back a bit, away from her arm. He was uneasy and trying not to obviously stare at her wrist, longingly. "I said I didn't want any."

"You really gonna turn me away?" She placed her wrist to his mouth without waiting for an answer. He smelled the blood there and the change overcame him automatically as it touched his lips. That had never happened to him before, without control. He closed his eyes and forced his hands to remain on the ground, in the grass where he'd been resting them. So badly he wanted to grasp her arm and crush her wrist to his open mouth, but he barely parted his lips. Very gently and slowly he let his tongue explore the wound she had made. Just barely tasting the blood there.

It was so divine.

He could not do this now, here, with Felicity just inside. It just would not be right... would it? Or did it even matter? It *would* help. He didn't really have much of a choice, his body would not let him move away to refuse her. After an eternal moment of indecision, he sucked a little at her wrist and was rewarded with a few more drops of her exquisite blood. He refused to let himself bite her. He would take only what came. She made it very easy, pressing the wound so firmly against his lips, as though she could force the blood into his mouth.

He drew from her again, more strongly this time. Then, more again. His natural instinct was to bite her himself, to infect her with his venom and renew his mark, but he resisted. As difficult as it was, the blood was what mattered most. It was so good.

It was such pure strong blood, however unpure seeming its source. Drinking from her wrist as he was, it felt pure. Focused, perhaps was a better description. It wasn't colored by sexual intent, as everything associated with Sindy usually was.

The throat was such a sensitive and intimate area. To drink from the throat forced one's body into alignment with the victim's, making drinking from there, almost sexual by nature. But from the wrist, although still intimate, as drinking blood always was, was not nearly the same experience. It was only the blood, nothing else, and the blood was enough.

It seemed he spent quite awhile, gently sucking and feeding from her wrist, although he really didn't take all that much. He took only enough to quiet his thirst, enough to give him better control. He shifted back to his human state when he was able, and he kissed and then pulled away from her wrist.

She brought it to her own mouth, gave it a little lick and smiled. "Now, isn't that better?" She slowly ran her tongue over her upper lip. "I suppose reciprocation is out of the question?"

He stood and looked back down at her. "You suppose correctly."

She stood as well. "Can't blame a girl for trying." She gave him a quick glance up and down, smiling, as if to show him how much she appreciated his looks. "Enjoy your date."

He smiled back and shook his head at her audacity. "Thanks."

They both turned at the sound of Felicity and Ben emerging from the store. They were around the corner, yet to be seen. Sindy blew him a little kiss and walked up into the tree line behind the store, leaving him to meet them alone.

Ben and Felicity stayed together in front of the store for a moment, locking up he imagined. Once Sindy was gone, he moved around the building to meet them. As soon as he came into view, Felicity went to him, leaving Ben at the door.

"Cain, hi. Why didn't you come in?" She pouted playfully. "I was waiting for you."

"I know. I'm sorry. I was... delayed, talking to someone." She looked down at the ground. Ben finished setting the alarm and began walking towards them, to go to his car. Cain wondered if he had told her that Sindy was there. "Are we still on for the evening?"

"Yes of course, definitely. I'm not letting you off the hook that easy."

Ben approached them on the way to his car. Cain glanced up at him, while mumbling to Felicity. "Great... Good evening Ben."

Ben hardly even looked at him. "Goodnight." He continued on past.

Cain and Felicity stood in awkward silence for a moment, watching him as he walked. Once he was beyond their range, Cain turned to her and quietly asked, "Is everything alright?"

"Yeah, fine." She stared at him for a moment. "How about with you?"

She seemed a little anxious, uneasy. She had to know that Sindy had been around. He gave her a coy smile. "Wonderful, now that you're here." She smiled and on impulse, he took hold of her and kissed her. She was caught a bit by surprise, but was very responsive all the same. He didn't hold it long, but it was *very* nice. And his thirst was indeed gone, for now.

She gave him a dazed little smile. "I thought the kisses were reserved for the end of the evening?"

"Who made up that dumb rule? You don't plan to hold me to that do you?" She laughed and he suddenly remembered his promise not to touch her without her express permission. "I'm sorry, perhaps I should have asked..."

She laughed. "You're allowed to kiss me! You don't have to ask. I was just pleasantly surprised. You're always so restrained."

"Well, I thought I'd better get my kisses in now, while I still can. You might not be so eager, come the end of the evening."

He'd lost his joyful attitude as he said this last. "You keep saying stuff like that. Why don't you let me be the judge?" she whispered, as she stepped closer to kiss him again. Before their lips met however, they were startled by the sound of Ben's tires screeching as he left the parking lot.

After taking a moment to regain her composure, Felicity gave him only a peck on the lips. She then moved out of his arms to look around for his bike. "Are we walking tonight?"

"No, it's 'round the side." He moved towards the motorcycle and she followed. It was loaded just the same as the night before, with the picnic basket and her comforter on the back. "Shall we head back to the park? You wanted 'identical' right?"

"It is pretty spot, but we can go wherever you want. The location isn't exactly the focal point of the evening. All day I feel like I've been waiting for the other shoe to drop."

"Me too. I can't say I'm looking forward to finishing my history for you, but it will be good to have it over with. I don't suppose *you* have any deep dark secrets to share, to make me feel better?"

She smiled. "Sorry, not off the top of my head, but, I'll try and think of some on the ride over."

"Thanks."

~~~~~~~~~~~~~~~~~~~~~~~~~~~~~~~~

Half an hour later found them sitting on the tablecloth spread over the ground, in front of the little waterfall at the pond once again. Cain eyed Felicity playfully as he poured her a glass of wine. "So, out with it, your deepest darkest shame."

She laughed. "You'll be very disappointed, it's pretty tame."

"Well, that's not disappointing. That's a good thing! But I know what you mean. Tell me anyway."

She took a large sip from her wine glass and then put it aside. She took a deep breath, as though preparing herself for a very shameful confession. "I stole a bathing suit once. My friend Deidre dared me. She stole one too. I spent some of last summer in the Hamptons, on Long Island with her family. We were invited to this very important beach party. We didn't have enough money for new bathing suits though. All the really cool guys were going to be there, so you could imagine how vital it was for us to look absolutely amazing. So... we stole them." Cain just smiled and then poured himself a glass of wine. "I know it's kind of dumb, but aren't you even going to say anything? Ask me if we got caught?"

"You did *not* get caught. And you *did* look absolutely amazing," he supplied.

Felicity wore a puzzled expression. "Well no, we didn't get caught, but I don't know how great we looked. We had a lot of fun at the party, but neither of us got a 'cool' boyfriend out of it," she laughed.

"Those boys must have been blind." He laughed at her as she rolled her eyes at him. "Bronze bikini?" he asked, smiling at the memory of the snapshot in her room.

Now she looked thoroughly shocked. "Yes."

"Deidre's was blue and green. She's very cute, but you... You my dear, looked like a goddess," he told her with a smoldering smile.

Felicity began to look very alarmed. "Okay, you didn't even know me then. Besides, bright sunny day at the beach, so I'm thinkin' you weren't there. Please tell me that you can't read minds."

He grinned. "I can't read minds. There's a picture in your room, on the mirror."

She breathed a too obvious sigh of relief. "Oh yeah, I forgot. You've got a good memory though."

"The way you looked in that bikini, was worth remembering." She smiled and dropped her eyes from his. "Did you really not have a boyfriend?"

She shrugged. "I used to be kind of shy."

"*Used* to?" he asked with a laugh.

"You still think I'm shy? I thought I was making like this conscious effort not to be," she confessed.

"Well, then you must have been positively bashful before! Now, I'd say you're just a little timid," he informed her.

"*Timid?* You think I'm timid?" She pretended to be angry with him and before he knew it, she had lunged herself at him for a kiss. He fell back trying to kiss her, laugh and not spill his wine all at the same time. She lay on top of him, until the giggles were gone and a very real kiss took their place.

When she let him up again he made a great show of composing himself. "Thought you might feel compelled to prove me wrong. Worked like a charm." He smiled mischievously and took a sip from his glass. She began to grin as she realized that he'd set her up, but didn't really seem to mind.

She drank some more of her own wine and smiled at him. "It's after eleven. I'm sure you'd much rather spend the evening fooling around, but I want to hear the rest of what happened before I have to go home for the weekend."

She was right, though it pained him to admit it. It was time to continue his narration. He could put it off no longer. "I know, alright." He drew a deep breath and took on a more somber composure. "So... I was speaking of the winter ending in 1692. Terrible year. Many people died that winter. My beloved daughter Amelia was among them."

He sighed and spoke slowly, taking his time. "What I did not tell you, was that shortly thereafter, on the twenty first of February, 1692, I lost my wife Elizabeth as well."

"Oh Cain, I'm sorry," she said quietly.

"God forgive me, that I do not shed more tears for her. She was a good woman, my wife. She deserved more of a life than that. I should have tried harder to make things better between us. I should have been honest with her from the start, but now, it was too late. Their deaths weighed heavily on me. I took ill as well, and racked with grief as I was, I could hardly care for myself. In fact, to be perfectly honest, I had no desire to.

I *wanted* to die. I felt that I had brought about the destruction of my family myself. Who was I to deserve a loving family? I had betrayed them! The good Lord giveth, and so the Lord shall taketh away. That I should lose those I loved was only fitting punishment. And so I barely cared for myself. I lay in bed and simply waited for the fevers to take me.

Obviously, they did not. I felt the cruel irony in that, but I suppose it just was not my time to die. Although I might have, if not for Maribeth. Once the illness left me, I still wouldn't eat. It was Maribeth who saw to me. Even when I was mostly unaware of my surroundings, delusional with shock, grief and starvation.

Charles and Maribeth had been almost unaffected by the illness. Charles had taken sick for a little in early March, but then the spring came with its green herbs and healing. Charles recovered quickly and he and Maribeth breathed a sigh of relief that their household had been largely passed by.

They had gotten into the habit of coming to check on me each day, after my own family passed. They had wanted me to come and stay with them, so that they could better care for me, but I refused. Then Charles took ill and Mari spent most of her time healing him, but she did get into the routine of bringing me meals each night. Sometimes she would bring their girl Alice with her, the one that helped to keep the house for them. She brought her to keep up the appearance of propriety I suppose. That was rather a joke though, I was so weak.

I barely picked at the food. After awhile I just stopped eating altogether and left the meals untouched. I hardly spoke to the ladies when they came. I wanted nothing to do with Maribeth, or anyone. I was obviously growing thin, wasting away and Mari became worried. She tried to spoon feed me, but I refused her food. She would send Alice over with the morning's fresh bread, but I usually left it untouched. Although the smell was maddening, I still sought to punish myself.

Finally, Maribeth began to bring me a cup of broth along with the usual plate of food that I never touched. She would sit there on the edge of my bed with the cup. The first few nights I ignored her for an hour or so, until I eventually did yell at her to leave and then she would. But finally, one night she sat resolute and pushed the damn cup at me until I drank. After that night, it became like a ritual. Every evening, after seeing that Charles had his dinner, she would bring me a plate, which she left on the table and collect the mostly untouched one from the evening before. Then she would come into the bedroom with my broth and refuse to leave until I'd drunk it. It became easier just to drink the stuff so she would go away and leave me alone. I still wouldn't really speak to her though.

A few of the townsfolk came with Elizabeth's family to pay their respects, but I was unresponsive and cold to them. Once Charles recovered, he came to see me a few times, but I ignored him as well. I just couldn't face him. No one could understand the penance I had set upon myself, except perhaps for Maribeth. I had abused the trust of all those who had loved me. Now I could not even beg their forgiveness. They were gone and I should suffer for it. I did ponder the idea of confessing to Charles, to set things straight with him at least, but I hadn't the spirit for it, I knew that Mari would be the one to suffer. Although I did blame her as well, I had decided that the final choice had ultimately lain with me and *I* had chosen to commit the sin. I wasn't so cruel as to actively seek *her* punishment.

So things went and I suffered in a sort of limbo, if you will. Until one day, it was nearly April by then I believe, Mari had come to me in the evening, as usual. She was alone on this occasion. I lay on the bed, unresponsive as usual. She put down the cup and plate, and stood there, arms folded, staring at me. 'Christian,' she said, "tis time for you to live in the world again.'

I didn't meet her eyes. I don't know what made me answer her, when so many other times I had not, but I did, to tell her that the world held nothing for me now.

She actually seemed to get angry with me. I remember finally looking at her, because I was so very surprised to hear the harshness in her voice, when next she spoke. 'You, Christian Herald are being dreadfully selfish.' she told me. 'You may not need the world, but there are those in the world who need you. I need you. The truth is, something has happened, something that I cannot face alone.'

I have to admit that I had become accustomed to the sympathy and compassion that people had been speaking to me with, since my family's deaths. To hear her speak to me *this* way seemed a bit shocking. I was cross that she should think that she could pull me back into living for her own selfish reasons, when I'd no desire. I had no idea what she could be talking about.

'I am with child again Christian,' she said simply.

It took a few moments for the statement to register. Even when it did, all I could think was that it should be a happy circumstance. That some joy might come into our lives again, after so much loss. I knew she and Charles would be worried, whether she could carry the child to completion, but at least we could all hope. 'Mari that's wonderful,' I told her.

She looked at me as though I were truly delusional for such a sentiment. "Tis our undoing! The babe is yours.'

Again, I felt as though we were miscommunicating; that her words needed deciphering before their implications could be understood. It seemed impossible. Our tryst had been before Amy had even fallen sick. It seemed ages ago. 'How can that be? How can you know?' I queried.

She looked rather insulted that I could ask such a question. 'I've loved no one but you. Charles hasn't touched me since months before.'

'Not even once?' I asked, incredulously.

She seemed disgusted to have to admit it. 'Not even.'

'My brother *is* a fool,' I informed her.

'He may be a fool, but he is not a forgiving one. What am I to do?' she asked.

I took only a moment to consider. It seemed a clear sign from God. We must admit our wrong doings, go before my brother, disclose our infidelity and try to put things to rights. The lies would then plague us no further. We should beg forgiveness and carry the secret sins of our past no longer. This I did tell her, though she seemed far less embracing of the idea. 'We are to confess. Charles may be hard hearted of late, but he did love us once. We shall throw ourselves upon his mercy and then you shall get yourself to bed, and stay there. Your only mission is to rest and prepare yourself to birth this child. Don't think and worry on life after, 'tis only the babe that matters now.'

She became very quiet and forlorn. 'Christian, you know that I cannot. My body does not work as it should. 'Twill be only enough to ruin us, not bring forth life.'

I sat up and took her hands into my own, in my lap. 'Mari are you sure there is life within you now? There is no mistake?'

'I am certain.' She stood and flattened her dress against her stomach, that I might see the slight new bulge there. It had been very well hidden amongst her welter of skirts, but it was undeniable, now that she showed it. I know that perhaps she would have expected disappointment, that there was no hiding our deeds of the past, but I could feel nothing but excitement and elation. That was my child! The only thing that had ever truly made me happy, was my daughter, Amelia. Now here was another chance, a baby living within her, so that I might have another chance to be happy again.

She seemed very puzzled by my excited grin. As though she'd expected me to be angry with her. 'Mari, how has he not known already?' I asked.

'He barely looks at me these days.' Again, she looked shamed to tell me.

'He must know immediately! You need to take to bed now, before you've done too much. You must take care of this child, so that it might bring some joy back into our empty lives.'

'*Our* lives? It may be your babe, but I am still his wife Christian.'

'I don't care if Charles claims the baby for his own, only that I might be a part of its life.'

'Christian, you overestimate your brother's compassion. I do not really want to confess, but I cannot hide who the child came from. 'Twill be obvious in retrospect. Even if I *can* bring this child into the world and *if* Charles accepts to raise it, I would expect that you are the one person that the child will never see.'

'What do you mean?'

'I know him. Far better than you these past years. He's changed. He's not the same man that you knew. He has become cold and unforgiving, your brother. He will hate you. He will send you away from us.'

'He can't. Not *my* brother. He would never turn me away. Things will be hard between us, but that needn't concern you any further. As I said, your only worry should be the child now. We shall go and speak to Charles, together. Do not worry.'

She did seem relieved that she shouldn't have to face him alone. 'Christian,' she asked, turning to me and looking quite serious, 'do you love me?' She didn't let me answer though. 'Do not say, 'tis not a fair question. Let us go and do what we must.' She still looked as though she thought I was foolish to think that Charles might forgive us. She was right."

"Did you?" Felicity asked.

Cain was startled back to the present. "What?"

"Did you love her? Maribeth?"

After a moment, he smiled. "Yes, I suppose so. Of course, if you'd asked me at the time, I'd have told you no. I cared for her well being, of course, but I'd have said that she was spoiled and stubborn and her personality was totally unlike a woman that I would love. Later on, I might even add conniving and manipulative to the list.

But that's the funny thing about love. They say love is blind, but that isn't always the case. People your heart chooses to love, sometimes have traits you would consider to be glaring faults. You are not blind to them at all, but when you truly come to love someone, those traits simply become part of a larger whole. Just a few aspects of someone you love. And because you love them, you can see past those things, to the person inside. You may disagree with their decisions, they may do things of which you disapprove and you may even dislike them a lot of the time, but you don't stop loving them. I know I don't, anyway.

When someone has your heart, 'tis not a simple thing to dismiss. It doesn't even have to be romantic love, in fact it holds true for families a lot of the time, but most people feel that they *must* love their families. They do things for their family more out of a sense of duty, than for love. To *really* give your heart to another, with no obligations, or assurance of its return, is a scary venture. But I do think that's an important lesson in life, to learn how to love. Some people really don't know how, not truly."

"That's so... discerning; perceptive and sad. She loved you too I'll bet. The way she took care of you and wouldn't give up on you... but I guess it was never meant to be. She was trapped in her marriage with Charles and you had already been so hurt by your loss. Admitting that you loved her would have just made things worse for you. You had already betrayed your wife and brother, and her presence must have just been an awful reminder of that.

I don't think that I would have liked her very much, but I do feel for her. All that she went through, losing all those babies and being trapped in an unhappy marriage. Then to not even be able to hear that someone she loved, loved her back... It's so tragic and depressing, for both of you."

Her eyes looked as though they were tearing and her face held the most forlorn expression. He leaned forward and gave her cheek a quick caress. "Surely you didn't expect the story of *my* life to be a 'feel good' sort of affair, did you? Because I did give you a disclaimer at the beginning, if you remember."

Now she smiled, though it was still a watery sort of grin. "I'm sorry; I guess I'm getting too invested in the characters," she said archly.

"Well, there may have been much trial and heartache along the way, but if you're at all worried, so far, it has a happy ending." That made her laugh. "Shall I go on?"

"Please," she said, eagerly.

They both took a moment to drink from their wine glasses and then he continued. "Well, I don't know how I expected Charles to react. I guess I thought there would be a lot of yelling. A furious rage that would eventually spend itself and then he would calm and we would carry on.

It must sound foolish, I know, that I would think that he could forgive us. You have to realize that I had spent the first seventeen years of my life getting into trouble, and Charles was always the one to bail me out. He was the peacekeeper, the buffer between me and the world. I would have fun without a care for the wrath brought down around me and Charles would help to hide it from father, smooth things over and make things right. I had gone to him for everything, my whole life.

My father was gone now, after having shunned me, even if he had meant it to be only symbolic. I had only Charles. I could never imagine him turning his back on me, even if only for a lesson, as father had tried to accomplish. The greatest betrayal I had ever felt from Charles, was when he insisted we come here, to the colonies. And even that was for my own good, I could now see. Charles always had my best interest in mind, but it had never before been *him* that I'd transgressed against.

When we told him, he barely even looked at Maribeth. It was as though he had only expected as much from her. He stared at me, long and hard. Then he quietly told me to get out of his house; he never wished to look upon my face again. As I said, I'd been expecting a fight. I was prepared to throw myself at his mercy and agree with terrible accusations and outbursts. I didn't know how to handle this silent anger. He turned from me, and would say nothing more. I tried to engage him in an apology and plead forgiveness, but the only thing he would say was 'get out'." Cain couldn't keep the plea for empathy from his voice, as though Felicity ought to agree that Charles should have forgiven him. He did not really feel that way, but it was difficult not to look for understanding from her.

She was unmoved. "All he had ever done was help you, and you betrayed him. *You slept with his wife.* What did you expect?" Felicity looked as disgusted with him as he felt with himself.

Cain had acceded to his guilt in all of this, in his own mind, long ago. So long ago, that it simply seemed a 'given'. It was something that he'd not really thought of from Charles' point of view in a long while. It was just taken for granted in his memory as something that had *happened*. Other things in his life seemed so much worse. It was true, what he had done in sleeping with Maribeth, was lecherous, but he had let himself forget about it a long time ago, in light of newer sins. "I suppose he had every right to hate me. I should never have expected otherwise.

So, he told me to get out. I wanted to stay, because I was afraid that he would turn his fury upon Maribeth when I left, but I was also afraid to say or do anything more to make things worse. He wanted me out. To stay would only bait him. Mari's eyes pleaded for me to remain, but I left.

I did wait outside a little, ready to come to Maribeth's aid if needed, if Charles' anger got out of hand. I don't know what I thought I would do. I was still so weak from lack of food and grief, but I would not let her take the brunt of it, if I could help it.

He didn't really yell much at her either though. I did hear him call her an ignorant whore. He told her that he thought she was very stupid to have bothered to tell him. That she should have simply waited for the baby to die, like all of the others, and then he need not have known."

"Oh my God, that's horrible!"

"Cruel, I know, but nothing that she couldn't handle. If anything, Maribeth was always strong. I felt for her, but I knew that the hardest thing right now would not be for her to hold back tears, but to hold her tongue. She was more one for vicious arguing than quiet weeping. Thankfully she was smart enough to keep silent. He sent her to bed and that was the end of it, that night.

I went home. There was nothing more for me to do. Ten days. I waited ten days, desperate to know how she faired. I tried to regain my strength. I made myself some meager meals with what dry stores I had left. I did feel myself slowly beginning to return to health. The illness had left me unharmed, it was really only my own refusal to eat or get out of bed that had kept me weak. From Charles and Maribeth, I heard nothing. I saw no one. They did not even send Alice over with bread any longer. I was afraid to approach their house and rile things up again, so I waited.

Then circumstances did present for me a solution of sorts. I'd gone into town, for something or other. There I saw Nan. You may remember that she was the girl that we had employed some five years before, to help Elizabeth during her pregnancy. Well, she was a *girl* no more. I believe that she was about twenty by then. Still unmarried, but I knew she was being courted. Anyway, she saw me and came to give her condolences over Liza and Amy. She seemed worried for me, I must still have looked terribly thin and pale. She asked if there was anything that she could do.

I told her that as a matter of fact there was. Now that I was alone, I could use someone to cook me a meal each day and take care of some light housework for me. If she could be persuaded, I would pay her well. She and her beau needn't worry for appearances, she could come while I was out at work in the fields. Do some wash and cleaning, then leave me a meal to heat later for supper. It would all be very proper and advantageous to us both.

What I was also thinking about, was the fact that I knew that Nan was still good friends with Alice, the girl in Charles and Maribeth's employ. I say girl, but that's really untrue. Like Nan, she also had grown. Alice was a married woman now, but still went once a day to help with the baking and such. Once I could re-establish a relationship with Nan, I would explain that Charles and I had had a falling out. She needn't know details, just that I knew Mari was with child and I would be appreciative if she could speak to Alice, and tell me of Maribeth's well being now and again.

Nan did agree and things worked out as I'd hoped. I was able to get news relayed to me every other day or so of the state of things in Charles and Mari's home. Maribeth was indeed still with child and had taken strictly to bed. She seemed to be doing well, although she did ask to call out the doctor for every slight alarm. Charles often became annoyed with her over it.

Confidentially, Nan said that Alice felt bad for Mari, because Charles did not seem hopeful or even very happy for the baby at all. She assumed that he was just worried that the child would not be born. I however, was certain that it was quite the opposite. I don't think Charles had ever expected the child to live. Now that it looked as though Maribeth might succeed with *my* child, when all of his had failed... I did become worried for the future.

In the meanwhile, as my health returned, I began to throw myself back into working the farm. I never saw Charles. He'd hired hands to work in my absence. The spring had come whether I was ready for it or not. We weren't wealthy any longer. We did rely upon our crops, but we had enough money for all the help we needed. My working again did lessen the load, but I never heard anything from Charles about it.

If possible, it seemed I felt my family's loss all the more now. Life was trying to get back to normal, back into routine and yet I was all alone. There was no one for me to come home to, only a covered dish on the table and a note from Nan.

I worked from dawn until dusk when I could. Only when there was work to be done, could I try to forget. Evenings, I would come back to the house and collapse in despair. I tried to force myself to eat whatever Nan had prepared, because if I had no energy, I could not work. If I could not work, I would be trapped in the house with my grief and my worries all day.

I was ever desperate for news of Mari and the child. The baby would be expected mid to late October. Here it was, end of May and she was still well! In my heart, I rejoiced for that, but I also felt an ever-impending doom. Would she really carry to completion? What would Charles do when the baby was born? He still had not spoken to me. I saw him once from afar. He had turned and walked away. Would he really keep this on forever? He had to let me see the child. I felt desperate that he just had to let me be in its life. He knew what it would mean to me, didn't he?

Then, one day soon after sunset, there was a carriage come up my drive and then a knock at my door. I was very anxious as I opened it. No one ever called upon me and I thought perhaps that something had happened.

It was a man in a suit. He introduced himself as being in Charles' employ. He apologized for the hour, but explained that he was told he would only find me at home after dark. He'd a case full of papers that I was to sign. Charles wanted to take over my half of the farm and my house. I was to leave town and find myself a new life elsewhere. I laughed at the man. It was ludicrous!

The man assured me that my brother was fully within his rights, in asking me to leave. In fact, my consent was a mere formality. He could force me to leave if I resisted. You see, it was still his name on the deeds to our properties. In effect, without his grace, I owned nothing! As you can imagine, I was flabbergasted. I would not believe him, but he showed me the legal documents for proof.

Among those papers, I was also dumbfounded to find information on the balance left in my account back in England. It was emptied. At the age of twenty-one, I had gained access to it. I had used the account on occasion, but it was still a joint account with my brother, who had now taken it all. I was penniless, homeless, alone and in total shock over it all. I sent the man away. If Charles thought to rob me of my life, he could bloody well come and throw me out in person!

I know that it must seem that I had ruined his life, from his perspective. He felt I'd ruined his relationship with his wife and then gotten her pregnant, branding him a fool, but to be honest, he hadn't a relationship with her anyway. It was still wrong of course and perhaps I was just feeling selfish, but I couldn't agree to the severity of his reaction. No one else would ever know that the child was not his. I didn't know what else Mari might have told him, but as far as I knew, he was only aware of our one tryst, not the ongoing affair we'd had years past.

To be honest, I had no idea really, what he felt. I don't know how I would have felt if our roles had been reversed. I don't think I had ever really felt about someone, the way that Charles had practically worshiped Maribeth when they had first wed, but now their relationship had deteriorated into a hollow facade of a marriage from what I could see. I hadn't been the cause of their troubles. Surely, Charles knew that. It was only true, that I had done an absolutely terrible thing in taking advantage of the fact that his marriage was already weak.

But now he sought to ruin my life in return? What had he to ruin? God had already taken from me the only people I had ever loved! My family was gone! What should I care any longer for money? But he knew I also loved the farm. He saw me out there every day. He knew that it was the only way that I kept myself sane. So he would take that too? Take my livelihood and make sure that I never got to see his wife again, or know of our baby, all in one fell swoop! It was unacceptable! I didn't care how wrong I was or how much I'd hurt him; I would not allow him to do this.

But before anything else, I needed to see Maribeth. I wanted to see her for myself and to know that she and the baby were alright. I had to speak to her of this, find out what she made of it all. She might not even know of Charles' plans. Once I thought it over, I realized that it was very likely that she'd no idea.

I wondered absently if Mari had thought to ask Alice for information on me as I had done over her. I had the baby as motive, but I suddenly realized that perhaps I did care a bit more for Maribeth herself, then I'd previously let myself acknowledge.

It began to take shape in my mind that perhaps the two of us would be happier to rid ourselves of Charles' influence altogether. Run off and start a family of our own, leaving Charles' anger far behind, a distant memory.

Living where and doing what? I was a pauper now. Should I hire myself as a farm hand and work for someone else's profit, leaving Maribeth home alone to sew all day and night so that we might survive? No. There was no way I could consign us to such a life. One thing at a time. I needed to see her.

I waited all the next morning, purposely working in sight of their house, hoping to see Charles' carriage head out for town. Finally, I was rewarded in seeing him leave. I went to Maribeth straight away. Alice met me at the door. She was a bit flustered and apologetic in telling me that she'd specific standing instructions to turn me away if ever I came. Maribeth heard this from the bedroom however. She told Alice to let me in, in spite of what Charles had told her. Alice still had reservations, until Mari threatened that if I were not allowed to come in, then Maribeth herself would be forced to come out. Alice would not have risked hurting the baby. She said she would leave on some errand and know nothing of my visit.

I went to the bedroom and there she lay. I can't say that I felt a rush of romantic love as I saw her, but a great wave of relief did wash over me, that she was indeed alright. Her stomach evidenced that the baby was well also. I just stared for a moment in disbelief. She did look to be doing very well. In fact, upon laying eyes on me, she positively glowed. She put her hands to her belly and beamed at me. 'It's growing Christian. I've never come this far! Do you see? Come, you can feel it!'

I couldn't help it, I had to go and place my hands upon her. How could I not? I remembered doing the very same with my own wife five years before. A magical experience. I felt it too, after a few impatient minutes. I felt the baby move!" Cain had to pause for a moment, a strong smile of remembrance upon his face. "She was so thrilled, we both were. Moments like those... that's what life is all about." He took a deep breath and looked up to see Felicity staring at him intently. Cain had never truly shared his thoughts and feelings on these things with anyone before. As he noticed her gaze upon him, he felt as though her eyes could see into his very soul. He sincerely hoped as he went on, that she would not be too frightened by what she would see there.

"Anyway, I knew that we hadn't much time. We needed to talk. As I had suspected, Mari knew nothing of what Charles had done, in closing my account and trying to strip me of my home. She was appalled, although not entirely surprised. She hadn't known, but she had predicted he would react thusly.

I never mentioned the idea of running off. She was the one who asked me. 'The Manor. Once the baby is born, I want to go back to Herald Manor, Christian. You are a Herald still. If we could wrest it from him somehow... return to Canterbury. I've had quite my fill of being a farmer's wife. I'm meant for better than this, you know I am, as are you.'

I wasn't so sure of that. Perhaps she did belong elsewhere, but I loved the farm life. Of course, without my family it was a bit empty, maybe a change would do me good. I still could think of the Manor as home. Anyway, it was a moot point. 'The Manor is still in his possession Mari, we cannot gain it from him. He will stand in our way, whatever we were to try and do.'

'Then we must remove him.'

She said it clearly and coldly, as though it was something practiced in her mind. I didn't even know what she could mean at first. When the implication hit me, it was so horrible and yet so like my own thoughts the night before, I knew not what to say. I never would have spoken that myself and I hadn't even thought of it consciously. I'd ideas of leaving him, not *killing* him, but now that it had been said, I had to admit that it seemed to make perfect, if brutal sense. All of our problems neatly solved. It was absolutely dreadful to even consider, but consider it I did.

Then I told Maribeth that I couldn't do it. I told her that our happiness was not worth a man's life. That we would find another way. She never said another word about it. She didn't try to convince me, she just looked at me for a few moments, thoughtfully. I knew that although I had spoken out against it, she was certain that the idea hadn't left my mind. She knew me well.

I left, telling her that I may come again if I could. I went back to daily life, but every time that I was reminded of my brother, that awful idea surfaced. It wouldn't leave my thoughts. It hovered there, like a poison fog.

The man in the suit came back. He said I had less than a month to collect my belongings and remove myself from the property. Preposterous! He had documents and things showing that I would then be removed by force if necessary. I had until the first of July. I laughed at that date. Convenient. I had worked all spring to plant, and I would be removed just as work finished. Plenty of time for Charles to find the help he would need for harvest. Then in the autumn, Charles could reap the fruits of my labor. When I told the man as much, he replied to me, off the record, that I could take Charles before a judge on that fact, and be reimbursed for my work, from the profits of the harvest. However, he also said that in dealing with my brother, he knew that this was a highly vengeful situation. He would advise me to let it go. My brother was prepared to be as hurtful and devastating as possible. I should leave for greener pastures and be happy to be rid of him.

Rid of him I would be. I honestly began to entertain the idea. I can't even say that I thought to beset upon him in a rage, killing him in the passion of anger. This was a cold and calculated thought process, of how best to remove this man from my life. I won't tell you of the things that I considered. I never spoke to Maribeth again either. I hadn't the chance to see her alone and I didn't want to provoke Charles any further. I knew that Maribeth would not be distraught if Charles disappeared from our lives. That was all that I felt I needed to know."

Cain was watching Felicity to see her reaction to his words. She said nothing, but stared at him with a rattled discontentment over her wine. Most likely, she had thought that the deaths on his hands had not begun until *after* his change; that his experience as a murderer had come with, and because of his vampire nature. That would indeed have been easier to forgive, he was sure. He was terribly sorry to disappoint her. He continued.

"Of course I had not totally given myself o'er to the plan. I did love my brother still, my brother of the past anyway. I swung back and forth over the issue constantly. I still tried to think of some way that we could simply leave, without finding ourselves destitute, but nothing seemed plausible, and the days were quickly passing. Besides, I could not hope to move Mari in her state. Whatever happened, she would need to remain at home until the baby was safely born.

Finally, I convinced myself that I could not become a murderer. No matter what Charles had tried to do to me, what I had already done to him was bad enough. I would not repay his past years of kindness with death at my hands.

I decided that I would leave peacefully. I would do what I could to set up a new home elsewhere, doing my best to remain in contact with those who could relay information to me of Maribeth. Perhaps I could even convince Charles that if he wanted me to leave, he needed to give me some money for a new start. Once the baby was born, I would return for them. Then we could steal away, Maribeth the baby and I, to live in my new home. I would need to see Maribeth again, to be sure of her, but I knew that she would gladly accept the idea. It may be difficult, and it would certainly not be Herald Manor, but I would care for her and the child. She knew that at least *I* had a loving heart.

I began to prepare my things for a move. I wouldn't bring much really. I finally nerved myself to gather Elizabeth and Amelia's things. I had let no one touch them. Now I brought them to Liza's father, at the church, and asked that he give them to a family who might need them.

I kept nothing of Liza's, although sometimes I do wish that I had. I did however keep Amelia's prized possession, her porcelain doll. I'd bought it when she'd turned three, ordered it from England, although everyone told me that it was too fine a thing for such a little girl. They'd told me that I should get one of cloth, until she was old enough to care for it, but I wouldn't listen. She had carried it everywhere. She treated it like a person and it never got even a chip, she was so careful. The doll's name was Harriet.

So, Harriet went into a box with what few other things I would keep. I went and knocked on Charles and Mari's door, one week before I was to leave. I knew Charles wasn't there. Alice answered once again. I told her that I knew her concerns, as I saw her shaking her head and worrying over disobeying my brother, again, but that I'd be leaving town soon and needed to say goodbye. She couldn't refuse me. I told her to relay to Charles my request for a meeting the next day. She agreed and then left for me to speak with Maribeth in private.

When I told Mari of my plans, she was a little disappointed in staying in the colonies, but as I expected, she professed that she'd be far happier with me than ever she would be with Charles. So it was set. She would write me letters if she could. If not, she would ask Alice to write. Nothing revealing, just a general report of her health and the baby's progress. A few weeks after the baby was born, when Mari felt able to travel, I would come for them.

The next day, the man in the suit returned. I should have known better than to expect Charles himself. I made my proposal, that if Charles should truly hope never to see me again, it was only fair that he give me back the money he had stolen from my account. I would need to buy myself a house and some land elsewhere; otherwise, he could expect to see me here in town, living as a farm hand with a neighbor.

I don't know if perhaps Maribeth had already approached him with the idea or not, but the man was prepared already to do just that. They had anticipated my request and were going to oblige, as long as I promised to leave town. And so, it was settled.

I decided that I should travel some distance from our farm before choosing a place to settle. Not only did I not want any reminders of the past years to intrude, but I also had thoughts that it would make it that much more difficult for Charles to find us, come the time that Maribeth would join me.

I ended up in New York finally. Not far from where we are now, believe it or not. I had just enough money to purchase a modest homestead with a plot of land large enough to work for profit. The house was unfinished and needed much work, but it would do. In fact, I was glad because it gave me something to focus on while I waited for the months to pass.

I sent a letter to Alice at her home, to let her know where I had settled. I asked again for her to please send me any news. I received a response from her not long after, stating that she was glad that I had begun my life anew and wished me all the best. Charles and Maribeth were doing well, her pregnancy progressing nicely. I should rest assured that she would send me updates now and again.

So, time went on. I worked on my house and began to establish myself in this new community. I also prepared a field as quickly as I could, and did some planting, that it was not too late for me to have some small crop come fall. I received another letter from Alice a few weeks later, saying that all was well. It seemed that things would work out as I'd hoped. Then the messenger came.

A messenger arrived with a letter from Alice, highly unusual. I immediately feared the worst, that Maribeth had lost the baby, but once read, it revealed news that might almost be considered worse from my point of view. They were gone! Alice informed me that Charles had unexpectedly sold both of our houses and the farm, and they were leaving for England! By the time I got the letter, they would be on their way. She gave me the name of the ship, port and departure time. They were to sail on the 'Glory' out of Delaware Bay, but they had left at first light yesterday morning. They were gone!

What the hell was Charles doing, making Maribeth travel in her condition? Why were they going back to the Manor *now?* Did he know of our plans? He couldn't. Did it mean so much to him that I be deprived of the pleasure of ever seeing her and my baby again? He was putting her on a ship for such a long and arduous journey... he was going to kill my child!

I hastily scrawled and sent back a short message to Alice, thanking her profusely for the information. I then set about trying to get details about the passage route of the ship 'Glory'. After a harrowing search, I found that luck was with me still. I'd a slight chance to catch them. The ship had three other stops to make before its main crossing. It was scheduled to stop in Keyport, New Jersey. That was not all that far from my new home actually, but they would have landed there today and were going to sail again in the morning. It was very doubtful I could get there in time. The ship would dock again up in Massachusetts however, to drop off some of its cargo to the port at Salem. Then it would stop once more at Kennebunkport in Maine and restock its own supplies before setting out to cross the Atlantic. I would try to meet them in Salem. It would be quite the frantic scramble, but with a good horse and a bit of luck, I might catch them before they were truly gone. It was worth a try. I did not relish the idea of trying to follow them across the sea back to England. I was terribly afraid that my child should not survive it. That was a last resort.

So I chose my fastest horse, a beautiful palomino stallion, packed some supplies for the journey and wasted no time in setting out for Salem, Massachusetts. Once there, if I succeeded in catching up with Charles and Maribeth, and indeed was able to work things so that Mari would return with me, then I would have to purchase a carriage for the return trip. I could never expect her to travel on horseback. I wouldn't bring my own carriage now, for speed was of the essence. I would worry about the return trip once I got that far. My only thoughts now, were of reaching them, before it was too late.

I raced through forest and field, from town to town. I won't keep you in suspense, but tell you that I did indeed make the dock the night before they were to set sail. Although I was desperately certain the whole time that I wouldn't. In fact, even though I had arrived a few hours before they were to leave, I still could hardly believe my eyes when I saw that the ship was indeed still there.

It was the middle of the night, almost two in the morning. Now that I had actually made it to my destination, I had no idea what to do. I studied the ship from a respectful distance and saw that there was a man there, keeping watch. It was he, whom I would have to approach. There was just no way that I might sneak aboard and spirit Mari away, although I would like to. I'd no idea where to find them and surely Charles would be with her. I thought for a moment and then brought with me a small saddlebag as I went to try and gain access to the ship.

I hailed the man and inquired if this was indeed 'The Glory', and whether I might find the Lord and Lady Herald aboard, as it was imperative that I see them at once. Of course, the man was surprised that I should seek to come aboard at so late an hour. He told me that it was out of the question, as only passengers were allowed entrance at this time. The ship would sail at dawn.

At this news, I became quite agitated and told the man that if he had been unaware, the Lady Herald was with child. I was a physician, and had been called to look upon her one last time before they debarked on their journey. I had expected to arrive earlier, but was unavoidably detained. I was quite concerned that perhaps the lady was not well enough for the trip, and I must be allowed to examine her before they set sail. I waved my bag for emphasis, hoping that the dark would help to hide the fact that it was not really a doctor's bag.

This did seem to shake him a bit. He believed me I was sure, and it was obvious that he had noted Maribeth's condition. Still, he was uneasy to allow me aboard to bother them in the middle of the night. After what he said next however, I knew that I must get onboard immediately. He said that although he believed a final examination to be an excellent idea, he really thought that I should wait until Lord Herald came back aboard. He had not yet returned from 'The Ship's Tavern', a local pub, and the man had not been told to expect me.

Charles was not even on board! He'd left Maribeth to go and get drunk over his disappointments in us? If only we could leave before his return! I pleaded with the man as to the urgency of my visit. I was due to be somewhere else in the morning, and could not possibly wait for dawn to board this ship. The examination would take only twenty minutes or so. The baby's life could depend on it!

Finally, he decided to risk it. He would accompany me on board and we would inquire whether the lady would see me. When we reached the passenger's quarters, I had him inform her that Doctor Christian wanted to see her. Thankfully, she allowed me in.

I had woken her of course, but she was powerfully pleased to see me. I wanted to interrogate her as to why they were making this journey *now*, or at all! Had she any idea how dangerous this would be for the child? But we hadn't time for any of that now. Charles could return at any moment.

Maribeth knew my thoughts anyway and told me simply that she'd had no choice. Charles had given her no time to find a way to relay the news to me. She was amazed that I'd found my way here. Apparently, Alice had taken it upon herself to inform me, as Mari hadn't even the chance to speak to her before they left.

She was more than willing to leave with me, back to my new farm if that was what I wanted. She wanted only what was best for the baby, that we become a real family. I must know that this baby was most important to her. Charles had hired a mid-wife, to make the journey with them, or else he knew Mari would refuse to come. She was asleep in the next room.

I wanted Mari to leave with me straight away, but she began searching the room frantically. It tortured me to see her, six months pregnant and rushing about like that. I tried to make her tell me what she was looking for, so that I might find it for her. She wanted a box. Charles had a metal box that he kept their valuables in. It was hidden in the room and there was something that she wanted from it before we left. She wouldn't tell me more, but I helped her search, to no avail. Finally, I persuaded her that we must leave without it. She actually looked undecided for a moment, but I took her hands and kissed them. "Please Mari..." I begged. It was time to go.

As we made to leave the ship, I was concocting in my head some story for the watchman, of how Mari was unfit to travel and I would take her to an inn, but the man was nowhere in sight. We left unseen and made our way off the ship to the dock.

We were so close. The dock was long, and deserted. I had left my horse tied amidst the trees some little distance away. I had thought to take Mari riding gingerly sidesaddle, as I walked the horse to a place where we might camp for the night. Then we would find her a proper carriage the next day and be gone. Unfortunately, it was not to be.

Charles returned, his timing impeccable. He approached the dock even as we stepped off of it. He was drunk. He started yelling at his 'fool woman', daring to come out looking for him in the dead of night. He would return when he was good and ready. Apparently, he'd thought at first that I was just some escort to accompany her, from the ship. It took him a moment to even recognize me. When he did, his eyes went wide, and then his mouth became a vicious snarl and he actually sought to charge at me and knock me from my feet.

I'd never seen rage overtake Charles like that, though I'd seen it in others many a time, back in my more mischievous days. There was a time or two that a man had come rushing at me with fury in his eyes back then, for being in places and doing things I'd no right to be. But it was a decade since someone had come at me that way, and I was no longer a child, but truly a man. I backed away in surprise and he actually shoved Maribeth aside as he hit me. He knocked me right off of my feet. His ferocity astounded me. I hit the ground in bewilderment as to what I should do, as I hadn't initially planned to fight him, but the fact that he'd put his hands on Mari stifled any empathy I might have felt for his position.

I couldn't even speak to him. He was like an animal fighting blind and started pounding his fists to me, wherever he could connect. Mari, upon seeing him beat me so, became terribly distraught and did the stupidest thing she could have done. She tried to get him off of me.

She began pulling at him and screaming for him to leave me alone. I tried to tell her to get away, but I don't believe she even heard me. I was rather busy just trying to regain my feet before I became too badly injured, so that I might fight back.

Charles turned on her in an absolute fury. He grabbed her off of him and threw her to the ground calling her a filthy whore. Rather than leave it be, she still screamed back at him like a common fishwife and not the lady of noble bearing that she should be.

I flew at him and hit him once or twice, but before he would take notice of me, he kicked Maribeth as she lie there on the ground... hard. Some detached part of my mind saw it and knew that it was a very calculated and intentional strike. It was her swelled stomach that took most of the blow.

I saw positively red after that, there was no coming back from it. I beset upon him with the sole intent and purpose of killing him. I think he knew it too. We fought brutally. Charles and I were evenly matched in size and strength, but I was five years his junior, and he was still quite drunk. He did fight well though, I must give him that. When it became clear that he wouldn't win, he tried to circle me and find a way to run past, to the ship I suppose. I guess he thought to get help. I don't know how no one heard us, but we remained unobserved. I wouldn't let him by when he sought to pass me. In fact, I gave him a swift punch to the side of the head.

It was then that I heard her, Maribeth. It seemed as though she spoke directly into my ear, although she still lay crying some little bit away. 'Finish him Christian.' I don't know, to this day if I heard it only in my head or if Maribeth actually spoke the words. Charles was dazed and thrown off balance, and before I think I even realized consciously what I was doing, I kicked him over the side.

I don't think I'd meant to do that at first. Truthfully, it all happened so fast, it's rather hard to sort out now, but at the thought of what he'd done to Maribeth, I believe I only thought to kick him back, as he had kicked her. It was only when I heard him hit the water with a loud splash, that I realized what it meant. Charles could not swim. The water was not terribly deep here at the dock, but the tide was coming in and it was deep enough. He was drunk and I'd just punched him in the head hard enough to deliver a concussion. I stood there for a moment in shock, listening to the waves. Then I did think perhaps to go after him, but when I reached the edge, he was gone. I couldn't even see where he had disappeared to under the water. Then I heard Maribeth scream.

It cut through the dazed shock like a knife. I spun to see her digging at her skirts and she screamed again as though she had been stabbed. I ran to her of course, but I knew even before I reached her, what it would mean. She was trying to get the folds of her dress out of the way so that she might see her legs, but had to stop and double over in pain.

There was nothing I could do at first, but hold her until it passed. When she was able, she lifted her skirts away. I'm sure we both expected to see her thighs dark with blood, but that wasn't the case. They were wet though, her skin gleamed in the moonlight. I didn't know much about childbirth, but the doctor and Elizabeth had told me some, before Amelia was born. I remembered that there'd be a rush of fluids to mark the time when the baby would come. Maribeth's water had broken.

This could not be good, it was far too early, but at least it wasn't blood. I lifted her to her feet and we made our way off the dock into the proper town. I helped her walk and half carried her when needed. Twice we had to stop along the way as her body was wracked with contractions. I pounded upon the first door that we came to.

It was a fisherman's home, he and his wife and children awakened by our furious knocking. I quickly made known our situation, and they were kind enough to let us in and give Mari a bed to lie on. The man went rushing out to fetch the local doctor as his wife helped to calm Maribeth. She had her eldest daughter make a tea that she said might help to stave off the labor and soothe her body back to rest. The contractions however showed no signs of slowing, but instead came harder and faster as we waited for the doctor to arrive.

When he finally did come, it was obvious that the baby would also be arriving shortly. There was nothing the doctor could do but try to ease the birth." Cain became very quiet and still for a moment, lost in his thoughts. Felicity sipped her wine and waited patiently for him to go on.

"The wait wasn't long, and my second child was born. We had a boy." Cain tried to swallow past the lump in his throat. He would not lose his composure this time, but he resolved that he would not give in to his urge to skip ahead in the story, past the memories he had not called up for himself in so long. His voice became quiet and confidential as he recalled the sad wonder with which he had viewed his little boy.

"He was *so* tiny. Perfectly formed, with ten little fingers and toes. He was quiet, but alive, kicking and wriggling, but I knew he was *too* small. Mari knew it too. The doctor only needed to look at us to know that he needn't try to explain.

They have such miracles these days; such modern wonders of technology; special beds and boxes to keep a baby warm and great machines that can breathe for a child whose lungs were not quite ready yet. Of course, we'd none of that then. He couldn't breathe well at all, not even to cry properly, and we knew he'd almost no chance of survival.

I held him, while they attended to Maribeth. She was still cramping and bleeding, but they told me not to worry. It was normal and she'd be alright, it would stop soon. As for the baby, he didn't last more than an hour or so. Died in my arms, he did. Maribeth wouldn't hold him, even after she was better recovered.

It was as though she didn't want to become attached to him. She wouldn't even give him a name. I wanted to name him, but she refused to let me. It was as though she was in denial and just wanted to forget it all as quickly as possible.

He died, and they took him away. Maribeth asked them to take care of it for us. She didn't want details. Baby Herald was all they called him. I never told anyone, not even Mari, but... I wanted to name him Daniel. That was his name... Daniel."

Cain paused to wipe the tears that had filled his eyes and to drink more of his wine. Felicity looked silently heartbroken for him. He took a deep breath.

"I guess I wasn't meant to be a father." She didn't say anything, but reached over to squeeze his shoulder for a moment in sympathy. He noticed she said nothing about Charles, not that he'd given her much of a chance. That's how it had happened though. Maribeth had begun labor before he himself had even had a chance to really acknowledge his brother's death in his mind. Charles' death would not remain entirely forgotten at the time however.

"Just after the dawn, there was a knock at the door. It was someone come from the 'Glory'. As soon as I realized, terror struck my heart and I was forced to remember the other events of the evening. As I sat quietly by Mari's side, I could hear them from the front room, and they never even mentioned Charles' disappearance. They wanted us to know that the ship would be sailing shortly, with or without us. Maribeth was sleeping, and the man of the house came quietly to fetch me.

For a moment, I feared it would be the watchman from the night before, but I couldn't be *that* unlucky. It was someone that I did not recognize, nor they me. I came to understand that the people of the house had assumed that *I* was Maribeth's husband. Of course they had, why wouldn't they? My name was Herald and I acted 'the father' of the baby. The only person who had seen me approach the ship, knowing that Charles had not yet returned, was the watchman. I don't know what he ever told anyone, but it seemed to have been accepted that Mari left the ship in the night for the baby. Charles was assumed to have met her in town, and now they must have thought me to be him.

The porter who came to us now, brought two suitcases of the Herald's belongings from the ship, and a message from the mid-wife Charles had hired for the journey. I had totally forgotten about her and for a moment, I felt terribly stricken that perhaps if we had gone back to the boat she could have helped us, faster than the doctor in town could.

But no, I realized that in all reality that she would not have been able to do anything to prevent the baby's early birth. In fact, it was a good thing we hadn't seen her. For she would certainly have been able to tell someone that I was not Charles. As it was, she didn't even know that I existed.

She sent word now of her condolences. Unbeknownst to us at the time, when the baby was born, the man of the house had sent word to the ship for us, of our whereabouts and condition. That's why they weren't even looking for Charles. They thought for sure he was here. The mid-wife wanted us to know that she was greatly sorry for our loss, but that she would still be making the passage to England as planned. We could still have our room back aboard the ship if we'd like, but they would sail within the hour.

I was so dazed by the night's events; I could hardly think what to tell them. The doctor gently advised me against continuing the voyage, for Maribeth's condition. She should recover and have time to accept our loss and grieve properly before making such a journey. I simply nodded my head, happy to follow whatever advice I'd been given. I couldn't really expect us to board the ship anyway. They weren't looking for Charles now, but surely *someone* onboard would know that I was not him. How would I explain Maribeth leaving her husband behind to take me in his place?

The porter left and the doctor went to check on Mari. I was about to follow, when the lady of the house put her hand on my arm to stay me. She asked me quietly if I'd seen anything unusual just before Maribeth's labor had begun. I was stunned for a moment and then told her that I had no idea what she could mean.

I was worried of course, that someone had heard the fight that had taken place, so I was quite unprepared for what she said next. She asked if perhaps I had seen a specter or an apparition, the visage of someone hovering above Maribeth, as if to curse or harm her. Mayhap an odd animal or bird had been in the area?

As you can imagine, at this I was thoroughly confused. What on earth could she mean? I apologized, told her that I had seen nothing of the sort and knew not even, what such a thing would mean.

She took me to the corner, as though to whisper a great secret. 'Witches', she breathed. She gave me a knowing nod as she saw my eyes grow quite wide at the word. 'The Devil has been busy, doing evil works here in Salem. 'T'would have been best had you never left that ship of yours, to set foot in this God forsaken hamlet. The Lord help us, but the Devil is run rampant here these past months. Some have hung for it already, but still they've not yet routed him out.'

She said "Twas most likely witches what caused your baby's death.' Did we know anyone here in town? Have we had ill relations with any townsfolk we might have met? Perhaps we'd like to file a formal report?

I hardly knew how to respond. Was she serious? I remembered now that I had heard of a woman being hung for a witch, hereabouts, but I'd dismissed it as foolishness and of course, I'd had more pressing personal matters in mind of late. Finally, knowing not how else to respond, I thanked her for her insight. I told her that I'd no wish to report any mysterious happenings, but that I would surely tell someone if I remembered anything of note.

I returned to Mari a bit bemused. I found she was awake and the doctor had apparently just finished examining her. He announced she was recovering nicely and left us to talk in private. Well, let me tell you, she would ask or say nothing about the baby. I tried to console her, but she would not grieve nor be consoled. She wanted it to disappear into the past, to have never been.

After a time of silence, she fell back to sleep, she was exhausted still from her ordeal to be sure. I sat, trying to understand her affected cold and heartless attitude and then I left that she should rest. The lady of the house invited that I join them in a meal, after which I went back to sit by Mari's side. Before long she did awaken and asked of the state of things.

When I told her about the ship, she grew positively frantic! I thought she should be happy that no one would be the wiser for what had happened. Now we could travel back to my home in New York and try to resume some sort of life. I couldn't understand her desperation.

The box. She still wanted that box that Charles had hidden in the room onboard. She had me search the luggage left for us three times, but of course, it was not there. The ship's crew had packed only those things that were in plain sight. The doctor came to tell us that he'd be leaving and begged for Maribeth to rest, but she shooed him away with barely a glance.

The ship. She demanded that we go after it. I thought she must be mad. What could be so important? I assumed she wanted some family heirloom from the box, a piece of jewelry, or something of sentimental value. I refused to speak to her of going after it until she told me exactly what she was searching for.

Would you believe it was money? I should have known. Wealth and status were always so damn important to her. Charles had put all of the profit from the sale of the farm and our two houses into that box. Bloody stupid if you ask me. He'd never heard of a bank? But they were going back overseas and he wanted to have it with him. He didn't trust anyone on the boat to guard it for him, so he hid it himself. He'd told her so, though she hadn't been privileged enough to know where.

The ship would be docking only one more time before setting out across the Atlantic. It would stop in Kennebunkport Maine, and we would be there to meet it. Maribeth was resolute. If I would not accompany her, she would find her way there alone.

She insisted that physically, she was fine. I didn't quite believe her, for I knew that Liza had needed a few days to recover from Amy's birth, but I also knew better than to challenge her. She would rather die than let me prove her wrong. She said that she would rest in bed until I could purchase her a horse and make ready to go, but she was going. She wouldn't take a carriage, that would tie us to the roads, when through forest may be quicker at times. She was hesitant to try and have my horse carry us both. It would be a close thing and she wouldn't take the chance of weighing him down too heavily to run at full speed.

Maribeth's not a woman easily argued with, and after all she'd been through, I knew better than to try and go against her wishes. A bit of checking did reveal that the ship had left as scheduled, a few hours before. So I found myself looking for a horse and supplies. I ended up purchasing a fine chestnut mare from a man in town. I added a few things to what supplies I already had, including a good map of the area, and made ready to go. I tried to convince her to let me go alone, that she should await me here, but she was adamant that I not leave without her. I think she actually questioned whether I would return!

Before sunset, I stood with much trepidation, and aided Maribeth in mounting her horse. We'd profusely thanked the couple at whose home we'd stayed, and asked that they keep our luggage until we might return for it. I wanted to stay here the night and begin our travels with the dawn, but Maribeth wouldn't hear of it. The ship already had a full days' travel ahead of us. 'Twas a straight easy run up to Kennebunkport from here for sailing, but the boat would stay in harbor for a full two days. We might make it if we hurried.

Once again, I found myself chasing that bloody ship. Warnings rushed about in my head, given by the lady of the house at our departure. 'Stick to the roads and be mindful of spirits and animals of the night. Perhaps they would not be angry with us, for we'd not turned against them to the courts, but the Devil will strike whom he will, with oft' no rhyme or reason. His witches are a wily lot, and know of ways to strike unseen.'

Of course, we paid her no heed, but set off at a harrowing pace. Upon studying our course, I saw that we could not take a direct route, but would often be forced to make detours around inlets and towards bridges over rivers and streams. Maribeth chafed at each setback that I showed her on the map, but refused to be deterred. To be honest, I was much more worried that she not break her neck, than to whether we should catch the ship. At this point, I hardly wanted Charles' money.

In fact, if no one learned of what had happened to Charles and he was simply declared 'disappeared', eventually Maribeth and I would inherit the Manor, and any other holdings he might have had left; a fact that I pointed out to Mari as we traveled, but she was too impatient to wait. What if they discovered that there had been foul play? The money in the box was a sure thing. It was hers, and she wanted it... now.

We didn't get very far. We were still in the outskirts of Salem actually, when our journey met its abrupt detour and eventual end. We had crossed a field and entered a forest, because it was a quicker route than the winding road. The brush was light, and even with the dark we were able to keep a good pace through the tall trees, when our horses suddenly stopped and became terribly skittish, refusing to go on.

A man stepped out from the trees, although I didn't know him for a man at first. He was thin and bald, very withered and old. The wane moonlight that shone through the branches above seemed to bounce off of his head and bath him in an otherworldly glow. He seemed so gnarled and old, one would think him a goblin or bogie of the forest, but he stood there and looked at us, and then he did seem only a man.

I don't know why I was so frightened of him, as I said, upon closer inspection, he did *look* human, but the way that he stepped out and smiled at us with an odd and malicious gleam in his eye, told me that he was indeed evil. I didn't know it then of course, but this would be my first encounter with a vampire.

I'm sure it was only a moment, although it seemed to occur in slow motion. He looked at me, gave me an evil grin, and then looked to Maribeth. At that precise moment, her horse became spooked and took off into the woods. The old man grinned at me once again and then took off after her.

Of course, I followed. How such an old man thought he would keep up with a horse, I'd no idea, but somehow they quickly lost me. I was not to learn what he was until much later, and even a vampire is no faster than a man through the woods, but I realize now, that the man must have had some slight telepathic talents and was using them to try and direct Mari's steed.

I've met vampire's who laid claim to such powers, although never anyone skilled enough to do anything truly impressive. The power does not always come with vampirism, as I've never evinced a bit of it myself, if not through venom, but some do have it. I believe that is how he did manage to chase them out of my path. Clouds covered what little moonlight there was and I was left in the dark, picking my way through the forest. I was following the sounds of Mari's mare crashing through the brush, when I heard the animal let out a piercing shriek, and Maribeth herself screamed.

What could have happened? Had he caught up to them? But what could he have done to the horse to make it wail so? I could do nothing but follow the last echo of Mari's scream. I heard nothing after. I was desperate to find her but knew not what to do. I wouldn't yell and reveal my location, for surely I was close. I must surprise them, but... nothing. Finally, I did begin to yell and scream for Maribeth. Still, nothing. I searched and I searched and could not find sign nor sound of them.

It must have been hours. Dawn arrived, and I had found nothing. I was truly beginning to doubt my own sanity. In fact, a very clear and frightening idea occurred to me. What if I had not caught their boat? What if I'd never re-encountered Charles and Maribeth? The fight, kicking Charles over the side, Mari's labor pains, the baby... what if it were all some grand delusional dream? Here I was alone, wandering through the woods. Could I prove that any of it had ever happened, to anyone... even myself? I was just a lone man riding through the forest, same as two days before, before everything. It was mind numbing to think about.

Then, at last, I came upon Mari's horse, riderless. Thank the Lord that I was yet still sane! I was quite surprised to find the mare alive actually, after the scream she'd let out in the night. I think now, that she must have been rebelling against an overload of mental commands from their pursuer. Or perhaps he had changed before her and she was frightened, knowing him for a predator, for she wasn't greatly injured. She was wandering between the trees, looking for something to graze upon.

The mare seemed totally unharmed at first. Then I did notice upon closer inspection, that she'd a small wound on the side of her neck, a bite of some sort. I'd no idea what would have done that or what it could mean. She seemed none the worse for it. Where was Maribeth?

Then my heart seemed to stop in dread. The saddle... it was covered in blood, but after a moment's reflection, I realized that although it worried me, it was no proof of foul play. It was from Maribeth's riding most likely. Her poor battered body had only just endured the birth of a child, however small. Riding should certainly have been forbidden by the doctor had he known she'd be so foolish. She'd caused herself to bleed again. It was upsetting, but not nearly as much as her continued absence. Again and again, I bellowed her name into the unresponding forest.

Had I any knowledge of vampires at the time, I would surely have realized that it was Maribeth who had drawn the creature right to us. She'd been bleeding rather heavily and the scent must have driven him to follow us like a summons.

I knew not what to do. I wandered the whole day screaming and searching, until finally I had to concede that she was lost. I would not spend the night out here alone. I would go to town and perhaps I could get others to help me search in the morning.

I went not back to Salem, but the next town over, to which I was closer. I thought it best I not return to Salem anyway. If Charles' body had been found, I'd be wanted for questioning. Besides, the last thing that I wanted was to be drawn into some trial over witches killing my baby and now stealing its mother. For I did wonder if witches it was, although I did not care to stand before a court o'er it.

I'd never before heard of a man being called a witch, but he didn't seem merely a man either. Perhaps 'twas Satan himself who'd stolen her away. How else had they so thoroughly disappeared? I was entirely beside myself.

I found an inn at which I could stay, and did gain help in searching for her come the morn'. I don't really know what the men whose aide I enlisted really thought of my tale. They did admit to hearing of many strange happenings of late, but as days went by and we found not a trace of her, I could not ask them to keep looking. At least I had her horse, as some sort of proof that I was not entirely suffering from hallucinations. Maribeth *had* been with me, and now she was gone.

I was aimless and unsure what to do after we stopped looking. Cold as it may sound, I won't say that I missed her terribly as a companion. Ours was never a great romantic love. In fact, our relationship throughout the years had been a strange one indeed, if you stop to think o'er it. It had begun with indifference and even petty jealousy over Charles' attention. Then it ranged through friendly camaraderie, to lust, to angry condemnation and finally a desperate sort of clinging to each other; to help weather the storms of Charles' wrath and simply so we should not be alone in the world. I never saw us as 'soul mates' or two people emphatically in love with one another. We knew each other well and understood each other. Without each other... we each were frighteningly and undeniably alone.

I spent the next week at that inn. My days sleeping late and staring out the windows at the forest, my nights by the hearthside in the tavern. I would scarce notice those around me, but sit and gaze into my ale as though it held great unfathomed secrets of life. I would stay as late as they would let me, and then go to bed and dream of that wrinkled old man and Maribeth's scream mingled with that of her mare.

Until one evening, after the fire had burned low and the serving wench had sent me to bed; I went to draw the shutters closed over the window against the bright, nearly full moon, when I saw something outside that nearly stopped my heart. There was a figure making its way through the woods to come out into the field at the side of the inn. It struck not fear in me, for it stood tall and upright, nothing like the creature that had stolen Mari from me. It was a person moving steadily, and although I could not yet see its features clearly, it was definitely a woman by the long full skirts of the dress she wore.

I could scarce let myself hope for it to be true, until the woman stepped out of the trees into the field under the moonlight. Even in the odd blue light of the moon, I could see a glint of fiery red in the long hair falling over her shoulders. Maribeth!

I could not stop to think of how she could have come here or be unharmed after all these days gone. It was Maribeth! I ran from my room without jacket or hat and through the empty tavern out into the night. As soon as she saw me, she stopped dead in her tracks. I didn't even think it odd that she didn't run to meet me, but when she started to back away, I called to her in confusion.

My calls were unanswered. She was clearly glad to see me, but still she turned and headed back to the cover of the forest. What could I do but follow? Stories floated through my mind of the will-o'-the-wisp, an elusive light or spirit thought to lure people into the woods, to lose their way and vanish never to be seen again. The idea of witches sending out an apparition of a deceased loved one in order to draw the grief stricken into a trap, wanted me to pause for caution.

But this was no glowing spirit. This was no elusive vision of loveliness, garbed in robes of white. Lovely though she was, it was simply Maribeth, just as I'd seen her last, except that her hair had come loose of the braid she had worn. She was real. I saw her clothing snag upon branches she passed and her feet made noise on the forest floor, although slight.

She was just beyond reach and as I put on a desperate burst of speed, I did touch her. She was solid and whole. 'Maribeth stop!' I pleaded desperately as I finally caught her and turned her to face me. She looked into my eyes and seemed dazed and almost terrified. I had no idea what she could have been through, but I tried to console her.

I pulled her to me with such force that it's a wonder I didn't hurt her. I sobbed and I laughed and I kissed her hair. I rambled nonsense of how she was safe now, and I would care for her and everything would be over and behind us. Eventually I managed to move her hair away and find her soft skin on which to place my kisses of joy. I don't know how long my lips covered and tasted the place where her throat met her shoulder, but after a time, I felt her kiss the side of my throat as well. I suppose you can imagine what next I felt."

Felicity was enrapt; her forgotten glass half raised to her lips. Her own mouth slightly open and her eyes wide. As Cain's attention fell upon her, she closed her mouth to swallow and she tried to stifle a chill that ran down her back. "She bit you," she whispered.

Cain nodded slowly. He stared at her in thought for a moment. "I won't describe that to you. You *know* what that is." His eyes darted about guiltily for a moment before they settled back on hers. Felicity had still not ever confided in him, her own impressions of his bite. He wasn't sure how she thought of it, though of course *he* remembered it fondly. He was fairly sure the experience itself had pleased her, although she may never admit it, but had she also been so frightened that she would not even consider discussing it with him... or repeating it? Smarter to avoid the topic, to be explored another time... or never again. Why couldn't he get that straight in his mind? It should not be repeated, but forgotten.

At least he thought so, but still she asked, "Is it always the same? It's not, is it? Not for everyone."

He forced himself to answer shortly, without emotion. "No, it's similar for most, but in some ways it differs. It's a very personal experience." His eyes could practically read the memory from her own. She'd been thoroughly enthralled and loathed to admit it. He would move on with his tale of the past, to avoid having to speak on more recent events.

"The next I knew, I was in pitch darkness with the cool scent of deep earth all around me. I was unsure if I was even alive. Thought I was dead and buried, I did.

A light flared. There was Maribeth, looking terribly worried, with a lantern and shelves of jellies and jams behind her. I was so confused, that I had to close my eyes again. My thoughts wouldn't sort themselves. Things were hazy and I felt as though I was drowning in foggy recollections. My body felt terrible heavy and my eyes didn't want to stay open. All I could want was rest.

'Christian?' Maribeth's voice cut through the delirium of half-sleep. I *was* alive then, but where were we, what had happened? I couldn't remember.

'Christian!' This time there was clearly panic in her voice. What was she so worried over? Suddenly I did remember, some. I remembered Charles, and the baby, and her disappearance, and following her through the woods this very night, and then something had happened... to me, but I could not recall what, the memory stopped there.

'Christian please! You must answer a question for me.'

It seemed terribly hard work just to open my eyes, but I did. Yes, jams and jellies. We were in someone's root cellar, I came to realize. I couldn't fathom how we might have come to be here though. My eyes found Maribeth once again. My, but she did look distraught. The dim light of the lantern made her face look gauntly thin and her eyes were red-rimmed and bright with tears.

'Yes?' I managed to whisper.

'Oh Christian!' She was so relieved that I could still hear and respond to her. I must have been drained very near to death. 'Christian, do you love me?'

I closed my eyes again. She shook me to look at her, and tried to make me sit up. 'Do you love me Christian?' I couldn't imagine why she'd be asking me this now. In fact, I was so bewildered by everything that it took me a moment before I even realized that she expected an answer. 'Do you?'

I can't really say that I pondered the question. I was hardly in the frame of mind for thoughtful response. I simply know that I opened my mouth and the word that came out was... 'yes'. She let me go, and I gratefully dropped myself back to the hay strewn floor to close my eyes. I very happily would have died just then, but Maribeth wouldn't allow it.

'Drink. Drink Christian. If you don't, you'll die! Drink it Christian, I won't let you leave me!'

Maribeth... again. 'Damn that woman' I thought, 'couldn't she just let me be?' Do you know, that I instantly felt as though I had traveled back in time? Funny how our minds seek to protect us from truths. I was positively convinced that I had traveled back in time. Maribeth's pregnancy, Charles' death, the loss of yet another child, none of it had ever happened. Of course it hadn't! I was sick, remember? I was grieving over the loss of Amy and Liza. I wanted to die and Maribeth *still* would not leave me alone! All I wanted was to close my eyes and be left to die, and that woman kept pushing at me her bloody broth!

I opened my eyes to tell her just that. I was so powerfully angry! Who was *she* to tell me that she would not let me die! 'I don't want your damn soup!' I yelled at her. Obviously, she found me delusional and then took matters into her own hands. When I did manage to focus my eyes to see what she offered, it was to see not a cup of broth, but her own torn and bloody wrist that she brought to my lips.

I hadn't even the patience with myself to think how odd that was. I simply declared myself insane and closed my eyes again. She pressed her wrist to my lips and forced the blood to my mouth, and then... all else was instantly forgotten and forgiven. I drank."

"You drank her blood?" Felicity's voice was full of quiet awe and revulsion.

"I did. That's how it's done," he confirmed.

"But... you were still human," she said in disgusted confusion.

"I was, at the time," he agreed.

"But, didn't you... resist; find it... appalling?" she asked.

Cain gave her a little smile. This was a conversation for a later date. "No. It's not something I can really explain. It's more something that you have to... experience." She seemed a little frightened by that remark.

He pretended not to notice, and went on. "Anyway, that is how it is done. To create a vampire, ideally you would want to replace all of the humans' blood with that of their maker. Obviously this is not an exact science and seems almost impossible to carry out, but to give a person too little vampire blood, is to let their body die. That is how those unfortunate zombie creatures you've seen are created. Lesser amounts can allow the body to become brain dead, produce mild to severe retardation, or simply allow memory loss or a range of cognitive disabilities. If a vampire is to retain their present state of mind, lucidity, there can be no true death or disruption, but a seamless transition from one state of being to the other.

In order to allow this, the candidate must first be as nearly drained of blood as possible, without allowing true death to occur. Then that person is given back all the blood lost, mingled with that of the vampire, but this alone is not enough. For a sure and thorough change, it must be done not just once, but over and over again, until the blood of the vampire and its chosen one are so mixed as to be indistinguishable."

Felicity was still not quite with him. "So you drank her blood, while you were still human, *again and again?* Wasn't there a point where you were recovered enough to think clearly? Wasn't there a time when you thought 'What the hell am I doing?'"

Obviously, she was refusing to understand how he could become caught up in the sheer passion of it all. She wouldn't face her own recollections of being bitten and he was almost afraid to try and describe it to her. Felicity spoke again before he could try again to explain. "She bit you again, didn't she? Only this time, you had to understand what she was, right? Weren't you scared of her?"

He was careful not to show any expression. Had Felicity been scared when he'd bitten her? Her body certainly hadn't reacted in fright. "It was Maribeth," he said with a shrug, by way of simple explanation. "When she bit me the first time, I hadn't seen her change, and truthfully, I didn't really remember it all that well. Too much had happened. I believe I must have been in shock. The second time she bit me, again I didn't see her face.

Until that point, I did *not* know what she was. It was only after she began to draw the blood from my body, that I realized what she had become. I must tell you though, I'd no fear of her. In fact, if you really want to know my thoughts at the time, I realized that she had been transformed, that she was not human any longer. I came to understand that she had instead become something made to prey upon humans. That was clear, and all I could think, was that *even in this, she was magnificent.* I may have seen many faults in her as a person, but as a lover, and as a vampire, I had felt that she was beyond compare. I was not frightened but enraptured that she could even now have such an effect on me."

The way in which Felicity looked at him, was not with understanding or sympathy. She did not pretend to misunderstand him, but rather seemed to deny that she could empathize. Finally, she asked, "When did it happen? Did you know you would become a vampire? How did you *change?*"

"After she drank from me the second time, I would drink again from her. I watched with amazed wonder as she did show me her vampire features and bare her fangs. She did this not menacingly, but as an honest display, so that I might know her now for what she was. Also, so that she might tear her own skin for me, to drink, reopen the wound at her wrist. There were no words spoken, none were needed. It was then that I truly understood. It wasn't as ghastly as I might have thought it should be. It was just like puzzle pieces fell into place, and I understood. She made the tear and I drank without hesitation, it just seemed right somehow, that I should.

When I was done, she drank from me again, and left me severely weakened and empty. It was almost painful to feel the lack of blood within me, although I didn't think that I should die. It wasn't the heavy grogginess that I'd felt when life had been truly slipping from me before, but I knew that I *needed* the blood within her. I was positively desperate for it. She had paused for rest before she would open her vein for me, and I became impatient. Before I could even recognize what was happening, I began to change myself. I felt a sudden fierce ache in my upper jaw and my eyesight grew blurry.

I felt a flash of pain as my jaw exercised its new hinge. It moved for my new fangs to become exposed. The next thing I knew, my gums were tearing to allow new hollow slivers of sharpened bone to come through, and my fangs extended. Then I became terribly disoriented because the colors of the room seemed to suddenly shift, and Maribeth turned blue."

Felicity had been listening with an almost cringing sort of revulsion. Cain almost had the impression that she *felt she ought to* be disgusted, more than she actually was, but this clearly caught her by surprise. She forgot to be disdainful and sat forward with clear curiosity. *"Blue?"*

Cain smiled. "My eyes, they changed. We see heat, and blood, when in our vampire state. I'm sure you've seen such things in movies, or on television, heat vision cameras or whatever, but it's much clearer than that. The details don't suffer nearly as much. I could still perfectly see the expression upon her face. I could count every eyelash if I'd a mind too. They were just the wrong color. Very disorienting as you can imagine.

Maribeth's body was outwardly dead, cold, and so I saw her in blues and greens, but the blood within her stood out with a strong deep red color that beckoned me to come for it. It was as though I could see nothing else. At her throat was a strong thick band of it, just beneath the skin, and I pulled her to me, thinking of nothing but drinking it.

As my fangs touched and then broke through her skin, sliding through her flesh so easily, all I could think was how wonderful it was, that she needn't open the way for me any longer. And so... I was reborn a vampire. All because a woman asked me if I loved her and I was fool enough to say yes.

To be perfectly honest, I don't believe changing me had been her original intent. I don't know exactly what happened to her the night she'd disappeared. She never would speak of it. That remains her story to tell. I don't know how or why the old man changed her, or how it was that she came to be alone after, but alone she was, and just like myself at the time, I think the prospect of being alone terrified her. I believe she came to look for me, only because she knew not to whom else she would turn.

She wanted to see me, to show me and make me understand what had happened to her. I don't think she meant to harm me, but when I pulled her to me and held her the way that I did... I had kissed her very throat. I don't know how much she understood of what she was. I don't believe the one who made her had been much of a teacher. I know that later on, all that we learned of what we had become, we discovered together.

The temptation to drink from me must have overwhelmed her. When she did pull away, she must have been horrified by what she'd done. Do you have any idea how hard it must have been for her to leave me breathing at all? Of course you don't! The will she must have possessed to stop herself...

Anyway, she had taken me to the place she herself must have hidden by day. I can hardly comprehend the strength of will and determination that it must have taken for her to carry or drag me there. I am not a light man and she herself was surely not a woman accustomed to such work, but she knew that we needed to go someplace where we would remain unobserved.

When she saw that I would die, she did the only thing she knew that would save me. She did that which had been done to her, when she herself had faced death, but only after I answered her question. Did I love her? Only if I truly loved her could I forgive her. Only if I loved her, could she feel justified in keeping me with her, instead of letting me go."

Cain gave Felicity a mischievous grin. "I often wonder what she would have done if I'd said no. I very easily could have you know, and Maribeth is not one to take such things lightly. She has a passionate nature and a wicked temper. I've a distinct feeling that I would not be here right now, had my answer not been to her liking. She does rather tend to take things to extremes. Even now, I'm unsure at times, whether she will fly at me in a rage or smother me with her affections."

Felicity's smile of amusement dropped and the narration of his story seemed to come to a screeching halt. *"Even now?"*

"Yes. She hasn't changed much, if anything she's gotten worse."

"She's still alive?" Felicity seemed very distraught at the prospect.

Cain smiled. "Well, not technically, but she's around." He furrowed his brow at her confusion. "We're *immortal* luv, remember? Those of us smart enough to stay out of harm's path anyway."

Felicity shook her head a little, as though trying to dislodge her previous thoughts. "I know, I just... I assumed that something had... happened to her. Where is she?"

Now Cain's grin broadened. Felicity looked as though she expected Cain to shout 'behind you!' and have a good laugh as Mari attacked her. "Nevada I think," he answered truthfully. "Last I saw her, she'd quite a spread there, out in the desert, just outside 'Vegas. Fancy's herself a showgirl now and again. She always was one to want attention.

Of course, that was back in '74... or maybe it was '73. Early seventies anyway. She may have moved again by now. We do that, move about. It's never smart to stay anyplace for too long, no matter how fond of it you are." Felicity was quite openly very relieved. She seemed to have worried that he'd still been seeing her or something. "We don't keep in touch. Even when I saw her last, it was by chance. I only stayed the weekend." He added in a confidential whisper, "We don't really get along."

Felicity's face showed seeming understanding. "Oh, because of what she did to you."

"Oh, heaven's no!" Felicity still didn't get it. She saw Mari's changing him as some detestable act of malice. "Not at all! I bear her no ill will! She simply lives differently than I do. It makes it very hard for me to be around her, you know?"

Now true understanding came over her face and Felicity turned a bit pale. "Oh," she muttered. With a start, she suddenly looked down at her watch. Cain couldn't read it from his angle, but he knew that dawn was not far off. He'd been talking all night. She sat up straighter and took the last sip of wine from her glass. "Well, not quite the ending that I was expecting, but I'm glad that you felt you could tell me." She sounded very businesslike and began to put things back into the picnic basket, to prepare to leave.

He almost let her. He watched her begin to clear their things. She stood and brushed off her pants and ran her fingers through her hair. "Wait." She stopped and looked at him, expectantly. "There's more," he said quietly.

"I'm sure there is," she said with a smile. "But it's late. My dad's coming for me in the morning and I have to pack and stuff. You can tell me the rest when I get back."

"I'll see you Sunday then?"

"Sorry, three day weekend. I won't be getting in until late Monday night. I'll see you Tuesday. I'll come to you at sunset and you can take me out for a birthday dinner. Didn't you say you wanted to take me out for a 'real dinner' sometime?"

He smiled a little. "Yes, I did."

"Then it's a date. We'll talk more then, 'kay?"

Again, he almost accepted that. He almost let it go, but no, he had to do this now, and do it right. She deserved to know. She would be away from him for three nights. Her mark would be gone, and she would have time to think. She should know everything now. It was only fair. "No, it's not. I'll keep it brief, but I want you to know... now." She looked a bit shaken by his abrupt seriousness. She sat. "I've killed..." he began haltingly.

She gave him a little smile of understanding. "I know."

"Not just Charles, but others as well."

She took a deep breath, and sighed. "I kind of figured. You were turned into a creature that survives on blood. I assumed there'd been a few deaths on your hands before you figured out... well, how not to."

"No, you don't understand. It's not just a few."

He faced a straight stare. "How many?"

He shook his head. "I don't know."

"Ten? Twenty?...A hundred?"

He looked at the ground for a moment. "Do you remember when you were trying to estimate how many women I've bedded?" She blushed a bit at the memory of that conversation, but then just as quickly paled. "I've killed more than I've loved. Of that I'm sure."

"*Thousands?* You've killed thousands of people?"

"I drank their blood, all of it... and took their lives away. Maribeth and I together, we were like a plague. We left a wake of death behind, wherever we would go. Here, then overseas. We took back the Manor. We lived as horrid demons thriving on the blood of the humans all around us without thought or care for mercy or morality. When we were in danger of discovery we crossed the sea yet again, but still, we brought death with us like a silent companion. Every night of my life, for almost half a century, someone died... because of me."

She just stared at him for a very long time, searching his face as though she could find evidence that what he said was untrue. Finally, she seemed simply to accept it. "I knew. I knew that it had to be. I knew that in the beginning, you had to have killed to survive. For... fifty years? But that means for almost three hundred years, you haven't, right? You were only doing what you thought you had to. You don't hurt people anymore, right? It's okay... it's okay, I can accept that."

She was trying to convince herself. He knew how badly she wanted to. He knew that she would probably tell herself almost anything at this point, just to try and redeem him in her eyes.

He couldn't accept that. It wasn't real to her. "No, you don't understand. When you say 'they died, you killed them', those are just words.

You weren't there. You don't know. It was *real*. They were *people*. There were… bodies.

You say that I was only doing what I needed to survive. I suppose I did believe that, but I was a predator, and my prey… were mostly young girls; *girls like you*." He was forced to stop for a moment as he actually shocked himself into realizing just how like his old patterns his courtship with Felicity had been. Of course, it was drawn out over weeks instead of one whirlwind night, but still.

No, Felicity was certainly different. He really did love her. In fact, he loved her enough to know that he only wanted her to be happy. He wanted what was truly best for her. That was why this had to end… now. He spoke in a voice that trembled with the desperation of trying to make her understand. "Lovely young women, *so* like you, in the blush of youth, just starting their lives, full of hopes and expectations.

I would charm them, tell them of all the ways in which they were special. I would dance with them, talk with them, sometimes I even… loved them, their bodies anyway. But in the end, whether I bedded them or not, 'twas my deadly kiss they did receive, and it would end their lives.

I told myself it was a necessary evil. That I surely had a fixed place in the scheme of things in the world. God would not suffer me to live if it were not His will. I gave myself leave to prey upon others, night after night, after night.

And each night, when it was finished, I would be left with nothing but an empty shell of a girl. Pale and unmoving, never to smile, or laugh, or see her family again. And always before I left them, I would place upon their dead cold lips, a last parting kiss. I would thank them with a kiss, that they should have given their blood so that I might survive.

I was a monster. It is two hundred and seventy one years since I have killed someone for my thirst. That's a very long time. And yet, I feel a monster still. All of those lives, gone. For what? For me? There is no possible act more selfish or deplorable. Is it redeemable to human eyes? As I speak to you now, I come to realize something that I have known all along, although at times I do choose to forget. It is not.

There was more, things I'd meant for you to know, but what's the point? What I have told so far is more than enough to make us both realize that you would do far better in life without me.

I want to thank you, for being here for me, for giving me a chance to let it out. I've kept these things within me for so long, with no one to tell; no one with a human heart anyway, but I was selfish yet again, in ever thinking that you should try to forgive these things. It's terribly unfair. The only true forgiveness that I can hope to expect is through the Lord now. Who else can truly understand, accept and forgive the burden of *my* sins? Could a young human girl? How horribly wrong of me to lay this on you!

Felicity... the love that I have felt for you, and love it is; it has given me a peace that you cannot know. Happiness, to warm this dead heart of mine, something that I had long forgotten. Again, I thank you for that. And I want you to know that I expect nothing more.

I'm going to take you home now. And if you don't mind my asking... If I might beg you to allow me one more selfish act, well... I'd like to ask that you say nothing else. My story is finished. I don't want to speak of these things any longer. There is nothing you might say or do to try and comfort me. Anything you might try to utter, in understanding or acceptance... well, we both know that they cannot help. And if you might have something more harsh to tell me... well I can't say that I'd really like to hear that either, although I can't exactly stop you if you've a mind to tell me.

There's not much time left before dawn. I just want to see you home safely. I will return you, whole and sound, to your life, to your rightful place in the world, where I will not seek you again. At least I can do that much."

He stared into her tear-filled eyes for a moment, but it really was only a token pause. He wanted to be gone. He wanted truly to run from her, but he could not be *that* selfish. He gathered the rest of their things as quickly as he could. She stepped away from their ground cover and stood unmoving upon the grass, saying nothing. He was so grateful for that, that he was terrified to even look at her again, lest she speak.

Finally, after what seemed an interminable amount of time, he was ready to mount the bike. She got on behind him, silently and he sped off, to return her home... to her life.

Chapter 12 - Speechless

Felicity

Dorm steps
Just before sunrise
Saturday morning

She was speechless...

Felicity had sat and stared at him with mind numbing bewilderment as he finished his descriptions for her. Then she had stood, moved aside and stared some more, as he shoved the rest of their things into the basket and strapped it to the bike. In mute shock, she was staring at this man that she'd thought she knew, trying to figure out how all of his traits and features could come together to form a person who could have done those things.

Two hundred and seventy one years was a very long time. Did that make any difference? Did it matter at all? It's not as though they could ever be *un*-done. He'd had time to change, time to repent, time to become someone new, someone who would never repeat such horrid acts.

He was right. There was absolutely nothing she could say. She climbed onto the motorcycle and let him drive her home. When they reached the dorms and she dismounted the bike, she realized that she hadn't even thought to put on her helmet. It was still strapped to the back. She stood and stared at it.

He turned and she actually flinched. She hadn't meant to, but she did. He must have seen it, but he wasn't even turning towards her. He was getting her comforter off the back. He thrust it out to her without even looking. It wasn't done *un*-gently but she realized that he was trying to get rid of her as quickly as possible. From what she could see of his eyes, they looked moist and blood shot.

She awkwardly took the bundle into her arms and backed up a step for him to leave. He just sat there at first, staring at the handlebars. She realized that he was waiting to see her safely inside. He didn't want to face her, but was waiting to see her climb the steps to the door with his peripheral vision. She just stood there. She wasn't sure why, but she felt as though she wanted to force him to look at her. She needed to see his face again.

It was obvious that he almost wanted to wait her out. He didn't want to give in and face her, but time was on her side. The dawn was coming fast and he couldn't wait. Finally, he gave her a glance with undisguised guilt and self-loathing in his eyes.

She wasn't ready to leave. She opened her mouth, although she'd no idea what she'd say. He didn't give her the chance. Her revved the cycle to cover any words, and sped away. She watched his back recede until he was lost to her view.

She was still standing there a few minutes later, when she recognized the coming sun. A warm glow began to creep above the horizon in the distance, although all around her, the world was still covered in the odd blue and purple shadows of the night. He hadn't much time. She hoped he'd be alright. She wasn't really worried though. He was riding away from the dawn, shielded by ridges and trees. With the speed in which he'd left, it wouldn't take him long to be home.

She let herself wait to be bathed in the golden light of the sun for a moment, before she fled inside, to her room. She collapsed unthinking onto the bed and hoped for sleep to come quickly.

Once again, her father was a bit disgruntled to find that she was not nearly ready for him when he arrived. At least this time she was dressed. Of course, it was still from the night before, but he didn't know that. She didn't think it wise to explain that he should wait while she changed. She simply gathered her things for the weekend, and they left for home.

The ride took over an hour. She spent most of it staring out the window, unable to engage in pleasant conversation, or give detailed answers to her father's few probing questions. She told him she'd been up studying most of the night, big test on Tuesday. She felt bad to lie, but at least it explained why she was so tired, in a way that her parents would accept without question.

By the time that they actually did arrive home, she was able to put on a joyful face to greet her mom and listen to the latest family news. Her younger brothers made teasing remarks about her new freedom and dorm life. She responded with a few general comments about school and work to satisfy curiosity, and then went to her room for a nap.

Sleep would not come. She was still exhausted, but Cain's story in her mind would not let her rest. She retold the entire tale in her head. Carefully trying to remember and think through each part, each experience, as if she were him. What would she have done? His life before, although certainly not something that she could entirely approve of, she could accept. His affair with Maribeth, even the death of his brother, although awful events in and of themselves, she could live with those things. But what had come after...

He was not human any longer at that point. The things that he had done, the *way* in which he had done them, had to have been largely driven by instinct. She had to believe that, but was that only a convenient excuse? Surely, there was more to know, of how he'd lived, and the thoughts he'd had. It had to have been frightening and strange for him to discover what he truly was. Had he a choice? Surely he hadn't *enjoyed* killing all those people... No matter what he had felt then, he certainly agonized over it now. What would she have done in his position? Driven to distraction, desperation, by a thirst... for human blood. She had no clue.

She wanted to ask him how he had discovered the way in which he could live without surrounding himself with death. How had he learned to live without killing? She forced herself to look at a fact that she had deliberately kept from her conscious mind... She did not really *know* how he lived now.

Of all her questions and curiosities, that was the single most important answer that she never did seek to find. She'd blocked the question from her mind. She was afraid to know. When he had told her that he was giving her 'free reign', to 'ask him anything', the time had been perfect. She knew she should have asked him then, but she'd pushed the question from her thoughts out of fear. She'd queried him about his hair of all things instead.

The memory of the vision she'd had in the movie theater kept haunting her, the one in which she pictured him choosing victims from amongst anxious young girls like herself. Allie's words came back to her also. 'He's drinkin' somethin', he needs it'. The most likely explanation was that he drank from others, as he'd drunk from her, without hurting them. She did not know what he did or where he went before he came to her each night, or after. It seemed very likely that his thirst was satisfied by others.

Like the night he'd left she and Ben to go to Venus. She had not wanted to go. At the time, she was hesitant to see how he might react to Sindy, if she was there, but she had also worried that perhaps he had gone there planning to find another girl to dance with; a human girl whom he would then bring outside to kiss goodnight, and drink from. It seemed the obvious conclusion. He had all night, every night, until the wee hours of the morning to spend in bars and dance clubs. Someone as handsome and charming as Cain, would not have much difficulty in finding someone to take outside for a moment alone.

The cup; her one clue that she had clung to. When she had gone to his home, to speak to him about Ben, she had observed him drinking from a cup. It had been blood. It had to have been. He had made it quite clear that it was not coffee, and she had known that it was blood, but from where? Where could he get blood like that, to drink from a cup?

All she could think of was the hospital. They asked for people to donate blood all the time. In fact, her own school had just sponsored a blood drive last week. Did he have some sort of arrangement with someone, a worker perhaps? Did he purchase blood from some hospital employee in secret, or steal it even? Murderer or not, she could not picture the Cain that she knew, stealing anything.

It remained a mystery, but at least that idea sat better with her than the thought of him getting blood from another person directly. Would she *ever* know? She wasn't sure that she should see him again, but was terrified by the idea that she might not have the chance. She was horribly afraid that she would return to school to find that he was gone. What if he cleared out and left, disappeared, never to be seen again?

She was distraught over the things that he had revealed, but she was not ready to just let him go, not like this. Surely she needed time to think, and maybe she would decide that she never could look at him fondly again, but she didn't think so, and she didn't want him to take the matter from her hands.

She hoped that he would be there, upon her return. She wasn't frightened of him at all. Even knowing what he had done, she just could not believe that he would ever hurt *her*. Even knowing that there were many young girls, much like herself who had been deceived by him, she was unafraid. He *had* changed. It might seem unreasonable to anyone else that she should believe it, but she did. She knew that he had. He was *not* that monster anymore. She just wished she knew what had changed him so much, why his life had so totally turned around, into something that seemed selfless and good?

Was it a gradual change, or had something happened to reorder his life with sudden abruptness? There was a word for that... they'd just discussed it in English class. Epiphany. Yes, had it been that way? Had he experienced an epiphany, a sudden flash of insight, an almost religious revealing of another way of life?

He did behave as though he had a great belief and respect for God, like people you sometimes read about, who suffered near death experiences and then vowed to change their ways. Well, she supposed you couldn't get much nearer to death than Cain.

Christian; she felt the name suited him better now than ever. Why hadn't he taken it back? She almost instantly knew. The name 'Cain' was a reminder, to keep himself in check and be sure that he never sought to forget his past. It would be just like him, to force himself to face it every time he gave someone his name.

Felicity was unsure just how long she lay there, but it seemed suddenly that her mom was at the door, suggesting that she should get ready for guests soon, for dinner. Perhaps she'd like to shower and change? Her mom made the request lightly, but Felicity realized that the clothing she wore *was* terribly rumpled. She hadn't even really brushed her hair.

Her aunt and uncle were coming for dinner with her cousins, her older brother Eddie had just arrived home from his college for the weekend, and her mother announced, they were also expecting a surprise guest. After a moments irrational thought, that perhaps it was someone that she knew from school, she realized who it had to be. Deidre, finally! Her mother confirmed that it was so. Her best high school friend would be joining them for dinner to celebrate her birthday. She quickly got up to shower and change.

~~~~~~~~~~~~~~~~~~~~~~~~~~~~~~~~~~

Deidre didn't arrive until just before dinner, so they hadn't any private time to talk. Felicity's best friend of years past looked a little different than when they'd been together last. She still kept her dark hair in a short and sassy bob, but she had on way too much blue eye shadow and big gold hoop earrings. She was a little shorter than but nearly the same build as Felicity, usually somewhere between a size 12 and 14. Usually that was nice because they could share clothes, but Felicity didn't think that she would ever want to borrow tonight's ensemble. Deidre wore a pair of tight and really low-waisted hip-hugger jeans that did nothing to flatter her figure. She had paired them with a short satiny blue shirt that Felicity thought had to have been originally intended to be some sort of petite negligee. A change of scenery seemed to have changed Deidre some, but Felicity was glad to see her old friend again.

Felicity had thought that she would be very comforted to be at home, surrounded by friends and family. Familiar and ordinary things and people should be reassuring after spending all of her time talking about, fighting with and trying not to fall in love with vampires. Now that she had become more involved with Cain, she hadn't really wanted to spend time away from him, but the last month had been so unusual that she'd begun to think that it might be nice to have some time to be normal again.

It wasn't. It didn't seem comforting or a relief. It seemed boring and mundane, a waste of precious time. It just felt like there were more important things in her life to be focusing on. Even seeing Deidre, which she had waited for as though the girl could solve all of her problems, was a bit of a letdown. She and Dee were still good friends, and she was very glad to see her, but it seemed like her friend was very caught up in such superficial stuff. Dee wanted to know what the girls in Felicity's college were wearing, and what kind of music people around her were listening to; questions that Felicity could hardly even answer, as she hadn't really paid any attention to such things.

They hadn't much time to talk alone yet, but she could hardly imagine trying to confide in Dee, the real happenings in her life these days. She could just picture how it would be received, with odd looks, and then excited whispers and acknowledgement. It would be accepted as though Felicity were telling some sort of ghost story, the way that people claimed to believe in things like telepathy and paranormal experience, with an air of 'jump on the band-wagon' fervor and awe. They didn't *really* believe did they? It was all in fun. It always seemed to Felicity that those same people would probably want nothing but to get as far away as possible, if ever they were really faced with something supernatural.

Maybe Deidre would truly believe. She should give her the benefit of the doubt. Although most likely, her friend would be thinking that Felicity had lost her mind. Felicity did want to talk about Cain, though. Dee's opinion had always meant so much to Felicity in the past. Maybe she would just... leave out a few things. She'd have to feel it out.

After dinner came birthday presents. Her aunt and uncle gave her a cell phone, with her bills paid for the first three months. She thanked them profusely. At least she wouldn't have to sit out on the payphones anymore. Deidre had given her a dress, which actually did seem to suit her perfectly. It was a beautiful tie-dyed silk halter dress done in shades of blue and green. Felicity worried that it must have cost a fortune, but Deidre assured her that she'd bought it with a friend's employee discount and knew it would look gorgeous on her.

Lastly, her parents informed her that their gift waited outside. She dutifully followed them out front, unsure what to expect. When she saw it, she was happy, relieved and disappointed, all at the same time.

It was a car! She would finally have her own car! It wasn't really much to look at, but it was a car all the same. That meant that she would no longer have to worry about being accosted on the way home from work anymore, but that also meant that Cain would have no reason to escort her home... if he were even still around when she got back, but still, how could she not be excited? It was a car!

It was blue, but faded and a little dented on the passenger door, but for a first car, she couldn't really have expected much better. At least she didn't have to worry overly much about scratching the paint and stuff. Her dad informed her that it was a 1987 Ford Mustang, under his name and insurance, but it *was* really hers. He rode along in the back as she and Deidre took it for a ride. At least the driver's license in her wallet didn't seem so useless anymore. She'd taken driver's ed., and then agonized over and passed her road test, just to be told by her parents that they couldn't buy her a car just yet. College was expensive enough. It had been kind of a letdown.

Finally, they returned to the house for birthday cake and coffee, after which she and Deidre retreated to the kitchen to tackle the mound of dishes in the sink. Over the years, she and Deidre had eaten over each other's houses pretty often. Doing the dishes together was sort of a long-standing tradition. At least they'd have a chance to talk.

Felicity took up her station by the drain board to dry... whoever's house it was always dried - they knew where everything should be put away. Dee got started in the sink, with a smile. "See, it's just like we never left."

Felicity tried to smile back, but couldn't help but feel a little disappointed and annoyed that they hadn't spoken in so long. "I guess... but, I missed you."

Deidre seemed to realize the faux pas. "Oh, I totally missed you too! I'm sorry that I didn't write like I said I would, or return your phone call. I've just been real busy, what with classes and pledging and parties and stuff."

"Oh, did you get into that sorority that you wanted?"

"Yeah! It's so great! The sisters are really nice, and it's like instant popularity... especially with the frat boys! We get invited to parties like every other night! Total party school, my grades are gonna suck." Felicity smiled and gestured towards the running water in the sink, Deidre hadn't washed anything yet. She dutifully picked up a dinner plate to be scrubbed.

"So are you dating any of these frat boys?" Felicity asked.

"Not yet, but I do have a few prospects definitely worthy of a future 'maybe'. How about you? I notice you didn't bring a cute college boy home for dinner. Nobody special, huh?"

Felicity took the first plate to be dried and decided that she just *had* to talk about Cain. How could she not? "Well, I wouldn't exactly say that..."

Of course, Deidre immediately jumped for the information. "You've been holding out on me? Spill it!"

"Well, he doesn't go to college, and I definitely wouldn't call him a *boy*," Felicity informed her.

"Ooo, *all man*, I like it! So, how come he's not in college? Does he work with you?" Deidre asked.

"No, he's just...kind of *beyond* college," Felicity answered vaguely.

Deidre turned from the sink with a disappointed grimace. "He's *old?*"

"He's not *that* old." Felicity said defensively. "Well, he doesn't *look* old."

"Just how old is he?" Deidre asked skeptically.

"Like, Twenty seven...and he doesn't even look it," Felicity assured her.

"I guess that's okay," Dee said hesitantly.

"Glad you approve," Felicity answered with a chuckle.

"What's his name?" Deidre asked.

Felicity hesitated for a moment. "Cain."

"Cane? Like a stick?" Dee questioned with a raised brow.

Felicity rolled her eyes. "No, with an 'i'."

"Oh, Cain... Different, kind of sexy. I like it," Deidre decided.

All right, if she were going to mention him, she might as well try and get some insight. She wouldn't say anything incriminating, but she did want Deidre's opinion. "Dee, do you still think that people can't change?"

Deidre handed her the next dish with slumped shoulders and a look of disappointment. "He needs to change?"

"No! He already has. He's kind of got a...past," Felicity confessed.

"Who doesn't?" Dee asked with a smile.

"No, this is serious. Serious stuff," Felicity told her.

"Former bad boy huh?"

"To say the least," Felicity responded quietly, as she put away the plate she'd been drying.

"Well... *how* bad? What'd he do?"

No, definitely not going there! "I don't really want to get into specifics..." Felicity began.

Dee faced her again. "It's *that* bad? How long ago are we talkin' here?"

"Oh, ancient history," Felicity said with quick assurance. "Really ancient."

"That's good. Do *you* believe that he's changed?"

Felicity thought about it for a moment. "Totally."

Deidre did not seem entirely convinced. "Well, *I* never trust guys like that, but *I've* been known to be wrong...a lot. Is it something that's gonna keep comin' up, like...haunt your future, long term?"

Felicity sighed. "That's another obstacle. I don't really think long term commitment is going to be an option."

"Why? What, is he skittish?" Dee asked.

Felicity stifled a laugh. "No, not at all. It's not his fault, it's just... He's kind of... he's got this... disease."

"Oh my God, he's dying?" Dee asked incredulously.

"No! He's not going to die from it or anything. It's not even a disease, really. It's more of a condition. Like an allergy," she added lamely.

"What's he allergic to?" Deidre asked.

"...Sunlight," Felicity supplied haltingly.

Deidre's mouth fell open in shock. "Oh wow, I've heard of that!"

"You have?" That was the last thing Felicity had expected to hear.

"Yeah, on the Discovery channel. It's really rare. These people have a deficiency, an absence of pigment or melanin or something in their skin. If they go outside in the sun, they get like instant skin cancer, so they only go out at night."

Okay, close enough. "Wow. Yeah, that sounds pretty accurate."

Deidre scrunched up her nose and asked hesitantly, "He's not like...albino or anything, is he?"

Felicity laughed. "No, he's not albino, and it's not like he's sick or anything. He just has to be careful about some stuff. He's got this drink, like... medication that he has to take every day. Then he's fine."

Her friend looked thoughtful as she washed another dish. "Well, I guess you could work around that, it's do-able. Still, it might be kind of weird, once you have kids and stuff."

"Oh, he can't have kids."

Dee gave her the finished dish and turned to face her disapprovingly. "Alright, wait a minute. This guy's got such a bad past that you can't even tell me about it, he's *old*, he can't go out in the sunlight *and* he can't have kids? You're not givin' me much to work with here, Felicity."

It didn't sound very appealing did it? "I was just getting all the bad stuff out of the way first. There's good stuff too!"

"I should hope so. Is he *hot* at least? I mean, *he'd have to be!*" she said, turning back to the sink.

"Oh yeah! *Very* hot," Felicity assured her.

"Describe..." Deidre demanded.

Felicity closed her eyes for a minute, picturing Cain in her mind, not that it was a difficult image to call up. She felt as though she knew every line of his face by heart. "He's got long, sandy, light brown hair."

"How long? Like, Fabio?" Deidre asked.

"No! More like, surfer dude...except, no tan," Felicity added.

Dee laughed. "Right."

"Shoulder length, I guess, in layers. Oh, and his eyes... Deidre, his eyes are the deepest, clearest blue, like the Caribbean sea."

"Yeah, yeah. People always say that."

Felicity looked at her in earnest. "No, *really*. I could drown."

"Oh my God, you're *drowning?*" Dee exclaimed.

"Oh yeah. He is so sweet..." Felicity said dreamily.

"Wait, wait. We're not up to sweet yet. More with the description," Dee interrupted her.

Felicity smiled again. "Um, well...his face is so gentle and disarming, like you would trust him with your life, really. He's got these little lines around his eyes that make him seem so approachable and understanding. Like laugh lines I guess you'd call them."

"Wrinkles. I call them wrinkles," Deidre said with distaste.

"*They are not!* Would you stop? He does not look old at all, I swear! What else? He's tall. Not very tall, but taller than me. Close to six feet, maybe."

"Okay, body?" Dee asked.

Felicity felt her cheeks heating as she couldn't help smiling. "Nice...*very* nice, broad shoulders, good strong build. Not heavy, but definitely not skinny either. I mean, he's muscular, but not like a body builder or anything."

"That's good. Trust me; never date a guy who loves his weight bench more than you," Dee warned her.

"No weight bench. He's clean shaven and *so* good looking..."

"Mmmm. Okay, now we're up to sweet. Continue."

"Oh, he's kind and quiet, but not shy. He's got this... presence. Like he doesn't even have to say a word, but when he walks into the room, everyone else might as well be invisible! He's so commanding and confident, but he's not like, haughty or arrogant or anything. He's just sweet and unassuming and sooo *sexy!*"

"Felicity! You are *so* smitten! I've never heard you talk like this about anybody before. Usually I'm the one gushing, and then the guy turns out to be a total loser."

"Trust me; he's got his faults, but loser he is not. Oh and Deidre, he is so romantic!"

Dee rolled her eyes. "*Romantic?* Guys are only romantic in the movies. I need an example. Like, where did you go on your last date?"

Felicity thought about how excited and impressed she had been by his thoughtful planning, that first night of their picnic. "The park."

"Cheap," Dee pronounced.

"He is not cheap! In fact, he's got money. Like, independently wealthy – money," Felicity informed her.

Dee stopped washing to look at Felicity in disbelief. "Are you kidding?"

She just shook her head and smiled. "But he doesn't like to show it off at all, which is cool. And the park was very romantic! It was kind of a picnic, at night. Candlelight, wine and cheese, by a waterfall! Oh, and that's not all. One night, he came to my window...on the second floor! It was like Romeo and Juliet! Only he told me that I was even more beautiful than *Juliet!*"

"He actually said that?" Dee asked.

Now Felicity tried not to smirk at Dee's skepticism as she described the occasion. "Not quite in those words. I think he said, 'Even *her* description pales compared to *my* beauty, because I am far lovelier than anything that Shakespeare ever dreamed of.'"

Dee's mouth fell open, her half-washed dish held under the water, forgotten in her hands. "Holy shit."

Felicity laughed with a nod. "You should hear it in an English accent."

"Hold up...he's *British?*" Deidre demanded.

"Yeah, didn't I mention?" Felicity asked.

"No!" Deidre gave her a playful shove with her shoulder, and then handed her a dish. "You should have told me that first! Guys get extra points for being European! Maybe even enough to see past all that other stuff. Are you sure this guy's for real? I mean, it sounds kind of...James Bond. Romantic British guy with a secret past that only comes out at night? It's a little much to swallow. 'Lovelier than Juliet?' Who talks like that?"

"I know, but he's so sincere, really. It doesn't come off as fake at all." She put away the dish she held and then retrieved the last pot off of the stove. "And he's been so honest. He's told me all about his past and everything, so I'd know just what I was getting into." She stood there in silence for a minute watching Dee wash the final pot. As much as Cain's past bothered her, she felt almost as though it was something that he had done in a past life. He obviously had spent the rest of his life trying to make up for it. He was a different person now. A person that Felicity could not just walk away from, no matter how stupid it might seem for her to stay.

She took the pot to be dried and stared at the floor as she turned it over in her hands with the dishcloth. After a moment, she came to realize that her friend was standing there watching her with concern. "Deidre... I don't know what to do. I don't know if I can really have any kind of future with this guy, but I am really falling for him... hard. And he *so* turns me on, like no one ever has. Every time he touches me, I just...."

Deidre quickly glanced around to be sure they were alone and whispered fiercely, "*Felicity!* Have you slept with him?"

"Not yet." Felicity put the pot away. "Come on...my room."

They quickly climbed the stairs and secluded themselves in her room, far from parental ears. They both kicked off their shoes and sat cross-legged on Felicity's bed. Deidre shook her head and smiled. "Well, losing virginity is not a topic *I've* dealt with in a while, but oh wow."

"I know. What do I do? This is probably going nowhere, but I can't help it. Whenever we're together, it's like... overwhelming."

"You're still on birth control right? I know you said he can't have kids, but better safe than sorry." She smiled as Felicity nodded yes. "I told you having irregular periods would come in handy one day! Was I right or what? Convince your mom to take you to the gynecologist to get birth control pills - just to regulate, while you're still young. Now that you're older, it's already in place and it's not even an issue. I'm brilliant!"

Felicity just smiled. Getting pregnant was one of the very few concerns that she did *not* have at the moment. "I shouldn't even be considering. He even acts like it wouldn't be right. I mean, he definitely would like to, but then he pushes me away. He thinks that he's no good for me. He's probably right, but I care about him so much and I'm so attracted to him. I can't just walk away."

Deidre smiled. "Well the sorority sisters have a test, to determine worthiness. They say if you're going to sleep with a guy, he'd better be a DAMN good man. It's one of those acronym things you use to remember stuff. Check this out:

D -	is for 'discreet'. The guy's gotta be, you don't want him going all public with it the next day like a jerk.
A -	is for 'attractive'. Sounds like you've got no problem there.
M -	is called the 'mourn' factor. Just how into you is the guy? If you left him, would he mourn the loss, or just move on? and...
N -	is for 'no regrets'. If you sleep with him and then the relationship doesn't work out, will you wish you hadn't? Of course you hope the guy sticks around, but if you're going to do it, you should be able to appreciate the experience for itself, with no regrets.

Not exactly, the kind of standards your mom might appreciate, but... what do you think? Is Cain a DAMN good man?"

"Well, by those standards, yeah. I guess he is," Felicity said.

"Really?!" Dee asked.

"Sure he is. I mean, 'discreet' isn't even a question, neither is 'attractive'. As far as the 'mourn factor' goes... sometimes it's almost like he's in mourning already, in thinking that he shouldn't be with me. I don't know, we left things kind of weird yesterday, but I think that we'd both feel devastated if we didn't see each other again."

"What about the whole no regrets things though? If you really don't think you have a future with this guy... I mean, this is not your standard situation. We are talking about your *first time*. I don't know if the whole 'DAMN' thing really applies. It's more like a joke than a real determination anyway. Would you really have no regrets?"

Felicity knew it was the kind of thing she should probably consider more carefully, but there was really no question in her mind at this point. "You know, I don't think I'd regret it in the least. Even if I never saw him again, I know how much he cares about me, I just know it. And I know that it would be an incredible experience unlike anything else. Which *could* be a drawback when you think about it. If I did sleep with him, I've got the feeling he'd leave some pretty difficult shoes for any other guy to fill."

"Felicity! I can't even believe you are talking like this! It's so unlike you! Just *how* far have you gone with this guy?" Dee asked.

Felicity laughed. "We haven't *done* anything really. It's kind of hard to explain, but when he kisses me... it's like, magic," Felicity described.

"*Magic* kisses? I've never had magic kisses," she said poutingly. "The guys I kiss are always too busy trying to figure out how to unhook my bra to concentrate on *magic* kisses. So when are you going to see him again?"

"That's just it. I don't know. I saw him last night, well... this morning. We spent the whole night talking and... well, I guess we kind of broke up."

"What?" Dee demanded.

"Well, he's so concerned about hurting me, with his past and everything. It's like he's trying to punish himself for things that he did so long ago, like he thinks I deserve someone better. He thinks that I should see him as this horrible person, and maybe I should, but I just don't," Felicity explained.

"Felicity, slow down. It's kind of hard for me to give you advice when I don't even know what you're talking about. Can't you tell me what he did? How bad could it be?" Deidre asked.

"It's bad. Really," Felicity admitted.

"Well, unless he's like a mass murderer or something, I don't see how it could be unredeemable," Deidre tried to assure her.

Felicity stared very hard at the flowers on her bedspread and didn't say anything. How was she going to explain this? Like she was going to try and tell Dee that it didn't count because he was a supernatural monster, being controlled by instinct at the time?

"Felicity? He didn't *kill* somebody... did he?" Felicity looked up, but couldn't quite keep the tears from her eyes, no matter how she tried. "Oh my God Felicity. He killed someone?" She didn't answer. "You have got to stay away from this guy. Do you hear me? This is not the kind of thing that you mess around with, no way. I don't care how charming, romantic or handsome he is, serial killers do not make good boyfriends! Have you gone insane?!"

"You don't understand, Dee. It wasn't really his fault. He's different now, it was so long ago!"

"He's twenty-seven Felicity, how long could it be? What'd he do it when he was ten?" Deidre asked sarcastically.

"Something like that. Look, the details don't matter. I truly believe in my heart that he is a good person. Don't you think a person deserves to be forgiven for past mistakes?" Felicity asked.

"Pretty big mistake! Besides what are you, his priest? Don't get yourself tangled up with someone like that. Even if he wouldn't hurt *you*, it can only lead to problems and heartache. Besides, you only know what this guy has told you himself right? How can you even know if it's the whole truth? I mean, I guess if he were going to lie, he wouldn't have told you at all, but still... Please Felicity, there are so many other guys in the world."

For the second time today, Felicity found herself speechless. Once again, she felt as though there was nothing she could really say. Nothing she could tell Deidre in Cain's defense was very likely to help. She certainly didn't think that trying to explain that he was a vampire was going to earn him any sympathy.

Her whole life she had always been so concerned about what other people thought, but this was different. No matter what Deidre, Ben or even Cain would say to try and dissuade her, she knew that she loved him. She *loved* him.

Felicity believed that the man he was *now* was worthy of her love and respect. She was in love with Cain and all else was secondary. Oh wow, isn't that exactly what Ashley had told her? Who would have thought she'd be following *Ashley's* advice?

She hadn't delusions of trying to spend the rest of her life with him... well not really. Silly fantasies like that did pass through her mind now and again, but she knew that in a practical sense they would probably not last, but Cain was a good man and she did love him. She wanted to be with him and why shouldn't he deserve to have the love and trust of someone who could accept him as he was?

Felicity looked at Deidre's face and had a terrifying thought. Deidre was going to tell her mother. Dee had been her friend since they were little kids. She could read every expression on the girls face with almost flawless certainty, and she just knew that Dee would be talking to Felicity's mom about this, if she could not handle it herself. That had to be prevented at all costs.

"I guess you're right. We didn't really have much of a future anyway, too complicated," Felicity agreed.

"I'm glad you've come back to earth. Find yourself a nice frat guy to hang out with. They're a little immature but at least their motives are usually pretty clear," Deidre told her.

"Yeah. You know, I probably won't see him again anyway. Like I said, we broke up. In fact, he was only in town temporarily. I got the feeling last night that he was going to leave soon. So I doubt I'll even bump into him again, now that it's over."

"That's good. You sounded pretty hung up this guy though, for someone you thought you'd never see again," Dee said skeptically.

"I know. I had these crazy ideas that I was going to try and go back early, convince him to stay or something, but I know that you're right. I should just let him go," Felicity said, carefully observing Dee's reaction.

"It's for the best," Deidre assured her.

She nodded her head and told Deidre not to worry about her. Felicity tried to pacify her friend as best she could, but knew in her heart that she had to go back to Cain. She could never leave things the way that he had. Deidre wouldn't be around for the rest of the weekend, she had stuff to do with her own family, but she did promise to try and keep in better touch. It wasn't long before Dee's mom came to pick her up and they said their goodbyes.

Felicity spent the rest of her time at home closed away in her room as much as possible. She thought about Cain and just what she would do when she got back to see him again. Maybe she could go back early and surprise him! She thought and planned and told her parents that she was studying for that test she'd mentioned. She hoped they wouldn't notice that she hadn't brought home any books.

Chapter 13 - Reality

Cain

Cain's bedroom
Monday night

Cain awoke with the sunset, stretched and smiled as he remembered the comforts and pleasures of the day before. Felicity was still sleeping, her naked body soft and warm against his cool skin. He reached his hand beneath the sheets to give her enticingly fully fleshed thigh a loving caress.

He looked up as another approached. It was Ashley, wearing nothing but a cross expression and a filmy negligee. He had spurned her advances and neglected her affections these past months. She was petulant and dissatisfied, but still she sorely longed for him. He gestured for her to join them in the bed, eager to be forgiven.

Felicity awoke as Ashley climbed into their love nest, but simply wriggled against him and gave his bare chest a quick kiss, unthreatened. She knew that the attentions of her body satisfied him well, but she could never hope to slake his thirst alone. His demands were too great, and so she was willing to share.

A sound at the stairway startled him at first, but then he remembered that he had no need for alarm. Ben was standing guard. It was Ben who came to him now, crossing the room in his self assured and prideful manner, but as he reached the bed, he knelt before his master.

The girls made room for Cain to lean towards Ben, as the boy tipped his chin to the side and upwards in an oft' practiced pose. He wanted Cain to drink, the venom his reward. Cain smiled as Ben closed his eyes and anxiously awaited Cain's bite. He would not be disappointed.

Cain's lips tasted the salt sweat and bitter aftershave of Ben's skin as his fangs pierced the flesh of the boy's throat. The scent of his body was so different from that of the girls', so strong and masculine. The blood that came rushing to his tongue was rich and sweet. Yes, this was why he kept Ben... the boy gave himself over, utterly subdued and eager to be dominated. It pleased him well.

The girls fought for space and snuggled closer to him, as drinking awakened and aroused his sleepy body and an erection came with the blood.

Cain awoke from the dream with a gasp, as the remembered taste of blood seemed to fill his mouth. He sat up in bed, alone of course. There were no pets beneath his sheets, no willing victim at his throat. Only his erection was real.

He threw back the covers and rose from the bed, disgusted with himself that he should long for such things, even in an unconscious state. No, these were his friends, not his slaves. He wanted nothing from them, not their bodies or their blood, only respect and friendship. He tried desperately to convince himself that it was true, although he probably did not deserve even that. He went to his refrigerator and prepared himself a drink, blood to quench his forbidden cravings and desires, blood to chase his dreams away.

Of course, Felicity was an exception. He *had* wanted *her* body, had he not? But that was different. He wanted her not as a pet, but as an equal. Her love, should be a willing gift, not a sacrifice. Was there a difference? It could not lead to anything real. Whether he let himself admit it or not, she would act as his pet in the end, wouldn't she?

Once physical play had been fully explored, blood play would be next. The rewards from such experiments would be so great, how could he resist? How could she? She knew what it was to feel his touch, when his mark was upon her. Once her body had been freely given, how could she not ask him to take her blood? The thrill of sex after marking was something that he had not enjoyed in so many decades. It was an exquisite experience, beyond description. He knew that once she was in his bed, she would come to greatly anticipate such pleasures. How could he deny her?

No. This train of thought needed to end, now. He had decided that Felicity should be left to her family and her life. He could offer her nothing towards her future. Physical pleasures amidst a euphoric, venom induced haze; these were false comforts and would eventually desert her. Then she would be left wasted and unable to carry on with her life, with nothing to look forward to but death at his hands. Whether it be death eternal or living death by his side, it was still an unacceptable end.

His relationship with her would end, now. He had spent the entire weekend secluded in his home and grieving the loss of his love. He knew it was necessary, he knew that it was right. Felicity deserved more from life than what he could give her, and *he* did not deserve her at all.

He'd entertained the notion of leaving town entirely, disappearing to take temptation from their path, but he just couldn't do it. He told himself that he still worried for Sindy's behavior, should he do such a thing, but he was unsure how much of that was true. He also rationalized that he must stay to protect Alyson. Mattie was his best and really his only true friend. Knowing that the woman Mattie loved may be in danger was an automatic obligation to stay. He would expect no less of Mattie were the situation reversed. So, stay he would... for now.

Besides, staying should not be a temptation for him any longer; he just needed to stay out of Felicity's way until Mattie returned, then Cain would leave. Felicity would certainly not come to seek him out again. He had told her the truths of his past and of the monster, the murderer that he had been. He had scared her away from him now. Felicity was a smart girl with a good level head on her shoulders. He did not flatter himself, that she would be seeking him out anymore.

He forced himself to drink the blood from his cup and tried to will his body back to a state of unready rest, but another unbidden feeling came upon him, the closeness of another, one marked as his own. Sindy approached, and his body recognized her with a willing eagerness that undermined his efforts to subdue it.

He cursed the twisted psychological ties that caused the impending opportunity for more of her blood, to be intertwined with his bodies physical expression of desire. *His body* saw her as a chance to fulfill its needs. *He* didn't really want to see her at all, but she had found his place of rest at last. He had thought that he might be so lucky as to avoid leading her to his lair. Her mark from him was almost gone, but luck was not with him. Whether she was led by her mark or she already knew her destination, he could feel her coming ever closer.

As usual, he'd worn only his sleep pants to bed. Now he found a large tee-shirt to pull over his head, and hoped that it was long enough to disguise his present state of arousal. He mounted the stairs to meet her at the door.

Yes, she definitely knew that he was within. She waited on the porch, not bothering to knock. She was unsurprised when he opened the door, and remained leaning against the rail with arms crossed and a familiar pouting expression upon her lips. He stayed within the doorway. "What do you want?"

She looked strange, different. Her eyes; she had not applied the shadows that she usually wore. He'd never seen her without her face painted. She looked so young! Not a child, but a young fresh maiden in the new bloom of womanhood. He found her extremely appealing this way, and his body fought even harder to express the fact. He changed his stance, self consciously and tried to keep his face sternly set. He could not judge her mood by her expression. She did not look very happy with him, but that was typical of her. "To talk, can I come in?"

He did his best to look confused and began to leave the house to join her on the porch. He gave a little shrug of nonchalance. "It was only a place to spend the day. What makes you think I've the authority to invite you?"

Now a little smirk came upon her face as she raised her eyebrows at him. "Come on Cain, you obviously live here. You probably even *pay* for it," she added with contempt. "You don't exactly strike me as the squatter type." She uncrossed her arms and stepped a bit away from the rail, expectantly. "So can I come in, or not?"

Cain studied her for a moment. My, but she looked lovely without all of the artifice. He chased the thought from his mind. She wanted an invitation into his house. That would certainly not be a wise move on his part. However, it was useless to try and keep up the charade; he could not really deny that he did indeed live here. "Not." Sindy rolled her eyes and let out an exasperated little huff. He ignored her annoyance. "What do you want?"

She squinted at him as if trying to decide just what to say. "Chris is gone," she finally blurted. He simply stared at her, trying to interpret why she should think this would affect him. He stretched out his psychic awareness. Chris was indeed not within his reach, but that didn't mean

240

anything. They didn't usually sleep within reach of his house anyway. Sindy grew impatient with his silence. "Did you *do* it?" she demanded.

Oh... she meant *gone*. "Why would I harm Chris?"

"Don't play with me Cain! It's not like you haven't threatened him before!" He could hear the tinge of panic and grief creeping into her voice. Yes, she *had* cared for Chris, as he had thought.

He met her eyes, trying to convey the sincerity of his words. "I've done nothing to hurt him, honestly. I haven't had a problem with Chris, for as long as he stayed out of my way and kept out of trouble. He's been smart enough to avoid angering me. Are you certain... Did you actually *feel* him die?"

Sindy looked panicked and confused. "I can't feel him at all! Can you?"

"No, but he may just be out of my range. It's further than yours, but not limitless. When did you see him last?"

She looked at the ground, annoyed with his inability to give her instant relief from her worry. "When I woke up last night, he was gone."

Cain sighed and gave her a little comforting smile. "That doesn't mean anything's happened to him." He paused, wondering whether he should call up the memory for her, and then decided that he must. "Remember Ernest?"

Her expression immediately became full of scorn and resentment. "My first apprentice that you heartlessly dusted, after breaking nearly every bone in his body? Yeah, I think I recall."

Cain closed his eyes for a moment and then gazed into her eyes to gauge just how hurt she had been by the act. She hadn't really cared much for the man, he was sure. He had been fairly mindless and very violent. Still, the death of a protégé was always painful. "You know that I hadn't a choice." Her mouth was set in a hard line of discontentment, but he knew that she understood it to be true. "Do you remember the moment that it happened? Do you remember what you felt, the precise moment that my stake entered his heart?"

"Besides my extreme hate for you? Yeah, thanks for reminding me of that torturous moment in time."

He refused to react to her words and instead tried to be comforting to her. "If Chris were truly gone, you would know. You would have felt it... no matter the distance."

She let that sink in for a minute and then gave up trying to be mad at him. Instead her worry returned, although obviously lessened from before. "Then where is he?"

Cain allowed himself to smile, even if it was slightly at her expense. "Perhaps he was just wanting for a change of scenery... or company."

Sindy looked astonished at such a suggestion. "You mean like... voluntarily? He wouldn't do that! He couldn't do that! He can't leave me!"

"Why not?"

"He's mine! I made him! He needs me! He couldn't live without me, he just couldn't!"

Cain tried not to be cruel, but still could hardly help but smile a bit at her insistence. "Well, if you haven't felt him die, then you will have to concede that he is... living, somewhere else... without you."

"Why? Why would he do that?"

A laugh escaped him before he could stop himself. "Is that a serious question? You treat those boys like so much cattle! Obviously you recognize Chris' higher level of intelligence as compared to the rest of your drones, but I've only ever seen you acknowledge it with extra responsibility or through giving him the brunt of your wrath when things are not to your liking. Do you show him that you care for him at all?

You needn't answer, because I can't say that I truly wish to know, but answer the question for yourself, in your own mind. Have you ever shown him any sort of real affection? And I am not talking about sex. I mean do you ever even bother to spend any time with him as a person? Talk with him, share some sort of relationship other than that of master and slave?"

Cain's dream immediately sprang to mind and he fought to suppress the memory, the feelings of comfort that it had brought him. That was not the desired order of things! It was sinful, wicked and wrong. These were people not pawns. Vampire or human, they should be treated with respect. Relationships between two people should be built upon mutual fulfillment, trust and admiration for each other. Every relationship Sindy had ever had, had been one-sided, he was sure. Had she ever sought to please another besides him?

She was staring at him thoughtfully, most likely reviewing her bond with Chris in her mind. She knew that Cain was right. Cain knew something as well, although he couldn't say how he could tell. He knew that she was ready to give up all of her guard, get rid of every one of them, and start anew without the safety net of others to support her. If Chris was going to reject her, then she would stifle that hurt by rejecting him as well, by rejecting all of them. She was done with them now. She wanted to learn how to truly share in an equal relationship... with him.

She was only afraid to ask again. Her past pleas to him were always underlied with a mocking tone. She'd always been unwilling to truly distance herself from her boys, in case he would not accept her. After the initial advances she had made upon their acquaintance, she had built an emotional wall around herself. She would not let his rejections truly wound her.

But he could see in her eyes that the wall was gone. Amazing how the absence of make-up made her expression seem so much more open, honest and easy to read. Maybe it was the absence of those shadows that was fooling him, bringing him to these conclusions, but it seemed as though she was just waiting for him to say the word. At his request she would free them all and come to him, in some ways as a student, but hopefully, eventually, as an equal.

She was still staring at him, her eyes softened, her anger gone. He thought of his dream again. Is that what he had to look forward to, if things went further with Felicity? Of course, he assumed that he had better control than to let such a relationship spill over to control the other humans in his life.

But why? Why should he think that it would stop with her? In for a penny, in for a pound. If he was going to keep one pet, why not two, or three? Why stop there? He thought of how Sindy had lived these past months. Human or vampire, what was the difference? Pets to do his bidding, keep him comfortable, fed, pampered and loved. No. He was a good man... wasn't he? He held himself above such temptations.

Sindy almost seemed able to read the conflict within him as she gazed into his eyes. Why did he make things so difficult for himself? Why did he torture himself with people and pleasures that he could not truly allow himself to have? Right here before him was a willing and perfect mistress. Well, maybe not *perfect*, but she would be willing to learn now, wouldn't she? She wanted to please him. She moistened her lips and spoke to him softly, hesitantly. "Cain... you don't like me very much do you?"

She seemed so lost and forlorn. He smiled at her, but didn't answer the question, except for himself. No, he didn't always like her very much, but sometimes you don't much like those whom your heart chooses to love. He wasn't willing to entirely give himself over to the possibility... yet, but it *was* a possibility. He reached to caress the side of her face. At first she almost stepped back from his touch, alarmed. When she realized that it was meant to be a loving gesture, she seemed very surprised indeed.

She moved forward into his arms and sought to kiss him, but he let her come close to him while turning his head and resisting her lips. He folded his arms around her in a chaste embrace. It seemed odd that she smelled of nothing really. Usually she was heavily adorned with not only paint, but perfumes as well. The faint scent of shampoo was still in her hair, but that was all. He held her lightly, cool and supple in his arms. There was no pulse or heartbeat to lure him, no living scent of sweat, but she gently pressed herself against him and he felt almost as though she was terrified to make a false move, to cause him to end the embrace.

Could she ever really make him happy? His body desired her, and the memory of drinking from her spurred him to want more, but her charms were so different from those of Felicity. Felicity's ways spoke of sweet, guileless innocent excitement, while Sindy was mischievous and manipulative. He had dealt with more than enough women like that in his life. At this point, women of sly and cunning wiles set off alarms in his head that he had learned to heed... the hard way.

Sindy's body, although desirable, was cold as his own, sterile and lacking the reactions that his nearness usually brought about in Felicity. When he held his human love, her heart would pound and her pulse would race; her breaths would come in sweet little gasps that let him know just how truly he did excite her. He could sense her body's physical desire, as it produced for him a welcoming moistness, that although he had never directly observed in her, he could smell all the same, with his heightened senses. These memories caused him to long for Felicity far more than he could want the woman in his arms.

It was with stubborn and deliberate refusal to acknowledge the ache in his heart for Felicity, that he leaned back to look into Sindy's eyes. He knew that the physical aspect of a relationship may at first seem the most overwhelming, but it was only a small part of a larger whole. Still, he *did* want Sindy, as a man, and the prospect of drinking her blood made her all the more appealing; something that he could acknowledge in himself without shame. It would not hurt her. She would enjoy it as much as he. Perhaps at some point he would let her drink from him as well, but that would be the final act of submission on his part.

He was most definitely not ready for such admissions. But smaller steps, to repeat actions already completed in previous times? Surely such things held no harm. She stared at him, awaiting his command. She would do anything for him, he knew. He let go of her, stepping back into the doorway of his home. "Come in."

Chapter 14 - Anticipation

Felicity

Tuesday afternoon
Downtime Cafe/Bookstore

Felicity had returned to school driving her own car (!) with her dad following behind, just in case. She had wanted to try and come back yesterday, with the pretense of needing more study time in the library, but her mom had remarked that Felicity was already working too hard, what with staying up all night on Friday to study, and now spending half the weekend in her room to study more. Her mother had insisted on taking her shopping instead.

So now, she was finally back, with her new car, cell phone, some new clothes and a few bags of groceries and things that her mom had thought she would need. All Felicity felt she had really needed was some perspective. With some time away to sort out her feelings, she had been very eager to get back.

At least Tuesday was a light school day for her, with only morning classes. She was at work now for the afternoon, but it was only from 12 to 4. Plenty of time to prepare herself and head to Cain's before dark.

Luckily Ben wasn't working, so she wouldn't have to put up with any of his snide comments, not that they could even bother her today. Nothing was going to bring her down. She had done a lot of thinking and finally come to a decision that she felt was long overdue. She was done with anxiety and worrying. That was not how she wanted to live her life. She felt she was finally seeing things clearly and now she could not wait to see Cain.

Felicity had ridden right past Cain's house on her way home last night. Her dad was following close behind though, so she had been unable to stop, and could only slow down as they went by. Her mark was gone now, she couldn't feel him at all, but she still felt an enormous surge of relief as they passed. His motorcycle was still there! Parked up at the top of the driveway, as always. If he were going to leave town, he certainly would not have walked.

Hopefully he hadn't left after she'd gotten back to the dorms. She hadn't been able to get rid of her dad until late, by then she felt tired and worn out from the car ride and endless contemplation over Cain. She decided that she would just have to trust that he would still be there tomorrow. She wanted time to prepare herself to see him, not to rush over there in the late hours of the night. Tuesday turned out to be a bright and sunny day. As long as she reached him before dark, she felt certain that he would still be there.

She was working with Lucy and the hours seemed to drag, but quitting time would come eventually... it had to! She could hardly wait to go home and change. She was going to wear the dress that Deidre had bought her for her birthday. She'd tried it on at home and it was perfect! It made her look so sexy and appealing, but in a casual and 'breezy' kind of way. As though she hadn't gone through too much trouble and her beauty was unintentional.

She had never really seen herself as beautiful before. She thought that she was pretty and was never *terribly* unhappy with her reflection, but 'beautiful' was just strong enough a word to make her falter. She had too many flaws for that.

It was kind of odd to look at herself in the mirror and notice all of the good things instead of immediately zeroing in on the bad. In the past, she always tended to focus on things that she saw as drawbacks, upon inspection of herself. She would have to 'psych' herself up and give herself mental encouragements to be excited about how she looked, when she dressed for special occasions.

But as she had looked in the mirror at home, wearing that green dress, she had tried to see herself through Cain's eyes. His eyes always lingered on her as though he could hardly bring himself to look away. From that first night in the gym she had noticed it. He never gawked or stared, it wasn't an obvious or uncomfortable thing, but she did notice that he liked to look at her.

It made her see herself differently. Thinking of how he would see her tonight, made her smile. However, she was still stuck at the register for now. Trapped for another interminable half an hour.

Time dragged on. At 3:53 she couldn't take it anymore. It's not like they were busy. "I'm going to get ready to go," she called to Lucy as she headed for the lounge. Lucy didn't argue, not that Felicity gave her much of a chance.

She rushed back to the dorms to get ready. It felt odd to be driving home instead of walking. The DownTime was so close to the dorms that she felt as though she was there in seconds. That suited her just fine, she wanted plenty of time to dress and do her hair, and still arrive at Cain's well before sunset.

She struggled to carry everything in one trip, too impatient to have to go back. When she finally made it into her room, she dumped everything onto the spare bed. She instantly began to undress and throw her clothes onto the floor. She donned her bathrobe and then, after a moment's pause for thought, began digging through one of the bags she'd brought home.

Finally, she found what she'd been looking for. She took the new scented body wash she'd bought while shopping with her mom, stuffed it into her toiletry case and headed for the shower. At least the bathroom was empty at this time of day, so she wouldn't have to wait.

She forced herself to take her time, and shaved her legs... twice. She wanted everything to be perfect. By the time she was back in her room, finishing her hair it was 4:45. A little later than she had hoped, but still at least an hour before sunset. She picked out the only panties that she had, that she felt looked even vaguely sexy, and got dressed.

By the time she was ready to leave, she felt as though she needed to force herself to stop and relax for a minute. Her heart was racing and she felt terribly rushed. That was not the impression that she was going for. She checked herself in the mirror one more time. She had to smile. She *was* beautiful. She put on a last spritz of perfume and left for Cain's.

Chapter 15 - Detachment

Cain

Tuesday 4:45 p.m.
Cain's house

Cain awoke from his restless sleep, to lie there in the dark of his room. At least there had been no more dreams. Then he remembered the reality of the night before, and that seemed just as bad, if not worse. He had invited Sindy to join him inside. Probably a stupid move tactically, but he was tired of tactics and fighting. If he couldn't defend himself against *her*, then he didn't deserve to live. He couldn't honestly say that he cared anymore anyway.

Her blood...he'd wanted it, and he'd known that it was something she was more than willing to give. He'd wanted to drown his thoughts in her blood and forget all else. So he had invited her in and she had not hesitated. Lying in his bed now, he replayed the events of the evening before in his mind.

Sindy entered his home with an odd glance about, noting his lack of furnishings, but said nothing. He followed, closing the door behind her. He locked it and then stood there, staring at the knob for a moment. He wanted to prepare himself, mentally. He wanted to let go of humanity, call forth the vampire within him to bid the thirst to come and drive out any other consideration. Being a man only brought him heartache and pain; better to be a monster. He did not shift, but confident that he could call it forth at will, he was ready.

When he turned from the door, she was shrugging out of her dress. That was not what he'd planned. He'd wanted only to drink. She had misunderstood...or maybe not. She had understood quite well, when he would not kiss her at the door, but once inside, she didn't think he would have the strength to refuse her.

She was right. He stood, a silent observer as the dress fell and puddled about her feet on the floor. She wore nothing beneath, save her black g-string panty, which stood out darkly against her pale skin. Out on the porch he had been too busy contemplating the lack of make-up on her face to notice that she had dressed sparingly as well. She did not wear her normal stockings and boots, but had only slipped her feet into a pair of flat black shoes. She must have been very concerned over Chris's sudden absence, not to have taken the time to compose her appearance to fit the image of herself that she usually held in her mind. It made her far more approachable and appealing to his eye.

She *was* exquisitely made, he would not deny. Her young, lithe body was tall and thin as was popularly desirable in these times. Her dark straight hair lay full and long down her back, with a few locks straying over her shoulder to partly conceal her left breast. While not very large, her pert breasts were certainly firm and full enough to draw his eye and demand his attention. She stepped out of her dress and shoes, starting towards him, slowly and deliberately. He had plenty of time to speak against her, but found that he had no words to say.

He wanted to be desirous, excited by her, and in fact his body did acknowledge her readily, but he felt sick inside, depressed and cheated that this was not his love, but a poor substitute. If she noticed his lack of enthusiasm, she never let it show. Sindy brought herself to him with the air of an offering. When he did not push her away, she took it as acceptance. She rested her hands lightly on his chest, bringing her lips to his, eagerly. He couldn't help but respond; why shouldn't he? He was a vampire, an undeserving beast plagued by guilt and a thirst for sin. How could he ever fool himself to think he should be allowed happiness with a human girl? Another vampire was the only solace he should dare to hope for. *This* was his destiny, was it not?

He closed his eyes and tried to lose himself in Sindy's kiss. He didn't plan to try to deceive himself that she might be Felicity. Even if that *had* been his intent, it never could have lasted. Sindy's kiss was far more fevered and urgent. Even when taken with passion, Felicity had never sought to nip his lips with her teeth, or so boldly explore his mouth with her tongue. The venom was evident in Sindy's kiss as well, although it was not really all that strong to *him*.

After a moment of kissing him fervently, Sindy began to nip and bite at his lips with increasing frequency and need. He knew what she wanted. She wanted to change. She desired his blood as much, if not more than he wanted hers, but she would not shift without his leave. So she gave him play bites and awaited his consent, afraid to anger him into turning her away. As he hesitated in responding to her playful provocations, she reached up to clasp her hands behind his neck so as to more firmly bestow her attentions. He was increasingly aware of her hardened nipples rubbing up against his chest, but at the moment, the blood within her called to him more strongly than her body ever could.

She left his lips to nip at his throat with teasingly human bites, the pain of which only made him long for more, imploring him to allow her to sample his blood. Cain had already drunk from her twice before, and now he would again; there was no stopping it, but he just was not willing to give himself to her fully yet. He felt that he should, if only to emotionally seal his fate, but it was too soon, he couldn't go through with it. The blood was always so personal, an undeniable bond. He held her back from him for a moment to look into her eyes again. She seemed desperate for his approval, for his permission for her to have him, all of him. It seemed terribly unfair of him, but he would not drive himself to something he was so unready for.

His body. His body he could give her, willingly. It could be disconnected from his heart, to hold no lasting or bonding emotional ties. It would have to be enough. He shook his head gently, to show his dissent. He would not allow her his blood. She seemed very disappointed, but then he shifted to his own vampire state and pulled her roughly to him for another kiss. Apparently, that satisfied her; she accepted and returned it vehemently. Then *he* was the one to nip and bite, but *he* drew blood with his play. He continued to score her lips when he could, but then he found her tongue.

If it was painful, she never let on. It was only a moment. Then he could truly taste her precious blood mingled with the venom in her kiss. It fueled him, brought out desires that he always kept so carefully under control. He spent all of his nights trying to be gentle and kind, punishing himself for past sins, allowing himself only the very slightest of pleasures.

Not this time; he had refused to give himself to her emotionally, but that did not mean that she could not please him. She would be his outlet, in her he would satisfy his physical needs, if not his emotional ones.

He pulled back from her suddenly. She was at once startled and chagrinned that he would push her away, but then he pulled off his shirt and she smiled at him with knowing eyes.

He did not speak to her, and was very glad that she followed suit. She simply stripped herself of her thong to reveal the small inverted triangle of dark curls beneath, and then came towards him again. He remained still and silent as she approached and removed the last of his clothing for him. He stood, looking down at her as she helped him free his legs of the sleep-pants he'd worn. She smiled upon seeing him ready for her. She gave his body a few caresses and kisses, taking him into her mouth once or twice, in a well-practiced and expertly pleasing manner, but as good as it felt, it was token. She really wanted *him* to initiate. So after a parting kiss, she then looked up at him with supplicating eyes and simply lay down on the floor, waiting for him. She moved to place his discarded pants beneath her head, a thin and inadequate pillow against the hard wood.

As his passions grew in urgency, he never even thought to take her downstairs. The bedroom was *his* sanctuary. His bed was a personal creature comfort that he was unwilling to share with *her*. This was not for comfort, this was more like a necessary evil; an outlet for his desires and aggressions so that he could remind himself of his true nature, stop pining for a human woman he should not have, and move on.

He needed to release all of the anger, frustration, guilt and remorse that had held him prisoner for so long. If Sindy wanted to bring that out of him, so be it. Her comfort was not his concern. That's what flashed through his mind as he saw her there on the floor. He hated himself at that moment.

Sindy must have seen it in his eyes. She quickly rose and brought her lips to his ear. "It's alright, take it out on me...I can handle it." He closed his eyes and gave her a gentle push away, downward. She dropped back to the floor and he followed, unhesitating. He ran his hands over her breasts and down her torso, smooth, cool and firm. He let his fingers skim the inside of her thighs and stray deeper between to find her already slick with wanting him. He poised himself over her with his fangs at her throat, to take body and blood together.

As he entered her flesh, all concerns fled his mind. He did not need thought. Mindless succumbing to instinct was all that was necessary. He drank her blood and indulged himself in her body, his hips pounding with a rhythm set by the flow of her blood over his tongue. After only a short time, he took his mouth from her throat. Although her blood was sublime, he did not wish to weaken her. His drinks this night were only for play, not for reprimand. There was no deeper meaning, to any of it.

He was blissfully able to ignore any thoughts that these acts should mean more...until he made the mistake of opening his eyes and looking upon her face. What he saw there frightened him. Sindy's eyes were slightly moist and she was looking at him with such a soft expression as he'd never seen from her. She loved him. She really did.

He hastily withdrew and once more, she seemed distraught and forlorn, but he would not disappoint her; he would not send her away. He wished that he could ask her to shift to her vampire state. He did not want to see her as a woman. He wanted her to look like the monster that he felt he was, to assuage his guilt and ease his mind, but he could not ask her to change without offering his blood. She wouldn't understand.

Instead, he raised himself up from her, and gave her a slap on the thigh paired with a tilt of his head. She understood perfectly. He wanted to turn her from him, to be taken from behind. He did not want to see her face. He wanted them not to be lovers, only vampires, creatures of instinct. They should act like the animals he felt they were.

He was able to lose himself then. He entered her once more and become not a man but the beast within. He was never a truly violent creature and wouldn't really hurt her, but he used his body as an instrument to convey all of the unrequited need that he had held for so long. He thrust his fears, frustrations and torment away from him with every forceful, pounding stroke of his body into hers.

Leaning forward a bit, he gently but firmly wound his hand into her hair and pulled her upwards until she arched her back and brought her body up to meet his. He then let go her hair and sank his fangs into her shoulder, that he might taste her yet once more.

He knew that when the blood came, his climax would not be far behind, and did briefly wonder if *she* would be satisfied, but then he felt her fingers gently brush beneath him as the silence was broken with her moans. Her hand left his body for her own, and he realized he needn't have worried for her. If he were unwilling to ensure her pleasure, she would take care of herself. He should have known, it was just like her not to rely upon him, even in this.

The moment came when thought was truly gone and briefly, they were joined as one, both of only one focus, oblivious to the rest of the world. His lips left her shoulder to let her bend forward once again and support herself on all fours. Into her, he poured all of his grief, shame and self-loathing, until he felt an empty shell, incapable of feeling anything else. She tilted her face downward further towards the floor, pressing herself back against him so strongly, that he could scarcely keep upright, and then...it was done.

After a moment or two, she fell forward to the floor and he sat back upon his heels, weary, spent and wanting only to be alone. He watched her change colors as the spectrum of his vision shifted and he became human once again...to the rest of the world anyway.

He stood without a word. Sindy knelt there for a moment on the floor, afraid to look up at him, it seemed. He stepped back from her a few paces. He had a feeling she knew, that he wanted to send her away.

Finally, she stood and turned to face him. He could not really decide if she looked pleased with him, or upset by his harsh and abrupt performance. She said nothing though, thank God. He did not think that he could face sweet sentiments *or* tears, not now. He hadn't really expected either from her but was very relieved just the same.

She just stood there looking at him, as if she were trying to figure him out, and for a moment he feared for what *he* might say to her. He'd no desire to be cruel, but he also had no patience for tenderness right now, should she ask him if she might stay.

She crossed the room to retrieve her clothing, donning her panties and then stepping into her dress. It was a simple garment to pull up and zip. He put his own pants and shirt on as well. It took just a moment, and then they were again fully clothed, as though nothing had occurred. The room smelled not of human sex, but only water and salt, mixed with venom and blood.

Now he did feel awful as looked at her. The guilt he'd thought was gone, was instead trying to return and plague him for yet another sin, but she smiled and came to him before he could say anything. She looked up into his eyes with understanding beyond her years. "You don't have to try and pretend," she said quietly. "It's okay...I know."

Her professed acceptance made it seem all the more disdainful. When had she learned to read him so well? She turned and left. He hadn't even said a word...not since 'Come in'.

~~~~~~~~~~~~~~~~~~~~~~~~~~~~~~~

He had spent the rest of the night at home, alone. He went downstairs to shower, and then lay in his bed, disgusted by his actions, but trying to tell himself that things were as they should be. What should he want with love anyway? It had only ever in his life led him to trouble, grief and heartache. His love for his daughter Amy was the only pure love he could ever claim. Other than that, not even once could he say he had ever loved to a rewarding end, for anyone. Never had he felt that his love had given anyone true joy or happiness, least of all himself, not past the first stages of it anyway. His love always turned others sour and hurtful in the end. Why not just start out that way and be done with it?

He was an inhuman beast, undeserving of human love. Sindy would serve him as a woman when he felt that he needed one. He was not totally unfeeling towards her. On the contrary, he often wondered if he did feel the start of something between them, but compared to Felicity's love that he had lost, it seemed so slight. Although he was loathe to admit it, because of the way that he had treated her, he did believe that Sindy loved him...in her own unguided way. So what if he did not truly love her back, yet? Perhaps that would come in time. If not, maybe love was an unnecessary ingredient for a relationship between dead creatures anyway. Perhaps that was why all of his past loves had failed...he had loved them too much. He could exist in a relationship with Sindy without it.

Or maybe it was better just to be alone.

The day came, and then the night again. He slept, he woke, he drank pale and impersonal blood from his refrigerator. He focused on turning himself back into the disconnected and guarded being that he had been before Felicity had ever come into his life. Human emotions had no place in his existence. If he could not expel them, then he would do his very best to lock them away.

He had an odd thought, a picture in his mind of his body as seen from a knowing perspective. On the outside he appeared human, handsome and finely made. Of course, it was a lie. Inside of himself, he felt as though he were a hollow and false creature behind a clever disguise, empty, and made up of so many rooms, storage spaces and closets, every one with a locking door.

He spent his whole life collecting things to try to fill him, experiences to make him feel whole, but they always turned sour. He found himself filled not with the love and joy that he sought, but with much darker fare. Behind each door was yet another emotional scar, a secret, a sin. Death, sex, sorrow, grief; these were the things that he kept locked away from the world, things he often kept locked away from himself. He was usually so good at that, keeping everything locked up tight and just carrying on.

Now and again, he would meet someone, someone different, special; someone who could touch his heart...someone who had a key. Different people opened different doors. Some made him think of his failed marriage, some made him remember Amy, or Charles. Most simply would bring to mind the face or personality of a victim, long dead and gone, because of him. Yes, he had many closets in his mind filled with those. And then he would visit the secret shame that they exposed. He would take it out, turn it over in his mind, be forced to face it, and remember.

They never stayed, the ones with keys. And in the end, he would be forced to close the doors that they had opened, and carry on. He would spend some time 'tidying up', putting things back to where he could ignore them again. Secluded and shameful, he would do his best to push everything back to where it had come from and go on.

He ought to be pretty good at it by now, but Felicity had opened so many of those damn doors! How had she managed to bring all of that out of him? Why did he let her? Actually, it had been his own stupid idea. He'd thought that perhaps each sin could be revealed and dealt with, so that he could let it go, rather than keep them all. Somehow, in his mind, he had believed that if he emptied everything out for her to see, he could somehow clear it all away and then fill himself with gifts from her instead; gifts of hope and happiness, but he had been thinking only of himself and not the larger picture for her. And now, while all of these things were still exposed to his mind's eye...an emotional mess strewn upon the floor, now he'd gone and started adding more. How could he even have room for yet another sin, another shameful act?

That was the strange picture in his mind of the mess he felt inside. He had thought that long ago he had dealt with all of this. Very purposefully and intentionally he had brought it all out, before the Lord. It was so long ago. September 12, 1734, a date that he did remember well, although it had seemed an evening like all others at the start. The year before, he had begun to feel guilt and remorse with the deaths he caused. It had begun as a slight faltering now and again, but it grew. It got so each time a victim's heart would stop, he felt cold and fearful inside that he had truly become something evil. He became more and more shameful of his actions, until he could hardly carry on.

It was growing difficult to hunt and feed, he felt so convicted of his sins, but he needed the blood and could not go without it. He had tried to speak of it to Maribeth, but she had only laughed and told him to 'stop behaving like a human, with tears in his eyes and worries in his heart. Didn't he realize that he should be beyond such things now?' ...Had she no heart of her own?

Cain had tried to ignore it, but it was becoming increasingly unbearable. He could not just pretend to be above such things, as she seemed so easily to affect. Eventually, there came a night when he just could not do it. He had a willing woman in his arms. He had fascinated and delighted her with pretty words and wine; she would be his to take, it would be so easy. He'd never had much of a problem finding victims. Sometimes he almost felt that they sought him out, it was his honest face he supposed, but when the moment came, he was convicted, forced to see himself as nothing but a bringer of death. Was that his true purpose in the world, to dash the hopes and dreams of others and steal their lives away?

No! He had cried out against it, pushed the girl from him and run. He'd run far from the town through farms and pastures. Finally, he'd found himself among a field of cattle and unable to run further, collapsing upon the grass. What could he do? How could he live?

He'd sat there for hours, pondering his existence. He'd thought of other predators in the world, the wolf, the snake. They had no mercy for their prey. They lived oblivious and carried out their natural course, why couldn't he? He just sat and watched the cows, sleeping on their feet. An interesting memory had come to mind, just a slight snippet of information really, but it changed his life.

A short while back, somewhere in their travels, he and Maribeth had been at a tavern. Once their revisit to England had ended, they'd returned to the new world and had frequented practically every pub and tavern along the eastern coast in their nightly hunts. This one was just like every other, but that evening there was a man there, who considered himself a learned man of animal classification. He was entertaining his fellow patrons with tales of odd discoveries in the animal kingdom. Among the many oddities that he relayed, was the story of a bat recently discovered to live off the blood of animals, biting sleeping cattle and licking the blood from their wounds.

It was only briefly mentioned, a fleeting bit of information meant to impress and shock the others, but it had stood out in Cain's mind. An animal that lived off the blood of other animals. The idea had made him feel a little less alone in the world. It was proof in nature that his existence was not entirely an aberration.

As he had thought of that animal tale, while sitting in the field, an idea had begun to form. Why could *he* not live from the blood of animals as well? It seemed almost amazing that he hadn't thought of it before. He had lived from the flesh of animals as a man. The notion of drinking animal blood was not entirely distasteful. Carrying it out would be another story. He'd stood and approached one of the cows nearby, the animal completely unaware of his presence, in sleep. He had spent a very long time contemplating the animal, and how he could take the blood from within.

Eventually, he'd done it. It was not nearly so graceful or pleasing as feeding from the woman he'd hunted earlier would have been, but the discovery had been made. His body would accept this substance in lieu of the other. It had filled him and quieted his thirst. It would serve.

He'd come home elated, excited to bring Maribeth his news...and she'd thought him positively insane. It was then that he made another startling discovery. She had known. She'd known all along.

That first night, when she had been abducted by the old man, her sire, the night that she had been born to this life, she had learned to drink animal blood. After she'd been turned into a vampire, the man had given her a victim from whom to drink her first blood not his own, her horse. She had drunk from the mare, her very own horse and then sent it out to wander the woods come the dawn. The mark that Cain had seen upon its neck had been from Maribeth's very own new fangs.

He was shocked and appalled. He had completely forgotten the bite upon her horse's neck. Maribeth had known all along that they could prey upon animals to survive, *and she had never told him!* She had seen what he was going through, trying to deal with his remorse. She'd known he would be sorely grateful to have an alternative to their nightly hunts, but the experience of drinking from an animal had been distasteful to her, and so she had never shared it. She'd let him suffer.

That was the beginning of the end for their relationship. He and Maribeth grew further and further apart. He had refined his methods into ways more civilized, and she had thought him a fool. Eventually, they'd parted company. At that point, he could not even say that he would greatly miss her.

So he had continued to live from the blood of animals. His conscience was greatly eased, but the past did haunt him still. It became, yet again, too much to bear. He had been alone in the world at the time. He'd no idea how other vampires might deal with such things. The few he had met, professed attitudes much like Maribeth. They were untroubled by their deeds. He could take no cue from them.

He tried to think of what he would do if he were human. He would go to a priest and confess his sins, but of course, he was *not* human. To do such a thing in this inhuman state would not be wise, but maybe a priest was unnecessary to intercede. Such a confession was between himself and God, was it not?

At first, he'd thought to simply pray by himself at home, but it felt disconnected and false. He would visit a church. He and Maribeth had learned long before that to touch a cross was to feel pain, a very literal translation of the fall from grace that he had perceived within himself. They had never attempted to enter a church.

He had made his way there at nightfall; there were evening services in session. He lost the nerve to go in. Finally, he satisfied himself with sitting outside. He went around back, into the little cemetery there and sat in the grass, listening to the hymns drifting out through the windows from inside.

He wondered at the ability to walk on such hallowed ground, and whether it was proof that to enter the church would not mean his instant destruction. He decided that his intent was pure and his heart set upon repentance and redemption. That being the case, God would certainly show him mercy and allow him entrance.

He didn't try it. He had sat in the cemetery, confessed his sins aloud, wept and prayed over each memory, each transgression. At the time he had felt them taken from him, he really had. He'd become so broken and grief stricken that he had almost believed God would no longer suffer him to live. He'd lain on the ground and waited to be struck down. He had wanted to die. Instead, he had felt as though the weight was lifted, his sins taken away.

He did not receive death at God's will. He received instead, a vision. That was when he had received the notion in his mind to change his life. He must find a way to take the existence that he had, and use it for good.

He had gone home and thought of how he might act on such an idea. The fact that he no longer killed was not enough. He needed a true reversal, a way to give back, that which he had taken. He'd found ways to be useful in the world. Not just protecting humans, that was a short-term goal. He'd begun to seek out other vampires. That was when he had begun to think of himself as a teacher. He'd begun to think of himself as an instrument of God; a servant to help bring about Divine will in the dark and dreadful world of the living dead.

'We must be meant for more', he would insist. He had no idea what that purpose might be, but to him, one thing seemed certain, to stop the killing of humans was the first step. From that might evolve a larger goal at some point. Perhaps that part of the plan was not for him to know, but he'd felt that he had a mission, a duty, and he went to it with unshakable will. At last he'd felt that he was forgiven and his guilt could be replaced with the knowledge that he was doing good works.

Obviously, he had not as fully let go of his guilt as he'd thought. It had come rushing back to him as he'd relayed his tale to Felicity. He used to be satisfied with what he was. Perhaps it was not the sort of life he would have planned for himself, but he was content in the fact that he was doing good, he made a difference. He had a proper place in the world, to his mind.

There were lonely periods, sure. There were times when he transgressed and acted on ideas of his own, and strayed from his goal, but those times had not been allowed to keep him happy. Those transgressions always led to heartache in the end. He would then feel repentant and shameful, and be led back to his cause.

Now he felt so confused. He wanted to do the right thing, really he did. He wanted what was best for Felicity, and he also wanted to keep on traveling and helping others. That required a life separate and apart from human ties. At first his lonely needs had led him into temptation once again, into thinking that maybe she could join him. She could travel by his side, human, or as a creature like himself and they could continue his work together. He deserved that much didn't he? The life of one girl was nothing compared to all of those that she could help, with him.

That was a selfish rationalization. The end did not justify the means. She should not be deprived of her life, on the pretense that it was necessary to help others. It was not a necessary measure; it was a lonely act of selfishness. It was good that he had sent Felicity away and would not see her again, though it made his heart ache. It was the right thing to do. He could find solace in another of his kind, killed not by his hand. Sindy had certainly shown interest in being his companion...even if he didn't love her as he did Felicity. Or, if not, he could carry on alone. That might be better.

He was unsure of how he would face Sindy when next they met. He knew she wouldn't hold anything against him. He suspected she never thought to expect more from a man. Tender expressions of love, were most likely foreign to her. He should seek to change that in her life, not reinforce it.

He would need some time to think upon the course of action that would best benefit them both, and then decide if he could actually carry it out. He needed time. He had no stomach to seek Sindy out again anyway, not for a little while at least. He supposed he should surface to find whether she was planning on keeping her boys, or sending them out on their own.

She hadn't mentioned freeing them, that had been his own speculation, but he did need to know her intentions. The last thing he needed to deal with, was six spurned rogue vampires roaming his town. He would have to let her know that if she planned on freeing them, she should seek his help.

Not a favored aspect of the job he had set for himself, but not an unfamiliar one either. If she were to free them, he would need to asses each one on its own merits, as an individual. If he felt it sapient enough to live peacefully, fine; let it go and try to make an existence for itself elsewhere, but if it were functioning on a very low intellectual level, as most of hers were, it should simply have to be destroyed. It might seem cruel, but if they could not discreetly and properly care for themselves, he could not let them endanger others. From what he could tell, only Chris and Luke would make the cut.

Then he remembered, Chris had left. Cain wondered what had finally driven him to independence. Most likely it was Sindy's interest in Cain. She had finally given Cain her blood. Of course, it was not really willingly the first time, but Chris was surely not given details. Cain felt a little badly for causing strife between them, but would not let himself believe that he was the sole contributor to Chris' departure.

He was actually sort of glad for Chris. He'd often felt bad for the boy, although they were usually on opposite sides of an argument. Sindy had always treated him indifferently and he seemed aware enough to deserve better. Luke wasn't given any better treatment, but at least he never seemed to notice or care.

Cain wondered what a difficult time Sindy might have in controlling the rest of them now. He'd noticed that she had begun to leave them in Chris and Luke's care, more and more often as time wore on. She'd been craving more time alone...to spend with him, but in doing so, she had relied upon Chris heavily. Luke was no marvel of common sense and Cain doubted that he could ever handle them alone for any amount of time; probably one of the reasons that she had not been loath to leave so quickly last night, he realized. She had needed to get back, before something went wrong without her.

So these were the thoughts that he busied himself with, as he spent the day alone trying not to think and dwell on his love lost. He was really rather startled when he heard the knock at his door. The sun had not yet set...it was not even six in the evening yet. He stretched his mental awareness, but could find nothing close enough to be on his doorstep. Whoever came was unmarked.

Perhaps it was only a salesman, or someone with a mistaken address. He would ignore it. The knock came again, then again...louder. He waited quietly, with an impending fear coming upon him. There was only one human who had ever knowingly knocked upon his door at this house...

Felicity. Could it be? No, she wouldn't return. She had to have been disgusted and appalled by his account of his actions of the past. He had frightened her away and told her that he would no longer be a part of her life. He'd thought for sure that she would avoid him now. She was a smart girl.

Girl...she was only a girl; that was an aspect of her that he had not really reckoned with. She was sensitive and intelligent, mature for her age and made good decisions most of the time, but there was something that he had not really taken into account, she *was* a teenage girl, in love...with him. Irrational was practically the definition of a teenage girl in love. How unaware and unthinking must he have been not to realize that? She called to him now. "Cain? Please answer. I know you can hear me. Please?" It was definitely her.

He was frozen, unsure what to do. He should have left. He had known it in his heart, and yet he had stayed. He could not see her though, it would be selfish and wrong to give in to such desires. He had sent her away for her own good, and needed to hold firm in his decision. She knocked again.

Had he the detachment to leave her pleas unanswered?

Part 3

Battles and Bliss

Chapter 16 - Don't think

Cain

Tuesday 5:15 p.m.
Cain's house

Cain agonized over his indecision as Felicity knocked upon his door. Why had she come back to see him? She knew he was a murderous monster. He had no choice in being a vampire, and though he did choose now to resist killing humans for blood, it could not erase his past.

She was temptation incarnate, whom he would do better to stay away from, and he could bring a lovely girl such as she nothing but hurt and heartache he was sure. To allow himself to be with her would perhaps endanger her very life.

He knew he shouldn't answer the door. He should shun her, let her go on her way, to live her life. "Please, Cain?" He could hear her call quietly from up on his porch. Did he really think he had the resolve to ignore her?

He waited a few interminable moments and then had to concede that he did not. He could never turn a deaf ear to *her*. He would have to go and talk to her, try to send her away, although he knew that was unlikely to occur.

All of the comforting that he had tried to give himself, consoling himself that he had done the right thing in sending her away... was lost. It was gone and forgotten the moment he heard her voice. God, but he was so weak. He went to her. He did not know what he would say or do. He still told himself that he would ask her to leave, but he knew she wouldn't listen without persuasion that he may not be strong enough to carry out.

He opened the door to reveal her standing in the sunlight on his porch. "Hi," she said softly. Once again, he was enrapt by her beauty. She wore a lovely dress of green and blue, and tiny little sparkling diamonds in her ears. Her hair was wound up off of her shoulders, with some sort of oriental hair sticks with green designs on them, just visible towards the back, holding it in place. The dress showed off her smooth shoulders and just enough cleavage to be truly enticing without being too revealing.

Her throat was bare. He tore his eyes from the spot to find her eyes, an earthy green. She gazed at him for a moment and then smiled. "Aren't you even going to say anything?"

He fought to find his voice. "You look... stunning."

Her cheeks flushed gently pink with her pleasure of his compliment. "Thank you," she said quietly.

He felt so bewildered by her presence, when he had been trying so hard to accept that he would not see her again, and why was she dressed so? "Are you just coming from somewhere?"

Now she rolled her eyes and laughed. "No stupid! It's for you. Aren't you supposed to be taking me out to dinner, for my birthday?"

He vaguely remembered mention of such plans, but that was before he had finished his tale. He'd thought them irrelevant. He hadn't planned to see her again; surely she'd realized? Even if she did think he was taking her to dinner... he was unsure of the time, but the sun was certainly still shining brightly outside. "You're a few hours early."

"I know," she said with a secret sort of smile.

He closed his eyes a moment and tried to gather his strength. That was a smile, hard to resist. He looked at the ground, instead of her face. "I hadn't expected to see you again. I mean, I didn't think we *should* see each other. I thought you'd understood."

"I know." She looked down as he finally did try to meet her gaze, a little uncomfortably, but she then seemed to raise her courage and looked him in the eye. "I've been doing some thinking too. Want to know what I think?" He gazed at her and gave a slight nod, although he was fairly sure what she would say and that it would be better for him to not hear it. He should shut the door and make her go. Of course, he didn't move.

"I think," she said as she moved a bit closer, and he leaned a bit away, "that you and I..." She moved forward again. She didn't wait for an invitation, or for him to even back away for her to enter. She simply began to walk forward as she spoke, causing him to back away almost involuntarily. He was afraid to touch her and he moved back before her more surely even, then when she'd driven him with the cross. He stepped backwards until he met the wall, and she stopped just shy of his body. "We both think too much," she concluded.

She brought her lips to his and he felt powerless to prevent it. He stood stunned and unsure how to proceed, so torn with indecision. He shouldn't, he really shouldn't. She didn't realize where it might lead; how it could ruin her life to be with him. It also truly bothered him that this was the second time in just as many nights that such a thing had occurred. Her actions so echoed Sindy's that it was frightening. The thought of *his* actions with Sindy made him feel ill.

Felicity sought his attentions now, just as he had so sorely longed for, when Sindy had been the one to approach. It *was* Felicity who kissed him now, and he could hardly even kiss her back. He turned his head away. "I don't think..."

"*Don't* think. Why does everything have to be so well thought out, be perfectly planned, and make practical sense? There are some things in life that I don't want to analyze, I just want to experience."

He looked into her eyes then, with a lump in his throat from the sick feeling he got in remembering the night before. *Now* Felicity wanted this? He didn't deserve her, not in the least. He shook his head sadly. "Not with me," he whispered.

"Yes, with you." She adorned his lips with kisses once again. Sweet, soft cajoling little kisses that tempted and persuaded him that nothing else could matter more. This time he stopped fighting her, although he did not really give over to it. After a few moments, he ended it though. "I can't. I'm no good for you, really. I don't belong in your life."

She wouldn't back away, but instead rested her hands lightly on his shoulders. "This isn't my whole life, it's one day."

He gave a small smile and shook his head. "And tomorrow?"

She smiled back and gave a little shrug. "What's one more day?"

He laughed a bit and shook his head. "No, see living for the moment is really *not* a good thing for me. It's sort of what got me into this mess. I'm trying to avoid repeating past mistakes."

Again, she sought to bring herself to his lips. "It's not a mistake," she whispered as she kissed him.

Again he felt himself beginning to give over to her, and again he tried to stop it. He should be strong. He knew what was right, even if she didn't. "You should go," he told her quietly.

She stepped back from him, just a bit. She looked very stern and determined. It unnerved him a little, because he knew that she was not planning to leave and he would be rather hard pressed to convince her, without hurting her. Then he happened to glance at the place on the floor where he had been with Sindy. He hadn't meant to, but as he glanced at the spot, the memory flashed before him. The wonderful young woman before him now, deserved more than someone like him.

She spoke with serious intensity. "Do you really *want* me to leave?" Phrased like that, he could not answer. "Tell you what, I'll go. I'll leave, and I will never come here again... if you can do one thing for me." He made his face a stern mask as he waited for her to continue. "Tell me honestly, that you *don't* love me."

He closed his eyes for a moment, and then opened them to look at the floor. He had to do this, she had to go. He met her eyes, trying to make his own tell her nothing, cold and impersonal. "I don't love you."

Felicity never took her eyes from his, although her own were soon covered with a sheen of tears. She stared at him for a moment, then she tried to smile. "You're a really rotten liar."

As the words left her lips, he felt his face begin to crumple. He had meant to hold on to his stern expression, but it just didn't work. "Yeah, I know."

"You can't send me away." A single tear fell to her cheek as she spoke, and he couldn't take his eyes from it. "Because, I love you."

He just couldn't stand to break her heart. He knew that in the end, to send her away now might be the less painful choice, but he just couldn't do it. He loved her more deeply than any other woman he had ever known. Their future may be uncertain, but he could not deny her now. He took her into his arms. At first it was only a hug, a crushing embrace. Her heart was pounding against him and he almost felt as though it were trying to pour all of her love out to him in morse code against his chest.

Then she snuggled her face into his chest and began to kiss him there. At first through his shirt, but then she raised herself to find his throat. Her kisses moved upwards until her lips found his own and she kissed him with an intensity that surprised him. It was far more urgently seductive than any other kiss he could ever remember receiving from her.

Finally, he made her pull away so that he might speak. "Shouldn't we..."

"Go downstairs?" she asked eagerly.

He laughed. "I was going to say - close the door."

She turned to see the open doorway. The sun had lowered a bit and was sending a slanting slice of sunlight down upon the floor into the house, uncomfortably close to where they stood. An elderly couple was walking past outside. She smiled and giggled. "Oh yeah, sorry." She quickly went to close the door and then rushed back to his arms. "*Now* can we go downstairs?"

He glanced back to the spot where he had been with Sindy and grimaced. He hoped she didn't notice. "Yes, please."

Chapter 17 - No regrets

Felicity

Cain's house
Tuesday 5:30 p.m.

Felicity eagerly followed Cain downstairs, elated and amazed that she had been brave enough to say the things that she had practiced to herself earlier. She had known that he loved her, but had been terribly worried that he would not admit it. He was so bent on protecting her from himself. She had been right too. He had tried to deny his feelings, but she knew. Thank God she'd had the courage to call him on it. He loved her. She'd known.

As he reached the bottom of the stairs he began to cross the room, to light the lamp, next to the bed. She followed right behind him, and as soon as he turned it on, she practically threw herself into his arms. He was very startled. He must have thought that she'd remained by the stairs. Or maybe he just didn't expect her to be so forward.

But she had already decided in her mind that she should surprise him with her boldness. She remembered his story. What stood out in her mind now, were his descriptions of Maribeth. He had obviously been extremely attracted to her. Her brazen desires had most definitely turned him on. Felicity wanted to do the same. She wanted him to find *her* irresistible, in the same way that he could not deny his need for Maribeth. So when she kissed him, it was rushed and urgent and trying to convey impatience for the act that she was actually a bit nervous to carry out. She was certain that she wanted to, but she was nervous all the same.

Her experience with guys was not totally lacking. She'd had some hot and heavy dates out on the cliff over-looking the slate quarry, where kids in her town had parked to make-out, but those experiences only went so far. Cain was an older and *much* more experienced man. She didn't want him to think her naive. She was determined to be bold and unhesitating, as opposed to her usual timid self. She threw herself into his arms and practically propelled him onto the bed. Once there, she pushed him to lie back and moved to lie atop him, as he had caused her to do, that night on the stairs. This time she was unafraid of pressing into to him too strongly, letting things go too far. The longer they kissed the more aware she became of his body. She was amazed at how clearly she could feel him. Her silk dress and his thin sleep pants could hardly conceal how badly he longed for her.

With a very deliberate decision to carry on with her boldness, she began to move her hips against him. She brought her hands down to find the hem of his shirt and pushed them up underneath. After only a moment, she came back to the hem and began to tug and pull his shirt up. He sat up a bit to let her, and she pulled it to under his arms, but as it came up higher, she was still unwilling to end their kiss yet. Finally he sat up fully and broke from her, laughing. He leaned back, with arms up, to let her pull it over his head. She did, and threw his shirt to the floor. His chest was broad and smooth.

Once again, she attacked him with kisses, as though unable to restrain herself. This time it was the waist of his pants that she tugged at, trying to pull them down almost violently. He stopped the kiss and leaned back to look at her oddly. "What are you doing?"

She was a little put off by his question. What did he think? "Taking your pants off."

"Why?"

What kind of question is that? He seemed almost amused. "Because... I want you." After a moment's thought she added, "I *need* you." She was trying her very best to sound desperate and sultry at the same time.

He simply cocked an eyebrow at her. "Really?"

She eyed him for a moment as he seemed to be trying to read her true feelings. She refused to back down from her plan. She thought of all the things Cain had told her about his past experiences with women. She had paid close attention. He'd thought his wife's 'appetite' for 'bed sport' was sorely lacking and had been thrilled when Maribeth had 'hungered for him as a man' and attacked him with sheer desire in her eyes. Felicity would not disappoint, she wanted to thrill him. "Really. I *need* you, I do."

He gestured for her to let him up. She did, and he stood from the bed. He moved to stand to the side of the bed right next to her and she turned to face him, sitting. He wore a bit of a smirk on his face, but then composed it to be very serious. "You do? Isn't this moving a bit fast for you?"

She looked up at him indignantly, annoyed that he should question her. "I know what I want," she insisted with a confidence she didn't really feel.

He raised his eyebrows a bit and then after a moment of thought, wore a smug smile and said in a commanding tone, "Show me."

She was a little shocked by his attitude, but tried not to let her face convey anything but desire. When she did not immediately respond, he pulled down his pants and was revealed before her. Even though she fought to remain unfazed, she knew that her eyes had gone a bit wide. He was right in front of her face, erect and undeniably, nicely endowed. He took the pants off and then stood there unmoving, waiting for a display of her *need*.

Felicity was very close to trying to please him. Her hand even hovered before his body for a moment, but then she dropped it to the bed and looked up at him in annoyance. He had to know that she hadn't much experience. Exactly what did he expect from her? This was her first time! It was supposed to be romantic, and he was going to stand there and *order* things from her? "Why are you making this so difficult for me?" she asked.

He immediately dropped his stern composure and laughed. He seemed almost relieved. "*There* you are! The Felicity that I know and love, who doesn't take orders well. I was hoping that you would surface. That domineering girl who was kissing me, while trying to pull the shirt over my head and rip the clothes from my body... I don't know who *that* was, but it wasn't you. Why are you trying to be someone that you're not?"

She dropped her eyes to the bed. "I wasn't..."

He spoke to her tenderly. "I know what you were trying to do. I'm glad that you want to please me, but don't. I love you for who you are. Don't do things, only to try and impress me." He brought back the stern and commanding voice. "Do you know what I want you to do?"

Felicity kept her eyes lowered, chastened. "What?"

He put a finger to her chin, to tip her face and make her look at him. "Whatever *you* want. That will please me. Have faith." She smiled at him and then as she began to look back down, she turned from him, a little embarrassed. His erection had lessened a bit during their talk, but he was still right in front of her and impossible to ignore. He gave a little laugh. "Now, if you'd like to further your explorations of my body, I'll certainly be happy to oblige, but do you think you might come up here first and give me one of *your* kisses? I do sorely miss them."

She smiled broadly and stood up on the bed. She came into his arms, although the bed now made her slightly taller than he. He wrapped his arms about her waist and they kissed. A comfortable, familiar and wonderful kiss, that grew strong with passion unforced. After a few minutes she gave a little pull for him to lie down with her on the bed. He quickly did so and their kisses continued. She was still fully clothed, but she could easily feel him pressed against her. He was so hard! She was a bit shocked with herself at how much that observation did excite her. He stopped kissing her and rolled to the side.

"Your lovely dress is getting all wrinkled," he told her.

She tried to move back towards him. "I don't care," she said with a smile.

"Well, *I* do. Do you think I'm going to take you out to dinner later, looking like a street urchin?" She laughed and he gave her a playful shove to get up from the bed. "Go on and take it off for me, will you? But that's not an *order*, mind you. Just a suggestion," he said with a chuckle.

She stood and moved a few steps from the bed, facing him. After a moment's mental preparation, she reached behind her lower back, and unzipped the dress. The bodice of the dress was tight, but the material was gathered and shirred to a seam that ran up the middle, rather than being smooth. The result was that it created a sort of slanting stripe design. It was beautiful. It also had helped her to be less self conscious about wearing it without a bra.

The top of the bodice split to create two broad straps that fastened behind her neck, and left her shoulders bare. She brought her hands up behind her neck and opened the hook that held the top closed. She stood there for a second, and then let the dress drop. She wore no bra beneath, but she did have on pink cotton bikini panties, and full pantyhose. She looked down at the floor as she felt her face grow flushed.

Finally, she met his eyes and spoke. "Sorry about the plain panties and stockings. I wanted to get sexy ones, you know, like with a garter belt? But I was shopping with my mom, and I didn't want to have to try to explain a purchase like that." He laughed a little and smiled at her lovingly. She took off the pantyhose, but wasn't quite ready to remove her underwear. She left them on, and looked up at him again.

"Well, don't leave it on the floor," he said, nodding towards her dress. She rolled her eyes and picked it up. She moved to drape it across the bar, and then turned back to face him. She just stood there; holding in her stomach a bit and watching him run his eyes over her body. She tried not to be too self conscious. He hadn't hesitated in the least when revealing his body to her.

He smiled. "So, are you going to torture me further, standing all the way over there as I gaze upon your perfect body, or are you going to come to me?" He still lay on the bed, propped up on one elbow in a very casual pose.

She rolled her eyes and mumbled quietly. "*Perfect* is a little strong a word."

He rose from the bed and went to meet her, since she hadn't immediately come to him. He put a hand on each shoulder, smiled at her and whispered, "No, it's *not*." He then took her into his arms for a kiss. It felt so good to be enfolded in his arms, the absence of clothing making it something special and new. He leaned back again to look at her. "Stop worrying so much about the impression you're making."

She smiled to herself. "Don't think."

He moved his head to make her meet his eyes. "Are you sure this is what you want? Don't feel you need to prove to me, your love."

She snuggled a little closer against him, very aware of his exposed body, pressing against her. "This is definitely what I want. I guess I was just going about it the wrong way. Think we could kind of... start over?"

He laughed. "Well, I don't plan to get dressed again."

"No, that's okay." She laughed as she began to kiss him again and bravely let her hand wander from his back, down to give his butt cheek a little squeeze. "That really won't be necessary." He laughed a bit, but then their kiss turned much more serious. As passion began to dominate over silliness, she moved her body to the side a bit and let her caresses come around his thigh to find his penis.

He didn't question her boldness this time. His kiss became far more passionate as she let her hand explore him, and then begin to stroke and gently squeeze him in a way that she was sure he would enjoy. After a moment he did stop the kiss to question her. "Am I meant to believe *that* is an *in*experienced hand?" he asked breathlessly.

She gave a little laugh and met his eyes, while continuing her motions. "I'm a virgin, but I haven't been living under a rock," she answered smugly, glad that she had honestly surprised and impressed him on her own, without artifice.

"Is that so? Because by the look on your face when I disrobed earlier, I would have thought differently." Now he wore the smug smile.

She dropped her eyes with a giggle. "Was it *that* obvious?"

"I found it delightful."

A few more giggles escaped her as she tried to decide how to explain herself. "Well, this is going to seem kind of stupid..."

He spoke with a voice quiet and sincere. "Honest thoughts expressed cannot be stupid."

She stopped giggling long enough to answer seriously. "I've never actually *seen* a man's body before, not in person I mean."

He did look a little surprised. "Are you telling me that the eyes that belong to *that* hand have never seen what they touch?"

She rolled her eyes as she dropped her hand from him, and her face turned red. "Well, it's always been in the dark, in a parked car."

"Always?" he asked in amusement.

"Three times," she admitted.

"M-hmm." He smiled and gave her a little kiss. "Well, I commend you, for your honest admission." That brought forth her giggles again. She felt as though her confession must have sounded absurd to him. He continued. "Feel free to look all you like, but do me a favor?" She tried to compose herself and meet his eyes. "Do try to stop giggling first. It's not very helpful to a man's ego." Of course, that only made her giggles worse.

She eventually composed herself sufficiently to speak. "Don't try to tell me that *you're* self conscious? Even *I* can tell that *your* body really is perfect."

He shook his head a little with a modest smile. "I have the same fears and worries as everyone else. I'm just a bit more comfortable in my skin because I've been in it for so bloody long."

"Well, in case you were wondering, I'm very impressed."

He smiled and shook his head again. "I'm glad to hear it, but it's really not about that. I don't want to impress you. I want to love you, fully... unhindered, as I have *so* wanted to these past weeks."

She nodded and said quietly. "Yeah, that... that sounds *really* good."

"Alright then. Less talk, more kisses." They began their kisses once again and after a moment, he stooped to put his arm under her legs and scoop her off of her feet. They continued to kiss as he carried her to the bed. He put her down and then stopped to study her for a moment. She lay in a half-sitting position, propped up a bit by her elbows. She was surprised when he came forward not for another kiss, but to touch her hair. He plucked the sticks from it and let it unwind, down onto her shoulders. He held the hair-sticks up for her to see. "I don't think I'd like to roll over onto one of these," he said with a smile.

Oh. They were wooden, and each sharpened on one end, like the stakes that he used. She hadn't even realized. "Sorry."

He laughed. "That's alright. An ounce of prevention and all of that." He put them on the bar, where they would not be lost, and quickly returned to her. "Now... what else might I remove?" he asked teasingly, looking at her panties.

She smiled, and gave him a slight nod. He hooked one finger into the band at each hip and she lifted herself enough for him to take them off. He let them drop to the floor and came back for more kisses.

She had felt his venom beginning to affect her a bit more with each kiss, bringing about a slight haziness and helping to lower her inhibitions. She worried that it might get stronger, making her feel almost 'drunk', but as their kisses continued, it seemed to level off, reaching an equilibrium that kept her a little light headed, but not distressingly so.

As he lay down upon her, she couldn't help but tense with nervous apprehension. He noticed and raised himself up a bit to meet her eyes. "Relax. I'm not going to *thrust* myself upon you, unready. We're wanting for pleasure, not pain." He gave her a quick kiss and she smiled. "Have trust, never fear," he whispered. He brought his lips back to hers to continue their kisses. Before long those kisses did travel from her lips. For a split second she held her breath as they traveled down her throat. He hovered for a moment, at the place where he'd bitten her, but then gave her a kiss there and moved on.

His lips found her breast and he began to kiss and suckle her in a way that she found incredibly arousing. It was unexpectedly exciting, considering the absence of desire she'd felt the few times she had allowed herself to be groped there by boys back home. Her nipple began to tingle and harden a bit as his attentions grew stronger. He moved from one to the other, and then after a few minutes, resumed his travels downward.

After covering her belly with kisses, he gently parted her thighs. Again she tensed in anticipation, but held herself open to him. As he explored her there, with tongue and kisses, she wriggled and thrilled to what seemed such a forbidden act. She felt a warmth come upon her, that she had at first thought to be his breath, but then she sadly realized that he wasn't really breathing.

The venom. She was feeling it on her skin, just as surely as it was in his kiss. It caused only a slight warmth and a bit of tingling, but considering where he placed it, it was amazingly effective. Not that it was very necessary; she had never felt such desire in her life before this day.

When he came back to her she felt as though she were truly ready for him, although he simply lay atop her lightly and met her lips for more kisses. For a moment, she was startled when she realized that she could taste herself in his kiss, but she decided not to be unnerved, and accepted it as natural to the experience.

His hand found her then, and began to rub and caress the secret and hidden folds above her opening in a way that made her long to take him within her. His mouth left her lips and he spoke quietly. "If you don't mind my asking, has anyone ever ventured into such territory for you?" As he asked, his finger did tease and just barely enter her.

She sucked in her breath and took a moment before answering. She thought of the time that she *had* allowed another to touch her there romantically. Unfortunately, it had been anything *but* romantic. It had been ungraceful, bungling and blessedly brief. That uncomfortable experience was far removed from anything she might feel now, she was sure. "Nothing worth remembering." Surely he heard the remembered disdain in her voice.

She could almost feel his smile as he let out a little breath of a laugh. "Don't be disheartened. This shall erase the past." He brought his lips back to hers and continued to rub his finger against her until she became impatient, in thinking that he would never allow it to fully enter. She *was* beginning to feel the desperate urgency that she had tried to convince him she had felt earlier, but this time there was definitely no artifice necessary. When he finally did let his finger go further, she found she was practically moving herself down upon him, in an attempt to satisfy her need. He removed his hand far too soon for her liking, but then she realized that this was only the beginning.

She found herself very surprised, when rather than lie atop her, he rolled aside and looked up at her, hopefully. "Perhaps, a kiss or two of your own... to ease the way?"

It took her a moment to understand what he meant. He wanted her to kiss his body and make him wet for her. She moved lower on the bed, to be next to his hips and took then him into her hand. After a few exploratory kisses, she took him into her mouth. It seemed odd that he could feel so soft, smooth and cool, and yet so hard all at once. She did her best to please him, it was a little clumsy and awkward, but he didn't seem to mind. He didn't even let her go on very long really. "It's enough," he said quietly. She was afraid that maybe he was disappointed with her motions, but as she looked at his face, she realized it was quite the opposite. He couldn't wait much longer.

She thought that he would lie over her again, but instead he motioned for her to climb atop of him. She was sure that he noted her look of hesitant confusion, but he only smiled and nodded reassurance. She settled herself onto his thighs, thinking that maybe he wanted her to fondle him some more, but he sat up to put his hands to her waist and brought her forward to sit on his stomach instead. He then had her lean down for another kiss. That's when she realized what he really had planned. "But... I thought... I should lie down again," she said uncertainly, as she sat back up.

He smiled up at her doubting expression. "I want *you* to do it. After all, it is your maidenhood, you deserve the honor."

Now she was nervously uncertain, at the prospect of being made to take the lead. "But, I can't. I mean, I won't know... it won't be good."

He raised a hand to caress her cheek. "Trust me, it will be wonderful." He looked thoughtful for a moment, and then smiled. "Dance for you."

The sentence almost brought tears to her eyes as she remembered fondly their first dance. It had been so freeing and honest and like something from a dream. She came down to his lips and their kisses, at first sweet and loving, did become increasingly passionate again. He placed his hands upon her hips, and took great care in positioning her just shy of being truly astride him.

He gripped her hips a little more forcefully, and began to give her a rhythm. He moved her ever so slightly forward and back, so that she could feel his manhood press at her opening, and then all but leave her, again and again. His hands then left her hips to wrap gently around her lower back, as she continued the motions on her own.

She was pleased to find that as she moved, the slight friction of his lower stomach rubbing against her, between her legs, brought back the eager desire she had felt when his hand had caressed her there. She became bolder and felt him begin to enter, as she pressed down harder against him with each backward motion. Her body was moist with anticipation as she imagined how it would feel, but she only barely took him within her, taking her time.

She opened her eyes to look at his face. Cain's eyes were closed, but she knew that he was in pleasurable torment. It must seem torture that she would hesitate and tease him so. But then he opened his eyes, and smiled at her with such loving and patient desire, that she knew he would try to wait forever until she was ready, if he could. He needn't worry, she couldn't wait another moment.

With a brazen thrust, she brought herself down upon him. She let out a small cry as her body stretched to accommodate him, but the pleasure far outdistanced the pain. She froze there for a moment, and then tried to go further, but his hands moved back to her hips and stopped her. He moved her upwards instead, and then down, recreating their prior rhythm. His passage into her was much eased this way. With each stroke she let escape a small sigh of amazement and pleasure that he was indeed moving deeper within her. She soon found herself moving faster and further until she was taking him in as fully as possible.

She found rocking motions for her hips and rhythms so pleasing that she felt like an exotic dancer upon him. Twice he brought his hands to her hips again to stop her, and she realized that she was exciting him to the point that he must pause, lest their experience end too soon. She tried to wait patiently for him to let her go on... it was maddening.

He let her continue and she found herself voicing quiet moans of delight that, in her usual shyness, she had never thought she might utter. He answered them with his own, and together they moved until she felt her pleasure grow and build into an unimagined explosion of amazing ecstasy. She cried out, bucking and pressing against him, smothering his throat with kisses. She was shocked at how largely she had underestimated what she would feel.

Just as her own rapture began to subside, his hands again found her hips, to move her strongly upon him a few times, and then he lifted her from him. She swung her leg off of him, to lay snuggled next to him on the bed. Felicity watched in amazement, as evidence of their passions spilled out from him, onto his stomach. She held herself pressed as close against his side as she could, while she tried to calm her gasps for breath.

She couldn't help but feel curiously proud as she lay with her head on his shoulder and studied his body. He was obviously well satisfied. She looked up at him and smiled. "Wow," she said with a grin. He opened his eyes and smiled.

"I fully agree." He lay unmoving for a moment, and then turned his head to her for a kiss. "I *do* love you," he whispered.

She felt as though she could not get close enough to him as she continued to kiss his shoulder. "I love you too," she replied.

After studying her with a curiously penetrating gaze, he leaned over her and then moved down her body until his hair brushed her hips while he placed a light kiss upon her abdomen. He ran his hand down her thigh to the knee and then gently edged her legs open as he looked up at her, longing for her consent. "May I?" he breathed.

She was a bit startled when it occurred to her what he might be after, but she simply nodded and lay back to close her eyes. His tongue gently explored her, collecting evidence of her former maidenhood as she felt the comforting warmth of venom renewed once again. She reveled in her newfound lack of inhibition as she allowed herself to be at ease with him there. Just as she thought he might urge her desires to awaken yet again, he took a deep shuddering breath and returned to lay next to her, gazing steadily up at the ceiling. She studied his obvious inner struggle for self-control as she tried to calm her newly racing heart. After a moment, he tilted his head to see her unreservedly running her eyes over his body.

She looked away a bit shyly, to have been caught so obviously observing his anatomy. He reached an arm out to enfold her, but she gently wriggled from his embrace with a smile. "I'll be right back," she explained, as she headed for the bathroom.

"Think you might throw me a towel?" Cain asked.

She quickly found one and tossed it to him, before she ducked into the bathroom for herself. When she emerged, he was lying on the bed facing her, the towel on the floor.

She quickly padded across the room and jumped onto the bed, making him bounce about and laugh. Then she grabbed the sheet and lay down next to him, covering them both. He eagerly took her into his arms for a kiss. After a few minutes, they lay quiet, her head on his chest. She peeked up at him and smiled. "That was... unbelievable." He just smiled. She made her voice stern, teasing him. "Do you realize that all these weeks, we could have been doing that this whole time?"

He laughed. "That thought had occurred, yes." He smiled at her. "It's alright. I told you it'd be worth the wait."

She laughed and kissed him. "Can I ask you..."

"Anything," he assured her.

"Well, just now..." She smiled in thinking of their actions. "Why did you wait, until after I was done? I mean, why didn't you let it happen while you were still... while we were together? And why did you move me away? You couldn't have been worried that you'd... get me pregnant, right?"

He smiled, a bit sadly she thought. "No. You needn't worry about that with me. Although I do think you might have asked beforehand, if you were wondering."

"I wasn't, until you did that."

"Well, put your mind at ease. The ability to have children is gone in me. This body is no longer equipped. It can't carry diseases either, so that's something else off your mind. No worries." She should have been relieved, but she felt bad for him. It seemed very bittersweet. Truthfully, though it may have been foolish of her, those thoughts hadn't even entered her mind. "As to why I moved you, well... I thought *that* an experience better explored next time."

"What do you mean?"

"The venom. It's in all of my bodily fluids. I understand it can have quite an effect." Her eyes went a bit wide at the thought, he just shrugged a little. "I wanted you to know what it was like, without that. As much as possible, anyway."

She tried to hide her smile at the hint of promise behind his words... next time. She snuggled closer to him for more kisses. "Well, maybe we should do some more experimenting then," she said with a sly smile. He laughed.

"Please, I may not be human, but even my body doesn't regain strength *that* fast."

She laughed as well, but then turned to him, seriously. "I love you. My first time couldn't have been more perfect."

He smiled. "Well, it's a first for me too, you know."

She rolled her eyes at him. "Yeah, your first time *with me*."

"It *is* a first. I've never had the distinct pleasure of de-flowering a virgin before. Well... other than my past wife that is, but she saw such things as little more than her wifely duty. Trust me, that experience was *nothing* like this one. Yours is the only virginity I've tasted as a vampire. In a life as long as mine, *firsts* are rare to come by. The fact that you entrusted the experience to me, is something that I will always look upon with fond memory, and a flush of pleasure." He had seemed so happy and light hearted at first, but after a moment, Felicity could swear he was fighting tears.

"What's wrong?" she asked in quiet concern.

"I wish I could freeze time. Stop things right here and live only in this moment, but things always change in time. Everything but me. Loving you so much, only distresses me more to lose you."

"I'm not going anywhere. In fact, I'm pretty sure I've got at least fifty or sixty good years left in me." She tried to make him smile. It didn't really work.

He swallowed and closed his eyes for a moment, before meeting hers again. "Not planning to live much further beyond that, are you?"

She knew what he meant. She looked down at the bed sheets for a minute, and then looked up with sad seriousness. "Not really... no." She gave a little shrug. "Still... it seems pretty long to me. Could be fun while it lasts." She gazed at him thoughtfully. "No regrets."

He gave a little laugh, as a tear fell onto his cheek. He wiped it away and then took her into his arms again. "It may not be long, but it will be unforgettable, I promise you that." He tickled her beneath the covers, to chase away any impending gloom.

They rolled about a bit, laughing, tickling and kissing until thoroughly exhausted. She lay against him trying to catch her breath, and looked up at him naughtily. "So... when do you think you'll be ready for more?"

He laughed. "What, do you plan to cram all of your experiences into one evening? When I said our relationship may not be long, I didn't mean that I'd be leaving at sunset, besides, I owe you a dinner. You must be starved after such activities."

"Actually yeah, I am." She looked at him oddly for a moment. "Are *you?*"

He smiled at her concern. "Don't worry, I'm alright." He nodded his head towards her clothes at the bar. "Why don't we put some clothes on, and I'll take you somewhere worthy of that beautiful dress?"

She kissed him once more, before leaving the bed. "I'd like that."

Chapter 18 - Reservations

Cain

Cain's house
Tuesday evening, sunset

Cain and Felicity stood in the doorway of his home, arm in arm, and watched the sun's brilliant rays dip below the horizon. Cain turned to look at her and lightly touched the curls of her beautiful hair, all wound up again with her oriental hair sticks. "Your hair looks so lovely this way, but I hadn't realized... it'll be ruined with the ride. Sorry."

She turned to look at him with a smile. "That's okay. I'll drive."

He looked at her in confusion for a moment, and then his eyes found her car, out in front of the house. "A lady of independent means are you now? Congratulations. Still, now I'll have no excuse to escort you home from work in the evenings."

She gave a little laugh. "That's just what I thought, but it's okay if you still want to come and visit. I know how addicted you are to your coffee."

He smiled. "Trying to trade one addiction for another, I suppose." He took his leather jacket from a closet by the door and then paused, as if to offer it to her. "Do you need it?"

"That's okay; it doesn't really go with my dress," she said with a laugh. "Mine's in the car."

"I suppose I ought to wear something a little more suitable as well." He reached into the closet and traded the leather for a sports jacket.

"Very nice," Felicity said, giving him a smile and a kiss.

As the bright colors of the sunset began to subside, and the sky became shades of lavender and dark blue, Cain took her by the hand, and they went out to the car. Felicity seemed very surprised to find that she had to invite him into it, just as she had her room. Cain shrugged. "It's your personal space."

"Good to know. Come on in. My space is your space."

He directed her to a restaurant, saying it was a bit far, but surely it would be worth the drive. Honestly, he had no idea where to find a fancy restaurant locally. He'd never had need of such knowledge. The place that he thought of now, he had paused at just before entering this town, back in early June. He had been following rumors and headlines, trying to locate the vampires which turned out to be Sindy and Ernest, wrecking havoc hereabouts, back in the spring.

Normally he would seek out bars and seedy pubs in which he could listen for gossip and scan for other vampires, but as he'd passed this place he'd been travel weary and wanting for a break from the road. No lesser places offered and he had thought it wouldn't be too extravagant to treat himself to a nicer experience for a change.

It was a very dignified establishment. In fact, he'd paused to take a dress shirt and jacket from his pack, to don before entering. He'd hoped that the fact that they'd been terribly wrinkled would go unnoticed.

He'd mostly drunk wine and only picked at the appetizer he'd ordered, but it was nice to feel himself among a more civilized crowd than he was used to. He normally found himself only in the worst parts of towns and cities. Truthfully, he purposely did not treat himself to better on most occasions, as it was not something he ever wanted to get too used to again.

But this time with Felicity, he knew that it would be perfect. He had dressed accordingly and had her stop at an ATM machine along the way, so that he might withdraw some money for the evening. He rarely kept any large amount of cash at his house. He had learned to limit himself; he didn't need it for much more than books and blood anyway.

They reached their destination, Felicity carefully guiding them into the parking lot. Her driving was a bit slow and unsteady, but they did make it in one piece. He had to smile at how much he'd forgotten what it was like to have new experiences in life. To see her having encounters like these for the first time, made him feel young again.

The lot was quite full and as he opened the door for her, he noticed that the restaurant was rather full as well. It was as nice as he remembered and Felicity gave him a surprised little smile. The maitre d' met them at the desk to ask for their reservation.

"As it happens, we haven't got one. I was hoping perhaps you might seat us anyway?" The man was already shaking his head in disapproval as Cain spoke, and telling them that he couldn't possibly find room. Cain took a hundred dollar bill from his pocket and discreetly gave it to the man with a handshake. "I do understand, but I hope you'll check again. It's my lady's birthday you see."

Of course, the man became suddenly quite accommodating and before long they found themselves at a private VIP table a bit away from the dinner crowd. Felicity seemed a little amazed at their service. As Cain ordered them a bottle of the finest wine with two glasses, their waiter became a bit uncomfortable. "I'm sorry sir, but I don't believe she's old enough to be served." He turned to ask Felicity, "Do you have ID miss?"

Felicity looked embarrassed, but before she could answer, Cain spoke to the man. "Terribly sorry, but I believe she's left it at home. It is her 21st birthday though. Perhaps you would be so kind, as to overlook her lack of identification for us?" As he said this, he gave the waiter a hundred dollar bill as well.

Felicity was obviously not comfortable with this. "Cain, it's alright, really. I'll just drink soda."

He wouldn't hear of it. "Nonsense. It's your birthday."

Cain looked back to the waiter, who was very apologetic. "Forgive me, it was my mistake. Obviously the lady is mature enough to order as she likes."

Cain gave a small smile and nodded his head once in approval. "The wine then." He looked to Felicity and she didn't argue, but when the waiter left she looked much less pleased.

"Cain, you didn't have to do that."

He beamed, taking her hands in his across the table. "It's your birthday."

"I know, but, I just... I'm not very comfortable with the way you're throwing money at people."

He became severely chastened and sought to take back his hands, but she wouldn't let him. "I'm sorry. I just wanted everything to be perfect for you."

"I'm here with you. Being together, *that* makes it perfect."

"You're right, of course. I am sorry. I tend to do that with money, that's why I don't use it all that much." Cain knew that it was true. There had been times in his life, when money had easily paved a very tempting path for him, one he had decided a long time ago, not to follow. It was shameful how easily it came back to him. He ventured a smile at her for forgiveness. "I do hope you'll order whatever you'd like for dinner, though. *I* don't plan to eat all that much, so it shouldn't be too outrageously expensive," he said with a smirk.

She rolled her eyes. "I don't mind if you want to spend *some* money on me. I just feel weird about using it to get people to do what you want."

"Forgive me. I'm just so bewildered," he said with a little laugh. "Being here... with you, this isn't *at all* the evening I had planned. In fact, I still feel very irresponsible for letting you seduce me earlier." Felicity began to blush fiercely and turned her eyes from him with a smile. "I had been trying to resign myself to the fact that I should leave you alone from now on." She met his eyes again, looking a little dejected at his words. "But you *are* irresistible. Please don't think that I am at all unhappy at the state of things, I'm just a bit lightheaded I suppose. Everything seems upside-down from the way I'd thought it would be, and old habits are all too easy to fall back on."

"Old habits? You mean using money to get what you want? That doesn't sound at all like you. Was that back when you were at Herald Manor?" she asked.

"No. Well yes, but I wasn't really thinking of when I was human. I was referring to when we went back to England, Maribeth and I... after."

"Oh," she replied quietly.

"After regaining the Manor, we lived rather atrociously for a while I'm afraid."

The waiter arrived with their bottle of wine in a fancy little bucket of ice on a stand. He put their glasses onto the table and opened the wine for them. He then poured a bit into Cain's glass for him to sample.

Cain did so, and once his approval was given, the waiter filled his glass the rest of the way. The man then made a great show of pouring a glass for Felicity, and waiting to see if she would enjoy it as well. Felicity hesitantly raised the glass to her lips for a little sip. She gave the waiter a small smile and a quiet 'thank you', after which, he said he would return shortly for their dinner order, and left.

The waiter had barely left the table, when another young man came over to fill their water glasses. He was grinning broadly at them the entire time. As soon as he was finished, the waiter returned with a warm loaf of fresh bread, on a little cutting board with a bowl of butter and a fancy little knife. "Have you decided upon your dinner selections?"

Cain smiled at Felicity, who was just staring at the table. She had not even opened a menu yet. "I think we'd like another moment."

"Of course sir, take your time."

The waiter left, and Felicity closed her eyes and shook her head. "What?" Cain asked.

"Now they're going to be tripping over each other trying to serve us and people are going to stare.

"No one's staring," he replied with a little laugh. She just looked at him in disapproval. He shrugged. "I'm sorry, please don't be uncomfortable." He nodded towards the menu on the table in front of her. "What would you like to eat?"

"I don't know," she said sullenly.

"Come on." He tried to get her to smile. "Please? I've been depressed enough for the both of us, believe me. This should be a happy occasion. Don't let me have spoiled this amazing day." She looked up at him with a smile. "You know, most young ladies would be very flattered and excited to have a man throwing money around on their behalf."

Felicity knitted her brows at him. "If you were looking to flatter someone, then you should have asked Ashley."

That brought the dream that he'd had to mind. Odd how the mind unburies and translates improper desires. Felicity was right, what was wrong with him? "You are absolutely right."

"That you should have asked Ashley?" she asked playfully.

"Of course not! I'm behaving terribly. I'm telling you, this unexpected happiness has put me all out of sorts. Brooding really is more my thing. I've had a lot of practice, gotten rather good at it." Now she laughed. He loved to see her smile. "Can we just forget this and start over, like you had asked me earlier?" Every time he even hinted at their earlier activities, it brought a blush to her cheeks. She was so delightful, sweet and innocent. He sorely hoped that they could both still look back on this time fondly, when all was said and done.

"Consider it forgotten," she said quietly.

She opened her menu, but seemed to be having trouble making a selection. "I would offer to order for you," he said, "but it's been so long, that I haven't even a clue what to recommend. Although most say that you can't go wrong with lobster. Do you like lobster?"

"I've never had it."

"Not even a taste? Even *I've* had lobster. Tell you what, order something you know you'd like, then I'll order the lobster, and you can have a bit of both."

"Okay, but you have to eat some too. Otherwise I'll feel funny about it."

He laughed, but agreed. "Anything for the birthday girl."

The rest of the evening went very nicely. The service was of course impeccable, and although it was a little much at times, Felicity didn't mention it again. She also thoroughly enjoyed the lobster. When she ordered a slice of cheesecake for dessert, the waiter asked him quietly if they should put a candle in it and sing to her, but Cain graciously declined. This sort of place was probably not the type to do such a thing, normally, but if Cain had asked, he'd no doubt they would have had every employee in the restaurant, crooning 'Happy Birthday' for them.

Cain knew that Felicity was not one to want such attention. Especially after she had admonished him for seeking special service to begin with. He watched her eat her dessert quietly as he drank his coffee. "Full day of classes tomorrow, I suppose?"

"Yeah. English Lit., Anthropology and Chemistry. And then I get to go to work! The fun just goes on and on."

Cain smiled. "So, you'll be done around 9:30?"

"Actually, I'm off at 8."

He laughed. "Perfect, I'll only have just woken up a bit before then."

"You are so lucky. You can do whatever you want. It must be nice not to have to answer to anyone, not to have any obligations."

He gave her a very serious stare for a moment. "No, it's really not. Why else would I have piled so many responsibilities upon myself? Feeling *unaccountable* is a very dangerous state in which to live, believe me."

"I guess, but I don't think carrying the weight of the world on your shoulders is the solution either. Sometimes you sound like you feel responsible for the behavior of every vampire there is. You'll never be able to change them all, you know. Not that it isn't a noble cause, but... I don't think you should have to sacrifice your own happiness to do it."

"I remember, you wanted me to 'take a break and have a life for a while', right?"

"Well, yeah. I mean, why couldn't you? Stay here with me for a while. We could hang out, kill a few years..."

He chuckled. "Years?"

Felicity smiled. "Wow, my friend Deidre is right. She has always maintained that all guys are automatically afraid of commitment, no matter what, like it's preprogrammed or something. *You're immortal.* You have lived for over three centuries, and you're afraid to give up a few years?" She laughed. "Not that I'm like *proposing* or anything. I don't want you to think that because of today... I'm going to start expecting stuff from you. I know it sounds like I'm kind of pushing the fast forward button here, but I have to say, your inherent alarm over the idea is kind of funny."

Cain smiled, but this time it was rather melancholy. "You can inform Deidre that she is mistaken. I'm not afraid to give you time out of my life. In fact, if I'd the chance, I would stay with *you* for all eternity." Cain was not very heartened by the look on her face. Felicity very suddenly dropped her smile and looked seriously shaken. Obviously she wanted to be *with* him, but being *like* him was not an option she was considering.

He had already known. He had sort of hinted at it earlier, and she'd shot him down, but he just couldn't stop thinking about it. Especially since his 'leave her for her own good' strategy, wasn't exactly going as planned. Felicity did not seem open to the idea of changing, to be with him fully. He would have to let it go... for now. They had time. "Be unconcerned, I *do* love you as you are," he said, without giving her a chance to comment. "We should get going. I've been irresponsible enough for one day. I won't be remiss in getting you home at a decent hour on a school night. As far as my 'taking a break' goes... we'll see. I can't make any promises."

"You have to." He raised his eyebrows, questioningly. She held his gaze in grave severity. "Make me one promise, it's all I ask."

"What's that?" he inquired.

Her eyes became moist and she took a deep breath as she looked into his eyes over the table. "Don't ever disappear on me. I know, at some point, you're going to feel like you have to leave. I don't know when that's going to be, and I hope it isn't soon, but I can't just pretend the day will never come. It's okay. I mean, I don't *want* you to go, but I guess eventually you'll have to, but you have to tell me. You have to say goodbye. You can't just *disappear*, okay? Promise? I want you to promise."

Of all the things to ask... she was a smart girl. Vampires are notorious for disappearing. Things not going well in a certain town, an identity? Just disappear and go start new somewhere else. It would be very hard for Cain to say goodbye to *her*. If he were going to leave her, disappearing might very well have been his choice, but he had to make the promise and remove that option. He wouldn't refuse her, right now, he would give her anything. "I promise."

~~~~~~~~~~~~~~~~~~~~~~~~~~~~~

The evening was at an end. It was decided that Felicity would drop him off at home, but not come in. The temptation would be too great to stay, if she did. They would see each other tomorrow.

As she drove him home, Cain could not help but replay their tryst in his mind. He had to smile at the sweet innocence she had tried so hard to hide. It had been a great pleasure to initiate her into such exploits, but no matter what they did together in times to come, she would always seem chaste and innocent to his mind.

As they neared his house however, any thoughts about chastity or innocence immediately fled his mind. Sindy; he could see her mark and feel her presence growing ever stronger as they drove. When they turned up his driveway, they could both see her standing at the rail up on his porch, waiting for him. Felicity parked the car in the driveway, staring coldly through the windshield. "Looks like you have company."

"Perfect. I should have known that this was going far too nicely to be an evening in *my* life," he muttered drolly.

"What do you think she wants?" Felicity asked.

She was still just standing there... staring at him. She did not look thrilled at his company. He turned to see Felicity staring at him as well. He shrugged. "She probably wants to pout and sulk some more about my not letting her kill Ben."

Felicity's expression immediately softened. "Thanks again for that."

He dropped his eyes from hers. "My pleasure," he mumbled guiltily. "I'll find out what she wants and then send her away. You don't have to stay, I know it's late."

"Did you... not want me to stay? Maybe I should; see if there's anything going on that Ben should know about."

He should have known she wouldn't want to leave. Woman's intuition. "No. You can certainly stay a bit if you want. I just thought you'd like to avoid being subjected to *Sindy's* company if at all possible." She was just looking at him blankly. Wonderful. "You coming?" He began to get out, as though everything were fine.

"Yeah, I'll come." Great.

He waited for Felicity in front of the car, as Sindy watched silently from the porch. Felicity came around to him and made sure to take his arm, he noticed. He remembered how Sindy had remarked on their body language in the past. It shouldn't be very difficult to read now. Surely that was Felicity's intention, whether or not it was a conscious one.

Sindy just stared at them stonily as they approached. Again she wore no make-up. It made her look curiously vulnerable, but he knew better than to think she was any less dangerous for it. He prayed that she would refrain from upsetting Felicity too much, or saying anything truly hurtful. It was probably a lot to ask from Sindy though.

They climbed the few steps to his porch, and Sindy uncrossed her arms and gave him a very deliberate knowing look, with a hint of a smile playing about her lips. She knew that she held a lot of power in that moment. She loved it. "Conference over?" she asked. Obviously they had been discussing her in the car. She had to know that he wouldn't have *told* Felicity though.

He kept his eyes on hers and silently begged for understanding from her. His mark was still upon her, renewed during their tryst, but her body did seem to be learning to fight it; it was not all that strong. He was very glad of that, it would have been very distracting and only made things worse. "Were you waiting to talk to me about something?"

She gave a slight smile. "Yeah. I just came to *talk*." She paused for a moment, glanced briefly at the cement beneath their feet, then back to him. "Chris has been gone for three nights, without a trace. You seen him?"

Thank God he did not need to breathe anymore, because he surely would have been holding his breath and then let out a great sigh of relief. She wouldn't say anything, bless you Sindy; he tried to tell her with his eyes. "No. Sorry." He meant that in so many ways.

He wasn't sure if she understood, or accepted it. She certainly didn't acknowledge it in any way. "If he comes on your radar, you'll let me know, right?"

"Yes," Cain assured her.

"Thanks." She folded her arms again and took her eyes from his to look at Felicity. It was the first time she'd really done so, since they came up on the porch. She gave Felicity a very obviously appraising look, and then seemed to notice and appraise Cain's appearance as well. "You guys are all done up nice. Celebrating something?" she asked, with a smirk.

Once again, Cain tried to beg her silently. 'Please Sindy, leave well enough alone. Don't spoil it now.' But all he said was, "It's Felicity's birthday." Felicity seemed to squeeze his arm just a bit tighter, though she still did not say a word. He was grateful she would let him handle it. Sindy may be feeling generous towards him, but if Felicity were to bait her, she may decide not to hold back.

Sindy gave a sarcastic sort of laugh and smiled. "No shit. Mine's next week. Although it doesn't really seem to mean as much once you're *dead*." She glanced at Cain. "I won't expect a present." She pushed past him and went down the steps to the driveway. "See 'ya 'round." She gave a dismissive wave over her shoulder without looking, and left.

Cain stood and watched her for a minute as she walked down the road, until Felicity asked, "Think it's anything serious?"

He turned to look at her incredulously. *"What?"*

"She said Chris was missing. You think something happened to him? Something important's going on?"

"Oh. No. If he had died, she would have known. She's his sire." Felicity looked a bit confused. "Sindy *made* him. That makes her his sire, or whatever you call the female equivalent. 'Dam' I suppose, but most vampires just use 'sire', male or female." Felicity was looking at him in amusement. He was rambling, most unlike him. "Anyway, if he'd died... she would know. He probably just got tired of being her 'whipping boy' and left. Can't say I blame him."

"Yeah, who'd want to have to spend eternity following around after her?" Cain tried to smile, but it was an uncomfortable venture. Thankfully, Felicity wasn't even looking at him. "I can't believe how young she looks with no make-up! What is she, fourteen?"

"She's not *that* young. She was sixteen I think, not all that much younger than you. She certainly was not a child. Anyway, appearance is no indication of age for *our* kind. She's older than you are now." Cain realized that he was perhaps protesting too much. He stopped talking and refrained from looking back at the road to search for Sindy's figure in the dark.

He found Felicity's eyes and reminded himself how lucky he was to have such a woman as she, even if it was only temporary. "I won't ask you in, because I know where that would lead. I shall practice restraint, but I will see you tomorrow... and don't expect restraint from me then," he added with a smile.

Now she smiled as well. If she had any suspicions about his relationship with Sindy, they seemed to have been dropped. She came into his arms for a kiss. "I'm looking forward to it," she whispered.

They kissed for a bit longer and then he gently pushed her away. "You had better leave now, or I may not let you."

"Careful, I may call you on that," she threatened.

He pulled her back for another kiss and then whispered, "Good night." She whispered, 'good night' back, turned and left.

He couldn't help but glance back down the road, as Felicity entered her car. Sindy had vanished into the woods. Felicity blew him a little kiss and then he went inside, closing and locking the door behind him.

Chapter 19 - Sympathy

Felicity

10:30, Tuesday night
Felicity's car

Felicity started the car and began her drive home. What a day! As the oddness of seeing Sindy left her mind, she began to think on much fonder memories of the day. They had done it! She and Cain had made love! She was no longer a virgin and no longer felt as though he might see her as a child. It had been so amazing and perfect! Of course, she felt a little silly for trying so hard at first to prove her eagerness to him, but she was glad he had forced her to stop and just be herself, even if he had done it in a slightly disconcerting way.

He was so wonderful, the way that he was with her, once the preliminary awkwardness was out of the way; awkwardness that was all *her* doing of course. She should have just trusted him to lead things to begin with, so that it wouldn't have been awkward at all. He was so gentle, sweet and non-threatening, making everything an amazing new experience instead of something to be intimidated over; like the way he had given her total control over the actual act, so that she would gain confidence in herself and become more comfortable with their actions.

She'd been shocked when he'd wanted her to be on top of him. She never would have dreamt that was how it would be, but he had known that it would be right for her, for this first time. Once they were engaged in it, she felt truly bold and unafraid, no need to pretend. It had been perfect. When their actions had culminated in her orgasm, she had felt as though it was her love for him which was exploding within her, to become something all encompassing and unequaled.

Why did he have to be a vampire? Life was so unfair! She wished they could have a normal relationship. She wished that he were human, so she could introduce him to her friends and family as her boyfriend... or maybe, fiancé. They could have a beautiful wedding, and children, and... a life together. That would never happen. Not with him. She knew that. Still...

No regrets. She could not have chosen a more perfect man to give her 'maidenhood' to. He was so sensitive and loving. The way that he had spoken of it as a great honor... 'de-flowering a virgin', it had made her smile. She loved the way he spoke, his odd mixture of archaic speech and modern slang, it was so quaint! She did love him, no matter their uncertain future. Sharing the experience of making love with him was something that she would *never* regret. At least they could be together for a little while. He *had* said that there would be a next time... The venom. Oh wow, there was an interesting thought.

She turned into the dorm lot and parked the car. She got out and locked the door, having indecent thoughts and speculating on possible future escapades. When she turned to cross the lot to the dorm, she was more than a little startled to find Luke stepping up to meet her. "Hey pretty girl."

She froze... keys in hand, and wondered what she should do. He didn't advance on her, but stopped a little apart from her and kept talking. "I know you, you're Cain's friend." He smiled. "I remember you from the field. You're pretty." She was just about to take a deep breath to yell for help, but Luke realized what she meant to do and looked curiously desperate and upset. "Wait, wait, take it easy! I just wanna talk, just to talk."

She eyed him warily for a moment. She remembered what Cain had said about lesser vampires sometimes suffering from a kind of brain damage. She wasn't sure how competent Luke was, or what he would do, but she *had* to be smarter than him. If things got physical, she was unsure what would happen, better to let him talk. "What do you want?"

He seemed relieved that she would listen. She studied him as he spoke. He was young... when he'd died. Fifteen or sixteen at most. He had a very handsome young face, cheeks still fleshed out with a little 'baby fat'. Although he wasn't a really heavy guy, he looked solid. He was hardly taller than Felicity, but definitely stronger. His hair was a mess of dark curls, and his brown eyes seemed very large and hopeful. He spoke with a voice nervous and uncertain.

"Chris. You know my buddy Chris? I don't know where he is. Nobody will tell me where he is. I can't find him. Have you seen Chris?"

Her eyes softened towards him, he seemed so lost. "I'm sorry," she said sympathetically. "I haven't seen him."

He moved a step closer and pleaded with her. He spoke with an urgency and cadence to his voice that seemed unnatural. He had always seemed like a regular guy to her, but she'd never spoken to him. Now she realized that he was probably not quite the boy he used to be in life. Of course she had not known him before, but something about him was just a little *off*.

He went on. "Are you sure? 'Cause, Sindy said he wasn't dead. She swears he's okay, but I don't know where he is. He wouldn't go nowhere without tellin' me." He stopped speaking for a moment to ponder the ground, and then looked up at her as if just noticing her again. "You know Chris, right? He's my best bud. We *always* hang together. Sindy says he left, but he wouldn't leave without me. Only I don't know where he is."

He seemed to be getting more upset as he spoke. Felicity used a calm and reassuring voice, as though he were a child. "Don't worry. I'm sure he'll come back. You should go and wait for him, so he'll know where to find you."

Luke didn't seem to be listening. "You know what *I* think? I think Cain took him. Cain doesn't like us much. One time, when Sindy wasn't listenin' to him, he said she was lucky he didn't turn her into dust. He said that. I remember."

Luke's eyes were beginning to look a little wild; Felicity took a small step back from him and tried to make her smooth calm voice cut through his growing panic. "It wasn't Cain, Luke. Chris is still alive, he just went somewhere. He's fine. Cain even told Sindy that, just tonight. He's fine."

"Sindy always believes Cain. I think she likes him better than us now. Cain can see us even when we're real far away. He *always* knows where we are. He knows where Chris is, he just won't tell. I'll bet he knows." Luke was beginning to look more than a little upset, more than Felicity wanted to try and handle, but he was standing between her and the dorms. They were still at the bottom of the hill in the lot; a little far to be sure someone would hear her in time if she yelled. She was sure he could catch her if she tried to run, better to get into the car, where he couldn't follow. She tried to seem casual, as she took a step back towards it.

She'd locked the door! Damn! She'd never be able to work the key in the lock before he was on her if he snapped. She'd have to talk her way out of it. "You know what? Why don't *I* ask Cain for you? I bet he'd tell me. He likes me you know... a lot. Wait here. I'll go ask Cain and then I can find Chris for you, okay?"

Luke got very angry. "You think I'm stupid?" She took another step away as he raised his voice, and was backed up against the car. "You don't like us either, do you? Sindy's the only one ever likes us, and she won't tell me where he is! You probably won't tell me either."

She had found her car key and tried to put it in the lock, but now Luke came forward and grabbed her wrist. "Let go of me." She tried to sound very strong and controlled, although she felt her own panic rising inside.

He didn't let go. "You gonna go see Cain? Cain always tells me 'no'. I'm supposed to stay away from him. I think he knows where Chris is."

"Let me go. I'll find Chris for you, I swear." She tried to pull her wrist back from him as she spoke, but he was too strong for her. His eyes got very wide as an idea seemed to come upon him.

"You could give Cain a message for me. Sindy told me not to ask him. I wanted to ask him about Chris, but Sindy said no. I bet *he* took Chris away. He doesn't like us, but he likes *you*. You could give him a message for me."

"I'll tell him whatever you want, just let go!" She was still trying to pull away, but he held her wrist firm. She couldn't really struggle much without touching his body, he was standing very close. She had the notion in the back of her mind that she should try not to rub up against him if at all possible; she didn't want him getting any other ideas.

He had seemed preoccupied as he'd held her wrist, very strongly but almost forgotten to his attention. Now, he suddenly focused on her face with an eerie smile. "Not *that* kind of message."

That sent a chill down her back. "Luke, think about it, you'd better leave me alone. If Cain knew you were touching me, he'd kill you. I'm *his*."

Luke looked confused for a minute. "I can't touch nobody that belongs to somebody else. Sindy told me that, and it makes my head hurt. I don't like that." He looked at her oddly, with new awareness. "But you don't belong to nobody. Maybe Cain doesn't like you so much anymore." He smiled at her new alarm. "I like you." As he finished the sentence, he shifted to his vampire state, smiling broadly to show her his fangs.

She screamed and brought her knee up to his groin as hard as she could. It surely hurt, but he didn't let go. He just squeezed her wrist harder, and pulled her to the ground with him as he fell to his knees.

Felicity's own knees hit the ground hard, and she dropped her keys. She tried to jerk her arm away, while trying to also regain her feet, but Luke still refused to let go. Instead, he used his grip to jerk and twist her arm abruptly backward, so that even as he knelt on the ground in pain, she was thrown onto her back on the ground next to him.

The back of her head struck the concrete, making her see stars. Her free hand went to her hair, expecting to feel blood. What her fingers found instead, was much more promising. Her oriental hair sticks! She grabbed one with her free hand, and pulled it from her hair. Just then, Luke climbed atop her, pinning her legs with his knees. "You bitch, that hurt!" he said it in a dejected tone, as though she should feel badly for him. 'Sorry', she thought, 'sympathy's over'.

He still held his tight grip on her arm, and now reached for the other. She jerked both wrist and stick away, knowing that if he got both arms pinned, she'd be done for. He did manage to get a slight hold of her wrist, but it was an awkward grip. She brought the hand down towards her stomach, in close to her body. Luke didn't really fight her motion too hard. He had let go for an instant, to get a better grip around her wrist. He hadn't noticed the stick; he didn't know she had a weapon.

With a desperate prayer that she would have good aim, she strongly thrust the stick upward into his chest with all her might. He yelled and let go of the hand that was over her head, his arm flung out to the side in desperation. His other hand got a better grip on her wrist and tried to pull her 'stake' out of his chest, but he was laying on top of her. It was almost impossible unless he could get up first.

She must not have hit his heart. Not knowing what else to do, she desperately jerked the make-shift stake to the side, even as he fought to get it out. He put his free arm to the ground for leverage and tried to raise himself a bit, to get the stake out. As he did, she violently jerked the stake to the other side... and it broke. She heard it crack and splinter as his hand let hers go, to come away holding half a stick. She looked up to see why he'd let her wrist go, just in time to see his face... perfectly formed, of what looked to be solidified ash. He then exploded into a cloud of dust.

She turned away and the other half of the stick fell onto *her* chest, as his disappeared. She lay there for a minute with her eyes and mouth scrunched closed, trying not to breathe. Then she rolled aside as her lungs made her take in a huge gasp for air, causing her to cough and choke on ash. The idea of breathing in Luke's remains made her absolutely nauseous, and she had to get herself up and away from the spot. As she scrambled to crawl and then stand a few steps away, trying to catch her breath without getting sick, she heard someone coming from the dorms.

"I'm okay." Felicity tried to tell them, as she composed herself. She wasn't hurt really, although her head was pounding and her wrist was very sore.

It was Maggie, in her robe. She came running to Felicity, looking around frantically for an attacker. "Are you alright? What happened? I thought I heard a scream!"

Felicity brushed herself off and tried to think what she could say. She didn't want the police out here, making her give a statement, and searching for an assailant who had already been turned to dust. "I, um... saw a rat," she said lamely.

Maggie looked at her in disbelief, her eyes moving to take in Felicity's messed hair and dusty dress.

"I saw a rat, and I screamed, and then I dropped my keys. Sorry, if I startled you. I think they went under the car, so I was on the ground looking for them. I didn't find them." She just stood there for a minute, looking at the ground and wondering what Maggie would say. Then she saw a glint of metal on the dirty cement by Maggie's bare feet. "Found 'em!" she said as she plucked her keys from the ground. "Thanks."

Not knowing what else to do, she simply started walking inside. Her knees hurt from the fall, but she tried to walk fast, so that Maggie couldn't say anything else. She heard Maggie follow in behind her, but Felicity just kept straight on, up the stairs and into her room, and then closed the door.

She'd killed him. She had killed Luke, just like that. He was... *gone.* She wanted to rush back to Cain's. She wanted nothing more than to be held in his arms. Now that the fight was over and she didn't need to put up a front for Maggie, she felt delayed reaction coming over her. She felt as though she would begin to shake and shiver. She just sat on the bed with her arms wrapped around herself. Cain... she wanted Cain.

A few things kept her from him. First of all, she wasn't sure if she could sneak back out without being seen by Maggie. She was already certain that the woman did not believe her stupid explanation, and she wasn't sure what else she could say.

Secondly, she was still covered in ash; it clung stubbornly to the folds of her dress and made her feel ill. It wasn't as though it was only dirt... it was *Luke*. She felt as though she'd like to take it off and burn it. She needed to shower as well; her hair was also full of dust. She wasn't sure she could stand to be like this a moment longer, certainly not for the whole ride to Cain's.

Lastly, Sindy. Cain had said that Sindy would feel it, if Chris died. That must mean she could feel Luke the same way, right? Sindy must know that he had just died, here in front of *her* dorm. She did not relish the idea of meeting Sindy on the way to Cain's house, covered in Luke's ashes. No thanks.

She would have to wait for the morning. Right now she would strip and shower - making well sure that the front door was locked and bolted first. Then she would stay in her room, protected by Sindy's lack of invitation, and wait for morning. It was sure to be a long night.

Indeed it was. Felicity's sleep was plagued with dreams that were odd combinations of happiness and nightmare. They seemed to play over and over again, giving her no rest or respite. They began with pleasant memories, bed play with Cain, rolling and tickling beneath the covers, but at some point, he would roll on top of her, and suddenly become Luke. He would smile evilly and try to bite her. She always staked him before he did, but as he died, in that moment when his face had looked ash - he would turn back into Cain. It was then, that she would scream. At one point during her sleep she had thought the screams real. Desperate cries not her own sounded in her ears, but they soon faded from her mind, and the dreams returned to replay the scene over, yet again.

Chapter 20 - Comfort

Cain

Cain's house
Tuesday, just after midnight

Cain lay in bed with a book. He wasn't really reading it though, he had too many of his own thoughts, to concentrate on another's. The book lay all but forgotten upon his chest as he replayed the events of the day in his mind.

He'd considered going back out; it was still awfully early, but he felt as though he had enough to think about, without adding to the evening. He just wanted to sit quietly and try to actually be happy for himself for a change. That was such a rare thing for him. *Content* he had been... but excited, eagerly anticipating what each new night would bring, happy? Not in quite some time. Of course it was underlied with the guilty feeling that he was moving in the wrong direction, but how could something that actually made him happy for a change, really be wrong?

Felicity was a constant thought in his mind. She made him happy like no one else ever had. He tried to keep in his mind, the fact that their relationship could only go so far, and then he would have to leave her; but he still could not quite let go the slim hope that she might change her mind, further into things. Close association with him these next week's would ease her fears and show her the wonder of the pair they could become, if she might someday ask, to be made like him.

It wouldn't be a bad thing, if she chose it for herself, right? It's not as though he would ever force such an existence upon her. He knew that as an intelligent young woman, she surely had a bright future ahead of her, but if *she* decided that her future would be with him... True, it looked unpromising at the moment, but he could not entirely let go of that hope, no matter how selfish and unrealistic.

Even without thoughts of change, their relationship had a promising short-term future anyway. He dreaded the looming thoughts of where they may be a month from now, but right now, she wanted to be with him, and he was planning to thoroughly enjoy every moment of it, while it lasted.

Thank God, Sindy had chosen not to say anything to upset Felicity earlier. Certainly she would hold it over him later, but he could handle that. She must have decided that having Cain in her debt, would be more rewarding than her immediate satisfaction from telling Felicity straight out.

Of course, it's not as though he had *truly* been unfaithful. Although he did spend a lot of time with Felicity, they did not have an expressly exclusive physical relationship...until today. He never would have touched Sindy anyway, out of respect for Felicity and the simple fact that he was with Felicity because he preferred her, but he *had* told Felicity that he would not see her anymore, before he'd let Sindy approach him the other night.

Still, he knew how hurt Felicity would be if she knew. He and Sindy had very long lives ahead of them, if they managed not to kill each other. Sindy must realize that if she let his relationship with Felicity run its course, odds were that eventually he would leave her, or she him. One way or another, Felicity would be out of his life. Then Sindy would have plenty of time to try and pursue her own agenda with him, whatever that might be.

He was just so elated over the prospect of spending the next few weeks loving Felicity, that he did not want to think of anything else. He lay back on his bed and replayed the events of the day over in his mind, yet again.

There was a sudden pounding upon his door. He quickly sat up in bed. Could it be Felicity? Was something wrong? He put down the book as the pounding came again. This time he recognized a mark and a voice to go along with it. "Cain!"

It was Sindy. Cain's desire to rush to the door suddenly became much less urgent. She pounded again as he went to put on his boots before answering. He wasn't planning to let her in; he would go outside to talk. She yelled again as he started up the stairs. "CAIN! Open this damn door!"

He was just reaching the top, when he heard the terrible crash of glass shattering. He ran up the last two steps and rounded the corner to see Sindy's boot kick in the last of his large front picture window.

"What the bloody hell do you think you're doing?" he yelled.

She stepped through the remains of his window with clenched fists and an enraged scowl upon her face. He was standing there looking at her with outraged astonishment when she stalked right up to him, and promptly threw two fistfuls of dust into his face.

Of course he stepped back, waving his hands to try and wipe it away, and spitting to clear his mouth. When he looked back up at her in furious anger, she was still standing there glaring at him.

"That was *Luke*, in case you were wondering," she said with seething ferocity. "She killed him! **She fucking killed him!**"

"Who?" Of course he knew who she must be talking about, but prayed it was untrue.

"Who do you think? Your fucking girlfriend killed my Luke! That bitch is *so* living on borrowed time!"

"Sindy, calm down"

"Calm down? This *is* calm! I think this is a very impressive display of self control. You know why? **Because *her* precious heart is *still beating*,** just the way *you* like it, while my Lukey is ashes on the fucking ground." As she yelled, her voice had begun to deteriorate from screaming fury into trembling grief. She didn't quite cry, but took a moment to gather and compose herself.

"Sindy, I'm sorry. What happened?"

"I don't know." She practically growled the words at him.

"Well, then how do you know it was Felicity?"

She ripped something from her pocket. "I found *this* in his ashes, in the parking lot next to *her* car. Who do you think killed him?" she asked, as she thrust her find into his hand.

It was the broken top half of one of Felicity's hair sticks. Cain could hardly help but smile a little. "Clever girl."

Sindy smacked it out of his hand to the floor. "You insensitive bastard!"

"I'm sorry, but you know that Felicity isn't one to go looking for trouble. You'll have to admit that if Luke was hanging about in the dorm parking lot, it couldn't have been with pure intentions. She had to have killed him in self defense."

"Thank you. That's very comforting," she spat out sarcastically. "You don't give a shit what happened to Luke, you're just worried about whether or not he sucked her first."

Cain could not help but flinch. "I am sorry. I know how hard this must be for you, to lose Luke just after Chris has left."

"Don't talk to me about him. You said more than enough last night."

"About last night..."

"Whatever." She stood quiet for a moment, and then continued in a softer, gentler tone. "Why'd she have to go and *kill* him? He wasn't the sharpest tool in the shed, but that boy would do tricks like a puppy to try and please me; just to make me happy. Do you have any idea how many people in my life have ever just wanted to make me *happy?*" She glared at him for a moment, but spoke again before he could answer. "I'll give you a hint. It's a real short list," She held up one finger and then pointed it at him. "and *you're* not on it." He turned his face from her to look at the floor. "And once again 'little miss goody two shoes' has taken it upon herself to go and fuck it all up for me."

Her anger was beginning to build again, but she composed herself to look at him with a stone cold glare. "I came to you first Cain. You'd better appreciate that, because you have *no* idea how close it was, how badly I just wanted to...ugghhh. I don't even *want* her blood. I just want to snap her pretty little neck!"

"Sindy, I do appreciate your restraint, but she's surely in her room, where you're uninvited. You couldn't get to her anyway."

Sindy looked at him with an evil smile. "I don't need to get into her room. I just need to get into the building. She's gotta go take a piss sometime, believe me, I'd manage."

He stared at her for a moment. She was probably right. It was by her choice that Felicity lived. "Guess I owe you one."

She dropped herself to sit on the floor with a thump. "Pfft. You owe me more than that. Felicity, Ben, Alyson... I'm keepin' a tab. We live long enough, I figure you've gotta pay me back, eventually." He gave her a little smile and shook his head as he joined her on the floor. The smile quickly left his face however, as he began to worry for Felicity again. What must she have been through? Was she alright?

Sindy seemed to have read his mind. She took a deep breath, presumably to calm herself. "She's not marked."

"What?"

"Felicity, she's not marked. No one in the dorm had Luke's mark on them. *She* must have gotten *him* first. Since you're obviously just itchin' to rush over there and check on her, thought you'd wanna know."

Cain gazed at her thoughtfully and gave a grateful smile. "Thanks. Still, they may have taken her to the hospital."

"Na, I didn't hear any sirens, and the place would've been swarmin' with cops. I'm sure she's just *fine*." She couldn't help but add a sarcastic edge to her voice.

"Thank you," he whispered.

"This whole thing is really your fault you know... when you think about it. Luke may have been dumb, but it doesn't take brains to follow instinct. You really ought to mark her again." Cain lowered his eyes, she was right. "What's the matter? Don't tell me she's shy of you. 'Cause you two looked pretty cozy earlier."

Cain looked up at her wearily. "Can't you just *tell* all of them that she's off limits?"

Sindy gave a little laugh. "Cain, have you met them? Sometimes I think that I'm lucky they recognize me."

"Well I don't expect she'll be marked again anytime soon, so try to keep them away from us, will you?"

Rather than take offense at his request, she seemed to find his admission amusing. "Turned you down, did she? What do you see in her anyway? I mean, if she's not even feedin' you..."

"I'd like to think that there's more to life than blood. She makes me happy. Like you said, that's a rare and valuable thing... for any of us." He looked at her meaningfully, for understanding.

She shook her head with a smile. "Won't be for long though. Neither one of you can hold out forever. Even if you did, you'd probably wind up resenting each other for it and that kind of defeats the purpose, don't you think? Doesn't sound like 'happily ever after' is gonna be an option. So... what kind of 'happy' is that?"

"Temporary happiness, better than none. That's the theory I'm going with, anyway. At least our *immediate* future will be happy and satisfying. Even you could understand why I would be hesitant to let that go. I know you've had fleeting glimpses of what a happy relationship can be like. Of course, you'll have to forgive me for saying, you can't have been truly satisfied though, or you wouldn't still be looking for more."

"Yeah well, here's a big surprise. Happy satisfaction, the kind that *doesn't* come at someone else's expense... not something I've had much experience with."

Cain gazed at her sadly. "Come now, there must have some time in your life when you were happy."

"Yeah, like maybe when I was five." He tilted his head with a smile, as though she must be joking. "I couldn't have been much older than that when my dad started makin' me suck his cock every night. When I didn't, he would beat me, so... happiness, not all that familiar a concept."

Cain stared at her for a moment. That certainly explained a lot about the internal power struggle she seemed to have with every man she knew. Recreating abusive relationships... herself in either role. "I'm sorry."

She chuckled dryly. "So was he, when I came back and sucked him dry."

"And your mother?"

Sindy gave a dismissive little shrug. "She's already got so many holes in her, *I* could never compete. She likes heroin." Sindy watched his face for a moment. "I know what you're thinkin'. No wonder I'm so fucked up, right? Don't worry about it. I'll straighten my shit out eventually. I don't even need *you* to do it." She stared at the floor for a moment and then looked up at him with large, expressive eyes. "Sucks to be alone though. I'm not saying Luke and I had some great relationship or anything. His stupidity *was* pretty annoying most of the time... especially when it came along with its own special guilt trip, knowing that some of it was *my* fault, but we did make each other happy, and now I don't even have him." Cain leaned forward to try and put an arm around her, but she jerked away from him hastily. "I'm not exactly in the mood."

Cain looked at her in disbelief. Couldn't she imagine that he might want to touch her for reasons *other* than sex? "I wasn't planning to...

Forgive me, but *that* won't be happening again. I am with Felicity now. I was only going to try and give you a hug."

"What for?" Sindy asked skeptically.

"To comfort you. That's what friends do," he explained.

"Oh, *now* I'm your *friend?*" she asked with a sarcastic smile.

"*You* used the term before *I* ever did," he pointed out.

She furrowed her brow, trying to place the comment. "Oh yeah, back when I fed you that night, from my wrist." She smiled at the memory.

"I suppose *that's* on my tab as well?" he asked with a smirk.

She smiled. "Na, that was a freebie."

He laughed. "Thanks."

She got up from the floor and dusted herself off. "I'm gonna go."

He rose as well. "Back to the rest of your brood? Are they..."

"They're at home. I told them not to go out without me. We've got a TV, they'll stay," she assured him.

Cain laughed at the absurd vision of her nearly mindless zombies sitting eagerly gathered around the television. "I can't even imagine what your home life must be like these days."

She looked at him with a sly smile. "Don't even try, I'm sure the reality is more than *you* could handle." She started towards the door to leave, and then turned back to him with a thought. "Keep Felicity out of my way. I mean it. Self control's *not* one of my strong points."

~~~~~~~~~~~~~~~~~~~~~~~~~~~~~

Less than a half an hour later, Cain was perched on Felicity's windowsill again. She'd left the window open a crack. At first, he thought it was incredibly careless of her. Then he realized that even though *he* had climbed up here, most humans wouldn't care to try it. And another vampire wouldn't have the invitation to enter this way. Rather than open it, he only reached inside to part the blinds a little, for a clearer view. She was asleep in her bed, safe and sound, just as Sindy had predicted. He sat watching her for a moment, in glad relief.

He thought about Sindy's suggestion, that she should be marked. He wondered what Felicity might think about that? But it would move things forward much faster then he'd like. After the familiarity they had shared with each other's bodies, marking would be a much more intense experience *this* time around. It would be difficult to keep it short and unentwined with physical expressions of their love. It would bring their relationship to a whole new level... and that much closer to its end.

No. He must try to avoid it, for now. Although even without its practical reasons, the idea of marking her again was extremely tempting.

He decided not to wake her. It was the middle of the night, and she seemed fine. Let her rest. Tomorrow would come soon enough. He would wait to see her then, as much as he would rather climb into the bed with her now. More than anything, he wanted to enfold her in his arms, but the morning would come all too soon, and this would not be a safe place to spend the day. She would be alright. Let her take care of her obligations tomorrow, and come to him when she was ready. He blew her a kiss, as she had to him earlier, and left her window, to go back home.

Chapter 21 - Why did you buy me this?

Felicity

Felicity's room
Wednesday morning

Morning was a welcome thing. Cain. She wanted to go to him. She should go to class, but it hardly seemed all that important. She got up and dressed quickly, having showered the night before. She picked out a pair of tan slacks with a matching black, white and tan blouse, more because they were a set outfit requiring no thought, than for any other reason. She already knew it looked fairly nice on her, without having to study her reflection. She was just leaving her room, when she bumped into a girl from down the hall. Her name was Cathy, Felicity vaguely knew her from a class or two that they shared.

The girl quickly pounced on Felicity and wanted to know if she'd studied for their English Literature quiz this morning. Felicity had of course forgotten the quiz entirely and couldn't have even said that she cared right now. The girl walked with her out of the building, speculating about the quiz questions. Felicity was just about to explain that she was planning to miss the class anyway, when she saw their professor approaching from the faculty parking lot, next to the dorm.

"Good morning ladies. All ready for this quiz?" she asked, as she fell in with them to walk to class.

"I guess so," Felicity mumbled, and found herself being drawn across campus. Cain's would have to wait.

After English Lit., she had Anthropology. She figured she might as well go. Daylight had certainly given her a better perspective on things and she no longer felt the desperation that had come upon her when she'd cried herself to sleep last night. She was alright. Lunch would come soon enough and then she could go to Cain's. Now that she had a car, there'd be plenty of time. There shouldn't really be any *need* for him to know what had happened sooner. He, Sindy and any others involved were restricted until nightfall anyway. Besides, at least she actually liked this class. She was pretty sure she'd failed her English Lit. quiz.

Come the end of Anthropology class, she raced to the cafeteria and bought a sandwich and soda. She then shoved them in her bag and headed to Cain's. She climbed up his front steps, thanking God for the sunlight, when she noticed something rather upsetting on his porch. Glass, there were shards of glass everywhere and his large front window was broken in. She rushed the last steps to the door and pounded on it.

She tried the door, but it was locked. She thought about trying to climb in the window, when the front door opened from the inside. It was Cain, unharmed. She rushed into his arms. He backed away from the door with her and she let him swing it closed again. "Oh Cain, I thought something'd happened to you."

"Easy there. I'm alright. It's you that I've worried for. Thank God you're safe and whole, but I knew that you were, and I'd have braved even the sun if I thought you in danger," he informed her.

"What happened?" she asked, looking at the broken window.

"Suppose *you* tell *me?*" he suggested.

"Oh my God. Last night, Luke... I killed him," she told him haltingly.

Cain held her tighter, as though to protect her from dangers already gone. "It *was* you." He leaned back to look into her eyes. "But you're unmarked," he said with obvious relief. "Did he... hurt you?" he asked quietly.

"No... well, a little, but I'm okay. I killed him Cain. I actually killed him." She couldn't get the shock of it from her mind, now that the memory had resurfaced. This was not some nameless monster, 'us' against 'them'. Luke had always been considered an enemy, but still. She'd felt like she knew him a little and the way that he was, was not really his fault, but now... he was dead.

"What did he do?" Cain asked.

"He was all upset, about Chris being gone. I felt bad for him actually. I was trying to make him feel better and hoping that I could just get him to go away, but he had this idea that *you'd* done something to Chris, that you wouldn't tell. That's when he attacked me. He said he was going to give you a message, by biting me I suppose. Maybe he thought that it would hurt you, for not telling him what happened to Chris, I guess. I don't know, he wasn't making much sense.

I warned him not to touch me. I told him you'd kill him, that I was *yours*, but he wouldn't listen. ...I'm not *marked*." She couldn't help but feel panicky tears come to her eyes as she remembered her fear and their struggle.

"Oh Felicity." He hugged her tightly to him again, as he ran his fingers through her hair and kissed the top of her head. "But you defeated him. You defended yourself and kept him from you. It's all over now. You're alright."

She leaned back to look at him excitedly as she spoke. "My hair sticks! I used my hair stick to stake him. You gave me the idea. I'd wear them every day from now on, but I broke one."

Cain smiled. "I'll buy you dozens."

"Guess I should start wearing the vial again too," she said quietly.

He looked at her thoughtfully for a moment. "Yes."

"What happened to your window?"

"Sindy. She was none too pleased about your ordeal. Not to worry, I've spoken to her. I don't believe she'll bother you over it, but you might want to avoid her for awhile."

"I always do." Felicity shuddered and asked if they might go downstairs. She ate her lunch with Cain, who then sent her back to school. Only kisses were exchanged as he admonished her advances and told her she would see him when work was finished this evening. He offered to meet her, but she assured him that she'd be fine. Now that she had the car, it really wasn't necessary. She promised that she would be extra careful. He reluctantly agreed and said that he'd be home, boarding his window.

So she forced herself to attend Chemistry class, and waited for time to pass. She never believed that it would, but time went on, as it always does. Eventually her class was over, and she was off to the DownTime for her shift.

When Felicity arrived at work, she saw that Ben and Harold were both in the cafe. There were a few students at a table being served by Harold, while Ben worked behind the counter. She ignored them both.

Ben was emptying the last of a tray of rice pudding into the new tray, at the far end of the counter as she approached. He finished just as she reached the door to the lounge, and she heard him tell Harold that he was going on break.

She heard the tray clang in the sink as the door swung closed, and she thought for sure that Ben would be entering the lounge right behind her. She put her purse into a locker and quickly took off her jacket. Just as she was wondering why he hadn't come in yet, she noticed something on the table by the phone. It was a present, for her.

The little box was beautifully decorated, probably gift wrapped at the store, she imagined. There was a card lying next to it on the table, she opened and read it. All it said, in Ben's large, scrawling penmanship was:

Felicity,

Happy Birthday

- Ben

She was stunned. He'd bought her a present? What could he have gotten her? She immediately tore off the paper and became slightly confused as she looked at the small black box beneath. It was obviously from a jewelry store.

She opened the lid. Inside, atop a piece of cardboard covered in black velvet, was a lovely and delicate gold cross on a thin gold chain. It had a tiny diamond chip on the end of each arm and a slightly larger diamond baguette in the center of the cross. It was tasteful, charming and definitely not cheap.

She quickly closed the box and held it clasped tightly in her hand as she went out to find him. He was not in the cafe. Sure enough, she saw him through the window, walking to his car in the parking lot. She rushed to confront him before he could get in.

"Ben!" she yelled as she opened the door. He stopped at his car, slumping his head and shoulders. His hope had obviously been to escape unnoticed. He turned to face her as she stormed up to him, gift in hand. "Why did you buy me this?"

Ben gave a snort of disgust at her reaction. "You're welcome." He turned back around and unlocked his car door.

Felicity put a hand on his shoulder to make him face her again. "Thank you," she said sincerely. "It's beautiful. *It's too much*. You're barely even speaking to me, why would you buy me this?"

He squinted at her in annoyance. "Well, it's not like I bought it *today*." He gave a heavy sigh and dropped his eyes to the ground. "I got it back when I found out your birthday was coming. You know... right after the night we spent at Allie's." He still wouldn't meet her gaze. "I saw it, and it made me think of you. It was pretty and I thought you'd like it." He shifted his feet uncomfortably and then became annoyed again. "I couldn't find the receipt, so I figured I might as well give it to you. Happy birthday." The last was practically spit out, but it made Felicity smile. She was pretty sure that he was only pretending to be mad at her.

Ben began to open the car door, but she put a hand out to gently push it closed again. He looked up at her with a scowl on his face. "Thank you," she said again softly. "I love it."

He gave up his pretense of being angry with a little huff of breath and a smile. "Too bad you'll never wear it."

"Sure I will." She immediately opened it, took the chain from the box and fastened it around her neck. "See?"

Ben's face clouded again. "Yeah, in the daytime," he said in disgust.

"*Every* time I leave the house, from now on, believe me." Something in her voice drew his attention. He looked up at her questioningly. "Luke attacked me last night," she explained.

Ben was immediately alarmed, although she was obviously alright. "Oh man, are you okay?"

"I staked him," she said quietly with large eyes. She still could hardly believe she'd done that. It seemed very different from the first vampire she'd killed. It seemed more... real.

"No way!" he said it with quiet disbelief. "He's dust? How'd you manage that? Where was Chris, weren't you double teamed? They always fight together."

"He was alone; otherwise I wouldn't have stood a chance. Chris is missing, he just up and disappeared. Sindy told us last night."

"You're sure hangin' with the wrong crowd these days. Enjoy the cross. Sounds like you'll need it. Or of course, you could always ask Cain to bite you again. I'm sure he's just waiting for a good excuse."

She glared at him for a moment, not even dignifying his remark with a response. "Thanks for the gift," she said shortly and turned to walk away.

"Hey," he called out to stop her. She turned back to face him, but he didn't look any less disgruntled. "Sorry I've been such a prick." His expression hardly matched his words, evidenced by the fact that he couldn't leave them stand. "I still think you're being incredibly stupid! But, I'm sorry." It came out short and sarcastic.

Felicity gave him a disbelieving smirk. "Some apology!"

Ben was unfazed. "It's the best you're going to get, so take it or leave it."

"You are so arrogant!" Felicity studied him for a moment. He was trying very hard to affect indifference, but she knew he really did want to make up with her. "But I'll take it."

He looked up in surprise. "Yeah?" he asked hesitantly.

"Are you going to *stop* being such a prick?" she asked with a smile.

"That depends, are you *done* being stupid?"

She opened her mouth and slumped her shoulders with a short sigh. She was trying to give him an out and he had the audacity to think he would tell her what to do? "If you're asking me if I'm going to stop seeing Cain, the answer is definitely no."

"Then I can't make any promises."

"Why did I even ask? It was stupid of me to expect you to go against your inherent nature!" She turned on her heel and began to leave, as Ben slumped against the car with his arms crossed.

"Do you *really* think I'm a prick?" he yelled after her.

She stopped and stood there for a moment, as though thinking it over. Finally she returned, eyeing him appraisingly. "No," she said grudgingly as she reached him. "But you sure do a good imitation sometimes." He'd begun to smile, but stopped to roll his eyes at her. "Do you really think I'm stupid?" she asked.

Ben stared at her, assessingly. "You and Cain are getting pretty serious, huh?" She glared at him without answering. "Do I have to answer?"

Felicity crossed her arms as well and shifted her weight to one side, waiting expectedly. "Alright, go ahead."

"What?" he asked.

"Go ahead, I'm waiting," she informed her acidly.

"For what? For me to tell you you're being stupid? I think we already covered that," he said with a chuckle.

"I'm waiting for you to go all 'big brother' on me and give me a lecture on *why* you think I'm incredibly stupid. Tell me how you're just trying to protect me from my own naiveté."

"First of all, I don't *lecture!*" he insisted. Felicity let out a little 'Ha!'. Ben barely contained his annoyance and went on. "Secondly…" he growled, "I'm *not* your 'big brother', so stop calling me that; I hate it!"

Felicity's voice took on a mockingly sweet tone. "Oh, I'm sorry. How terribly insensitive of me! I should have realized that you would worry someone would overhear and think that you might actually be related to someone as dumb as me!"

Ben uncrossed his arms to push himself off the car in outrage, and then ran his hands through his hair as though exasperated. "Felicity! You are *so* far off base, I'm beginning to wonder if you really *are* stupid!"

"What?" she asked in confusion.

He just shook his head with a sigh. "Forget it. Do want to meet for lunch tomorrow?" The question sounded odd, considering he still had a bit of an annoyed growl in his voice.

She stared at him for a minute. "Are you going to lecture me?"

"No," he grumbled.

"Are you going to glare at me disapprovingly the entire time?"

"No," he grumbled again. Then he smiled. "Well, maybe just a little."

She rolled her eyes. "Yeah, okay." She looked back up at him with a smile. "Wanna go to McDonalds? I'll drive."

It took him a second to realize what she meant, and then he smiled back. "Somebody got a car for her birthday!"

She gestured across the lot with excitement. "Yeah, it's over there. The blue one."

He looked to see it and grinned. "You got a Mustang!"

She laughed. "Oh yeah. That's what you've got, right?" She glanced from his car to hers. "So how come they're so different?"

Ben laughed. "Well, duh. Mine's a 1965 Shelby GT-350 fastback, and yours is..."

"A piece of crap?" she interjected, helpfully.

Ben shook his head and smiled. "I'm thinkin' late 80's? 4 cylinder? It's still a Mustang, they're the best."

"It's a 1987 Ford Mustang, and it's blue. That's about the extent of my car knowledge. That and the fact that next to yours, it looks like a scratched and dented piece of junk."

He shrugged with a smile. "That's just cosmetic stuff, how's it run?"

Felicity shrugged in return. "I don't know. Okay I guess. Maybe you could check it out for me, let me know if it's any good? Help me fix it up a little?" she asked hopefully.

"Yeah, sure. I love a good project," he said with a quiet smile. "So, where's your last class before lunch tomorrow?"

"Abrams building," she told him.

"Cool, I'm right next door. I'll meet you in lot B, say 12:15?"

"Okay. What about Alyson?" she asked.

Ben looked unhappy that she should ask. "I don't think she'd care to join us."

"You guys still fighting?" she prodded.

Ben just moved his head noncommittally. "I haven't seen her."

"All weekend?" she asked.

"Since Thursday," he clarified.

Felicity became concerned. "Do you think she's okay?"

Ben nodded his head in reassurance. "Oh yeah, I'm sure she's fine. I've seen her car come and go over at Tommy's... I just haven't gone in."

"Why not?"

"I have nothing to say to her." Felicity sighed in disapproval. Ben looked as though he'd like to add something, but was hesitant. Finally he asked, "Do you know if..." He couldn't finish the question, but she knew what was on his mind.

"Mattie's not back yet. As far as I know, anyway."

Ben nodded thanks for her insight. "Just curious." They stood in silence for a moment. "Cain knows him, doesn't he?"

Felicity gave a little nod. "Yeah."

"What does he say?" Ben asked.

"What do you mean?"

"About Mattie," he clarified. "Does Cain think he's... okay?"

Ben's quiet concern for the friend he had lost, tugged at her heart. "Yeah. Cain likes him. Says he's a 'good kid'," she said with a little chuckle. "Shy, quiet, real nice. And he says he's never killed anybody, not *ever*. So, something else must have happened to David."

Ben winced at the mention of his murdered friend. "How the hell would he know?"

"I guess he wouldn't, really, but that's what he says."

They stood in uncomfortable silence for a moment, staring at the ground. When Ben looked at her again, she almost thought there might be tears in his eyes; not that he would let them fall in front of her. "I don't think I can do this 'Liss. Everybody expects me to just act like this is all okay and it's just not! This has gone so bizarrely *beyond* okay and I'm the only person who can see it! This whole situation has turned so bad and you guys act like *I'm* the one who's gone insane! Do you have any idea the danger you put yourself in every night? I can't just stand here and do nothing! I can't just *watch* while you..."

"Felicity!" It was Ashley, standing in the doorway and staring at them accusingly. Ben didn't turn to look at her. "You were supposed to be on like ten minutes ago! I wanna go on break!"

Felicity barely glanced in Ashley's direction. "Yeah, I'll be right in." Ashley stood there, sullenly for another moment before closing the door. Felicity looked back at Ben, who seemed to have composed himself. "Ben, I'm okay." He just stared into space until she wondered if he'd even heard her. "You should talk to Alyson."

He gave a bitter little smile. "Yeah, not going to happen."

"Why not? Ben?"

He wouldn't look at her. "Whatever. My break's half over and I have to go home for something. We'll talk tomorrow." Without another glance he got into his car. She was forced to back up and let him drive away.

Felicity was still standing there watching him leave, when Ashley leaned out the door again. "Come on Felicity! I wanna go eat!"

"Coming."

~~~~~~~~~~~~~~~~~~~~~~~~~~~~~~~~

Felicity watched the clock impatiently until finally, at a quarter to eight, she could hardly stand it any longer. It was another slow night, so what if she left a few minutes early – big deal. She headed towards the lounge, taking off her nametag on the way. "Ashley, I'm going to go," she yelled towards the shelves in the back. Felicity was in the lounge getting her stuff before Ashley could even have a chance to answer.

She came back out and gave a little wave to Ben as he was waiting a table, across the cafe. She hadn't had another chance to talk with him once he'd returned from his break, but she had an idea how she would set things right when she saw him for lunch tomorrow. Now, all she could concentrate on was getting to Cain's.She found herself eyeing the sides of the road warily as she drove. She almost expected to see Sindy around every bend, but she made it to Cain's without event. She was so excited to see him! The upset and worry from last night seemed to vanish at the prospect of spending the evening with Cain. In fact, she was planning to spend most of the evening in his bed. She felt so daring and indecent to even be thinking such things, but eager and excited as well. She felt like they had uncovered an entirely new aspect of their relationship. Knowing that it may not last all that long, made her feel as though she wanted to spend every last minute of their time together in his arms.

There was another thought in the back of her mind as well. Now that they had made love together, things were different. She felt as though they were connected in a whole new way. That the bond between them had become stronger than ever, intimate and close, almost like when she'd worn his mark.

Part of her did not really believe that he could leave her. Not now, not after feeling *this*. She knew that he had been very up front and told her that he *would* leave, and she did accept that, but there was a small irrational voice in the back of her mind telling her that after he had loved her like that... he could not really go.

She wanted to feel that again. That incredible closeness, that strong and unbreakable bond that she had felt with him... after. *During* was certainly amazing and unforgettable in its own right. Yes, she was certainly looking forward to some more of *that*. But after, lying next to him on the bed, she loved being snuggled close to him and sharing that peaceful satisfaction of being truly together. It made her feel as though she could very happily spend the rest of her life snuggling and giggling in his bed, without a care for the rest of the world.

She had always been so reserved about such things in the past. Loving Cain had been so freeing. It made her wonder why she had wasted so much time being shy in the first place. Of course, a certain amount of decorum was called for. Time to get to know him and to be sure of her feelings, had been necessary. But now that she felt that she knew him so well, what was the point of being timid? She had nothing to hide from *him*. She resolved to stop wasting time with reservations. He knew her... every inch of her. Shyness and hesitation just seemed silly at this point. Subtlety was just a waste of precious time.

She looked around cautiously before leaving her car. All seemed quiet, no one was in sight. As she mounted the front steps, she noticed that he had indeed boarded up his big front window by the door, from the inside. She was actually quite startled when the sound of loud hammering suddenly came from within. Apparently, he wasn't finished. She pictured him, holding up the sheet of plywood and strongly hammering in the nails... maybe with his shirt off. She shook her head, admonishing herself for such silly visions, better to go and see the real thing. She knocked on the door.

The hammering stopped and he opened the door almost immediately... fully dressed. Of course he was dressed. Felicity smiled at how foolishly disappointed she was. "Honey, I'm home!" she said in a chipper 'playing house' type of voice.

Cain gave her a broad smile. "Hello dear, how was your day?" he answered, copying her tone.

"Better now," she said with a sincere smile.

"What a coincidence, mine too." He took her into his arms for a kiss. They moved inside and by the light in the entryway, Felicity could see his hammer and nails on the floor by the window.

She leaned back to look him up and down. "Look at you, all up and dressed already. That was a very silly thing to do."

He laughed at her. "I had some errands to run. Some work to do," he said, nodding towards the window.

She smiled naughtily. "Well, I suppose we'll just have to get you undressed again, won't we?"

"Well, aren't we bold?" he asked.

"Yeah, it's something new I'm trying." He gave her a little disapproving look. "I'm not trying to be anyone else; I'm just... not going to be shy anymore. Let me know how it works for you." Cain shook his head skeptically, but let her pull him in for another kiss. "Come on, let's go downstairs." She took his hand and began leading him to the stairway. He seemed a bit bemused by her attitude, but suffered himself to be led to his bedroom.

Once at the bottom of the stairs, he went to turn on the light and she followed him into the room. As he turned back to her, she put her arms around his neck and smiled. "Now, where were we?" This time their kiss went on longer and became far more passionate, until Cain suddenly thrust her away from him. "Ow!"

Felicity felt a slight warmth at her throat and her hand shot to the spot... to find the cross necklace that she still wore. "Oh my God! I am so sorry! Here, I'll take it off!" She began pulling the chain around to try and find the clasp.

Cain was looking at it oddly, while lightly fingering the burn at the base of his throat. "That's new."

"Yeah, I just got it today. I totally forgot that I had it on. I am so sorry! Did it hurt?" she asked in concern.

"I'm alright. It's pretty," he observed.

"Oh, yeah. Ben gave it to me." Felicity was eyeing Cain's throat as she undid the chain and took it off. Cain stretched the collar of his shirt a bit, to keep it from rubbing the spot. "Oh God, it left a burn mark!"

Cain seemed unconcerned with his injury, and was looking at her strangely. "Benjamin did?"

"Uh huh. For my birthday. Do you want some ice?" she asked.

"No, and should I think it odd or be at all concerned, that Benjamin is giving my lady jewelry?"

She brought her gaze from his throat to his eyes, and smiled. "No. It's nothing." She held up the necklace in her hand for emphasis. As they both eyed it between them, she realized that it was too pretty to be so easily dismissed. "Well, I mean, it's not *nothing*. It's... very nice, but, it doesn't *mean* anything. It was just... for my birthday."

"Right. Next he'll be spiking my coffee with holy water." Felicity couldn't help but let out a choked little laugh at the idea. "I thought you two weren't getting along?" he asked.

"We made up," she said with a little unconcerned shrug.

"Oh. That's... nice."

Felicity's smile broadened. "Look at you, trying so hard not to be jealous! You're so sweet. You know Ben and I are just friends."

Cain eyed her thoughtfully. "You and *I* used to be just friends."

She looked at him in amazement. "*We* were never *just* friends."

"We weren't?" he asked.

"No! Not in my mind anyway," Felicity informed him.

He raised his eyebrows. "Really?"

"Yeah, where have *you* been? Wasn't it obvious?"

"Best you learn now, that when it comes to reading women, most men are a little slow. I'm glad it's obvious now," he said.

"Me too," she answered.

She shoved the cross necklace into her pocket, and moved to let him enfold her into his arms for another kiss. As the kiss ended, Cain leaned back to look at her again, seeming reassured and satisfied. She had to smile at the insecurity he had shown. As if she would ever want to be anywhere but here in his arms?

"So, you've been straight from school, to work, to me. Have you had any dinner?"

"Not really. I only had a fifteen minute break, during which I wolfed down some pasta salad, but I'm okay. I didn't want to stop for anything after; I wanted to come straight here."

"Are you hungry?" he inquired.

She gave him a sly grin. "Not for food."

She was pleased when he laughed in shock at her statement. "I have thoroughly corrupted you haven't I?"

"Who's complaining?" she replied with a smile.

"You really should eat something," he admonished.

"So, give me *something* to eat," she said with a smirk as she let her hands wander over his body. He wiggled away from her, seeming a bit off-put.

"Alright, this whole 'bold' thing, it *really* doesn't suit you."

"No?" she asked innocently.

324

"I don't think so. I meant did you want to go to a restaurant?"

"I know what you meant. I kind of wanted to have my *dessert* first. Fits with my whole new bold and un-shy attitude."

He rolled his eyes at her. "And what was wrong with your old attitude?"

"It was kind of blah. Shy and subtle seems like such a waste of time. Not much fun. This..." She moved closer to let her hands wander again, for emphasis of her words, "is much more fun."

He laughed and shook his head. "I liked your old attitude."

"You called me timid!" She pretended to be cross with him and pushed him down onto the bed.

He allowed it, but made a sad face, as though disappointed. "Yes, but to be honest, I rather liked timid."

She climbed atop him on the bed, straddling him. "Yeah? Do you like this?" she asked, as she came down for a kiss, after which, he gave her a bemused little smile.

"Yes, actually... I think I could grow quite fond of that."

"Quite?" she teased him, smiling.

"Yes. Very, very fond."

She kissed him again and then wiggled her hips against him. "Okay, these jeans... too thick and stiff. I like your P.J.'s way better." She gave him another kiss, pressing herself firmly against him. "Yeah, the denim has definitely got to go."

She sat up on him and scootched down his legs to grasp and undo his button and zipper. "Luckily, I can help you out with that."

He reached out to keep her hand from his pants. "Alright. Who are you, and what have you done with Felicity?" She laughed. "This is replaying an awful lot like yesterday. I thought you were going to stop trying to be other people?"

"Alright, I'll admit it. Yesterday, I *was* trying to imitate the attitude of another woman, who really seemed to turn you on." As though he couldn't guess who that might be. "But now, I'm really *not* being anyone else. It's me. Honest. This is just the 'me' that I don't let anyone else see. The side that used to be too shy to come out."

Cain raised his eyebrows and thought about that for a moment. "Intriguing. Right then, carry on."

She laughed and then continued unfastening and pulling down his pants. She threw his jeans to the floor and then went back to remove his underwear. She smiled up at him nervously, but resolved not to hesitate. She kept her eyes on his, and not what she was doing, to help ease her nervous butterflies. Unfortunately, that was probably not a good strategy. She simply pulled his underwear straight down by the band at each hip, and managed to snag them on his erection. She pulled uncomfortably before noticing.

"Ah!" he cried.

"Sorry!" She let go in flustered embarrassment.

"That's alright," he said through his laughter. "At least I know it really *is* you. If you'd managed to undress me too easily, I might wonder where you'd had the practice." She hid her face and shook her head in humiliation.

He reached up to pull her hands away and meet her eyes as he spoke. "Don't waste time and worries on embarrassment. We laugh *with*, not *at* each other. Do you think in three hundred and forty years, I've never had an awkward moment?" She smiled at him, though her face was surely still red. "Now, would you like to try again?" he asked with a chuckle. "Or shall *I* remove those for you?"

She tried to stop giggling. Why did things never go just as she imagined them to? "I think I can do it," she said with a little smile.

~~~~~~~~~~~~~~~~~~~~~~~~~~~~~~

Felicity snuggled closer under the covers, against Cain in the dim light of his bedroom. She'd thought him sleeping, but as she moved against him in the bed, he opened his eyes and gave her a contented little smile. She smiled back and then rested her head against his chest.

They had spent the evening in his bed, just as she'd fantasized earlier. It was surely well after midnight by now. The hours had seemed to pass in a dreamy haze of laughter, love and new experiences. She was only just feeling the venom fade from her now. He had not bitten her of course, but through his kisses and their love making, her body *had* been thoroughly infiltrated by it. The effects of the venom on her senses never quite reached the level of intoxication that she had felt the night that he *had* bitten her, but it did come close.

She tried never to think of that night. The memory of his bite was something she had tried to block out of her consciousness, not to be confused with the feelings that he stirred in her now. They did seem so similar, the physical desires he brought out in her and those brought about by his bite, but she refused to try and analyze it. The bite was on its way to becoming an indistinct memory, she'd like to think. That was the past, separate and unlike the natural and harmless enjoyments that they now shared.

She lay there, basking in the tender and peaceful contentment of their quiet time together, feeling totally empathetic to his sentiments last night, that he wished time could stop. This moment in time had to be preferable to anything that the future might hold. As though to prove her point, he spoke. "It's late. You should probably go."

She looked up and pouted at him. "I don't wanna go." He just smiled. "You wouldn't actually kick me out, would you?"

He reached around to take hold of her and roll her to lie atop him for a kiss. "You have classes tomorrow."

"So? That's like eight hours away. Can't I stay here, or do you really *want* me to go?"

"What I want and what should be, are two entirely separate matters. I know you must be tired. I however, am nocturnal and will be very much awake for the rest of night. If I were to let you stay, I would be utterly incapable of keeping my hands off of you." He squeezed her bottom to emphasize his point. "You'd get no sleep at all. Then the dawn would come. Knowing that I'll be trapped here alone all day, I really will be loathe to let you leave. You should go now. I won't have you missing classes for me."

"So I take a sick day, big deal."

He laughed. "Right, and one sick day becomes two and then three... Before you know it, your studies will have been totally neglected and you'll find yourself spending all of your time in my bed."

She cocked an eyebrow at him. "Are you supposed to be discouraging me from this? Because, you're doing a terrible job. In fact, it sounds pretty good to me." She wrapped her legs around him and snuggled her face into his chest. "I could be very happy, right here, cozy in bed with you, forever."

"I myself would be perfectly happy never to leave this bed again. However, *I* would be the only one to survive that scenario. *You* may get hungry after a while," he teased.

"I got a cell phone for my birthday. I'll order pizza."

He grinned and hugged her for a moment, and then gently rolled her aside. She looked up to see him with a quiet sadness in his eyes. He reached up to tap a finger upon her nose with a little smile and then it trail down to her lips for a kiss. "*Forever*, is not a word to be thrown around lightly."

She was a little disgruntled by his statement. They had never discussed it openly, she wouldn't really let him, but she knew full well that he would change her to stay with him forever, if she'd allow it. She also knew that he understood that she didn't want to. Not like that. It was like a little unspoken sore spot between them. One that was better ignored.

Felicity rolled to her side, facing away from him. She felt tears rising to her eyes, because she was not really the kind of woman that he wanted her to be. She knew that he loved her.., but she was human and planned to stay that way.

Cain snuggled close to her back and put his arm around her, to hug her from behind. He gave her a kiss on the cheek and whispered to her ear. "But I say you must leave not only for your benefit, but to fix it to be set in my mind as well. You have a life, a future, *outside* of my bedroom. That's a wonderful thing for you to look forward to. I'm trying very hard, not to forget that.

Go home, get some sleep. Go to your classes, do the things that you must. Tomorrow evening will come soon enough."

She smiled sadly. He did love her, even if she was human. He would accept her the way that she was. For the hundredth time she cursed the fact that he was a vampire and not just a regular guy. She wiggled herself against him and looked up to him over her shoulder. "Okay, I'll go, but... just one more hour wouldn't hurt, would it?"

He chuckled and pressed himself firmly against her from behind. "Now *that's* something that I might let you convince me of."

~~~~~~~~~~~~~~~~~~~~~~~~~~~~~

The next morning's classes seemed to go quickly, but that might have been because she was half asleep for most of them, by the time she had gotten back to her dorm last night, it was about two o'clock in the morning. She had found that she had to open the car window, just to ensure she would remain awake on the ride home.

When she had finally made it there, she had held tightly in her hand, the new stake that Cain had given her, as she crossed the lot to the dorm steps. She thought about how angry Sindy must be with her and was very grateful that Cain seemed to have intervened somewhat on her behalf. Sindy may not treat her kindly if they came across each other, but at least she was not there waiting in the parking lot.

Now she sat watching the clock and at 11:45, the instant sociology ended, Felicity was out the door again to her car. Ben's beloved yellow Mustang was still in the parking lot, not far from her own. She hoped his class ran late.

Felicity had to pound on Allie's door three times before she finally answered. She was still in her pajamas and stifling a yawn as she opened the door. She seemed very surprised to find Felicity standing there.

"Hi! Get dressed, we're going to lunch."

"We are?"

"Yes, my treat." Allie backed into the apartment to let Felicity enter. After a minute, she shrugged and went to get dressed.

Felicity wandered over to study some pictures on the wall as she waited. They were photographs; beautifully captured nature scenes of forests and fields, with the odd butterfly in the frame or deer in the distance. At first Felicity assumed that Allie had picked them up at a flea market or garage sale; but when she moved to look at a picture on the opposite wall she had a strange start of recognition as she recognized the little waterfall near the duck pond at the park. The same one where she and Cain had enjoyed their picnics. Felicity wondered who the photographer was.

"What brought this on?" Allie asked from the bedroom, as she changed her clothes.

"I haven't seen you in a while. Thought we'd talk." Allie stuck her head out the door and looked at her suspiciously.

"About what?"

"Well…" It only took Felicity a second to think of a topic Alyson might take fondly to. "Cain and I have been getting pretty serious. I thought maybe you could give me some insight on some stuff."

Now Allie came out in a tee-shirt and jeans. She sat on the couch to put on her sneakers and gave Felicity a sly grin. "Ooh, gettin' hot and heavy are ya? Let me tell you, vampire sex.., *best* you will *ever* have. Really. There is no equal."

"Allie! That's not really what I wanted to talk about."

"Why not? That's the fun stuff. It's not like I get to talk about it with anybody else." She sighed. "God I miss Mattie."

"Still no sign of him, huh?"

"No. He's got eleven more days and then I will be officially pissed at him."

"I'm sure he'll show. Are you ready?" Felicity asked.

"Just a sec, I wanna brush my teeth." Allie darted into the bathroom as Felicity impatiently looked at her watch. Only a few minutes before Ben would be waiting for her. Allie came out with the toothbrush still in her mouth. She pushed it to one side and spoke around it. "Are you marked?"

Felicity just stared at her for a minute, until Allie couldn't wait anymore. She went into the bathroom to spit and then came back out, wiping her mouth on the back of her arm. "Are you?"

"No." Felicity opened the front door.

Allie put on and zipped up her sweatshirt as she looked at Felicity's car in the driveway. "That yours?"

"Yes."

"Pretty," Allie replied sarcastically.

"Very funny, get in."

They got themselves settled in the car and Felicity headed back to school. As soon as they left the driveway, Allie started after her again. "So how come you're not marked, you wouldn't let him?"

Felicity glanced at her in annoyance. "He didn't ask."

Alyson rolled her eyes and leaned back to rest her knees on the dash. "Well it's not like you don't know he wants to."

"Allie, I didn't really want to talk about that either."

Now Allie was the one to become disgruntled. "You want to talk about you and Cain, but you don't want to talk about sex, and you don't want to talk about blood. What else is there?"

"Plenty, but I didn't really want to talk about Cain at all. That was just my cover."

Now Allie looked very confused. "Then who'd you wanna talk about?"

"You and Ben," Felicity informed her.

Alyson slumped down further in her seat. "You woke me up for that?"

"Come on, you guys are best friends. You can't stay mad forever," she admonished.

"I'm not mad," Allie said defensively.

"So what happened? You guys had a fight?" Felicity asked.

Allie shrugged. "It wasn't much of a fight really. It was the whole Vermont scenario again. He wanted me to go with him, before Mattie got back. I said no. He told me not to see Mattie, and I told him to go fuck himself. It was pretty straightforward really. I'm not mad at him, but I'll be damned if I'm gonna let him tell me what to do. Never have, never will."

"You guys have to talk it out. Somebody has to make Ben see that things are okay," Felicity told her.

"Well, that somebody ain't gonna be me. He won't talk to me; I know how stubborn he is." They pulled onto the college grounds. "Where are we going? You're taking me to school for lunch? Some treat." As they pulled into lot B, Felicity could see Ben at the far end, leaning against his car, Allie spotted him too. "Oh."

Ben was just checking his watch when Felicity pulled up next to him. She put the car in park right in the middle of the lot and got out. Ben spoke to her as she did, but she walked around to the passenger side rather than stop to listen to him. "Where'd you go, I thought we were going to meet here?"

Felicity ignored him and opened the door to pull her passenger out. That's when Ben saw Allie. "Ah, 'Liss what are you doin'?"

Felicity took Allie by the wrist and led her around the car, but she didn't bring her to Ben. She took her to the passenger side of Ben's car and made her get in. Now Ben looked pissed. "Get out of my car." Allie just slumped down in her seat, the same as she had in Felicity's car and wouldn't speak or budge.

Ben looked back to Felicity. "What are you doing?"

"*I'm* not doing anything. *You* and Allie are going to make up."

"Why?"

"Because you and I have made up already and you're way better friends with Allie than you are with me. So you can't be mad at her for dating a vampire, and still be friends with me while I'm dating one. It wouldn't make sense. You're the one who says he lives in 'logical reality'."

"I'd be more logical to just stop being friends with you again."

"Shut up. I'm going to McDonald's and you and Allie are going to follow me. And by the time we get there, you two better have made up, because I don't have any more classes today, and if you don't make up with her, I'm going to follow you around and bug you until you do."

Ben stared at her for a minute. Alyson spoke up from within the car. "Felicity, being followed around by you all day... not gonna be a big deterrent. Ben, get in the damn car. Otherwise *I'll* follow you around, and I *know* how to be a pain in the ass."

Felicity looked at him pleadingly and smiled. He never looked at Allie, but stayed staring at her for a minute or two longer. "Ben," she asked quietly, "please get in." He didn't say anything.

Allie leaned to look at her from in the car. "Just go to McDonald's, we'll be there"

Ben took his eyes from hers, to look at the ground and sigh. "Go ahead," he said quietly.

She left. Felicity sat in the McDonalds parking lot for fifteen minutes before they finally showed up. When they got out of the car, neither one of them looked very happy, but they didn't say anything.

When they got their food and found a table, she noticed that Ben made a point to sit next to her instead of Allie. They made mostly small talk as they ate their lunch, but at least Felicity got them talking again.

Chapter 22 - Thirst

Cain

Thursday afternoon
Cain's house

Cain lay in bed, waiting for Felicity to arrive. It wouldn't be dark out for a few hours yet, but he couldn't sleep. Their recent time together had made him so happy... it couldn't last. He hated to think that way, but he was becoming aware of an issue that he would have to face. His blood thirst, yet again, was getting in the way. He'd felt the beast within, longing for Felicity, each time they made love. It was getting stronger. It was growing into something difficult to ignore.

In his years of solitude, he drank nothing but animal blood, bought from the butcher, cold and impersonal. His body had become accustomed to that, it expected no more, but in the past three weeks, he had drunk from a victim, no less than four times. Starting with Felicity and ending with Sindy, he had given his body blood that, compared to that from his refrigerator, was absolutely divine. It truly *was* an addiction, the blood. The more his body had, the more it craved. It knew the difference... it wanted the good stuff.

It served as a good lesson to him actually. It was so long since he'd been in a relationship that allowed him to drink from another regularly. He had forgotten just how difficult it could be, to deny the vampire within, what it really wanted. He should not be so hard on the young ones, whom he so often tried to teach. It was harder than he remembered.

In the past, when a blood relationship ended, it was usually tied to emotional heartache as well. When his body admonished him for denial of his thirst, he had usually accounted it to his emotional loss. Purely physical withdrawal was not something he'd really thought much about. Now, his body was remembering the rich rewards of drinking from a host, rather than a cup. It wanted more, but he could not entirely blame his problem on the beast within. He knew that *he* was directly to blame for his blood desires as well.

Old habits die hard. His relationship with Felicity was not moving quite as quickly as things had gone with others in the past. Women that he had shared his bed with, he had always drunk from as well. It was something started back in the old days, when he used to hunt. Many of his victims had been 'ladies of the evening'. Thus it was a simple thing to pay them for their services and then take more than they had thought to give.

Even when he had ceased hunting, he'd still drunk from Maribeth during sex. Once that relationship ended, he had gone through the worst withdrawal period of his life, but he'd almost thought that it was the physical expression of his grief over her departure, being that he found it hard to openly emotionally grieve over her leaving.

Over the years he had entered into serious relationships with others, now and again. There weren't many, but they all had one thing in common. For the entire duration of his relationships with those women, be they human or vampire at the time, he had drunk from them during sex. It seemed a natural thing, done not only for himself, but often at their request. They wanted the venom, he wanted the blood. They both came to expect it and often it brought about the climax of their love making, for both of them. His body had come to expect it as well, why shouldn't it? That was only what Cain himself had taught it. The vampire within had come to learn that when his body engaged in sex, blood would be forthcoming.

He had assumed that he could disengage himself from that. That he could make love to Felicity and it could clear the other desires from his mind. Somehow he had not expected that it would only make them worse. Sindy's blood had helped to quench the thirst for a time, but that blood was just about gone from his system now. He certainly wasn't going to ask to drink from her again. He had planned to drink as much blood from his refrigerator as his body could hold, before seeing Felicity again, but it was not going down very well and he still worried that it wouldn't really help.

He got up from bed now, to try and drink some more. He wanted the evening to be perfect. He was unsure when she would arrive, but she had said she would see him before sunset. She wasn't working tonight, but she did have plans for lunch with Ben and Alyson, before she would come to him.

He tried not to let that bother him. It was a *good* thing that she had a life, outside, in the daylight. If she did not choose to stay with him, (and he had to admit that it seemed likely she would not), then he would eventually have to leave her. She would need friends and outside distractions, to help her to let him go. Still, he wished she had *other* friends. Benjamin, while close with Felicity, would never accept *him* as a friend. Ben could not see past the fact that Cain was a vampire. That made him not a mutual friend, but a sort of wedge between them.

Cain felt as though Ben was constantly speaking against him and doing things to undermine his relationship with Felicity. Giving her a cross for her birthday? It seemed an obvious slap in the face. Not that Cain planned to let the boy get to him, but it would be nice if Felicity did not spend *so* much time with him. It wasn't as though Cain were really jealous of Ben, but anyone who could spend the day outside in the sunshine with her, had something that he did not. The fact that it was Benjamin made it seem that much worse. It was depressing.

But away from petty thoughts and on to more important concerns. Luke's attack on Felicity had brought the blood issue further to his attention. She was not marked. He had decided to try and wait a while longer before marking her again, because he did not want to feed his inner vampire any more than he had too.

However, (and he was loathe to admit this to himself), he could not help but notice with a bit of indignance, that she did not even seem to want him to. He had thought that the experience of Luke's attack would spook her. She understood the concept of marking. She knew that it would help to keep her safe, and yet she had said that she would wear the vial, rather than speak to him of marking her. She did not *want* him to mark her. That should not bother him, but it did.

He knew that she had enjoyed the experience of his drinking from her. She would not discuss it with him and he'd been afraid to question her about it before she was ready, but he *knew*. So why was she so afraid to relive it? She must know that he would not really hurt her and she couldn't have the same concerns as he. She could not foresee how the dynamics of their relationship would change.

Was she in denial? Was she simply trying to pretend that it had not happened, that he was... human? Surely she wished that he was. Was she unwilling to face the truth? Had she been *that* frightened by the act, scared to realize that he really was *a monster?*

He forced himself to drink the blood from his cup and then went back to bed... to wait. The hours passed, he dozed on and off, listening for her knock upon his door. He got up, showered, shaved and dressed. Finally she arrived.

She was such a welcome sight to his eyes. Even in jeans and a casual shirt, she was lovely. He greeted and kissed her, and brought her downstairs. He was excited to give her the surprise he'd prepared. She sat on the bed, confused but eager anticipation in her eyes. He felt such silly giddiness as he went to get the package. "Stay there, I'll get it," he said as he went behind the bar.

"What is it? What's the surprise?"

"If I told you, it wouldn't be a surprise," he said with a grin. "I never did give you a birthday present," he said by way of explanation.

"You don't have to give me a present, besides, you took me out for that expensive dinner."

"That wasn't a present, that was just food."

"It was very nice," she said as he handed her his gift.

It was sadly bundled in newspaper. A child probably could have done better, as he didn't even have any tape. "Sorry, I didn't have any wrapping paper."

She smiled up at him. "You didn't have to go and get me anything."

"Well, I hope you won't be disappointed, but... I didn't. It's something that I already had, but I hope you'll like it, I think it suites you."

She smiled at him thoughtfully and unwrapped the paper. There was a black silk scarf, bearing a pink and white floral design inside. "It's pretty."

"The real present's inside the scarf. I didn't have a box either." he quickly explained.

Now she unfolded the scarf to find within, an antique hair comb. It was heavily encrusted with beautiful jewels. Tiny little diamonds, sapphires and emeralds in swirling designs, across the top. Her eyes went wide and she was obviously delighted.

He was so glad that she seemed to like it. "Before the thought even comes to your mind, let me say that... no, it did *not* belong to my wife, or Maribeth, or any other ex-girlfriend. Nor did I steal it from any victim long ago. I *inherited* it, from my aunt. It's mine. Shortage of girls in my family, guess it was thought that I'd give it to my wife someday, but I stuck it in a drawer and forgot about it.

I came across it again, during the estate sale when we cleared out the Manor. You know, we sold everything, before allowing tourists to come traipsing through. Anyway, I ought to have sold it, but it was just so lovely. *I* certainly had no use for it, but I couldn't seem to part with it. So I held on to it, all these years, although I didn't know for whom. As it turns out, it was you. I hope you like it. Happy birthday."

She kept fingering the jewels and turning it this way and that, to shine in the light. "Cain, it's *gorgeous, b*ut, it must be such a valuable antique by now."

"I don't know what it's worth, but the stones are real. And I do think that it's about four hundred years old by this time."

She looked up at him in disbelief. "I can't accept this."

"Of course you can. Please. I *want* you to have it. *If* you do like it, that is." She looked at him as if he'd be crazy to question whether she cared for the piece. He smiled. "Keep it, and when you look upon it, think of me. And make me a promise. If you truly do care for it, then don't leave it locked and hidden away in a safe deposit box somewhere. Wear it, when the occasion warrants. I'm afraid it can't be used for staking ill-mannered vampires, but I know it will look charming in those lovely auburn locks of yours."

She seemed to shake off the shock that had come upon her when first revealing the gift. Now she held it tightly in her hand and leaned to hold and kiss him. "Thank you! Thank you so much! I do love it, really!" He smiled and gladly accepted her kisses and hugs. He tried not to acknowledge the phrase that kept floating through his head... 'something to remember me by'.

He took her for dinner, to a more modest establishment this time, and the evening once again ended in his bed. He did not even let his lips wander to her throat this time, the temptation was too great, but their love making did carry its own rewards, and once again, he made it through. Still, he wondered if they would have to speak of his concerns sometime soon.

She trusted him, explicitly. Ever since the first time that she questioned his control. He had promised her that he would tell her, if things became too difficult. He felt his word was sacred. What else did he have if not his word and character? He would tell her, if he *had* to.

To be honest, he had hoped that she herself would have broached the subject by now. They had never even really discussed the bite that she had already received from him in the past. He had believed that once she was fully comfortable with him, physically, it would be something that she would be unafraid to talk about, but she had never even evinced curiosity, or asked for further explanation of the act. He would have to speak to her of it soon, lest he inadvertently make known his illicit desires and make things ten times worse. At least if they talked openly, he would know how she really felt over the issue.

She lay snuggled in his arms and he tried to think how such a conversation could even start, but no words came to mind. The night wore on. Finally, he found himself kissing her goodbye until the morrow. The topic would have to be broached another night.

~~~~~~~~~~~~~~~~~~~~~~~~~~~~~~~~

One night rolled into the next, and before he knew it, a whole week had gone by. He still hadn't brought himself to begin discussions of blood, but he was doing better. He was keeping himself very well fed, no matter how distasteful his meager fare seemed. The vampire in him still wanted more, but the prospect of losing Felicity due to fear, helped motivate him to keep things in check. He drank animal blood until it made him feel ill, refusing to acknowledge his desires to drink from Felicity. It was one of the most difficult things he had ever accomplished.

Their days and nights together seemed to pass in a haze of romantic outings, quiet comfortable evenings at home and ever ardent expressions of love in his bed. She had become confident and playful during their love making, and although the beast within him desired her strongly, the man that he was, was quite well satisfied.

Things were so comfortable now, normal and pleasant. How could he ruin it with admissions of thirst for her precious blood? He told himself that of course he would let her know, if it were truly a problem, but he didn't want to frighten her unnecessarily, he had things under control.

Another solution also came to mind. There was always Sindy. She had strictly avoided him since Luke's death, and he did not seek her out. He was unsure how she was spending her time, but it was not with him. She was still around; he did feel her now and then. She slept in the same location that she and her brood had used back when he'd first gone to find them, to protect Ben, but once the evening was underway, she seemed to prefer solitude. She never strayed all that far from her boys, surely their marks were usually within her range, so she could keep an eye on them he assumed, but she seemed more and more to be seeking physical distance from them.

Sometimes while out with Felicity, he would sense Sindy; though he wouldn't mention it, and they never saw her. He would feel her... alone, near Venus or just out in the woods, on the way from one place to another. He believed that he was right in assuming that she was growing tired of her boys. Especially now that Luke and Chris were gone, she did not seem to want to share her company with the others any more than necessary.

He could drink from *her*, that would quiet the beast within him for a longer time. The very idea felt indecent; that he would do so without Felicity's knowledge and that he would *use* Sindy so. It would be wrong, but it would solve his problem, for a while anyway. It was almost as though he needed a separate woman for each of the entities that he was inside. Felicity for the man, Sindy for the vampire.

No, that was not an acceptable scenario. He would have to consider it an option of last resort. For now, he would rely on his own self control, and hope that it remained strong enough.

Chapter 23 - Have a ball

Felicity

DownTime cafe and bookstore
Friday afternoon

Felicity stood at the register, waiting for Cain to arrive. It wasn't even really dark out yet, but she could hardly wait to see him. The last week had been such a romantic whirlwind of new experiences and old comforts, blended together to make the happiest time of her life. She had seen Cain at his home after school each day, or if she were working, he would come to the DownTime as soon as the sunset permitted. He took her for dinner, dancing, they'd even had another romantic picnic - with no serious or frightening discussion, only happy and wonderful time spent together. She wanted it to last... forever.

The finishing touch, to truly make the week perfect... no vampires, not a single one. Except for Cain of course, but she hardly even thought of *him* as a vampire anymore. She had not seen a single vampire since killing Luke, and that suited her just fine. Maybe they were afraid of her now? Probably not, but whatever the reason, she was very happy about it... it couldn't last.

She wore the vial faithfully and the cross from Ben as well. The vial hung a bit lower, on a longer chain than the cross. Together, she thought they looked very interesting. The cross so lovely and traditional, the vial also pretty, but exotic and unique. She had gotten many compliments on them both. She never went out without them and made very sure to take them off, upon arriving at Cain's. He surely noticed this new habit, but never commented on it.

She had worn the hair comb once, for an evening out with Cain. It was so beautiful! It really did work well in her hair and looked absolutely gorgeous. To wear it made her feel like royalty, a princess. She knew that she would treasure it always.

She loved the scarf as well, and wore it often. It had hardly seemed noteworthy next to the comb, but on its own, it was very pretty. She loved that she could wear it all the time, in her hair, or tied about her throat. She loved that it had come from him. She wore the scarf today, holding her long hair in a loose pony tail. It made even such a casual hairstyle, look charming and polished. Even Ashley had commented on how pretty it was, and Ashley was not one to give out compliments often.

Darkness fell, and Felicity found herself eagerly watching the door for Cain, as Ashley shelved books. Cain had returned to his habit of walking to the DownTime, when she was working. Then she would drive them back to his house at the evening's end. So she knew that it would take a little longer for him to get there, than when he drove the motorcycle. When he finally did arrive, he met her at the counter for a kiss hello. It began as a simple, and 'workplace acceptable' peck on the lips, but as he sought to back away, she threw her arms around his neck, over the counter, for a longer and much more intimate kiss.

Normally she would never do such a thing, not in public anyway, but whether it was conscious or not, it wasn't just his kiss that she coveted; it was the venom that she wanted as well. She had become quite fond of the dreamy euphoric feeling that his deep kisses could produce in her, however short lasting. They had not seen each other all day, and she had been waiting for that kiss. A simple peck on the lips would not do. The kiss ended, and he backed away from her with a slightly reprimanding look and a small smile. "You're going to get yourself in trouble. I'm going to find a book to read." He gave her a little wink and headed back to the shelves, giving Ashley a quick 'hello' as he passed.

Ashley came to meet Felicity at the registers. "You two certainly seem to have kicked it up a notch." Felicity just gave an embarrassed smile as she turned her eyes from Cain to the floor. "Things finally getting hot?"

"Like molten lava," she whispered with a giggle.

"Ooo. With *him*...I've no doubt." Ashley always persisted in asking her embarrassing questions about Cain, when he was in the store. Ashley assumed he couldn't hear them, and of course he could always hear the entire conversation. It had become almost a game to Felicity and she found herself answering more for Cain than for Ashley, most of the time.

Cain picked out a book to buy and Felicity rung it up with a demure little grin. Cain kept a remarkably straight face, but as Ashley walked away he raised his eyebrows. "Lava?" he whispered with a smirk. She just giggled and sent him over to the cafe.

Ashley came back, very obviously admiring Cain from behind, as he left. Felicity always tried to take Ashley's open attraction for Cain as a sort of compliment. At least Ashley didn't flirt with him in front of Felicity so much anymore, although she had no doubt, the flirting probably still went on when she was not around.

Felicity was certain that a man as handsome and charming as Cain could probably manage to attract the attention of pretty much any girl that he wanted. He was with her because he wanted to be, and by this point in his life, he seemed mature enough not to bother playing games. She didn't really worry about another girl stealing him away. Still, as much as she pretended not to mind Ashley's attraction to Cain, it *was* a bit grating at times.

Felicity decided to give Ashley a little disapproving look as she finally pulled her eyes from Cain. Ashley seemed completely oblivious. "Is he taking you to the Halloween Masquerade Ball?" she inquired with a smile.

Sore subject. "No. We're not going." She and Cain had discussed the dance the other night. He had informed her that he definitely would not attend an event centered on such a banal and offensive 'holiday'. She was more than a little disappointed.

Ashley seemed to think it was an absolute outrage. "What?! You totally have to go! I'm on the decorating committee; it's going to be awesome." Felicity just shrugged sullenly. "You have to make him take you."

"I already asked, he said no. He thinks Halloween is distasteful and heathen."

"No it isn't! What does that even mean?"

Felicity laughed and shook her head. "It's...kind of against his religion."

"Oh. Well that sucks."

Felicity just gave her a little nod. She didn't really think that Cain was listening any longer, but didn't want to say too much about it, just in case. "Are you going with Ben?"

"Of course. I have got that boy wrapped around my little finger. He adores me." Before Felicity had decided whether or not she should comment on that, Alyson arrived. Ashley noted her approach. "Oh look, it's the girl who thinks *every* day is Halloween."

Allie sneered at her. "At least I don't spend all of my time trying to look like a Barbie doll."

"That's funny, because you actually do look just like a 'Barbie' that I used to have, *after* my little sister tortured her with scissors and a magic marker." Allie just gave her a disgusted look and ignored her, thumbing through flyers and bookmarks on the counter. Ashley turned back to Felicity, who had learned to stay out of their frequent insult exchanges. "Anyway, I'm going over to Clarissa's Costume Shop tomorrow, to pick up my outfit. You should come; maybe you'll see something good. If you get the right costume, Cain won't be able to let you go alone."

"Thanks, but I was just going to skip it, really."

Ashley shook her head and rolled her eyes. "See, I tried to tell you. Once you let them think they've got all the power, you're done for." Alyson gave a little snort of a laugh, and went back to browsing through the bookmarks.

"Not everything is a power trip Ashley," Felicity answered. "He just doesn't want to go, and I respect that."

"Okay, but do *you* want to go?" Felicity glanced at Cain, who didn't seem to be paying any attention. She just shrugged. "Did he tell you *not* to go?"

"Well of course not, but I wouldn't go with anyone else. I know you date lots of guys, but I can't do that. I don't wanna go with anyone but Cain."

"So, go alone. It's not like you won't know anyone there."

Felicity just shrugged and decided to try and take the focus off of herself. "So what's your costume?"

Ashley gave her a smug smile. "Jeannie, as in 'I dream of.'"

Alyson snorted at her again. "Original," she said sarcastically.

Her comment was met by a sharp glare from Ashley. "With *my* hair and body, it's the perfect costume."

Felicity spoke up, a little apologetically. "There *are* usually one or two of them at every party."

Ashley seemed unconcerned. "So? That will just go to prove how much better *I* look in it than *they* do." Ashley glanced from one speechless girl to the other, and then at the registers. She opened one and took out a few twenties. "We need change; I'm goin' over to the cafe." She walked over, money in hand, as Allie and Felicity exchanged looks.

"Is she for real?" Felicity asked.

Allie rolled her eyes. "Unfortunately, and she's spending more and more time with Ben, which frankly, just makes me nauseous."

"He's taking her to the Halloween dance," Felicity told her.

"Well, that's one event that *I* won't be attending," Allie replied.

Felicity watched as Ashley walked behind the counter to the cafe register and promptly began draping herself all over Ben as he made change for her. "I wonder what Ben's going to be."

"You mean besides emotionally abused? Ben's always a super hero. He says that he thinks the girls like them, but I think he's just feeding his inner geek. He used to be big into comic books."

Felicity laughed. "Super heroes huh?"

"Oh yeah, he's been them all. Superman, Batman, Spiderman, various X-Men, the Green Lantern, he's been everybody. He's starting to run out of cool heroes though. I mean really, who's left, *Aqua man?*"

Felicity started to chuckle when she suddenly remembered something and dropped her smile. "Oh no!"

"What?" Allie asked.

"Poor Ben!" Felicity exclaimed.

"What?!" Allie repeated.

"I talked to Karen this morning, and Todd and Brenda are still together," Felicity explained.

"Yeah, so?" Alyson asked.

"So, they're going to the dance...as Captain America and Wonder Woman," Felicity revealed sympathetically.

Allie slammed her hand on the counter with a laugh. "Oh my God! Ben is gonna *die!*"

"I know. Maybe he and Brenda had more in common than I thought. I feel so guilty," Felicity admitted.

"Why? You didn't do anything," Allie assured her.

"I practically threw Todd at her. I feel terrible," Felicity said.

Alyson laughed. "Don't worry about it. Like he said, Ben could have gotten her back if he'd tried. I know he was trying to sound smug, but it's probably true. Ben's a pretty charming smooth talker when he wants to be."

"*Ben* is?" Felicity asked incredulously.

Allie rolled her eyes again. "Well he doesn't waste it on *us*." Felicity laughed and they both turned to watch Ben with Ashley. She had gotten her change but was now obviously working him over for something else. She was really trying hard too, batting her eyes and giving him pouty little kisses, while rubbing against him just so and whispering in his ear. Whatever she was trying to accomplish, Ben did not look very happy about it. It seemed as though he finally gave over, but continued to look very sulky and annoyed.

Allie seemed disgusted. "What could he possibly see in her? She is so vapid and shallow. They've started dating again and he's taking her to this dance, and *I* didn't even think that he liked her all that much."

"That's what *I* said!" Felicity agreed.

"I think the man's gone insane. I mean, I'm sorry, but even sex with *Ashley* can't be worth having to *listen* to her all day."

Felicity shook her head with a smile. "Maybe they have fun together."

Allie chuckled and gestured towards the cafe, where Ben was still looking sullen and aggravated as Ashley tried to make him smile with kisses and tickling. "Does that look like the face of a *happy* man to you? I'd better go rescue him."

Allie turned to leave, but Felicity put a hand on her arm to stop her. "Wait, what are you going to do? I mean, if Ben is dating her, then you really shouldn't say anything. It's none of our business."

"Oh, I'm not gonna say anything. I'm just gonna sit there and smile at her," Allie informed her.

"What's *that* going to do?" Felicity asked.

"Just watch, I'll bet she leaves in under a minute." With that, Allie left for the cafe to prove her prediction. She chose a chair from Cain's table without a word, turned it to face the counter better, and sat. Cain looked up curiously from his book at Alyson's arrival, but said nothing. Allie promptly began to smile at Ben and Ashley. They were probably wondering why she had purposely strode over to Cain's table to ignore him.

It only took a few seconds before Ashley said something to Ben and left, heading back to the registers. She seemed a little displeased when she got there. Felicity looked at her questioningly, but all she said was, "Don't you get another fifteen?"

The question caught Felicity off guard. Oh, her break. "Yeah, I do."

"Well, you'd better take it now, because at eight o'clock, I'm outta here," Ashley informed her.

"Okay." Felicity walked over to the cafe with a bemused expression on her face. She went to Cain's table and gave him a kiss hello. It was just a quick kiss this time, but he quickly pulled back from it, as if to escape her leading him into more. She looked at him as though he'd hurt her feelings.

"Sorry, but I can't be too careful. You've become quite cheeky these days."

She giggled with a slight blush. She *had* been awfully bold with their kiss before. She sat down and stared at him for a moment. "Why do you come here so early? I won't get out for two and a half more hours. Aren't you bored?"

"Well I do have Alyson here, keeping me company."

"Yeah, what am I chopped liver?" Alyson chimed in.

"Did you want something?" Felicity looked up in surprise to find Ben at her shoulder.

"I get *served?*"

"Considering you didn't make it easy for me by sitting at the counter, yeah. You want something?"

"Sorry. Um, yeah. I'll have a cup of coffee."

Alyson chirped up, "Make it three." Felicity gave her a bit of an odd look, that she was ordering for Cain. Since when had they become so familiar?

Felicity spoke to Allie, as Ben left to get their coffees. "So you were right, she left. You didn't say anything?"

"Not a word," Allie answered with a smile. "You may have noticed that Ashley has a hard time being around me, without spitting out some depreciative comment or rude remark."

"I had noticed that, yeah."

"Well, she can't do that around Ben, because he always defends me and then she gets all pissed. So, rather than have to be nice to me, she just leaves."

Felicity and Cain chuckled as Ben returned with their coffee. "There you go," he said, setting one in front of each of them. He then looked pointedly at Cain. "Three coffees, hold the holy water."

Cain looked very annoyed as Allie and Felicity tried to hold in their giggles. Alyson reached up to stop Ben from leaving. "Would you get me a piece of pie?"

"What kind?" Ben asked.

"Whatever's not old," Allie replied.

Cain was staring disapprovingly at Felicity, as Ben left. "You *had* to tell them?"

Felicity smiled. She couldn't help but share Cain's remark, about worrying that Ben would spike his coffee with holy water. "It was funny."

"It was a legitimate concern," Cain said defensively.

"Not with Ben!" Felicity insisted.

"Still, you needn't go about giving people ideas," he mumbled.

"I'm sorry, forgive me?" She smiled at him and batted her eyes, feeling a bit like Ashley, in trying to get him to smile. Cain gave her a subtle little amorous look and took her hand from the table, raising it to his lips for a kiss. She was always so thrilled when he did things like that.

Ben dropped Allie's pie plate on the table with a thud, it was pecan. "Is that it?"

Allie questioned his annoyance. "What's *your* problem? It's not like you're busy." The one table of customers Ben'd had, had left a few minutes before.

Ben looked at Cain and then back to Allie. "That's because it's almost eight o'clock on a Friday night. Most people who aren't *required* to be here, have got better things to do."

Allie and Cain shared a glance and a smile, before Alyson answered. "Well, lucky for you, *I've* got the whole evening free. So I'm gonna spend it right here."

"What do you know? Me too," Cain added playfully.

Ben just shook his head with a groan and turned to leave. Felicity stopped him. "I heard you're taking Ashley to the Halloween Ball."

"Yeah," he answered shortly.

He didn't exactly sound thrilled. "Who are you going as?" Felicity asked.

"Major Nelson," Ben replied.

"Who?"

"Major Anthony Nelson, the astronaut from 'I Dream Of Jeannie'. Ashley wants us to match," Ben explained.

Allie opened her mouth in indignance. "You don't even get to pick your own costume? That sucks!"

Ben shrugged. "It doesn't matter." It looked to Felicity as though it might matter a great deal to Ben.

She was glad when Allie said something about it. "Ben! You love Halloween! Don't let her wreck it for you! What are you going to wear, a silver track suit and a fishbowl on your head?"

"No! It's a NASA dress uniform," Ben clarified.

"That is *so* lame!" Allie insisted.

"Ashley says I'll look dashing," Ben said defensively.

"Boooring. Ashley must not have ever seen you in the tights." Allie gave Felicity a confidential little smile and informed her, "He looks *really* good in tights."

Cain looked at Ben with an arched eyebrow. "When did you wear *tights?*"

Ben glared at him. "It was a Superman costume." He turned to Allie. "Shut up and mind your own business."

Felicity felt that she ought to say something before they started fighting. "So Allie, what are you going to be?"

Ben answered for her. "Allie doesn't *do* Halloween."

Felicity looked from Allie to Cain. "No wonder you two have been getting along so well."

Cain gave Alyson an amicable grin. "Ah, someone else who doesn't wish to support the celebration of Devil worship and hedonism."

Allie sat staring at him very oddly for a moment before answering. "No. I just think it's *stupid.*"

"Why?" Felicity asked.

"Everybody waits for this one day a year, just so they can get all dressed up in ways that would normally be socially unacceptable and not get criticized for it. It's such a joke."

"Isn't that kind of the point, to dress as something you aren't?"

"But that's just it, people treat it more as a 'come as you secretly are'. It's not like anybody tries to be scary anymore. They choose costumes that are really just expressions of their hidden innermost desires. Like Ashley's outfit. You don't think she'd dress like that *every day*, if she could get away with it? Halloween is just a convenient excuse for girls like her to drop their inhibitions without being ostracized for it."

Ben shook his head at her. "You should be a psychology major."

"I just speak the obvious truth. I don't have any use for Halloween. I'm *already* out there for everyone to see. I don't have to hide behind some stupid fake holiday. If I want my hair to be pink, I dye it pink. If I *wanted* to walk around half naked, I would and *I* wouldn't have to consult a calendar to do it."

Cain was looking at her with new admiration. "Well said."

"Thank you," Allie answered with a smile.

Ben smiled. "Going as a black cat?"

Alyson's smile disappeared. "Yeah."

Felicity looked to Allie in confusion. "Wait, I thought you didn't dress up?"

Allie sat back in a huff as Ben answered for her. "Tommy always makes Alyson work on Halloween. It's bar policy that all employees *have* to wear a costume." He looked to Allie. "You know he just does that to piss you off, right?"

Allie shrugged. "I wear a head band with ears and pin a tail to my ass, and everybody leaves me alone."

Ashley interrupted them by yelling across the store. "Felicity, it's eight o'clock! Come on, I wanna leave. Some people have a life *outside* of the cafe." She sounded very annoyed and sarcastic.

Alyson beamed a broad smile at Ben. "She is *such* a catch Ben, you must be *so* proud."

"Bite me Allie."

Ben took Felicity's coffee cup to the sink behind the counter, as Felicity returned to the registers. She offered Ashley a 'sorry', but the girl just brushed past her on the way to the lounge.

A minute later, Ashley came back out with her purse and jacket. She paused to give Ben a quick kiss goodbye, and then headed for the door. Just as she left the cafe, Ben called out to her. "Ashley, wait!"

Ashley turned, looking annoyed. "What?"

He hesitated for a moment, as though searching for something to say. "You can't leave yet."

Ashley was very irritated. "Why not? It's ten after." Ben just looked at her pleadingly for a minute, but she was having none of it. "Ben, I have to go... I have plans."

"Ashley..."

"It's Friday night and you won't be out of here for at *least* two more hours."

Ben now ignored Ashley to stare at Cain, who was deep in a conversation with Alyson. "Cain, go lock the door."

Chapter 24 - Payback's a bitch

Cain

Friday night
DownTime cafe and bookstore

Cain had been very involved in a conversation with Alyson about false personas and hidden identity traits, when Ben ordered him to go and lock the door. He had been very much ignoring Ben's altercation with Ashley, and now wondered why he was being dragged into things, and given orders no less.

Ashley stared at Ben in disbelieving shock. "Ben! Please, let's not make this messy. *You're* the one who didn't want to be exclusive. What, you get to date other people and I don't? It's Friday night!"

Ben was still ignoring her and staring at Cain. He started to come out from behind the counter. Ben's seriousness made Cain get up from the table and start for the door, but why had he asked Cain to do it? Felicity was much closer. As he reached the door and peered outside, a flash of understanding came upon him. Sindy was just outside and had been about to enter. Ben must have felt her coming. Rather than lock the door on her, Cain let her in.

"What the hell are you doing?" Ben yelled from the edge of the cafe.

Cain ignored him. Sindy seemed very distraught, pained even. She did not seem physically hurt, but she practically collapsed against the wall once inside. Suddenly her trace flared into existence in his mind, and he realized her distress. She'd been cloaking herself, through great mental strain, to get here undiscovered.

She looked up at him, disgusted with her lack of staying power. "I can't hold it. You'd better lock the door."

Cain did as she asked, as Ben came storming up to them. "*Now* he locks it?" Ben yelled to the others with his arms in the air. He stalked right up to Sindy. "Get the fuck out of my store bitch," he growled.

Ashley put one hand on her hip and gestured towards Sindy with the other. "Who is that?" No one bothered to answer her.

Cain spared Ben a warning glance. "Back off." Without waiting for a response, he turned his attention back to Sindy. "How far behind you?"

"They didn't know where I was going, they couldn't follow, but I'm too drained to keep up my cover. They'll find me before long.

"Who? What's going on?"

"They're all after me." She glanced at Ben and then back to Cain. "I *can't* go back out there. They'll kill me."

"Good!" Ben practically spat at her.

Cain gave Ben a fierce glare. "Think you might give us a moment?" Ben only backed up a step. "Who?"

Sindy was looking him in the eye, as she leaned her back against the wall. "It's Chris. He came back."

"When?"

"Last night. I went out on my own... shopping." By the way that she said it, Cain knew she meant for blood. He was more than a little surprised; he hadn't thought she was drinking store bought blood. "I was only gone for like an hour, but when I got back to the house, he was there." She glanced down at the floor and he could tell that she would rather not have an audience for her telling. She hadn't a choice. "I thought he wanted to come back, to be like it was, you know? But he started talking about status and stuff. He was all worked up, saying that 'sire or not' he shouldn't have to take orders from a girl. That it just wasn't right." She looked up to find Felicity in the store. Sindy's gaze landed upon her, behind the counter... if looks could kill, it surely would have been deadly. "Then he found out about Luke. Let me tell you somethin' honey. You thought you were livin' dangerously before? He's got *special* plans for *you*."

Cain gave her a little shove on the shoulder. "That'll be quite enough of that, bottom line please?"

"He's turned them against me Cain, all of them! How could he do that? They're *mine!* But they won't listen to me now, not like they listen to him. And he's got them all worked up and thinkin' they'd be better off without me! I take care of them don't I? How could they do this to me?

Chris told them that Luke, and those other dumb jocks that got themselves killed... that it's all *my* fault. Like I'm incompetent or something! He says that *I'm* gonna take orders from *him* for a change. He starts tellin' me to do all this stuff for him, and when I wouldn't he freaked!" She gave Felicity another dangerous glare. "Maybe I should have just done it."

"What did he want you to do?" Cain asked.

Sindy gave an evil little smile. "Like I said, he's got plans for your girlfriend over there. Real specific instructions." She chuckled at Felicity. "Man, you should have left Luke alone."

Cain was staring at her thoughtfully. "You told him no," he said quietly.

She looked up at him and shrugged. "I put it on your tab. Anyway we had this big fight, and he starts threatenin' me, like actually pushin' me around and stuff. So I call Marcus, to make Chris leave me alone, *and he wouldn't come!* Chris starts laughin' at me, tellin' me that *girls* shouldn't be givin' orders.

That's when I realized, they've got his mark Cain. That creep drank from my boys while I was gone! They listen to him; they've always listened to him, but now he's tellin' them to get rid of *me!* They're so stupid; they'll just do anything he says. He wants me out of the way, dusted! And he can make them do it!"

Ben smiled. "Sounds like I'm going to owe that man a favor."

Before anyone else could comment, Ashley approached them at the door, to address Sindy. "Excuse me, hi. Look, I'm real sorry that there's like people trying to kill you and stuff. That really sucks. You should like, call the police or something, but, *I'm* late for an appointment. So if you don't mind, I'm just going to slip out to my car, 'kay?"

Sindy just stared at her for a moment in disdain and disbelief. Cain shook his head, as though to clear it and then spoke seriously to Sindy. "You, stay here, don't move and you should probably refrain from speaking as well." Now he turned to Ben. "You, back off and don't do *anything*, until I get back." Cain went to take Ashley by the arm. "I'll escort you to your car."

Ashley smiled at Cain as though he were the only sane person in the establishment. *"Thank you."*

Ben moved grudgingly aside, but Sindy stood her ground in front of the door. "Cain, wait. Chris... he can cloak." She looked disgusted to admit it. "Better than *me*."

Cain rolled his eyes as Sindy stepped aside for him. "Wonderful." He looked over to Felicity, who hadn't said anything, but was looking rather nervous at the register. "You just stay put, I'll be right in."

There was a nervous moment of silence, as Cain and Ashley stepped outside and glanced around. No one was in sight. He let the door swing closed behind them and turned to Ashley. "Your car, it's the green one?" He nodded towards a little mint green VW Bug convertible.

Ashley began walking towards it, unconcerned. "Yeah, cute right?"

"Adorable, but you might want to put the top up." They reached her car without event. Cain stood there, keeping an eye on their surroundings, until he realized that Ashley still hadn't gotten in. She stood there, looking at him for a moment, until Cain opened the door for her.

She gave him a flirtatious little smile and got in. "You know, if you ever wanted to come for a ride... I'd be happy to take you for one."

Cain gave her a benign smile and a light touch on the arm. "Thanks. Goodnight." He tapped her arm before he backed away. "Put the top up."

He watched her as she put up the top and pulled out of the lot. As soon as she was off alright, Cain headed back inside. He approached the door to find Sindy against the wall as Ben held a stake to her chest. Alyson was standing behind Ben, arms crossed and Felicity was next to him, obviously trying to talk him into putting away the stake. Sindy stood with remarkable calm, her eyes locked on Ben. She seemed to be concentrating on him intensely. Cain realized that rather than choose a physical rebuttal to Ben's threat, she was using whatever slight mental control she might have left from her mark. Ben looked disgusted and nauseous.

Cain ripped open the door, stalked right up to them and grabbed Ben's wrist. "Can't turn my back on you for a minute, can I?"

Alyson spoke from behind them. "Sindy was eggin' him on. I thought he handled it pretty well. I would have staked her already."

Cain looked from Sindy to Ben. They both still seemed locked in their mental battle of wills. "Now children, let's not fight." He gave a little push on Ben's wrist with the stake, for him to drop the arm to his side.

Ben seemed to notice Cain for the first time, and lowered the stake. "She needs to leave. Why are you even defending her? Don't you actually *care* about Felicity at all?"

"I beg your pardon?" Cain responded in quiet outrage. "How dare you question my loyalties?"

Ben gestured towards Sindy with the stake in his hand. "Don't you see what she's doing? She tells Chris that Felicity killed Luke and then she leads him right to her. So now *her* problem has become *our* problem."

Sindy became indignant. "I didn't even know that Felicity was here!" She looked pleadingly at Cain. "It's not like that at all!"

Cain was just gazing at her steadily, unsure what to believe. "Convince me," he said mildly.

Sindy opened her mouth in disbelief. "I have been dealing with this *without you* since like ten o'clock last night, when I first ran from him. Why wouldn't I have just brought them to Felicity from the beginning?"

Ben was happy to answer and try to make her look worse. "Because she was in her room, where you and Chris couldn't get in. So you had to wait until you could find her in a public place at night. Like... oh, I don't know... **here?**"

Sindy looked as though she'd like to kick him. She turned back to Cain. "Cain, I didn't want to involve you at all, *believe me,* but Arif sent me away, and I don't know what else to do. There are too many of them for me to handle alone."

Cain looked puzzled. "You spoke to Arif of this?"

"Yeah, I went to him last night."

"And...?"

"And," Her shoulders slumped. Once again she seemed to loathe having to share her personal business with all of them. "He sent me away." Cain still stared at her, waiting for details. "He told me that while he felt responsible to protect me from *others;* my own brood is my own problem."

Cain raised his eyebrows a bit as Ben spoke. "Sounds fair to me."

Cain gave a little smile. "If I were wise, I'd probably tell you the same." Sindy just stared at him. She didn't bother to try and look hopeful or beg for his help. Apparently, she had decided that he would come to his own decision, and she'd rather hold on to her pride. "Since when does Chris know how to hide his trace?"

Sindy become uncomfortable at the mention of Chris' talent, superior to hers. Her voice was full of contempt. "I don't know. I never saw him do it until yesterday. I guess he's been practicing behind my back or something. I don't know how he got so good at it."

"Sounds to me as though perhaps *Chris* paid a visit to Arif as well. His new philosophies would certainly make good evidence for such a case."

Realization and scorn came over her. "That creep! Turning my own against me and then acting all condescending about it! It's not fair! They were mine! So is Chris! I made him, how can he turn against me like this?"

Ben moved a little closer, enjoying Sindy's distress. "Ain't payback a bitch?" he asked with a smile.

Sindy's anger flared for a moment, but then she fixed Ben with a steady stare and a sweet smile. Strange expressions flashed over Ben's features, before he composed his face into a blank mask. He gripped the stake so hard his knuckles were white and he returned her stare with his own. Cain moved to break their line of sight.

Ben closed his eyes as Cain watched him for a moment. Over Ben's shoulder, Cain noticed that Alyson seemed very interested in the exchange. Normally she became hostile very quickly in Sindy's presence, but right now she seemed to Cain to be curious more than anything else. As though she would really like to understand just what Sindy was capable of and how she did it.

Cain turned to Sindy. By the little smirk on her face, he was certain she was sending Ben the strongest indecent sensations and callings she could manage. "That's enough. End it, *now.*"

Ben brushed past his shoulder to face Sindy again. "She'd better, or I'll find a way to work through it. Keep it up and you're dust," he threatened, with a fierce growl in his voice and lifting the stake in his hand.

Cain let him stare her down for a minute before lightly touching the stake. "Put it away," Cain said quietly.

Ben looked as though he'd like to argue, but thought better of it and slid the stake into his back pocket. "Are you throwing her out or what? She might as well be a neon sign for anybody who wants her and Felicity, right?

They can see her? So put her out. Let them chase her around for a while, so Felicity can get home." He suddenly turned to Felicity in apprehension. "Can they... see you too?"

Felicity spoke for the first time during the events of the evening. She seemed a bit shaken. All she said was a quiet 'no'. Ben looked as though he didn't quite believe her.

Alyson spoke up in her defense. "She's not marked."

Both Ben and Cain looked at her curiously. It was Ben who asked. "How would you know?"

"She told me," Allie replied with a shrug.

Cain shook his head and turned back to Sindy. "He's right; you're going to have to hide your trace. It may already be too late, but you should try."

She looked annoyed. "I told you I can't."

"You did it well enough *outside* the door. So unless you'd like me to believe that you *are* purposely leading them here, you'd better do it again now." Their voices began to rise a bit, with the desperate knowledge that every moment lost, was bringing danger closer.

"Cain, I can't! I'm spent."

"It's easy enough. Once you get the correct shape of it into your mind, it can become effortless. I do it almost unconsciously."

"Good for you," she quipped sarcastically.

"Chris learned it quickly enough."

"I guess *he* had a good teacher."

Ben spoke up again. "We don't have time for this Cain, get rid of her!"

Sindy looked at Cain with degraded contempt in her eyes. "I can't do it. You never taught me."

Cain became impatient. "Well I'm teaching you now!"

Alyson's voice broke through his focus on Sindy. "Too late, school's out." Cain turned to see two of Sindy's football players at the door. In his distraction of breaking things up between Ben and Sindy, he hadn't even locked it again. Not that it mattered much; it was all glass, easily broken.

Cain cursed himself for a fool. He shouldn't have wasted time worrying about hiding Sindy's trace. They'd had time to determine her general location, and Chris wasn't entirely stupid. He had to have guessed where she might come in this area. He should have made Felicity and

Alyson get to safety, but he knew that Felicity would be terrified to be far from him, and without her in sight he would worry for a trap. Anyway, too late now.

The two at the door began pushing their way in, as Cain moved forward to shove the door closed in their faces. He locked it, but as predicted, they simply began to kick in the glass. As the first crash sounded, he heard an almost identical crash from across the store. The front window of the cafe came shattering in.

Cain turned to see that Alyson had produced a stake from somewhere, as Felicity raced behind the counter to the employee lounge with Ben close behind, his stake in hand. Sindy watched Cain pull a stake from his own boot, as the two at the door tried to come through. "Got an extra one of those?" she inquired. He tossed her the one from his hand, and took out another from his other boot. He stepped aside, as the two came through the door.

The guy closest to Cain must have been blindly following Sindy's trace. He was so focused on getting to Sindy that he did not even notice Cain, off to the side, until it was too late. Either that, or because of Cain's hidden trace, he simply thought Cain human and therefore of no immediate concern. Cain was able to stake him before the vampire even realized the threat.

Sindy seemed about to stake the one before her, when she suddenly dropped to the floor as though struck. The guy was upon her in a moment, but Cain attacked him from behind. The lesser vampire did see him and tried to push him away, but it was hardly adequate resistance. Cain dispatched him easily. As he did, he saw Sindy turn and wince.

He realized the problem. They were her 'children'. She felt their deaths as though it was her own physical pain. She would hardly be much use in this fight. He put out a hand to help her up, as his eyes found the lounge door in the cafe.

Ben and Felicity were emerging from the lounge, with more stakes and crosses. Apparently the weapons had been with their belongings, in the lounge. What they did not see, was the third football player waiting for them behind the counter. "Felicity, Ben, look out!"

As Cain yelled, the guy sprang at Ben, who had come through the door first. The two became engaged in a struggle as Felicity tried to get out to help. She was blocked in the doorway by their fight, though. Cain tried to imagine if there'd be any windows or other doors in the lounge, for someone to come through from behind. He'd never been back there.

Hoping Felicity was safe for the moment, he turned back to Sindy. He'd helped her to her feet, and she stood with the support of his arm. She looked up to him with a weak smile. "This isn't gonna be much fun."

He turned back to see Ben beating the hell out of his foe. Alyson was moving to join Ben and Felicity, when Ben finally staked him. Cain was forced to turn towards Sindy as she practically broke his arm in her pain. Cain was about to ask after her, when he saw two more vampires coming through the door. They were zombies; filthy, rotten and mindless, but advancing upon he and Sindy with grim determination. He glanced back to Sindy, who hadn't seen them and dragged her back away from the door a step, by her hold on his arm. "Are those yours?"

She looked up to see who he meant, and looked instantly ill. "I do better work than that, give me a little credit."

"Good, then you can fight them." She looked a little offended by his lack of assistance, but he had other worries. Two more zombies had come in by the window to the cafe. They must have followed the guy Ben had killed. Ben seemed eager to tackle one of them. Alyson and Felicity positioned themselves before the other one. They should manage. In fact, as he watched, he saw Felicity remember the vial at her throat. She handed Alyson the cross she'd been holding. Then Felicity quickly opened the vial, and moved Allie aside so that Felicity was directly in front of the thing.

Cain smiled, she was a smart girl, but he was unsure if the vial would help. Hopefully, the instinct driven corpse before her would feel loathe to touch her if she smelled of Cain's blood, but as Felicity was not traditionally marked, there was a good chance that it would not understand the meaning of smelling Cain's blood on her at all. Still, it couldn't hurt. The vampire wasn't decayed enough to suggest that it was totally mindless. It seemed pretty straightforward that the smell of another vampire on a victim should mark ownership... if the thing could even smell it. From what Cain could see, the vampire/zombie they faced must have been through some trying past event. Its face was very disfigured and it hadn't much of a nose left. Cain almost wished Felicity would pour the blood upon herself, to be sure.

Cain left the front entrance registers, moving towards the cafe in case the others needed assistance, but he also had in his mind, the fact that they had not yet seen Chris… or Marcus. *Cain* wanted to be the one to face them, if possible. Cain saw that Ben's foe seemed confused and Cain realized that Ben was still marked. That should serve to help protect him as well. He wished Allie had such assurance. His eyes searched the cafe. Where was Chris?

He heard movement from the back of the bookstore. He spared a parting glance at Sindy, before going to check it out. She had killed one zombie and was struggling with the other. It was a gruesome battle. She couldn't stake it because it was too close to her, holding her in a sort of hug as it tried to bite her. She grabbed at its hair, to try to pull its face back away from herself, but she only came away with a handful of loose hair and ripped scalp.

She pushed and struggled against the thing until she could get out from under it. Cain felt bad to leave her, but it wouldn't do her any permanent damage. It was too stupid to know how to really kill Sindy and it hadn't a weapon anyway.

Cain started towards the bookshelves, looking back to the cafe as he went. Ben had dispatched his 'vampire' and was moving to help the girls. They weren't really in distress. Using vial and cross, they avoided the zombie who was trying to get to them, but they didn't seem to want to touch it. He couldn't blame them.

Cain made his way into the labyrinth of bookshelves. He heard it again, someone was definitely back there. He tried to recall the various windows and exits where Chris might have snuck in. The back door should sound a fire alarm when opened. He approached the corner of each shelf warily, tense with anticipation. He finally reached the back of the store, and as he turned into last aisle he found… a boy. Well, a young man really, although rather short and slight of build; he was certainly not a vampire. He was huddled in the corner, hugging a large book. He wore glasses and was about Felicity's age. Cain sighed in annoyance as the boy spoke. "I was looking something up, for my history paper. Somebody broke the glass door. Did they rob the place? I was going to buy the book, I swear."

Cain shook his head. The boy acted as though he thought Cain might be a cop. "Come on, you don't want to be here." Cain was turning to lead the boy up and out the front, when he sensed four new traces enter the store. Damn, one of them was Marcus. "On second thought, stay here." Cain left the kid to run back up front. He got there in time to see Sindy fighting another zombie. He assumed it was a new one, and she had finished the one from before. This one was definitely better preserved and putting up quite a fight. How many of these things had Chris made?

Well, he knew that there were at least two more. He could feel them... with Marcus. The other two zombies and Marcus were just entering the cafe, after having come through the front door, but Cain's attention was instead instantly drawn to the cafe window. Chris was there. Cain saw him only for a moment. Chris yelled for Marcus, who turned to face him. Chris quickly surveyed the situation and seemed very disappointed that things hadn't gone better for him and his lot. Cain, Sindy and all of the humans within, including Felicity seemed unharmed. Chris certainly must have felt his zombies' deaths, but they would not have been as painful as the deaths Sindy had felt. The better made the vampire, the stronger the blood tie to its sire. Surely Chris was disappointed.

Chris called insistently again for Marcus and then disappeared from the window. He was indeed cloaked well. Cain could not feel where he went. He considered trying to give chase, but then he heard Felicity scream. Marcus was exiting through the window after Chris, but the two zombies had been busy making their way behind the cafe counter. Cain saw that his friends seemed to have killed the one they were fighting before, but Felicity had screamed because a new one had grabbed her by the arm, pulling her close. Ben was trying to beat it off of her, so that he might get an open shot at its chest. Meanwhile Alyson was struggling to keep the other one from backing her into a corner. She had out her stake, but seemed to be having a hard time getting to its heart.

Cain sighed; Chris and Marcus would have to wait. He wasn't sure that he wanted to tackle the two of them alone anyway. Marcus was so huge! As he started toward the cafe to help dispatch the last two, he was startled by Sindy. She took his arm at the elbow from behind. "I heard Chris. Is he gone?"

Cain glanced towards the front door. Sindy had finished the 'vampire' that had been there. He stopped to remove her from his arm. "Yes, and Marcus survives also." He looked over to the cafe to see that Allie had killed her foe, and Ben had pulled the other from Felicity. He had it backed up against the counter. Their struggle would certainly be over soon. Cain looked back to Sindy. "We're very lucky to have come out of this unscathed."

She backed away so that he could better see her. "Easy for you to say. You aren't covered in gore and zombie guts! Thanks for your help by the way," she added sarcastically.

Cain turned to face her more fully. "*You should* be thankful, very. Ben was right, you know. I'd have been smarter to put you out, and make you deal with them on your own."

"You mean *kill me;* because you know I couldn't have survived all of this alone."

"Hence the due gratitude."

"Oh. Well yeah, but I could have just killed Felicity myself last night. Would have bought *me* some safety. Just 'cause Chris didn't want to take orders, doesn't mean that he didn't *want* me you know. He'd have been very happy to have me by his side. All I needed to do was take Felicity for him. Then he would have treated me *real* nice. I don't care if she stays where I'm uninvited; I would have found a way. I could have bought some time, done it tonight, or tomorrow. You know I could have."

"That is why you are still alive, but if I find that you knowingly lead harm to Felicity again in any way... I'll stake you myself." Sindy stared back at him in dead seriousness.

"I'm done playing games. Really." Her eyes looked hopefully for his trust.

He hadn't the time or presence of mind to sort such things out now. He simply answered, "Good," and started back to the cafe, where the last of the zombies had been turned to ash floating in the air. Felicity, Ben and Alyson were dusting themselves off.

Sindy stopped him again, her hand lightly on his arm. "I don't suppose I could stay at your place for the day?"

He looked at her as though she must be mad. "No."

She shrugged, looking a bit disappointed, but not really surprised. "Just thought I'd ask."

He stared at her for a moment and then dug some bills from his pocket. He thrust them into her hand. "Go and find a hotel room, and practice your cloaking."

She eagerly tucked the bills into her bra, at the shoulder of her dress. "Thanks."

Ben spoke from behind him, emerging from the cafe. "She leads hoards of angry undead upon us, and you *pay her for it?*" Before Cain could answer, Felicity flew into his arms. She snuggled her face into his chest, and he couldn't help but enfold his arms tightly around her.

Allie reached them, and stopped to take a look around. The front door and large picture window in the cafe were both smashed in, glass was everywhere, and the floor and cafe counter were covered in the ashes of no less than ten vampires. Alyson began laughing, and they all turned to look at her in bewildered curiosity. By way of explanation she said, "Penten's gonna be pissed!"

Just then, they were startled by movement behind them as someone emerged from the back of the store. Everyone made ready for defense by raising stakes and crosses, and preparing themselves to meet... the young man with the glasses, who had been shopping in the back of the store before the attack.

He was still clutching his book, but dropped it to the floor, to put up his hands upon seeing his hostile reception. He stood there for a second in frightened silence, until weapons were lowered with sighs of relief. He looked questioningly at Cain. "Can I go home now?"

~~~~~~~~~~~~~~~~~~~~~~~~~~~~~~~~

TO BE CONTINUED

IN

ALMOST HUMAN

❧ THE FIRST TRILOGY ❧

VOLUME 3

EVOLVING ECSTASY

~~~~~~~~~~~~~~~~~~~~~~~~~~~~

If you enjoyed this book, please take a moment to leave a review online, on your favorite book review website!

You can join author/reader discussions about the series, and get updates on upcoming book releases for this series on the author's web site at:
www.MelanieNowak.com

Made in the USA
Columbia, SC
11 August 2023

21516815R00205